For Cousin Bill and Mrs. Dexter

SPOONER

Pete Dexter is one of America's great living novelists. He won the US National Book Award for Fiction for *Paris Trout,* two Penn West Awards for Best Novel of the Year (*Paris Trout* and *The Paperboy*), and the *Los Angeles Times* Book Prize for Best Novel for his last novel, *Train.*

ALSO BY PETE DEXTER

Paper Trails

Train

The Paperboy

Brotherly Love

Paris Trout

Deadwood

God's Pocket

SPOONER

Pete Dexter

Atlantic Books
London

First published in 2009 in the United States of America by Grand Central
Publishing, Hachette Book Group, 237 Park Avenue, New York, NY 10017.

First published in Great Britain in 2010 in trade paperback by Atlantic
Books, an imprint of Grove Atlantic Ltd.

1 3 5 7 9 10 8 6 4 2

A CIP catalogue record for this book is available from the British Library.

978 1 84887 339 1

Printed and Bound by Thomson Litho, East Kilbride, Scotland

Atlantic Books
An imprint of Grove Atlantic Ltd
Ormond House
26–27 Boswell Street
London WC1N 3JZ

www.atlantic-books.co.uk

SPOONER

PART ONE

Milledgeville

ONE

Spooner was born a few minutes previous to daybreak in the historic, honeysuckled little town of Milledgeville, Georgia, in a makeshift delivery room put together in the waiting area of the medical offices of Dr. Emil Woods, across the street from and approximately in the crosshairs of a cluster of Confederate artillery pieces guarding the dog-spotted front lawn of the Greene Street Sons of the Confederacy Retirement Home. It was the first Saturday of December 1956, and the old folks' home was on fire.

The birthing itself lacked cotton-picking, and grits, and darkies to do all the work, but otherwise had the history of the South stamped all over it—misery, besiegement, injustice, smoke enough to sting the eyes (although this was as invisible as the rest of it in the night air), along with an eerie faint keening in the distance and the aroma of singed hair. Unless that was in fact somebody cooking grits.

As we pick up the story, though, three days preceding, the retired veterans are snug in their beds, and Spooner is on the clock but fixing to evacuate the premises no time soon. Minutes pool slowly into hours, and hours into a day, and then spill over into a new day and another.

And now a resident of the home dozes off with a half-smoked Lucky in his mouth, which falls into his beard, unwashed since D-day or so and as flammable as a two-month-old Christmas tree, and it all goes up at once.

While back in Dr. Woods's office, Spooner is still holding on like an abscessed tooth, defying all the laws of the female apparatus and common sense—not that those two spheres are much overlapped in the experience of the doctor, who is vaguely in charge of this drama and known locally as something of a droll southern wit. But by now Dr. Woods, like everyone else, is exhausted as well as terrified of Spooner's mother Lily, and no droll southern wittage has rolled off his tongue in a long, long time.

It's a stalemate, then, the first of thousands Spooner will negotiate with the outside world, yet even as visions of stillborn livestock and dead mares percolate like a growling stomach through the tiny band of spectators, and Dr. Woods discreetly leaves the room to refortify from the locked middle drawer of his office desk, and Lily's sisters, who, sniffing tragedy, have assembled from as far off as Omaha, Nebraska, but are at this moment huddled together at the hallway window to have a smoke and watch for jumpers across the street, Spooner's mother rolls out of bed on her own and gains her feet, and in those first vertical moments, with one of her hands clutching a visitor's chair for balance and the other covering her mouth against the possibility of unpleasant morning breath, she issues Spooner, feet first and the color of an eggplant, the umbilical cord looped around his neck, like a bare little man dropped through the gallows on the way to the next world.

As it happened, Spooner was second out the door that morning, a few moments behind his better-looking fraternal twin, Clifford, who, in the way these things often worked out for Spooner's mother, arrived dead yet precious as life itself, and in the years of visitation ahead was a comfort to her in a way that none of the others (one before Spooner and two further down the line) could ever be.

And was forever, secretly, the favorite child.

TWO

Due to problems of tone and syntax, not to mention good taste (how, after all, are you supposed to fit a regular baby and a dead one into the same paragraph without ruining it for them both?), Spooner's birth was left out of society editor Dixie Ander's regular weekly account of local comings and goings in the *Milledgeville World Telegraph,* and the birth certificate itself was subsequently tossed by Miss Ander's unmarried first cousin, Charlotte Memms, who at this point in her career had worked without oversight or supervision for thirty-six years in the Baldwin County Office of Registrations and Certificates, filing and discarding documents as she saw fit. There was a soaking rain on the day that news of Spooner's birth arrived on her desk, and the afternoon before one of the Stamps niggers from down in the Bottoms had driven his turkey truck into town, parked in Miss Charlotte's just-vacated spot in the courthouse parking lot and promptly got himself arrested inside, sassing the county clerk over the poultry tax, and Miss Charlotte saw that truck full of turkeys in her regular spot when she came to work in the morning, half of them drowned, and decided then and there that she'd had enough—she was tired of being taken for granted and tired of people without manners—and so it happened that until the census board caught up with her the following year, the rule of thumb in Baldwin County was that you did not get born here without references.

Which is not meant to leave the impression that the birth went unrecorded. In Lily Spooner's log of unspeakable ordeals, it was never lower than number five, and Lily, it could be said, had made her bones in matters of the unspeakable and knew the real goods when she saw it. And was wolfishly jealous of what was hers. And had Spooner's brother only hung around a day or two, long enough to break bread, as they say, the tragedy might very well have made it all the way to the top.

Even so, no one even casually of Lily's acquaintance thought of suggesting that he appreciated what she had endured, certainly no doctor or relative, and if some afternoon a month or a year after the event, perhaps in the throes of an asthma attack, she suddenly compared the grittiness of birthing twins—she lost one, you know—to a battlefield amputation, who was going to argue the point? You? Are you crazy? She said things like this just daring someone like you to say something like that. Daring you to say anything at all. And you wouldn't, not even if you were standing there in the uniform of the United States Army, sprouting ribbons and medals on your chest like rows of porch pansies and peeking over the foot of her bed on stumps. You wouldn't, because hanging over this opera was the strange possibility that she *had* suffered beyond what you could understand, or imagine, and to demonstrate her vantage in the field, she could easily refuse food for a week and simply live off bad luck and misfortune. And how would you feel then?

But hold on a minute, you're thinking, sustain life on nothing but bad luck and misfortune?

To borrow one of Lily's many lifelong expressions which always ran an involuntary shudder through Spooner, you darn tootin'. Bad luck and misfortune. You probably have to see it for yourself to see it, but the model is there in any grade school history book, in the carefree wanderings of our predecessor, the migratory Sioux, happy as a clam out on the prairie, employing every last bit of his buffalo right down to the molars. Which is the way you live off misfortune and bad luck, using *everything*, the same way you live off the pitiful salary paid to public schoolteachers. Waste not, want not.

Which could have been the family motto, if the family had had a motto, which it didn't. As the cowboys say, they is some things you can get a rope around and some things you isn't.

So in fairness to Spooner's mother, it was an exhausting delivery at the end of an exhausting month: the heartbreak of Eisenhower over Adlai Stevenson (again), followed by the death of her father, followed by the sudden and mysterious illness of her husband Ward, followed by this luckless, endless labor leading to the death of Spooner's better-looking twin brother Clifford, her firstborn son.

And what came next? What did she have to show for her suffering?

Spooner.

Warren Whitlowe Spooner, five pounds, no ounces, fifty-three hours just getting through the door. Dr. Woods, who had predicted an easy birth, was humbled by and unable to influence the struggle taking place on his table and, before it was over was visiting the silver flask (Sigma Alpha Epsilon, University of Georgia, class of 1921) in his locked desk drawer so often that he'd quit locking it and was reduced to encouraging prayer and trying to keep the uneasy peace among the various family factions who had traveled to Georgia to help out, due to Ward's sudden and mysterious condition.

As for Ward, he spent the entire fifty-three-hour delivery at home with Spooner's sister Margaret, too weak even to drive Lily to the clinic when her water broke. And in spite of his previously unblemished record, the whole episode sniffed of neglect to Lily, but due to her own condition she was unable to get to the bottom of it then, and had to put off the investigation until later. When, of course, it was too late.

"Sometimes with twins," the doctor said that second day—several times, in fact, as he drank and forgot what he'd said before, "they isn't either one of them that wants to come out first."

THREE

On the same day Warren Spooner was born, December 1, 1956, a 360-pound, eight-term U.S. congressman named Rudolph Toebox jerked up out of his seat on the forty-yard line at Municipal Stadium in South Philadelphia—a hot dog vendor would tell the first reporter on the scene, "Dat big man come up outde heah like he hook on to a fishin' poe!"—rising to almost his full height before turning over in the air and flopping back onto two of the most expensive seats in Municipal Stadium, where he died sunny-side up across his wife's lap, in a sleet storm, during the third quarter of the Army-Navy football game. Her name was Iris.

The wife didn't scream or try to save him, only sat where she was, motionless, letting the news settle, watching the sleet glaze over Rudy's glasses, her tiny, gloved hand resting across the expanse of his stomach. Dead weight. Two Teddy Roosevelts. Her mind took a strange drift, as it tended to do in moments of embarrassment, and she pictured how much worse it might have been if this had happened earlier, in their room at the Bellevue-Stratford, where Rudy, as was his habit, had been standing at the window looking down at the common folk, naked as a jaybird save his cigar and the pair of python-skin cowboy boots he was wearing everywhere these days and which he could not get into or out of by himself. Could she have gotten him dressed before she called for help? Or even taken off the damn boots? And what if he'd fallen the other way, through the window?

She noticed the stitching had come out of his zipper, and the button at the waist had popped off. He was always outgrowing his pants. Big-boned, his mother said. But then, his mother was also big-boned, in that same way. His father, at the other end of things, had been pint-size and full of squint, one of those mean little fellows you run into now and then out west, always spoiling for a fight, who just can't leave a woman with a wide bottom alone.

Iris shifted out from under the press of his weight and he rolled off her knees and wedged between her shins and the seat back in front of them. Pinning her legs. A little air came out of him; it sounded like he'd sighed.

He was dead, though. Her people were all ranchers from west of the river, and she recognized a dead thing when she saw it, had seen the exact expression that just crossed her husband's face a hundred times in the slaughter shed, where the animals that they kept for themselves were butchered and, eerily enough, where Grandma Macon also cashed in one afternoon, in front of her, attending to the slaughter of a pig. In those days it was Iris's job to scrub down the floor with bleach before the blood congealed and turned slippery and left the scent of slaughter in the cement. Like anything else, pigs could be dangerous when they smelled it coming.

On the morning she was remembering now—it was sometime in the week after Christmas—she'd stood in the doorway with a hose and a bucket and a mop, the nozzle leaking a spray of icy water through her fingers, and watched the look of dying drop over the pig's face—like a cloud had crossed the sun—and then, with that same miraculous speed of shadows and clouds, cross the room to Grandma Macon and pass over her face too, as abruptly as the squirt of the animal's blood had a moment earlier jumped into her hair.

Grandma Macon's expression turned into that expression when the bottom drops out of your garbage bag. Iris had seen it enough to know that by the time you felt it coming loose, it was already too late—egg-shells, Kotex, coffee grounds, a Band-aid with body hair stuck in the adhesive, that little bag of turkey organs they stick inside the bird at the factory, like they were sending it out into the world with a sack lunch—and there was no stopping it then. The mess was there for anybody to see, and had to be cleaned up.

And the people in the stands around them were beginning to move now, some trying to get away, some calling for doctors, one man shouting, "Air, give him air!" The embarrassment of dying, the odor. My God, he'd messed his trousers.

"Air!" the man shouted. "Air . . ."

They had been married, Iris and Rudy, in a little church overlooking the great river and its valley, an old windmill creaking outside a stained-glass window propped open with a chalkboard eraser. Thirty-one years together, and now this.

She was forty-seven; he was forty-nine, the only man she'd ever suffered. She reached down to him, wedged in against the seat, and took the glasses off his nose. She put them in her pocket, thinking, *Just like that.*

FOUR

On the upside, even at the moment itself, it was not hard to see that there would be life after Toebox. Not that Iris didn't care, only that she would clearly survive. She found it was hard to take his death personally.

This was also the feeling back home, more or less, when word reached his constituents. It was like Montgomery Ward had gone out of business.

Not that Toebox was particularly worse than the other great public servants of his time, and in fact was in some ways probably better, at least kept in closer contact with the people. He probably knew a thousand of them by name—he had a trick of memory that helped him match names with faces—and this trick had naturally fostered in him the conceit that he was irreplaceable, which is a common enough conceit in the business, although in the hard light of day, Rudolph Toebox, like so many of his colleagues, was exactly as irreplaceable as the laces in your shoes.

He was drinking peppermint schnapps out of a leather-covered flask when the end came, sweating even in the cold, and had been trying to distract himself from an oncoming bout of food poisoning ever since he ate the hot dogs at the beginning of the second quarter. Three of them, heavy on the sauerkraut and onions. And now the same gimped-up little nigger harnessed into the aluminum box had reappeared at the end of the row of seats and was standing there, trying to get his attention, trying to sell him three more.

"Three mo', big man. Three mo' . . ."

The congressman ignored the vendor and concentrated on the problem. As it happened, he was known in Washington as a problem solver, and had his secrets for that too. One secret, actually, as at heart, like so many other distinguished public servants, he was a surprisingly simple fellow. A one-solution man, in fact.

No sudden moves.

That was the ticket. Long years of public servitude on behalf of one of the vast and barren regions of America—a thousand speeches at one-room schoolhouse graduations, at co-ops and churches and VFW halls—had taught him firsthand the nature of life on the prairie, and he had come to understand that nothing out there, not beast nor fowl, liked things to move suddenly; that sudden movement was always an invitation to stampede. Cattle, geese, bison, chickens, the common man: They were all the same, and now, in a moment of insight just before the end, he saw his theory also applied to diarrhea. Who knew, it might have been the key to the universe.

Too late for that, though. The seats he'd been given, wonderful as they were, were fifty yards from the closest bathrooms, and there was not a chance of making it. He didn't have the time; he didn't have the strength. He was weak in a way now that went beyond all the ways he had been weak before. In Toebox's final moments, he could not have lifted his own bosom.

Which was why, even suffocating in his coat, he hadn't been up to moving around enough to take it off. Instead, he sat inside it and sweated. The coat was made of vicuña and had been given to him for Christmas the previous year by the nation of Bolivia, along with a matching hat. Iris didn't care for the hat and worried that it made him look like a Communist, but Toebox wore it anyway. He loved hats, and here, if you'd like to see it, is a list of the ones she cleaned out of the Washington apartment later that week after she got back from the funeral: an Elk's cap, an honorary deputy sheriff's hat, a mortarboard he got from the state university where he received his honorary Ph.D., several Stetson cowboy hats that were presented to him as mementos for serving as grand marshal of various parades and rodeos in the western regions of his district, a Brooks Brothers fedora he was given—along with a pin-striped, double-breasted blue suit—when he toured the plant, a Beefeater's hat like the ones the guards wear at Buckingham Palace (a gift from the British ambassador to the U.N.), a Japanese helmet with a bullet hole through the side—the only one he paid for himself—and a yarmulke he got at some Jewish deal that he never did find out what it was supposed to be about.

Back in the home district Toebox was known variously as A Man of Many Hats and Your Voice in Washington and The Working Congressman—there were highway signs that said those things everywhere you went—but while he was in fact many-hatted, and undeniably had a certain voice in Washington (forty-yard-line seats to the Army-Navy game spoke for themselves), the only work he'd ever done that you could call work was a stint in the U.S. Navy, where his specialty was waxing floors. Toebox's floor waxing occurred in 1942, early in the war, and led to a Purple Heart when he stepped into a puddle of water as he operated the waxing machine, briefly dancing out into the land of cardiac arrest, then was brought back more or less along the same route, when a medic hooked up his toes to the same outlet, more or less inventing the defibrillator. After that, he would not even plug in a toaster, and was eventually designated Section 8 and sent home to Iris.

And there, as the district's first war hero returned live from combat, he ran for and was elected to public office, and spoke mysteriously of the hidden scars of war, and while he was not reluctant to wear his medals and ribbons at parades and VFW speeches and appearances at high school gymnasiums, the specific incident behind his own hidden scars Toebox would not discuss. More than once some smart little crapper in the audience asked if he'd smothered an enemy grenade—there was always one at every school assembly bringing his size into it—and he would eye the kid for a long minute before he answered, pointing him out for the principal to deal with later, and say the same thing: "The real heroes didn't come back, son." Which would shut the kid up, all right, and as a rule dropped the rest of them into a respectful silence too.

The farmers and ranchers in Toebox's part of the country were appreciative of his visits to their children's schools and his stand against higher taxes to raise the salaries of teachers and other public workers, and liked his billboards and his short, snappy-looking wife, and he was elected again and again.

His district was the entire state, a flat, dry rectangle of prairie and plains out in that part of the country that is all rectangles and plains, and occupied by farmers and ranchers and the salesmen in ties half a foot wide who followed them, selling them Oldsmobiles and John Deere tractors. Yet, in spite of the congressman's prairie roots, and hers, Iris decided to have the body buried at sea. Perhaps because of his service in the navy—he'd won the Purple Heart, after all—or perhaps it was the expense. It was not the cheapest thing in the world to ship 360-odd pounds across the country, especially refrigerated, which in itself seemed like a ridiculous waste of money at this time of year. Iris had spent her twenties in the Great Depression and had seen hard times and was tight with a dollar.

But whatever the reason she decided that her husband should be returned to the sea instead of the prairie, the point here is the way things happen—in this case, the end of the congressman and the beginning of Spooner—the long way around telling you that after a sparsely attended funeral, Toebox's casket was driven to the naval station in South Philadelphia, and the next morning loaded on board the U.S.S. *Buck Whittemore*, a 2,800-ton Forrest Sherman–class destroyer under the command of Commander Calmer Ottosson, a polite, soft-spoken farm boy from South Dakota turned wunderkind at the U.S. Naval Academy at Annapolis, turned youngest commander in the United States Navy, and now, still polite and soft-spoken, plainly an officer on the fast track to the top.

Except things morbid and unexpected happened one after another that day on the *Buck Whittemore*, and after that day, the only place Calmer Ottosson was going as far as the navy was concerned was back to wherever he came from, the sooner the better.

And which accounts, indirectly, for how he became Spooner's father.

FIVE

Calmer Ottosson had not received the coffin containing Rudolph Toebox gladly. The congressman came with reporters and photographers, for one thing, and a widow and a congressional aide and other congressmen and their congressional aides, and Calmer, who didn't like on-board ceremonies in the first place, or, now that he thought it over, on-board politicians, resented the waste of money and time just to drop one over the side. In this way he was unlike most of his classmates back at Annapolis, who were drawn into the service by ceremony and/or the uniform itself.

But then, Calmer was bare-bones itself. Except for physical-education classes, he'd had no social life at all at the academy, no girls, no card games, no sports, no fistfights, very little self-abuse. He was reclusive and self-reliant, never comfortable asking for anything, even the salt and pepper. His only authorized activity beyond the ordinary academic life of a midshipman was caring for the school's mascot, Bill, a sweet, low-key angora goat whom he fed and groomed throughout his junior and senior years, and for whom he kept a secret, oddly romantic diary entitled *The Quiet Yearnings of Bill, a Castrated Goat.*

He held himself to a short regimen of nightly calisthenics and taught himself to write with his feet. This foot writing was accomplished by holding a pencil between his second and third toes (counting from the inside out), and before he gave it up he could write in script or block letters and even turn the pencil around and erase his mistakes.

He was a natural student with a tireless curiosity and could stay awake forty-eight hours and still think clearly over an exam. He played the piano and did square roots in his head, and could read sheet music and in some way hear it almost as if he were remembering it.

He kept these things to himself and kept himself apart, yet never seemed to stir the kind of resentment and misunderstandings that you might expect, this sort of person in this sort of place. And nothing about this ever changed. Sixth in his class at Annapolis, first at flight school in Memphis, and right to the end had no enemies below or above.

If the question occurs to you as to how or why a human being teaches himself to write with his feet, it began, at least in this case, with a letter from home. Calmer's mother wrote all the letters and cards that came out of the house, and he received one every week, Wednesday or Thursday, usually six pages long, as it was her habit to compose a page a day, usually after the supper dishes were done, and rest on the Sabbath. The letters were full of weather forecasts, crop reports, news of broken drive belts, what the coyotes had killed while she and Dad were at church (*My, but the varmint has got Father's dander up this time! He's still setting up there in the upstairs bathroom window with his 30-30 and a flashlight, wouldn't even come down for supper . . .*), stories of broken fences and heartburn, car wrecks, tractor accidents. And newspaper clippings. Sometimes it seemed like she'd clipped the whole *Conde Record*. Winners and losers of the turkey shoot down at the Rod and Gun Club, football scores, honor rolls, high school graduations, marriages, births, obituaries. The letters were always signed *Love, Father and Mom*.

It was toward the end of one of her letters, after a detailed, strangely nonpartisan account of a monthlong battle of wits between Father and a weasel that was raising cain in the henhouse that she dropped in the news about Arlo:

I suppose you heard by now that Cousin Arlo finally run out of Luck with that polar bear in Minneapolis and had Three Fingers de-gloved on his left hand, which I am given to understand means the bear got it all but the Bones, which the docs proceeded to Lop off at the hospital anyways. He made all the papers and the UPI news wire, and said he didn't blame nobody at the Zoo, lest of all the bear, who was just doing the job she was hired to do. Just his luck to be left handed! I am certain he'll be looking at those missing fingers for the rest of his Life, and think about what a darn Fool he was to be getting drunk with that crowd in the first place. But that's Arlo for you, the one that's always got to find out everything for himself.

And off this news, Calmer taught himself to write with his feet. More out of curiosity than sympathy, wondering what he would do if he lost his own fingers. As the fitness reports always said—right up until the day he was ruined—Calmer Ottosson was an officer prepared for contingencies.

But more to the point, teaching himself to write with his feet was the sort of thing he had been up to all his life. Making his own fun, as the great writer called it.

But then, like the great writer, he'd grown up alone.

An adopted only child on a break-even two-hundred-acre farm fourteen miles southeast of Conde, South Dakota, a tiny spot up in the northeast corner of the map near Aberdeen, who at seven years old enjoyed sitting barefoot in a plowed field, balancing his father's helmet from the war on his head and firing his single-shot Remington .22 into the air, correcting for the breeze as the little puffs of dust appeared in the spots where the bullets landed, trying to bring one right in on top of his head. He was a child who listened to what he was told and never bragged about his good marks at school or his shooting, just as years later, at the academy, he never mentioned that he could write with his feet. Not to anyone there, not in any of his letters home. Not even the ones to Cousin Arlo, although Arlo would have been tickled to hear of it—Arlo was everybody's favorite, and not just because he led a colorful life and visited the twin cities and Chicago and came home with stories on himself, but also because, unlike the rest of them, he knew how to accept a compliment without feeling indebted, which led to family resentments. Most of them wouldn't smile if you gave them the Nobel Prize. On the other hand, Arlo was a damn-the-torpedoes drinker, especially at family celebrations, and Calmer didn't want the relatives hearing about his foot writing at a baptism or a funeral and coming away thinking that he'd got so fancy in college that he was having fun these days off the misfortunes of his own cousin, which would just kill his mother.

Once in a while, though, alone on a Saturday night, he might take off his shoes and socks and stand on his desk, ducking his head to accommodate the ceiling, and write a letter:

> *Dear Arlo,*
>
> *Greetings and salutations! Mother wrote with the happy news that you have finally quit biting your nails.*

Or something of that nature, which was the nature of Calmer and Arlo around each other, and had always been. Calmer was no mischief maker himself, but he had an appreciation for those who were, and even when his luck ran out and he lost all the things he'd worked for and was drained empty, he never quit trying to see himself in the world as Arlo did, as part of the story.

SIX

If it is fair to say that Calmer Ottosson got where he was in spite of an inclination to avoid human entanglements, it is also fair to say that he got where he was because of it, loners and leaders so often turning out to be the same people. This solitary bent was his nature, but it was also a practical thing. Humans, he'd noticed early on, even before the academy, followed best when they couldn't see who was leading.

There was another reason for keeping apart, demonstrated in his awkwardness at finding himself off duty and in the proximity of the same men who took his orders. He accepted this awkwardness, knowing better than to try to change it, knowing his shyness was as set in him as the shape of his head. On duty, though, there was no shyness; he was fair with people and respectful, played no favorites, kept no enemies. Kept to himself. Privately, he did not trust even the best of them to do their jobs, particularly at sea, and constantly took the ship's signs himself, often knowing instinctively where trouble was coming—the engine room, communications, the kitchen, the mood of the crew—even before it arrived.

He did these things quietly and in order of importance, leaving time enough during the day to do his own work too.

How he kept this schedule was anybody's guess, except that for a human being Calmer could do with very little sleep. Beyond that, what was most in his favor was an innate sense of how things were put together and the way one part affected another—an engine, a horse, a septic tank, an outbreak of flu on ship—if a thing had moving parts, he could find a logic behind the movement, and when it broke, he would see how to fix it.

He was slower to see himself in the same way, though, and it was only later on that he came to understand that he'd done too much of the work himself, kept to himself too long. It had affected his judgment, this being alone, and led to what happened, and made him see things that were not there.

SEVEN

The sky was still dark when the congressman was de-
livered to the pier, not a glimpse of light in the east. The congressman
arrived in a gray Cadillac hearse, the driver an old man in a black suit and a
jet-black toupee who owned a funeral home on South Broad Street and did
quite a bit of business with the navy. Calmer came off the ship to personally
supervise the unloading and introduced himself to the undertaker.

"Calmer?" the undertaker said. "I never heard that one before." Then
he squeezed Calmer's bicep and said, "You ever done any piano moving,
sonny?"

It was a few minutes before six in the morning, and there were already
eight or nine reporters on board, along with half again as many photographers. It was cold, and the newspapermen were all down in the galley,
some of them eating, some of them drinking laced coffee against the chill
of the morning, talking about the stories they'd covered that were better
stories than this one.

The casket was made of mahogany and weighed, fully loaded, something over five hundred pounds. It emerged from the Cadillac dark and
gleaming (rollers had been installed at the business end of the vehicle, and
they rang faintly as they spun) and was gathered up into the hands of as
many sailors as could squeeze in to grab hold. Wherever Calmer went in
the navy, it was always the enlisted men—not the officers—who went out
of their way not to disappoint him.

He signed for the congressman and shook the funeral man's hand—it felt as small and fragile as a child's—and the casket was placed carefully in the center of a platform attached by four lines to a windlass operated from the deck of the *Buck Whittemore*.

Calmer checked the lines himself, then motioned to the operator, and the platform lifted slowly into the air, Calmer leaning farther and farther back to follow its progress. There was a whining noise from the electric motor and the platform climbed slowly into the fog and then stopped. The noise changed pitch and the platform jerked sideways, commencing a swinging motion that continued even as the casket dropped slowly toward the deck.

Calmer followed this motion from the ground, sensing that the windlass operator was unsure of himself in the fog, wishing he were operating it himself, and almost at the same moment this thought arrived, he saw two of the supporting lines go slack. Then, in a kind of slow motion, the platform dropped open about sixty degrees and stopped, and Calmer, who decided later that he must have been under the influence of the undertaker's question about piano moving, in fact thought of a grand piano, somehow turned upside down, the lid falling open. And then saw the piano player tumbling out of his own instrument.

And as Calmer imagined falling piano players, the casket dropped silently through the fog, and then began landing, three distinct landings—two crashes and a tremendous thud, like God himself had fallen out of the nest, a noise that hung distinctly in Calmer's memory all day.

———

The casket and its lid and its various hardware were strewn across the deck, reminding Calmer of a pecan nut stomped open. The congressman himself was lying belly up across a stairwell in the attitude of a man offering his face to the shower, or the Lord, looking for all the world like somebody with nothing to hide.

On the bright side of things, beyond having come apart the casket did not appear damaged, so the problem was only a matter of reassembly. And what could be assembled once could be assembled again.

Calmer issued orders quietly, and there was an equally quiet, insectlike scramble of sailors over the body and the various parts of the casket, and a moment later the body and the various pieces of the casket were below deck and Calmer was surprised to find himself washed in relief at having it all out of sight.

———

Calmer went into the room and locked the door.

The congressman's body and the pieces of his casket were lying across two tables used for butchering. The room was airtight and refrigerated, ventilated from the ceiling. Enormous sides of beef hung from hooks, pale blue and shiny, and there were boxes of poultry, cheese, eggs, thousands of pounds of perishable food. The congressman looked vaguely uncomfortable, his hair unmussed and perfect, decked out in a pinstriped Brooks Brothers suit which, truth be told, did him no favors, figure-wise, an effect enhanced perhaps by the fact that he was barefoot, his feet a color of blue similar to the hanging meat, and swollen well beyond the recognizable shape of human feet, as if they had been squeezed out of the pants' legs like toothpaste.

Calmer used a thin nylon rope to hold the box together while the glue set, looping it top to bottom like some country girl's suitcase.

He closed the door behind him, hoping to borrow another hour against the moment the coffin had to be untied and brought back up on deck. He found his body singing with optimism. The box would hold—it should hold—although the pallbearers would have to carry it on their shoulders now because one of the railings had broken off the side and would never support the weight of the full casket. It could be done, though. He'd lifted the body and gotten it back into the box alone; six men could get it up onto their shoulders. The hard part would be navigating the stairway back to the deck. He pictured how that might go and

experienced a brief sagging in the singing optimism department, and behind that came a knee-buckling weight which is the burden of optimism,
at least when optimism flies in the face of common sense and perhaps the
laws of physical science.

And now he remembered that three of the pallbearers would be politicians—a member of the House from a district adjacent to Toebox's and
two of Toebox's aides—and Calmer tried but could no longer remember
what there had been to be optimistic about in the first place. Politicians
for pallbearers? The effect of cold temperature on quick-drying glue? A
ship full of reporters and photographers?

Thinking these thoughts, he turned a corner and very nearly flattened
Iris Toebox.

EIGHT

The moment he laid eyes on this woman, a shot of desire fired somewhere so close to Calmer Ottosson that he could feel the concussion, and a whole tree of blackbirds rose at once into the sky. Which is the romantic way of saying that he just wanted to row her across Lake Michigan.

Iris was wearing a black coat over a black dress and a hat with a veil that was not yet dropped over her face. He had seen her picture the day before in the *Philadelphia Bulletin*, but it had not prepared him for this. She was not beautiful so much as flawless. Everything perfectly in place, perfectly in balance. Perfect calves, perfect ankles, perfect feet—although he couldn't actually see the feet, which were inside the shoes setting off her ankles and calves.

And the wings beat in his throat. All the panicked birds.

On her arm was a second lieutenant named Jerome Jensen, to Calmer's knowledge the worst officer on his ship. A man of breathtaking incompetence, no attention span, in love with detail and procedure and the uniform itself, and who habitually wrote up enlisted men for the smallest infractions and informed confidentially on his fellow officers.

It spoke of them both perhaps that Jensen had no whiff that he and Calmer were not eye to eye.

On reflection, Calmer would see that in regard to what happened that morning vis-à-vis the widow Toebox, it was his own imagination at fault; he had never imagined that even Jensen could make a botched job of greeting the congressman's widow. Calmer had intended to meet her himself but after the loading accident wanted as much time to put the congressman and his box right as he could get, and so had turned it over to the first officer he saw, which was Jensen. It seemed like a good idea, in fact, as Jensen looked like an officer and always wore his uniform spotless and freshly pressed. Calmer was very clear with the orders: Greet Mrs. Toebox when she arrived at the ship, apologize for Calmer's absence, escort her to Calmer's quarters to await the burial. Make her comfortable. Offer her coffee or a drink, something to eat if she wanted it, the morning papers, and then leave her alone.

He had given these orders slowly, patiently, and Jensen had nodded along just as patiently, yet here he stood, slightly behind her in the passageway, looking confident and not a little self-satisfied.

"Commander Ottosson," he said, "may I present Mrs. Toebox. She has asked to be with her husband."

She smiled and offered Calmer her hand. Pale, tapered fingers lay cool and light against his palm. Her wedding ring had been moved to her right hand, which he remembered was the custom of widows back in his part of South Dakota, too.

He tried not to look at Jensen, afraid he might strangle him. "Allow me to offer you my quarters, Mrs. Toebox," he said, and now he did glance quickly at Jensen. "It's warmer, and there's something to drink. I'm sure you'll be more comfortable."

"Thank you," she said, "but I prefer to be with my husband."

She spoke directly and evenly, and her voice did not begin to break as he thought it might. She waited a moment longer, then smiled politely and looked back at Jensen. "This way, you said?"

"Yes ma'am," and he nodded at Calmer as if he had everything under control. She started around him in the direction of the storage room. She was smooth and perfectly balanced, giving nothing away. Bereaved as a house cat, from her outward appearance.

He stood a moment watching her from behind, aching to protect her—always his first impulse with women who attracted him. He realized this was not an ordinary impulse, not even faintly tangent to sexual intercourse, but there it was and had always been. Except this time there were birds and the ache to protect her mingled with the woman's scent.

He got to the door first. "I'm afraid there was a small accident bringing the casket on board," he said. She didn't seem to hear that, just waited for him to open the door.

It was colder inside than he remembered. The casket also seemed different now: lying over the tables against the far wall, tied up like a hostage. Moisture had condensed on the lid.

He sent Jensen to get Mrs. Toebox a chair, and for a few minutes he was alone with her in cold storage, and the panicked birds pounded in his throat.

She seemed to think he had other things on his mind. "I'm quite comfortable here, Captain," she said. "I'm sure you have more important matters to address."

"Commander," he said, "I'm only a commander." He saw that she didn't understand the difference, but he was satisfied just to have set the record straight. He noticed that she hadn't remarked on the condition of the casket or asked what sort of accident he'd meant.

He heard himself say, "I understand your husband was a navy man." Polite conversation for Calmer was like dancing, trying to remember the steps.

She gazed at the casket, and he couldn't read her at all.

"He was in the war," she said. "He got the Purple Heart."

And then Jensen came back with a chair, and as time passed it occurred to Calmer that everything he had ever been and done was aimed at this single morning, that she was what he had come this far to find.

———

The *Buck Whittemore* cleared port at Philadelphia at 0800 hours and headed for deep water. Calmer reluctantly left Iris in cold storage and went to the bridge, checking the course and the radar. A light fog lay over the water, but a breeze was coming up from the south, beginning to clear it off, and he could see into it almost to the curve of the earth. His eyesight was still exceptional; the doctors at flight school had never seen anything like it.

He thought of the widow Toebox down in the storage room alone with the corpse, sitting next to it in the chair Jensen had brought, her legs crossed, feeling the roll and the size of the sea. And thought of the way she presented herself, even in mourning, as if nothing from life had laid a finger on her yet. In his experience the widow's appearance was an oddity for a woman who had grown up on a ranch. As a rule, ranch work—like farmwork, there wasn't much difference for the women—left its mark on them early, even if they married and moved into town. The womanly side dried up ahead of time, and year by year what was left was distinguishable from the men, who also were drying up, but more slowly and in a different way. Which is to say the men dried up mostly from the work, the women from the worry.

The wives of Calmer's cousins, for instance, were all wrung out by now, most of them still only in their thirties. Arlo's wife was sunshine itself, but already whiskery and the best arm wrestler in the family.

But nothing about the widow Toebox reminded Calmer of any of his cousins' wives. He pictured her now inspecting the casket—which he hadn't quite gotten shut all the way, leaving the width of a dime between the box and the lid, a crack he expected would be hidden by the flag—and then had another picture, which he had been picturing on and off ever since he'd seen the photograph of Toebox and his wife that ran with the obituary in the *Evening Bulletin*. How had it looked, the act itself between the congressman and his small, tidy wife? From the photograph in the *Bulletin*, it must have looked like a fat man fucking a mattress.

And as that image came and passed, Lieutenant Jensen meandered up onto the bridge, blowing over the surface of a cup of coffee, and sat down casually on the corner of the map table.

Calmer was still picturing the widow alone in the meat locker, and seeing Jensen he was suddenly unsure if holes had been drilled in the floor of the casket. The holes should have been drilled at the funeral home, but the old undertaker was plainly in some prolonged state of distraction, in the way old men sometimes were when the great distraction of their lives was no longer much of a distraction and they saw what was left. Or, to put it another way, they'd let go of pussy matters only to find themselves confronted with the big picture.

Calmer wondered if the big picture looked different if you'd been putting bodies in the ground all your life.

He looked around the wheelhouse, and everyone save Jensen was at work.

"Lieutenant," he said, and Jensen stood up and saluted. He hadn't noticed Calmer when he walked in.

"Yes, sir."

Calmer motioned him closer and spoke so that the other officers and men couldn't hear what he was saying. He did not chastise officers in front of each other; ordinarily he didn't have to chastise them at all. They knew he was paying attention, and for most of them that was enough. "I have something for you to do," he said.

"Yes, sir."

Calmer saw him begin to smile and had a corresponding impulse to pick him up by the neck. Instead, he moved a few inches even closer and was pleased to see a look of alarm cross the second lieutenant's face. "I want the coffin prepared for burial," he said.

"Aye-aye, sir."

"Wait, just wait. I want you to go back down to the storage locker and station yourself outside the door. Am I clear so far? You are outside the locker, she is inside, the door is shut."

"Yes, sir."

"A few minutes ahead of the ceremony, I will arrive to escort Mrs. Toebox to the deck. After we are no longer in the locker, you will enter the room and check the coffin to make sure holes have been drilled into the bottom. There should be ten or twelve holes, one inch in diameter. If there are not, you will drill them yourself. Are we clear?"

"Aye-aye, sir. Ten to twelve holes, one inch in diameter."

"The casket is lying between two tables, so you won't have to move it to gain access to the bottom."

"Yes, sir. No problem, sir."

Calmer studied him a few seconds longer. He thought of calling him off the job and doing it himself. Just drilling the holes with her there in the room, but then he imagined the drill bit breaking through and slipping in too deep, pulling spiraled flesh out of the bottom of the box.

No, he thought, *not with her in the room.*

Still, he tried to cover his bases. "This is not a matter in which you are to exercise personal discretion, Lieutenant," he said.

"No, sir."

Calmer studied him a moment and then nodded, dismissing him, and went back to the helm, lost in the image of the congressman having at his poor smothering wife.

———

He cut the speed to three knots, the ship rolling now in five-foot swells. Approaching the spot. He went to collect the widow.

Jensen was outside her door, as ordered. He knocked once, waited a moment, and looked in. To his enormous relief, she was still there. He felt ridiculous. What had he expected?

———

The crew was assembled in parade dress all along the port side of the deck. The reporters and photographers had come up from the ship's galley and were clustered together, apart from the sailors. Calmer stood with the widow and as he watched, one of the photographers, an old-timer in a duck hunter's hat and a black cigar took the cigar out of his teeth, leaned over the side and vomited, some of it blowing back onto his pants and the cameras hanging from his neck. He put the cigar back in his teeth, pulled a handkerchief out of his back pocket and dabbed here and there around the cigar to clean up his mouth and chin, and then knelt and began working on his shoes.

Calmer hoped the rest of the media wouldn't begin chucking breakfast too, which was the way it sometimes went. Somebody yodels and a minute later you've got an avalanche. He couldn't protect her from that.

There was motion behind him, the honor guard emerged from below, and behind it the coffin bearers and the coffin. Three sailors, three civilians. The coffin was draped in a flag of the United States. Calmer had not seen who'd brought the coffin up from the meat locker to its present spot, but two of his healthiest-looking enlisted men now lifted it from the deck and set it carefully on the coffin bearers' shoulders. Among the bearers were the congressman from the neighboring district and the two Toebox aides. The color guard was all from Toebox's home district and had been brought on board with the widow and politicians for the ceremony. There was no official beginning, but the procession to the side of the ship began and the crew came to attention, and a moment later even the members of the press fell silent, and in the quiet you could hear the flags overhead snapping in the wind. The coffin bearers, meanwhile, sailors and civilians alike, took short, stumbling steps under the weight, and the ship pitched and rolled. The wind had moved to the north, and the ship's bow was no longer directly into it.

The civilians had all taken one side of the box, and the sailors from Toebox's home district had taken the other. The sailors were taller than the civilians, and stronger, and that side of the box was riding half a foot higher than the other. Calmer now saw disaster everywhere he looked.

The congressman from the neighboring district had turned red, as if he were holding his breath, and then he stumbled, and the whole civilian side of the casket seemed to stumble with him. The scene earlier on the deck came back to Calmer, the casket lying in parts and the congressman face up, a quizzical cast to his expression, as if there were something about all this that he still didn't understand.

Calmer stood beside the widow Toebox, and she moved slightly in to him, her shoulder touching his arm, but he could not be sure if she had wanted him closer or if it was only the rolling of the ship. She did not pull away, though, and the spot where they connected issued some sweet, unknown buzzing.

The casket bearers reached the spot and set the casket down. Relieved of his load the congressman from the neighboring district pitched violently and pulled the flag off the flag-draped coffin in an effort to save himself from the fall. And Calmer felt her still there against him, slightly pressed in to him, all of her attention straight ahead. Did she even know they were touching? He did not move even an inch, afraid to lose the connection.

He tried to think of something to say but nothing came. Small talk again. The honor guard stood at attention behind them, rifles at their sides, and then he did think of something—he saw he could tell her to cover her ears before they fired off the salute. It felt like a blessing, this small thing he'd been given to say. He saw her gaze shift to the mechanism that would release the casket into the sea. Beyond it the sea looked as hard and gray as the side of the ship itself.

The ship's chaplain stepped forward and set about putting death in perspective. Not the end of things but the beginning. She moved slightly away and stood next to the casket, laid her gloved hand on top.

Calmer noticed Jensen then, off to the side in his dress whites, his mind a hundred miles away. Calmer remembered that he'd once heard him say the navy was his life.

The wind was picking up, pressing the widow's skirt into her legs, revealing her as clearly as if, in the same clothes, she'd just been pulled out of a swimming pool. She did not fuss with the skirt or turn away from the wind. She stood, her hand resting on the casket.

The chaplain finished his opening remarks and two members of the honor guard stepped forward to remove the flag, folding it into a tight triangle—the folding took a long time because of the wind—and then laid it in the widow's hands. She accepted it awkwardly, as you might take a baby if you were handed one with a loaded diaper. Then she stepped back to the place she had been before and again leaned slightly in to Calmer's arm, as if they'd made up after a quarrel.

The congressman from the neighboring district came forward now, holding a Bible. He faced her, smiling kindly, and then opened to Psalm 19 and began to read. It turned out he'd been a Bible thumper himself before he got into politics. He had to speak up to be heard over the wind, and to hold the page with the flat of his hand to keep it from blowing him into the New Testament, and after he finished, he put his hand on Mrs. Toebox's shoulder and then bent toward her and spoke into her hair. Calmer could not hear what he said. The widow stepped back and shook her head, and the congressman nodded to the chaplain, and then the chaplain nodded to another officer, who nodded to an enlisted man, who saluted the officer and tripped the mechanism that sprung the board, and in that exact moment, the wind died and the world held its breath.

The board dropped, the sound of the casket sliding off into eternity was like a long jump shot getting nothing but net, and then followed a moment of silence so long that you could almost think something had snared the box on the way down.

Finally, though, the splash. As if together they had willed it to hit the water. Calmer relaxed and could not even guess at what he had been afraid had gone wrong. Gravity?

He was watching her when the casket hit the water, and saw no flinch at the sound, no reaction at all, and saw that she would hold together. Like women of the prairie from the very beginning of the prairie, who buried their husbands and stood their ground. Mrs. Toebox was no faint heart.

The officer who had nodded to the enlisted man who released the coffin now called the honor guard to attention: by naval regulations, a three-gun salute. "Ready," he said.

Calmer leaned closer to her and for a moment felt her hair blow against his lips.

"Aim . . ."

"You may want to cover your ears," he said.

"I'm sorry?" she said.

The rifles went off, not quite in unison, and after the concussion there was a moment like the moment after you hit the water from the high board, when all the noise in the pool is suddenly mute. The widow herself seemed unaffected. She had not moved an inch at the sound and now returned her attention to the wall of gray sea.

He felt the tickle of her hair across his skin, and then, perhaps due to the soft fog in his ears from the rifle noise, perhaps not even hearing the words himself, he choked out, "Iris . . ." And somehow butted her just over the temple.

She fell back a step and turned to him with a quick, strange look, touching the spot where he'd butted her and then the guns went off again and seemed to remind her of where she was, and her gaze softened and moved back out in the direction of the sea, where her husband was settling into his eternal digs.

Calmer had not moved an inch, as slow as the widow to realize what had just happened.

"Excuse me. I'm terribly . . ."

And then stopped, realizing she was paying no attention. It was possible that the rifles firing and the head butting had rendered her deaf. She still stared out into the endless water, her gaze moving slowly aft as the ship made its three knots, and now the wind came up again, but from the other direction, the south. Weatherwise, a strange, strange day.

The guns fired again, this time catching him by surprise, and he realized he'd lost count. Not just of the firing of the rifles, but of the day itself. The details didn't seem to have any order.

And when he looked at her again he saw the same confusion in her expression, as if she were lost or didn't understand what they were doing. And the chaplain, what was wrong with the chaplain?

The widow finally spoke. "Excuse me," she said, as if nothing had happened between them, as if a moment earlier he hadn't butted her and breathed her name into her ear, "but isn't it supposed to be sinking?" She had a sweet, flat twang that reminded him of home.

The chaplain, for his part, looked like a mink in a trap, willing to chew off a foot to get loose. But then he was timid for a chaplain, at least by comparison with the other chaplains Calmer had known, and Calmer thought it was a good thing that he'd chosen a career in the navy, as he would have a hard time of it out in the civilian world, where a man in his line had to be able not only to sell but close the deal.

Calmer moved a little closer to the rail then and saw the casket, riding in the water like a cork. Behind him, she was speaking again but addressing the chaplain now. "Pardon me," she said, "but is something out of the ordinary?" The chaplain appeared terrified of being pulled further into this mess than he was.

And the casket rolled in the ocean, as seaworthy and tight as the *Buck Whittemore* herself. "Will somebody *please* tell me what's going on?" she said, sounding more ragged now, as if the whole sorry episode, starting back at the Army-Navy game, was all catching up with her at once.

Calmer smiled in a reassuring way, stalling for time to think.

She raised her voice. "Will somebody here please tell me what's going on?"

He said, "Mrs. Toebox, it might be best if you went below deck . . ."

She stared at him flatly and then turned to the chaplain and said, "Do you have a cigarette at least?" She was used to getting what she wanted, Calmer saw that now, but it only made him want to protect her more.

Second Lieutenant Jensen appeared with a pack of Chesterfields and a lighter. Calmer waited until he'd lit her up, and then took Jensen by the arm and steered him a few yards away. Until this moment, Calmer had never in his career put his hands on a man under his command, not in anger. He'd broken up fights, he'd shaken a sailor or two awake on watch. He'd caught thieves and loan sharks and extortionists and sent the worst of them to the brig. He'd had men go crazy and grabbed them before they could jump, and once a petty officer named Oliver Irwin had tried to throw him overboard during a Saturday-morning inspection. Calmer had wrestled him down ten feet from the side of the ship and held him there until he'd stopped kicking. The kid was the smallest sailor on board, and three times as strong as he looked. A farm boy too. Calmer still smiled at that, remembering how close Oliver Irwin had come to throwing him over the side.

He squeezed Jensen's arm, which was so soft as to feel boneless. "Mr. Jensen," he said, "did you prepare that casket for burial?"

"Yes, sir," he said. "I checked it over."

A look passed over his face, though, and Calmer saw that he couldn't remember if he'd drilled the holes or not.

"Do you have an opinion as to why it's floating?" he said.

"Sir?"

"I said, why is it floating?" He heard his own voice now, which meant he was getting his hearing back. Jensen looked confused. "Why hasn't the casket sunk?"

Jensen said, "Sir?" and an instant later, without really meaning to, Calmer reached up and pinched the man's cheeks, squeezing them together, or as close to together as he could. This pinching formed Jensen's lower lip into a spout and a heavy line of saliva dripped out of it over Calmer's hand. He cranked Jensen's head in the direction of the coffin. He hadn't intended to take it so far, but once in a blue moon things happened on their own. His hand skidded across Jensen's cheeks, and then Calmer had his lip, and then let go suddenly, sorry now that he'd grabbed his face at all.

"Do you see it, Lieutenant?" he said. "Is it coming back to you now, what we're talking about?" The widow took a long pull on the Chesterfield, then flipped it over the side.

Jensen's eyes were tearing, and Calmer saw that he'd somehow bloodied his lip.

"Yes, sir," Jensen said, but he spoke indistinctly, something wrong with the shape of his mouth.

"Is it sinking?"

"No, sir."

"Why doesn't an object sink, Jensen? You went to the University of Minnesota . . ."

Calmer heard her behind him. "Has someone got another smoke?"

"It's made of wood, sir," Jensen said.

"Did you drill holes in it?"

Calmer saw it now. Jensen's lip was somehow stuck behind his front teeth, and Jensen took it in his fingers and pulled it out before he answered. "My suggestion, sir, would be to put a boat in the water . . ."

There were specks of blood on Jensen's gloves and down the front of his uniform. There was also blood on Calmer's hand, already tacky. He felt her watching him, waiting for him to put a boat in the water and rescue the casket. He couldn't, of course. You didn't put a boat in the water unless there was no choice. Especially in choppy water. You didn't risk lives to save a dead man, even a dead member of Congress.

Jensen began to say something else but changed his mind. He dabbed at his lip instead. The casket had crossed into the ship's wake to the starboard side and was getting smaller all the time, the polished wood catching the sun as it bobbed. The photographers were shooting away, the whine of their motor drives audible even in the wind.

Her eyes moved from Calmer to the casket and back to Calmer. But there was nothing he could do.

"Chaplain," he said to the chaplain, "would you escort Mrs. Toebox belowdecks?" But she was shaking her head even before it was all out of his mouth.

"No," she said, "I am the wife of a U.S. congressman, and I'm not going anywhere while you just let him float away . . ." She looked out into the wake, and the conversation was over. The reporters were writing in their notebooks; he couldn't say if she'd noticed them or not, and the casket bobbed in the sun like the kindling of some ferocious headache in the distance.

"He couldn't even swim," she said, as if that should have made it easier to sink him.

Calmer said, "Chaplain . . ." and the chaplain reached tentatively for her arm, but she pulled away the moment he touched her sleeve. The reporters were moving closer, trying to see what was going on.

"Can't we just pick it back up and try again?" she said. She'd been angry a moment before, but now she was only exhausted.

Calmer shook his head. "There's nothing to pick it up with, ma'am. I can't put a boat in the water, not in this situation. I promise, though, I won't let the remains float off into the ocean. But now for your own peace of mind . . ."

She closed her eyes. "No," she said.

Someone had given her another cigarette and she looked around for a light. Calmer had no lighter but the chaplain pulled one out of his pants pocket and cupped his hands against the wind and tried to get it to work. The wind was back up, though and his hands were shaking, and the lighter blew out again and again.

She waited, leaning forward into his hands each time he tried to light her up, and then took the lighter away from him and lit the cigarette herself. She drew the smoke into her lungs—Calmer was mortified to find himself staring right at her lungs, and then to realize he was still staring at her lungs—and then she closed her eyes around the feel of the smoke, perhaps trying to shut off everything else. She handed the lighter back to the chaplain.

"Please, ma'am, you keep it," he said.

She would not be talked off the deck. She either had to be carried off or left where she was. Calmer imagined the pictures in the newspapers, the widow kicking, teeth bared, her dress slid up until her panties showed. She held the cigarette at the very tips of her fingers and leaned a few degrees over the railing to look back on the casket, and the wind, which had shifted again, pressed the material of the dress into her bottom, which had conjugated itself into a perfect valentine.

He saw it then, that he'd misread her. She was frantic, but not over her husband; she was like some claustrophobic child who does not want to get on the elevator, and then, thinking of claustrophobia, he reflected on the clammy, loose press of Rudolph Toebox himself, mounting up. Yes, that was it. She was here to see him sink.

A moment passed, and then a look of loathing crossed her face and she breathed the words: "*It's coming back.*"

He willed himself to look another direction, spotted his gunnery officer and turned away from Mrs. Toebox to speak to him privately.

He was staring again. It was like catching a fingernail in a tear in the lining of your pocket—you forget it's there, and then you're snagged on it again. He sensed that she was about to break into tears, and sensed how much she did not want to cry here in public, and he reached out to steady her. And in what was already the strangest day of his life, the strangest thing yet occurred. She had seen him coming and moved slightly away, not wanting to be touched—he saw that too late—and his hand, which he'd stopped in plenty of time, circled back like some malfunctioned missile and went straight for her bosom. Her left bosom, his right hand. It seemed to him that the ship pitched, or some spasm had taken over his nervous system.

Another, different sort of loathing passed over her face, replacing all the conflicting expressions already there, and he realized that even if he knew what just had happened—he didn't, and never would—something as bad or worse would happen while he was explaining it. Calmer was not in any way a superstitious man, was the opposite, in fact, a mathematician who understood and believed in the laws of probability and chance, but on this day he and the universe had not started out even.

"Ready here, sir," the gunnery man said.

Calmer looked up at him, knowing there was no way out, and nodded. Only that, a single nod. It was quiet a moment, and then the clear metallic sound of the gun being cocked, and then a long burst of fire so loud that Jensen, still preoccupied with his bleeding lip, bolted and ran for cover.

The first rounds broke the water perhaps twenty yards in front of the casket, and led from there directly to the box, reminding Calmer of the trails left by geese as they tiptoed out of the water to take flight.

And then the box itself. The first round that hit blew the top, and it splintered and spun high into the air, and was still in the air as other pieces of the thing exploded out beneath it.

Time passed, and the splashing began as the pieces fell back into the ocean, and then that was over and the sea was covered with pieces of the package, and Calmer didn't see how it could do anybody any good to check what was floating and what had sunk.

NINE

The court-martial was a formality. He was convicted of dereliction and acquitted of conduct unbecoming an officer—several members of the crew having testified to the strangeness of the sea that day, to swells six feet high, and swore that, knowing their commander and knowing the ship, any groping that may have occurred could only have been accidental.

Calmer's appointed lawyer was a recent graduate of Rutgers law school who did not look old enough to vote and found reasons for optimism right up to the announcement of the verdict.

The trial itself took only two hours in the morning; the deliberations went on all afternoon. The lawyer was buoyed at each new half hour that went by in deliberations, and he seemed like a pretty nice kid to Calmer, just starting his career in the law, and Calmer wasn't up to telling him that the deliberations were only a courtesy, that he would be guilty on one count, not guilty on the other. It didn't matter which one they chose. He was out of the navy; he wasn't going to jail. He would probably be fined what the navy owed him in pay.

The court came back finally at five-thirty with dereliction of duty, and on reflection, Calmer saw it was the right verdict, and his only disappointment with the whole proceeding was that the widow hadn't been called to testify. They'd taken her statement by deposition. He still carried the sight of her standing on the deck of the *Buck Whittemore*, the wind in her skirt. He had not been able to forget the tenderness he'd felt, and would never completely shake the feeling that they'd come through a bad

time together and were in that way linked. Later on, he read that she'd
gone home to the prairie and was appointed by the governor to serve out
her husband's term.

———

Calmer went home too. He worked the fields for his dad, and in the
fall and winter helped Cousin Arlo, who had almost a thousand acres. He
lived upstairs in Arlo's house, in constant proximity to Arlo and his wife
the arm wrestler, and after supper they would all drink shots of Jim Beam
chased with Falstaff beer, sometimes playing whist, sometimes listening
to the radio, night after night. Arlo's wife liked to pop off the bottle caps
against the kitchen table, and sometimes the glass lip would come off
with it too, and she would drink the beer anyway, right out of the bottle.
Sunshine itself.

Sometimes, half a dozen beers into the evening, Calmer would find
himself falling into a quiet melancholy over the congressman's wife and
Arlo would see the change coming and send Arlene to bed, then put his
stocking feet up on the kitchen table—his white socks turned the color
of the earth after a day in the fields—and try to head off the sadness.
"Let me tell you about the bears," he would say.

He never asked what had happened, just let Calmer tell him about it
in his own time, his own way. Arlo was everyone's favorite, and there were
reasons for that.

PART TWO

Vincent Heights

TEN

Spooner was four years old. It was April 1961, and the family lived at the top of a long, gradual rise of land, half a mile above a sawmill on the outskirts of Milledgeville, in the last house built in a poor white subdivision of town called Vincent Heights.

The house itself sat on a sun-scarred, twice-tiered lot on a narrow dirt road that looped off the paved road running through the rest of the development. The dirt loop was not technically in city limits and for that reason hadn't been paved when paving came to Vincent Heights. His grandmother still seethed when she thought of it, the city coming out here with their surveyors and cheating poor old widows out of their pavement—the widows being the grandmother herself and Granny Otts next door. For that matter Spooner's mother was also a widow, although technically the paving had occurred before she and Spooner and his sister moved in.

As Spooner understood it, the move in with Grandma came a week or so after the paving stopped at the circle where they lived, and a month or a year—he couldn't keep it straight which was longer—after his father died of a stroke. He also didn't quite twig how a stroke killed you—his understanding of the word *stroke* was that it meant petting a horse. Maybe the horse kicked him, but in any case this was the sort of information he knew better than to ask about at home. There was a rule in his grandmother's house against bringing up the misfortunes of the past, which applied specifically to the matter of Spooner's dead father but not to the unpaved circle in front of the house.

———

And while Spooner ran loose in Vincent Heights, telling the neighbors that his father had been killed by a horse, Calmer was back out in the world, picking his way from town to town in a 1949 Ford sedan, from the prairie into the midwestern states, then the South, headed for Georgia and in no hurry whatsoever to arrive. It was only the second time he'd left South Dakota. He liked the cities more than the towns, stopping at libraries and museums, but sometimes an old tractor or a historical marker along the road caught his attention, and he stopped to look at those too. Some days his car broke down—usually it was the carburetor, which he rebuilt three times in a month, or the radiator or the water pump, which he also rebuilt—and he would pull onto a gravel road or into a stand of trees and open the hood, the engine pouring steam if it was the radiator, and jury-rig what was broken, taking his time with that too. He enjoyed the repairing as much as the driving—the logic of the work, of the problem itself, the solid, familiar feel of tools, of knowing even before he opened the hood what was wrong underneath. Fixing things himself.

He'd left South Dakota this time with six hundred dollars in his money belt and had another two thousand that he'd never taken out of a savings account at Girard Bank back in Philadelphia. The job waiting for him in Georgia paid seventy-two hundred dollars a year.

Oddly enough, he'd been to the town itself once before, had spent three days there one August during his flight training, waiting for a new rudder cable for his plane. The air was unbreathable but otherwise he'd liked the place fine. General Sherman had come through on his march to break the South's back and end the war, but for some reason he'd spared the town and its great old houses and orchards, most of which were still intact. There was a women's college now on the grounds of the old penitentiary square, and a military school where Calmer had been hired to teach.

Calmer had lost his rudder on a training flight out of Pensacola back in 1950, and put the plane down on a dirt road leading to a complex of square brick buildings just outside town limits, climbed out of the plane into a hot wind, and, still standing on the wing, heard voices calling to him from the windows. He looked up, noticing the windows were barred, and then began to distinguish the shapes of people behind them, waving hankies, cheering. For a minute he felt like Ted Williams.

To the east, there was a small fenced field—perhaps twenty acres—and shirtless men bent at the waist, out in the afternoon sun digging peanuts. Guards watching, some of them with shotguns, cudgels attached to their belts. Between the field and the main building was a poultry yard.

There were also shirtless men in the poultry yard, two of them hidden in the shadow of a henhouse. One of them was having sex with a chicken and the other one was standing with his pants down around his knees, an erection like a divining rod, waiting his turn. Why he didn't just get a chicken of his own, only the man himself might know. Maybe it was too much like a double date.

ELEVEN

The road in front of Spooner's grandmother's house was made of clay, orange and cracked open seven months of the year, so hot in July and August that you could feel it through your shoes. In October, after the first hard rain, it turned to mud, sometimes half a foot deep, and it would suck the shoes right off your feet. Nothing grew alongside the road that did not have thorns or stickers.

Behind the house was a shallow yard full of pine trees, a briar patch off to the side, a barbed-wire fence. After supper, Spooner was sometimes sent to sit on the porch steps to think it over when he'd broken some rule or another that day, this being his mother's idea of punishment, and from here he could look out over a cow pasture and the muddy pond where the cattle collected at night, and beyond that to the sawmill, its chimney leaking black smoke into the sky all day and all night. To the right of the sawmill, downwind, was the Bottoms, where the colored people lived. That was what Spooner's family called them, *colored*. His grandmother had fired a maid, who was a person of color herself, for using the word *nigger* in her house.

An older, plumper grandmother than Spooner's grandmother had the house next door, Granny Otts, who had a dog called a toy poodle even though it wasn't. She called it Bitty and painted its fingernails. She also had a granddaughter, Marlis, who was fifteen and homely in a way that fixing up couldn't fix. The granddaughter smoked cigarettes and said *nigger* and spit, and had pretty much given up on humans and spent all her time with her horses, Gypsy Lee and Scout. Spooner and his sister were not allowed near the stable. Marlis had no use for Granny Otts or Bitty or Spooner or Margaret or any other people or animals that were not horses, and when Spooner told her that his father had been killed by a horse she said, "Wasn't the horse's fault."

She had no friends that Spooner ever saw but had taught the older horse—Gypsy Lee—to kiss her lips, although she had to hold a sugar cube between her teeth to get the horse to do it. She cut school more than she went and spent all day in the stable and smelled like it, which was not such a bad smell, at least to Spooner. Hay and sweet manure. Granny Otts didn't mind her cutting school, but often sitting in the kitchen she said to Spooner and Margaret that she wished the girl would take the time to pretty herself up. "A little toilet water wouldn't hurt her chances," she said. And Spooner, who did not know toilet water except as water in the toilet, didn't see how it could hurt either. Granny Otts was still looking for a boyfriend herself and kept the bait in the water, never leaving the house without perfume and lipstick and jewelry, even to hang laundry. She liked to have Spooner and his sister inside for Kool-Aid and sandwich cookies she bought from the A&P, and seemed to favor their company over Marlis's, and never let them out of her kitchen without warning them to stay clear of the stable. Those horses were biters, she said, one worse than the other.

———

The house itself had five rooms, six if you counted the toilet, which Spooner did, but his mother did not. She complained about it regularly—living in five tiny rooms—and he regularly corrected her, listing the rooms one by one on his fingers. The last time he'd corrected her, she buried her face in a dish towel and distinctly screamed the word *shit.* Then she cried, "*God, how long can I stand it?*"

Spooner was alone in the kitchen with her at the time—his grandmother had a moment before walked out the back door and let it slam behind her because his mother said that Dwight D. Eisenhower was spending too much time on the golf course when he should be running the country—and he sat there motionless as she cried, feeling the scene blowing across his face, like a dog riding halfway out the car window.

And then he'd said, "Maybe Grandma will die," and his mother got up and wailed off into the back of the house and that night after supper he was sent outside to sit on the porch steps and think it over. And as he thought it over, it seemed to him that the words had just popped out, the way shit popped out of cows. She'd been crying into the dish towel, *God, how long can I stand it?* and he didn't know if he was supposed to answer or not—this being a dilemma that would follow him all his life, by the way—but in the end, being the one who'd made her cry in the first place by saying the bathroom counted as a room, he pressed himself to say something to make her feel better and so he said what he said, which was the best he could do. And now he was out on the porch to think it over.

And he continued to sit on the porch steps and think it over, and the house continued to have six rooms. He knew a room when he saw it, and he knew how to count. There were three closets in the house, one in each bedroom and one in the hallway, nine windows, six faucets. There were seventeen lightbulb sockets—three in one lamp in the living room—and thirteen electrical outlets in the walls. Each month, a new Shell pest strip was hung over the kitchen sink, laden at the moment with exactly sixty-two dead or dying insects, mostly flies. Thirty-one on each side. Spooner took a count every morning and every night, and brought spiders or june bugs in from the yard to keep the sides even.

The rooms were all small and poorly lit, even the kitchen, where he sometimes lay on the floor in hot weather and watched bits of dust floating in the shaft of sun coming through the screen door. The house was full of dust, and secrets, and rules, and these things he didn't try to count because they were countless.

There was the rule against feeling sorry for past misfortunes, against leaving the house without permission, against climbing trees, against being on the roof. A rule against setting fires. There were rules about standing up straight, how tightly he was allowed to buckle his belt, how much water he could use to comb his hair in cold weather, and the correct way to tie his shoes so that he wouldn't trip when he ran. He was not allowed to suck his fingers—he liked the two middle ones on his right hand—and he was supposed to address strangers as *sir* and *ma'am*, and he was not supposed to talk to strangers, and he was supposed to look strangers in the eye when he spoke to them. He was not supposed to cry. He was not allowed to let the screen doors slam. He was not allowed anywhere near the sawmill or the horses next door. There was a rule about how much sugar he could put on his cereal in the morning, how much peanut butter he could put on a peanut butter sandwich. There were even rules for sleeping. A clothesline was hung across the middle of the bedroom where he and Margaret slept, and in the night sometimes the blanket hung across the line would rise up like a curtain in the wind, and his grandmother would appear, her hair the color of the moon, unpinned and fallen the length of her back, and pull his fingers out of his mouth or his hands out of his pajama bottoms.

Living under the press of so many rules, Spooner was unnaturally jumpy for a child of his age, and often shivered in the aftermath of breaking one of the rules and getting away with it—there was never a question of not breaking the rules—for instance, climbing through a window and making it outside without permission. And he would shiver, even in August and July. Sometimes it was like the little shiver after he'd tinkled, and sometimes it was like the Shakers' coonhound coming out of the pond down in the cow pasture and shaking off the water. The animal was called Rex but would come to any name you called it, up to and including Fucker, and would chase a rock right into the water and then swim around in circles trying to figure out where it went. And when he finally gave up and crawled out, he would shake front to back, throwing a cloud a yard deep of water and mud and pebbles into the air, and if the sun was in the right place, Spooner would see a rainbow in the haze.

And that's what it was like when, say, he climbed out his bedroom window while his mother was in her own bedroom crying—he'd watched her cry once from a branch of the tree just west of the house, and it looked like she was eating her pillow—it felt like loose shoes and rainbows.

———

Spooner's grandmother belonged to a society for the protection of the native songbirds of the state of Georgia, and did volunteer work, sending out pamphlets every month requesting donations to exterminate feral cats. The pamphlets included scientific evidence that killing one cat saved 240,000 birds, some of them yet to be born—the society's theory being that dead songbirds don't lay eggs. When she could locate Spooner on pamphlet days, his grandmother made him sit down at the kitchen table and lick envelopes, and unless she cooked something worse for dinner, the taste of envelope glue would stay in his mouth until he went to bed.

While this was going on, Spooner's mother would be working at her job in the sociology department at the women's college, or, just as likely, in the bedroom with an asthma attack. She closed the door when she had asthma attacks, not wanting to be seen, and once he'd climbed the tree outside her window to see what one looked like and it was like watching a nap.

———

All the houses on Spooner's side of the road were built on a ridge, in a broken line perhaps thirty feet above the road. Spooner, Granny Otts, and next to her, old man Stoppard. A kid named Kenny Durkin lived one house farther south. Kenny was a foot taller than Spooner, already in second grade. His teeth lay across each other like scrap lumber, and he didn't get sent to the back steps to think it over for punishment; his father beat him with a board. Kenny's house had different rules and fewer of them: He was not allowed to get into his mother's under things, or steal from her purse, or act like a sissy, and when he was beaten it was usually on Friday, when his father and the other workers from down in the sawmill drank beer at the icehouse before they came home from work. Kenny

Durkin did not suffer quietly; you could hear the screaming and crying all over the neighborhood.

Mr. Durkin drove a truck for the sawmill, and went fishing on Sundays instead of sitting in church. He'd quit taking Kenny after Kenny got a hook in his foot and whimpered all the way home. Mr. Durkin did not like having a sissy for a son. He'd been in the war and killed, by his estimate, about a yard full of Japs, and on occasion was overheard to say he wouldn't mind killing a few more. He kept a pistol in the davenport cushions where he could get to it in case he saw one in the road, and when Kenny Durkin and Spooner were over there alone, Kenny Durkin would sometimes take the gun out and empty the bullets out of the cylinder, and sometimes he let Spooner hold one until he was ready to put them back.

Spooner liked the smell of the gun, but Kenny Durkin never let him touch it or even hold the bullet very long.

TWELVE

It was Spooner's estimation that he crossed the line into criminality on a Friday afternoon early in June 1961 and once across the line, had nothing left to lose. He was four years old, and nothing he'd seen so far indicated that the world was a forgive-and-forget sort of proposition.

Kenny Durkin had passed second grade and had been hanging around Spooner's house all day every day since school let out, the way the Shakers' coonhound hung around next door when Grandma Otts's toy poodle Bitty went into heat. Spooner's grandmother didn't like having the boy in the house and hid her purse whenever he showed up, but Kenny wasn't haunting them that summer to rob the grandmother but to hide. Kenny's mother had got tired of finding him in her underpants and her purse—it had got where she could not stand the sound of the beatings after she told her husband—and sent him outdoors to play in the morning as soon as he'd eaten breakfast, sometimes even in the rain, where he was a sitting duck for the whole neighborhood, as he was a soft child who cried easily and was terrified of boys his own age.

The Friday Spooner went bad, Kenny's mother and father were gone shopping and he and Kenny were alone for once in Kenny's house, sitting on the tile living room floor while Kenny aimed his father's pistol here and there around the room, sometimes at Spooner's head, making shooting noises as he pulled the trigger on the empty chamber. On the floor between them were the six bullets that he'd removed from the cylinder when he first took it out of the davenport cushions to play.

As it happened, Kenny Durkin was holding the gun an inch from Spooner's eyeball, slowly pulling the trigger, when the room exploded, or seemed to, the noise shaking the glass in the front window. Spooner fell over backwards expecting to die and glimpsed Kenny Durkin, terrified, dropping bullets as fast as he could collect them, and trying to load them back into the gun. Spooner heard car doors slam, and realized the noise was only Kenny's daddy's Chevy coupe, backfiring when his daddy turned it off. Maybe a little louder today than usual.

The car and the various noises it made were well known in Vincent Heights, particularly to Spooner, who had even ridden in it once when he went along with Kenny on Mr. Durkin's paper route. Mr. Durkin delivered the *World Telegraph* on Sundays before he went fishing, and took Kenny along to tote the papers up to the houses, particularly the two houses in the Bottoms, so he wouldn't have to sit in the driveway blowing the horn until the nigger inside decided to come out and get it. Mr. Durkin did not believe he was put on earth to service people of color.

Spooner recalled the car had a hula dancer with a grass skirt stuck onto the dashboard who shimmied when you poked her tummy. Kenny's daddy called her his good-luck baby.

Spooner glanced at Kenny, who couldn't seem to stick the bullets into the cylinder, and when Spooner looked back out the window, Kenny Durkin's daddy and mother were already started up the driveway. She was trying to get at a package wrapped in butcher paper that he was holding over his head, wrestling and giggling as they came up the driveway to the house.

Kenny Durkin, meanwhile, continued to scramble around like nine pups on eight titties. Spooner turned back outside and watched them wrestling—he'd never seen grown-ups wrestling before, not like this—and then somewhere behind him Kenny Durkin began to cry. But then Kenny cried all the time, once when he lost his skate key, another time when Spooner told him that everyone dies. And then again one Friday when Spooner's grandmother made him go home.

Now he heard Kenny Durkin say, "Why, Warren. You know you ain't supposed to be playin' with Daddy's gun. You know better than that."

Spooner turned and looked at him, but Kenny Durkin had already seen that blaming Spooner wasn't going to work and, hearing them just outside the door, pushed the gun and all the loose bullets under the davenport, then got up, leaving Spooner where he was, and ran to his mother as she stepped inside the screen door and hugged her around the waist. His daddy watched him, knowing unnatural behavior when he saw it. He said, "Goddamn, Charlene, you'll have that kid sucking dicks next," which was the way Mr. Durkin talked when he came home on Fridays, after he'd been down at the icehouse with the boys on the way home from the sawmill.

Mrs. Durkin was a fat, pretty woman with red hair, and she was out of breath and sweating from trying to get at the package. "Roger," she said, "watch your language. Little pitchers have big ears . . ."

It sounded to Spooner like she'd been drinking with the boys down at the icehouse too.

As Spooner watched, one of the bullets rolled out from underneath the davenport in a circle, and he stared at it a moment, then picked it up and put it in his pocket. Not on purpose, particularly, but at the same time knowing he was stealing a bullet. He was four and a half years old now, and Kenny Durkin's daddy's bullet was the first thing he'd ever taken that wasn't his, and he liked the way stealing felt.

The Durkins all walked back toward the kitchen, leaving Spooner sitting on the floor, thinking of stealing the pistol too. In the end, he couldn't think of a place to hide it, and got up instead and went into the kitchen to see what was in Kenny Durkin's daddy's package.

Mr. Durkin had laid the package flat on the kitchen table and cut the string with his switchblade knife, which had been used previously to finish off a few of the Japs. It was his lucky knife, and he never went outside without it. He had a lot of lucky things, in fact almost everything he had was lucky. Maybe he didn't keep anything around if it wasn't lucky. Carefully, he unfolded the paper. Spooner stood on his toes, trying to see what it was.

Cheese.

It was just cheese. All that wrestling for *cheese.*

The cheese came in a circle, bright orange, about half as big as the tabletop itself. Kenny Durkin's mother seemed to be trying to crawl over his daddy to get at it, which to Spooner, was like getting all het up over licking envelopes.

Mr. Durkin made two small cuts along the edge and handed the triangle that came out to Kenny's mother, still on the point of the blade. She took it off with her fingers and set it carefully in her teeth, as if she was trying not to hurt it, and then she closed her eyes and swooned a little bit, in love with this cheese, and made a certain mooing sound that Spooner had heard before but couldn't remember where.

Mr. Durkin took a minute watching her mouth, then cut a piece for himself, which he ate directly off the blade, and then one for Kenny, who was afraid of the blade, like his mother, and took it with his fingers. And then there was another piece for her, and for himself, and Kenny.

Presently, Mrs. Durkin stopped mooing and noticed Spooner standing there in her kitchen, and even though Spooner didn't like cheese any better now than he had five minutes ago, he did want to take a piece of it off the knife blade in his teeth.

She moved a step sideways, her considerable amplitude cutting the cheese off from his line of sight, and behind her Mr. Durkin began wrapping it back up. She smiled at Spooner and said, "You better run along, Warren. I hear your grammy calling you for supper." She licked three of her fingers, one at a time, and Kenny Durkin's daddy was watching her in a strange way again, even as he re-wrapped the butcher paper, and then he turned on Spooner and Kenny both.

"Go on, now," he said, "git." The way you might speak to the Shakers' hound if it showed up begging cheese in your kitchen.

Spooner went back to his grandmother's house and sat on the front steps, and presently his sister came home from playing with the Garrett girls across the road and sat with him. Mrs. Garrett had invited her to sleep over—for supper and then a drive into town for an ice cream cone—and Margaret was waiting for their mother to come home from work to ask permission. She wasn't going to ask their grandmother because Grandma could always think of something youngsters ought to be doing instead of what they wanted to do. She thought licking stamps was good for anybody.

Spooner was feeling left out—first the cheese, now the ice cream—and wouldn't have minded climbing a tree and letting what was left of daylight disappear. He looked back in the direction of Kenny Durkin's house, still ashamed at the way he'd been tossed out, and that night, with Margaret gone to the sleepover with the Garrett girls and his mother and grandmother asleep in the room they shared, snoring back and forth in there like pond frogs, he climbed out of his window and crossed the backyard barefoot. His yard, then Granny Otts's yard, then old man Stoppard's. The pine needles were dry against his feet and the ground beneath it had gone cold, and he heard noises in the dark that he'd never noticed when he was in bed with the window open.

He got where he was going and waited a long moment outside the back porch, staring at the screen door, thinking of Kenny Durkin's daddy, the way he'd looked at Mrs. Durkin right before he told Spooner to git. A cow bawled in the pasture like somebody had told it the future.

He opened the door wide enough to slip inside, careful for once not to let it slam.

The linoleum floor was colder than the ground outside, and the only light was the moon shining in through the window. He stood dead still, feeling electricity singing down his arms, right down to the fingers, and gradually he began to make out the shapes of things, and then the sounds coming from the back of the house. Sleeping sounds, heavy and wet.

He stepped and the floor creaked as his foot touched the spot, and he stopped in that same instant and remade the step, and this time there was no noise. The breathing from the back of the house was deep and uneven and loose. He saw beer bottles on the kitchen table and picked one up and drank what was left in the bottom. The lip of the bottle tasted like cheese, and the beer was warm and bitter, like vomit, and he willed himself not to gag.

He set the bottle on the floor, making sure it was down flat and wouldn't tip, and then stepped wide around it and farther into the kitchen. He went to the icebox and opened it and was instantly blinded—Kenny

Durkin's daddy had screwed an outdoor lightbulb into the back to re-place one that burned out. The icebox smelled of fish and something else, maybe of the Durkins themselves.

Spooner held still in the stunning light, listening, smelling, and then, just as he had in the dark, he began to distinguish shapes. The cheese was lying on the bottom shelf, the butcher paper held by a rubber band, and lying next to it were eight perch wrapped lengthwise in newspaper, the heads poking out the end, wide-eyed, like he'd just woke them up.

He took the package out, slipped off the rubber band, and pulled the butcher paper away. The paper fell to the floor, and he held the cheese in his hand—it was heavier than it looked—not sure what to do with it and then, by itself, the cheese began to sag, dropping like a divining rod, and then broke off, and made a noise when it hit the floor that sounded to Spooner like an atom bomb.

Steps in the hallway.

Spooner stood in the light of the refrigerator, waiting to be murdered. And then somebody smarter than he was seemed to take over, and he closed his eyes and held out his arms—the smaller piece of the cheese round still in his hands—as if he were sleepwalking. They couldn't mur-der you for sleepwalking.

A moment later, a door swung open, the pitch of the creaking hinges dropping slowly as the door swung, and then the door handle bounced softly into the wall. Spooner turned away with his arms still out in front of him, like he was playing a piano from a yard away, wondering if he should snore. And should he be walking back and forth, or did sleepwalk-ers just stand around in the dark holding on to their cheese? Moments passed, and the current going through him went cold, and then he heard the noise of Kenny Durkin's daddy's powerful tinkling straight into the middle of the bowl. (Spooner had been taught by his grandmother to sit down on the toilet seat and tinkle into the front, above the waterline, to spare the ladies of the house the sound of his urination.)

He stood frozen, his eyes still shut tight, and the tinkling went on and on, like he was in there filling the bathtub. Spooner's shoulders ached, and he began to feel the weight of his arms. A long time later, the pitch of the tinkling changed slightly, growing higher, fading, and finally playing out.

Mr. Durkin proceeded to spasms now, like his battery was going dead, and then there was a soft, flabby sound as he shook out the last drops. The toilet flushed and Spooner jumped at the sound.

He heard the footsteps again, but going the other way now, back to the bedroom. Spooner dropped his arms, and the aching in his shoulders peaked and then passed.

He had a bite of the cheese. In spite of the mooing Kenny's mother had done, it tasted about like all the other cheese he'd tasted, and it was at that moment, with the cheese still in his mouth and Spooner undecided whether to swallow or spit it out, that he noticed that even as Kenny Durkin's daddy had been tinkling, he—Spooner—had been tinkling too. His shorts were stuck against his leg, like something grabbing him in the dark, and thinking of being grabbed in the dark, he dropped what was left of the cheese in front of him on the floor, and the puddle he'd made splashed up onto his feet and shins, and then, not even closing the icebox, he ran for the door.

The screen door slammed behind him as he crossed the driveway into old man Stoppard's backyard, running blind and seeing all kinds of shapes in the trees, and a moment later he was in Granny Otts's yard, his shorts as cold as ice and sticking to his skin, pine needles and dirt and pine sap lodged in his toes. His throat threw out dry, grabbing noises as his feet hit the ground, that sounded something like crying. And then he was in his own yard, and then at his own window, and then crawling back into his own house.

He stood still then, listening.

Nothing.

His knee had been scraped, climbing back in, and it bled down his shin onto his foot. He put his shorts and underpants in the bathroom hamper and crept to the bedroom and then lay awake, his face jumping here and there all over, and the only sounds in the place were his own breathing and the pounding of his heart in his ears and the snoring from the other bedroom. His skin was wet with sweat and tinkle and chilled him as it dried. Time passed, and his breathing quieted and his bed turned warm, and he thought over what had happened, remembering the electricity singing through him the whole time he was inside the house, terrified and tinkling into his own shorts, amazed at what had happened. He thought it probably felt something like being famous.

———

By morning the following day, word had already passed through the neighborhood that the niggers had broken into the Durkin house and pissed on the floor, and Mr. Durkin was prepared to kill the next one he saw on his property.

THIRTEEN

The man who would be Spooner's father showed up in July, toward the end of the month. He did not intrude suddenly—Spooner had no memory of a first meeting—but one day was simply there, dropping in most nights after supper, and always with a can of olives or a sack of popcorn or a book or a Chinese finger puzzle, and then, perhaps to avoid being thanked, he might read them a story from the book or make a bowl of the popcorn (*white delicacies in a dishpan*, he said) or look around for something that needed to be fixed, or built. He kept his tools in a box in the trunk of his car, everything exactly in its place, and before he started he always changed into work clothes that smelled like work, hanging his clean pants and shirt on the bathroom door. Sometimes he let Spooner saw a little bit or hammer a nail, but he stayed close and ready to intervene, and Spooner saw that it made him nervous not to be the one holding the tools.

Afterwards, when he'd finished what he'd started and put away his tools and taken a bath if he'd gotten dirty, and Spooner and Margaret and Spooner's grandmother had been sent off to bed, he and Spooner's mother would sit together in the kitchen, talking and listening to the radio. Sometimes Calmer had a glass of crackers and milk. As for giggling and wrestling, like Mr. and Mrs. Durkin when Mr. Durkin brought home the cheese, Spooner never heard it. He had a spot near the heating vent where he could lie after Margaret went to sleep and hear them as if he were in the kitchen himself, and he never heard anything playful going on and did not expect to. Spooner was fairly sure that people like his mother and Calmer had more important things on their minds.

In spite of all the time he was putting in, Calmer was still not much relaxed and comfortable when he came over, particularly in the vicinity of Spooner's grandmother, who watched him like she watched the maid around loose change, and under her roof Calmer was always on his feet, possibly to keep himself a moving target. He opened doors and carried groceries and painted most of the inside of the house. He fixed every leak in the plumbing, every leak on the roof. He took a loose tooth out of Margaret's mouth, and read the poems she wrote, and before very long she was spending more time with him than Spooner's mother was. Margaret was a conversationalist in those days, full of questions, and Calmer had not gotten over the surprise of her yet, all the things she knew, the intelligence of her questions. She had her own diary, and sometimes they sat on the davenport together, Margaret and Calmer, and she read to him what she'd written, looking up to check his face when she came to the important parts. She cooked him soup and made her finger bleed trying to sew a button back on his uniform shirt. She'd been hugging him when he came in the door since the second or third week, and Spooner watched from a doorway, sucking his fingers, wishing he could hug him too.

Sometimes Calmer took Margaret and Spooner with him downtown on errands, or to his office at the school, and one night they went out to the football field to look at the eclipse of the moon through the school's telescope. Margaret knew the names of all the constellations. On weekends, he made popcorn and sat with them in the backyard, playing a game called Numbers. He would write down four numbers and leave a space for the fifth, and he and Margaret had to guess what came next and explain the rule the numbers were following. He took them for ice cream and to the drugstore for grilled cheese sandwiches. Spooner would eat some and stick the rest in his pocket when Calmer wasn't looking and give it either to the Shakers' coonhound or the old one-legged colored boy who came through Vincent Heights once in a while looking into garbage cans—either one of them would eat anything.

The first time they'd gone to the drugstore for grilled cheese sandwiches, Margaret had taken Calmer's hand on the way back to the car. She was eighteen months older than Spooner was, half a foot taller, twice as fast, twice as smart, and as far as he knew had been born knowing how to read. And pretty, even Spooner could see that she was pretty. Without knowing he was doing it, Spooner reached for a hand too, and got Calmer's little finger instead, and they walked that way to the end of the block, and then Calmer stopped and gently pried him loose.

"Men don't hold hands," he said.

"For the sake of argument," Calmer said one night, indicating the pasture beyond the fence, "let us say that yon cow is in need of shoes, a pair of saddle shoes perhaps." They'd all driven to Macon that week for shoes; Margaret was beginning first grade on Monday. They were sitting at the picnic table in the backyard, an hour after he'd finished the dishes. Spooner, Margaret, Calmer. The air was hot and wet and full of insects, and no fresher to breathe, even though the sun had dropped into the cloud of awful, sweet smoke that hung over the sawmill, completely out of sight.

Spooner turned to look and saw the last few stragglers ambling downhill to the pond, where they spent the night together in a pile. A pile of cows. Calmer reached under the table and took Margaret's bare foot in his hand. "Now, the problem, my dear," he said, "as you may already know, cows have quite dainty feet—like yourself."

Spooner squinted, trying to make out the cows' dainty feet, and Calmer turned to him. "But the real problem is that yon cow will not ride in the family car. It's undignified, it thinks, and they push and pull and beg and cajole, but the animal will not budge, and in the end it has its own way and it walks. Thirty-two miles."

At the edge of his vision, Spooner saw Margaret write down the number thirty-two. These days she carried a notepad and a pencil everywhere she went, getting ready for school. Calmer had gotten him a notepad too—like his new shoes, so he wouldn't feel left out—but Spooner had used it only once, balling up a few pieces of paper, trying to set fire to the patch of briars at the edge of the woods. He had very little use for a notepad otherwise—he couldn't write yet, not numbers or letters, and wasn't even much at drawing.

"And so beginneth the journey," Calmer said. "But miles pass, and time, and eventually, exactly halfway to Macon the cow stops."

"Why?" Spooner said.

Calmer shrugged. "Well, his feet hurt," he said. "He *is* barefoot." Which bent Margaret over until her nose touched the notepad, and as she giggled, a line of drool dropped from her mouth onto the paper and pooled. She'd lost one of her front teeth the week before and another one was looser every day.

"And after the cow has rested its feet," Calmer said, "it starts out and walks half the distance to Macon again, and again stops and rests its feet."

"When does it sleep?" Spooner said.

"It sleeps while it rests its feet, and then eats breakfast, and then walks half the distance left to Macon again. And the cow proceeds in this way, walking and resting, each time covering half the distance left. And one day it comes to a post office and drops a card to its friends back in the pasture, saying the weather is fine and the grass is sweet and it should be in Macon by . . ."

Calmer paused, looking from Spooner to Margaret. "But it doesn't know when it will be in Macon, and that," he said, "is the question. How long should yon bovine say it will take, each day walking half the distance left, to arrive in Macon?"

Margaret thought a moment and began her calculations, writing careful, perfect numbers down the page, writing and erasing, subtracting and adding and dividing. Numbers all over. Spooner watched her work a little while and then looked away, back to the pasture, and presently, feeling Calmer's eyes on him, he picked up his pencil and drew a cow. This was a distraction of course, as most of everything he did and said around

Calmer was, hoping this time around that Calmer wouldn't notice that he didn't know how to do problems, or even write numbers, hoping somehow not to disappoint him. And the last thing he would do, or even think of doing, in the face of this convolution of time and miles and cows and saddle shoes, not to mention his sister's furious calculations as she closed in on the answer, was admit that, as far as he could tell, the cow was never going to make it to Macon at all.

———

To Spooner's knowledge Margaret didn't lie or make mistakes, but he still had his doubts when she told him Calmer was going to marry their mother.

From what Spooner had seen—from what he'd heard through the heating vent—there was something his mother wanted from Calmer that he couldn't give her, no matter how many walls he painted or how many times he climbed up onto the roof to fix a leak, or how hard he tried to cheer her up. Lately, there were times when he came over and she didn't even come out of her bedroom to see him. Asthma, she said, and stayed in bed all day.

It was sometimes Spooner's job to take his mother lunch or a glass of water when she was sick, and she would be under a sheet in her nightgown, the room warm and thick with the smell of her sickness, and the skin on her throat pulling tight against the cords beneath it when she pumped in the medicine.

His mother had been sick in this way, off and on, for as long as Spooner remembered, and he worried that Calmer would notice the smell and not want to come back.

FOURTEEN

In the fall, Margaret started second grade, and Spooner was shipped out to kindergarten. That was what Calmer called it, *shipping out*, which it was called back in the navy.

His grandmother drove them to school that morning—his mother had an early class to teach at the college—and wouldn't let Spooner roll down his window; she didn't want the wind messing up Margaret's hair on her first day. Spooner's grandmother was a *no nonsense, young man* kind of grandmother, not the kind that gave presents, and he sat alone in the breezeless backseat of her old Kaiser, an automobile she could not shift without a noise that reminded him of the drill the dentist had used that spring to smooth out what was left of the front tooth he broke off falling into the curb in front of the bakery. Six stitches in his eyebrow and then the dentist. And now kindergarten.

———

Spooner's kindergarten and Peabody Elementary sat on the same street, a block apart. They stopped at the kindergarten first, and Margaret was too excited to wait and walked the rest of the way by herself. Spooner watched her go—skipping—thinking he might like school too if he could already read better than the teacher.

His grandmother put an Indian-burn grip on his wrist and walked him through a gate in a chain-link fence, then through a swarm of children's faces, some of them sticking out their tongues to be ugly. The place had a dirt yard and a small slide and a sandbox and a set of swings, things that were of no interest to Spooner at all. Beyond the playground was the school house itself, and she tightened her grip and pulled him straight ahead.

The teacher was named Miss Julie Tuttle and stopped him dead in his tracks. Miss Tuttle had black hair that shone like Calmer's shoes and smelled like flowers, and Spooner wanted to roll in that smell the way the Shakers' coonhound rolled in cow shit after he'd been in the pond. And something more than that, something he felt crawling all over him, like impetigo.

A shampoo. He wanted Miss Tuttle to give him a shampoo, and thus emerged Spooner's pecker into the untidiness of the universe.

Miss Tuttle was twenty-one years old, fresh out of college, and had chosen kindergarten because children of that age were cuter than seven- or eight-year-olds—cuter, smaller, easier to handle, more innocent—and was pretty much innocent herself, or at least unaware that a child still three months shy of his fifth birthday could already be connected in that dark, reptilian way to his pecker.

She took Spooner's hand from his grandmother, smiling down at him, and said something about meeting the other children. Spooner had no interest in meeting other children and wanted only to stay right there where he was with Miss Tuttle, or possibly closer. His hand was tingling now that his grandmother was no longer cutting off the circulation. She was behind him—his grandmother—and straightening him up, pushing her thumbs into his shoulder blades and reminding him to keep his fingers out of his mouth. She smiled at Miss Tuttle, talking about him like he wasn't there, and reported that his finger sucking started that summer when he fell and broke his tooth, which was a lie, and then patted him on the shoulder and headed back to the gate.

Miss Tuttle watched her go and then winked at him, as if they were in it together now, and said, "What a sweet little guy." She laid her hand on his hair a moment and tousled it, then led him back in the direction of the playground to introduce him to his new classmates.

And with his fingers in his mouth and his pecker doing the thinking, Spooner allowed himself to be led into the yard.

Two weeks later Margaret was sent home with a letter saying she was being skipped ahead into third grade, and on that same day Spooner was also sent home with a letter, the contents of which were never discussed in his presence, but after which Spooner was a kindergartener no more.

The complaint was only superficially that Spooner had been dipping his head in glue and finger paint so that Miss Tuttle would have to wash out his hair. The real complaint was that Miss Tuttle had noticed that while she was washing out his hair, his head rose up into her hand like a cat raising its rump as you stroked it, and it was not long before she noticed the little rise in his britches, and after that even the sight of his arrival at the schoolyard in the morning frightened and repelled her, and she went finally, in tears, to the principal. Who had been having thoughts of his own about Miss Tuttle, and expelled Spooner on the spot.

Spooner listened to his mother and Calmer talking it over in the kitchen that night. He and Margaret and his grandmother were all in bed. A school day tomorrow, but not for Spooner.

"Could you at least talk to him about it?" she said.

Spooner could not figure out what she had on Calmer, why he always gave in and did what she wanted. Even so, this time it was quiet a pretty long time before he answered. "You know, it's probably just a phase . . ."

She said, "Please, Calmer. Children aren't expelled from kindergarten because they're going through a phase."

She was in her other voice now, the one she used for arguing politics with her sisters and her mother, all of whom were Republicans and had no idea what it was like to barely scrape by, to have to watch every penny.

"The teacher's just a kid herself, barely out of school," he said. "She doesn't know anything about children."

But it was too late; she was furious, so mad at him he might as well have been rich. A few moments passed; he heard Calmer's spoon scraping against the side of the glass, finishing his crackers and milk. He always finished everything, down to the last bit.

"I suppose I'll have to take him to the doctor," she said. He'd let her down, that was clear as day—this by the way was an expression Spooner had picked up at kindergarten, so you couldn't say it was all a waste of time.

"I'll take him to see Dr. Woods," he said, "that's no trouble at all. I just hate to see you so upset when nothing's necessarily wrong."

It was quiet again, and then he said, "If you want, I'll have a talk with him too. I just don't think we ought to make too much of it . . ."

But Spooner's mother had made up her mind that something was wrong with Spooner and didn't want any arguments. A little later he said, "Are you all right, my sweet?"

"I've got some tightness in my chest," she said, not about to call him *my sweet* too. It sounded like it might be Calmer's fault. "I think I'll go to bed." Spooner heard her chair slide across the floor and then her footsteps going past his door on the way to her bedroom. Calmer stayed in the kitchen a few minutes, and then Spooner heard him scrape the glass again with his spoon, then wash it in the sink and put it into the cupboard, then let himself out the front door.

———

They went to the doctor's office on Saturday morning, Calmer and Spooner, in the same building where Spooner had been born. Calmer was wearing the heavy wool uniform that all the instructors at the military school wore at that time of year, with a tie and a folding cap. He had to drop Spooner back at home after the appointment and be at work by noon. It was warm for October, and Calmer took off his cap in the car and laid it on the seat between them. Spooner looked at the shiny major's bars, worrying about them falling off and getting lost. But then, Spooner worried constantly about losing things, his hat, his catcher's mitt, the bullet he'd stolen from Kenny Durkin's father. He worried that Calmer would lose his car and not come to see them, and he worried at the movies when

a cowboy rode into town and went into the sheriff's office without tying
the horse carefully to the rail.

For a long time they rode in silence, neither one of them knowing
what to say and both of them wishing Margaret were in the backseat,
talking a mile a minute, and then, as they parked, Spooner glanced at the
freshly painted artillery pieces across the street and had a thought. He
said, "Did you kill any Krauts in the navy?"

Calmer jumped at the sound of the voice, as if he'd forgotten Spooner
was there. This was only the second time they'd gone anywhere alone since
Calmer began seeing Spooner's mother.

Calmer took his time answering, and as he waited Spooner realized
that he'd broken the dead-and-dying rule. He wasn't supposed to talk
about dying, or mention dead people or dead animals he saw along the
road. He wasn't even supposed to think about anything dead.

"Germans," Calmer said. "Let's not call them Krauts."

"Mr. Durkin does. He says they were harder to kill than the Japs."

"Well, not everybody who talks like that knows what he's talking
about," Calmer said. He'd had a look by now at Kenny Durkin's father,
heard him over there beating the kid.

"He was in the war," Spooner said.

"A lot of people were in the war."

Spooner didn't see what he meant. "Did you shoot anybody in the
navy?"

They got out of the car. There was a fence around what was left of the
old folks' home across the street—it still hadn't been rebuilt after the fire,
or even taken down—and the smell of that night was never completely
out of the air.

———

Dr. Woods was as old as Spooner's grandmother and had been the
Whitlowe family doctor since he got out of medical school. He'd delivered
Lily and Uncle Phillip and two of Lily's three sisters and both of Lily's
children. He was now forty-six years in the same office, and swore that he

had never seen a more difficult labor than the one that produced Spooner. He mentioned this to Lily every time she brought in the boy for repairs, and it never failed to cheer her up to hear him say it.

As for the child, he was injured often and in uncommon ways. Dr. Woods had some experience with this sort of patient—they came young and old, men and women, rummies and churchgoers alike, people who would stand in line to get hit by lightning—and was of the opinion that Spooner would not live to see his majority.

And on the one hand, he considered it his obligation as a physician to prepare Spooner's mother for that eventuality, and on the other hand, the woman was high-strung and prone to asthma attacks, so instead of talking about the boy as he was sewing up his head or setting a broken finger, he usually brought the conversation around to what a pretty, well-mannered little girl she had in Margaret Ward. And smart? My Lord, smart as a whip. Dr. Woods and his wife had no children of their own, but he had been around them since the day he set up his practice and saw them for what they were—whole little people. Good or bad, handsome or misshapen from the start, and he allowed himself to quietly judge which was which, to despise the ones he despised. The little Spooner girl was an angel and the boy, well, he'd been there himself but it was still hard to believe they come out the same rabbit hole.

———

The man who brought the boy in was wearing a uniform from the military school, which meant he was a schoolteacher, and Dr. Woods only hoped Mrs. Spooner knew what she was doing. He did not think much of men as schoolteachers; he didn't care if they wore a uniform or not. In his experience, most of them deviated from the norm, and even if it wasn't that or something worse, not one of them ended up with a pot to piss in anyway, and if they weren't smart enough to see that, what business did they have teaching anybody else?

Still, the widow was asthmatic, and excitable, and had the two children, one of them this hellion, and he supposed in her situation you took what come along.

The schoolteacher was at the desk outside Dr. Woods's office, trying to persuade his receptionist, a middle-aged woman named June Oakley, to let him speak privately with Dr. Woods regarding the boy's situation. Miss June had married into an old Milledgeville family far above her own family's social station, then was divorced out of it, and having tasted the good life once, could not abide having her authority questioned by anybody common. Dr. Woods watched her a little while and when he saw that she was about to cry or quit—which she did once or twice a month—he came out of his office to head it off, and asked Miss June would she kindly take the boy back to the examining room while he and the gentleman spoke. He led Calmer back into his office and lit a cigarette.

The schoolteacher was ill at ease, and Dr. Woods did nothing to make him more comfortable. The room smelled of alcohol and warm vitamins.

"So, Major Ottosson," Woods said, "I perceive there is a certain amount of discomfiture regarding the situation heah which you do not see fit to disclose to my receptionist." Letting him know right off that he'd been to college too.

"I didn't want to embarrass anyone needlessly."

The doctor smiled at that and said, "No cause to worry there. That woman is got skin as thick as a barefoot nigger," then waited to see what the schoolteacher would say to that.

"I'm not sure it's even a medical problem," Calmer said.

"Well, as long as you come all the way down heah, why don't let's let me decide?"

Calmer shrugged. "They sent Warren home from kindergarten with a note for staring at the teacher."

"What teacher is that?"

"Miss Tuttle. He was putting finger paint in his hair so she'd have to wash it. She seemed to think there was something sexual—"

Dr. Woods stroked his chin and looked at the ceiling. "Well," he said, "I heard of something like this before, but never in a white family. Colored children, you know, they tend to start at an earlier age. Especially the girls."

———

Spooner was sitting in the examination room in his undershorts. Dr. Woods did not speak to the boy when he came in, and Spooner sat nailed to the spot, his bare legs sweating against the butcher paper they used to cover the table. They had been here before, he and Dr. Woods, and it was never pleasant.

Dr. Woods looked him over and then went to the cabinet and pulled out a long syringe and laid it on a tray. He always did that, to show who was boss. Next, he took out a thermometer and a small rubber hammer and a stethoscope. Then a tongue depressor.

Dr. Woods attached the stethoscope to his neck and approached Spooner from the side. He took the boy by the elbow, a little roughly, and placed the thermometer in his armpit and then closed it down. He put the cold end of the stethoscope against Spooner's chest. Spooner sat still while the doctor listened, then took deep breaths when Dr. Woods moved behind him and told him to breathe. As if he needed to be told.

He ran his fingers through Spooner's hair, looking for ticks, and then tapped at his knees to check his reflexes. He looked in Spooner's ears and opened Spooner's mouth and had a look down his throat. Spooner smelled cigarettes and aftershave and saw dried blood on the doctor's jawline where he'd cut himself shaving.

Dr. Woods took a step back and sat down on his stool. He picked up a pencil and a clipboard and then balanced it on his lap while he lit a cigarette. "So," he said, "what's this bi'nis heah all about?"

Spooner didn't care for sitting undressed in front of Dr. Woods. It reminded him of whichever chicken Major Shaker's maid had picked out for supper being carried off to the chopping block by the feet, all the other chickens in the coop watching.

"You start fires?" the doctor asked, referring now to the clipboard.

Spooner shook his head. He'd thought of it a few times, pictured the fire engines and the sirens, but that was after Miss Tuttle had asked the kindergarten class what they wanted to be when they grew up, and every boy in the class, Spooner included—she'd asked him last—said a fireman. Which seemed to be the right answer.

"You wet the bed?"

Spooner shook his head again, thinking of what had happened in Kenny Durkin's kitchen. The doctor stared at him a little longer, like he could read his mind, and then went on with the list.

"How about animals?" the doctor said. "You ever hurt somebody's kitty cat?"

Spooner was bewildered. He stared at the doctor, forgetting that the doctor was staring at him. He didn't reply, forgot, in fact, that the doctor had asked him a question.

Dr. Woods saw that he was on to something. "You like to hurt things, do you?" he said.

While Spooner continued to stare, the doctor's cigarette hung in the corner of his mouth, and he squinted with one eye through the line of smoke and wrote something down. Then he set the clipboard aside, put the cigarette into an ashtray and stood up. "Well, let's have a look," he said.

The doctor was sitting on a stool in front of Spooner, bent over like a doctor milking a cow. It went on a long time, the doctor not saying much as he poked around, humming now and then, and then finally, he leaned back, took off his glasses, and told Spooner to get dressed and look at some comic books in the waiting room while he talked to Major Ottosson. He said *major* like Calmer was no such thing.

Spooner got into his underpants and his shorts and shoes and went to the waiting room. There weren't any comics.

Dr. Woods and Calmer were in the office; the door was closed. Spooner sat in the chair nearest the receptionist and could hear every word they said. The receptionist saw what he was up to and gave him a look, but next to Spooner's grandmother she was an amateur at giving looks, and he ignored her.

"That's all I seen," Dr. Woods was saying. "One of the boy's testicles isn't dropped, and later on, when the child comes to puberty, you-all might have to address that." Spooner sat on the floor, positive he didn't want to address a dropped testicle. No idea in the world what a testicle was supposed to be.

"How complicated is the procedure?" Calmer said.

What did that mean, *procedure*? Spooner could hear the worry in his voice and could hear that he didn't want to be the one to tell Spooner's mother about Spooner's testicle, and you couldn't blame him for that.

"Generally, it's simple," Dr. Woods said. "Generally, just an injection at the site. And by then, of course, it might of already dropped on its own. Sometime they do, sometime they don't."

"But it's got nothing to do with the other thing," Calmer said, talking about the thing that got Spooner sent home from school in the first place.

Dr. Woods said, "Alas, who can say?"

Spooner heard Dr. Woods light up another cigarette.

"If I was you, sir, I'd have the child to a child psychologist, have the boy turned upside down and shook to find out what he had in store for me down the road. That way, you at least know what you got on your hands." Dr. Woods was not naturally a patient man, particularly with the schoolteacher class, but would always make time to exercise his authority over their lives. It was one of the few day-to-day pleasures still left to a physician.

Spooner got off the chair and sat on the floor. He put the middle and ring fingers of his left hand in his mouth, tasting the dirt off the floor.

"Here now," the receptionist said, "you can't sit on the floor."

———

There was a night that would stay with Spooner the rest of his life, Calmer hitting his thumb while he nailed a hand rail onto the back steps,

splitting the nail and the thumb open, blood dripping through the handkerchief Calmer had wrapped around it onto the steps, and while Spooner
was frozen to the sight of so much blood, Margaret had run to the bathroom without being told to do it and come back with gauze and tape and
a bottle of beer from the icebox. She taped up the bloody thumb while he
sat on the steps, sweating and drinking his beer, smiling as he watched her
work. Spooner realized conclusively that night that he would never catch
up with her and gave up trying.

Later, after their baths, she and Spooner both sat with him on the
steps, and Calmer pointed up through the pine trees at the constellations,
and she already knew them by name and could see the shapes in the sky.

Spooner squinted up into the same sky, the same stars, and saw nothing but the sky and the stars themselves.

———

Unaccountably, the weekend after the visit to Dr. Woods, Calmer took
Spooner hunting. The following Tuesday he came over during lunch for a
game of catch in the front yard, and it went on like that, hunting rabbits
and playing catch, all that month and then the next and the next.

They hunted in an empty field that lay beside a shallow mud lake a
mile from town, just across Macon Highway from the state reformatory
for incorrigible youth. A metal fence and barbed wire lined the circumfer-
ence of the field against escapee delinquents, and there were signs on the
highway that Margaret had read out loud last year on their regular trip
to Macon for new shoes, instructing motorists not to pick up hitchhikers, but cars stopped for hitchhikers all the same and the gate was never
locked. Spooner was hoping to see an incorrigible or two, but what escap-
ees there were didn't escape to camp out across the street. Most of them
headed for Florida.

Calmer never left the car where it could be seen from the road, did not
want to precipitate an escape attempt, and so always drove to the back end
of the lake and parked in a stand of pines. It about broke Spooner's ribs
laughing, driving where there was no road, bouncing over dead pines in

the weeds, and sometimes Calmer let him sit in his lap and steer. It was the best part of hunting, driving to the other end of the lake.

The gun was a Remington single-shot .22 rifle that Calmer's dad had given him when he was six, and the moment Calmer put it in his hands Spooner felt himself changed—the weight, or maybe it was the connection to Calmer as a boy his own size, or the smell of oil and gunpowder. He didn't care much for killing rabbits but thought he might like to shoot a snake. He also thought about being shot himself, winged in the shoulder, and pictured himself lying in Miss Tuttle's lap, his arm in a sling as she shampooed his hair.

———

In the end, all that got shot were the rabbits, but only three or four—no more than they would eat—and after that, they shot at bottles or cans. Calmer could hit bottles on the fence posts from across the lake, so far away that Spooner could barely make out their shapes. Calmer cleaned and skinned the rabbits in the lake, gutting them and then cutting off the heads and tails and stripping them down to purple muscles, leaving the fur and guts on the ground, inside out, and after he'd finished, what was left—the bare little bodies—did not look big enough for all the insides that came out of them.

They took the rabbits home in a pail, and it didn't matter who did the cooking or how long it lasted, or what vegetables and seasonings were thrown in with them, the animals came out of the pot as wiry as they went in, and even the smallest pieces were like biting into something still alive.

Something else about it too, back at the lake. Spooner had begun looking at the wet piles of fur and organs they left behind, crawling with flies and bees, and feeling uneasy about what they'd done, about leaving the evidence of it in plain sight. He never said anything about this feeling to Calmer—in the first place, as far as he knew he wasn't supposed to notice the rabbits were dead—and in the second place, he was afraid that anything he might say would get back to his mother, and there would be no more hunting.

As to the matter of playing catch in the yard, Calmer was not as good at catch as he was at shooting, and didn't have a glove of his own and sometimes missed the ball when it came right into his hands.

One night he heard them talking in the kitchen. He heard Calmer telling her that the balls Spooner threw had begun to break, and Spooner went to the closet and took the ball out of his catcher's mitt and looked it over but couldn't see that it was broken at all, and he wondered if Calmer was telling her it was so that he wouldn't have to play catch anymore.

There was no question about whose idea it had been, by the way, all this hunting rabbits and catch.

———

Months passed and still no one spoke to him directly regarding his expulsion from kindergarten, but he understood it was still on their minds and could see them watching him all the time, bathtime especially. He was no longer allowed to bathe with Margaret, for one thing, and these days if he got out of the tub and his mother or grandmother saw that his pecker was sticking out, Calmer had to come over during lunch the next day and play catch, even in the rain.

It didn't make much sense, but then these were people who looked up into the night sky and saw the shapes of animals in the stars.

FIFTEEN

Early in May, Calmer and Spooner's mother were married in the backyard. A preacher from the Methodist church downtown presided, not the Sunday-morning Methodist preacher but one of his assistants. Spooner's grandmother said they should have hired a Baptist. She'd gone over to the Baptist side some years earlier, even though the family had belonged to the Methodist church since before the Civil War. The Baptists, she said, didn't treat you like white trash if you had a reversal in fortune.

A month or so before the wedding Calmer suspended hunting and games of catch in the yard and spent every free moment doing touch-up work outside the house, painting the picnic table, raking pine needles, hanging decorations, and then, on Friday, while an assembly of Spooner's aunts and uncles and cousins were inside drinking lemonade and beer in front of the fans that Calmer had borrowed and set up all over the house, Calmer himself was making trips back and forth to his school to pick up folding chairs for the party. The chairs didn't fit easily into the car and it took four trips, and Spooner went along, carrying one chair while Calmer carried six, three in each hand.

At home, they put the chairs in rows in the backyard, then went back for more. When there were enough chairs, they collected two card tables Calmer borrowed from his friend Sibilski, who taught mathematics at the school, and then went to the A&P to pick up ham and cheese and Ritz crackers, then to a liquor store for refreshments.

All week the relatives had been coming into town, most of them checking in to the Baldwin Hotel downtown. In the days before the wedding, they arrived at the house in the middle of the morning, and Calmer worked like a crazy man, finding reasons to be somewhere else.

All the aunts from Spooner's mother's side showed up, and most of their children. Uncle Arthur, the famous concert pianist, flew into Atlanta from his home in New York, then hired a taxi to drive him to Milledgeville. He paid for all the family's rooms at the hotel.

There was no one from South Dakota.

One night after supper, with the relatives in the house and Calmer doing dishes in the kitchen, Uncle Don, who was a circuit judge in Birmingham, Alabama, had several drinks and offered the observation that in his experience, a man was best served to begin all endeavors boldly, particularly marriage. Not running errands like the maid. Uncle Don was a tiny, round-shaped human much admired in Birmingham legal circles for pronouncements of just this sort, issued in a resonant, deep baritone that didn't seem possible, coming from his small, soft body.

The air in the house was heavy and wet from all the relatives inside, and in this sort of proximity to each other the aunts were like high-strung dogs, snapping blindly at any movement out on the periphery, and if one of them took a step back—showed weakness to the others—it was *woe is me* for her.

On the other hand, the aunts were all tender for Uncle Arthur. He was famous and rich and talented—the living proof, in spite of the financial calamities and shame that had befallen the family when they were children, that the Whitlowes were still an accomplished and exceptional house. He got drunk and would laugh sometimes until he cried, and he hugged his sisters all the time, occasionally two at the same time (which, to Calmer's eyes, recalled priming chickens for a cockfight), but the sisters all seemed to take some pleasure in Uncle Arthur's hugging, even two at a time, although as a rule the family did not enjoy the press of one another's flesh, which is not to suggest that the sisters didn't hug and kiss hello and good-bye, as none of them wanted to be seen as the one who couldn't stand it, an unmistakable sign of weakness, and each of them understood that any such sign of weakness was an instinctive signal to the others to go ahead and rip out her throat.

Thus by the time the wedding rolled around, the aunts had been bris-
tling at each other and baring teeth and generally mixing it up for three
days, and their husbands had been trying to stay out of the way—all except
Uncle Don, who loved the sound of his own voice too much for his own
good and was roughed up several times when he didn't know enough to shut
up—and in the end things sorted out the same way they always sorted out,
which was that Daisy, the oldest, could still make the rest of them cry.

The wedding was short and hot, and afterward a spectacular bowl
carved out of ice arrived in a truck from Atlanta, and Uncle Arthur filled it
with champagne punch and then poured Spooner a glass and gave him one
of his black, European cigarettes. Uncle Arthur addressed him as *Warren, old
man*. Spooner's aunts sat in the folding chairs, getting louder as they drank,
two of them recalling that Arthur hadn't got them fancy ice bowls for their
weddings (not to mention the hundreds of pansies frozen inside it), and
remarking with some satisfaction on the growing number of bugs floating
in the champagne, and the pity that the ice had to melt, that the beauty of
it couldn't be preserved forever. And guessed how much it must have cost
him to have something like that trucked in from Atlanta.

And even now Calmer, newly married, went back and forth into the house,
making sure everybody had clean glasses and plates and all the Ritz crackers
they wanted. He did not stop moving once. Uncle Arthur was watching this
from the back steps, Spooner sitting on the step below him, each of them
smoking a black cigarette. Uncle Arthur put his hand on Spooner's shoulder
and said, "She's got him on his toes, hasn't she, old man?"

Calmer was passing the aunts a minute later when one of them, Violet,
the one who was married to Uncle Don and lived in Birmingham, Alabama, reached out and touched his arm to point out the puddle beneath
the table holding the ice bowl. "Calmer, dear," she said, "I think it would
last longer if you moved it into the shade."

The sun had shifted now, and the sisters had shifted with it.

Calmer went to the punch bowl and lifted it up without seeming to try, and then Uncle Don made to drag the card table into the shade of the house near the driveway, but tripped over a tree root as he backed up and fell on the seat of his pants and claimed to have broken his coccyx, but nobody paid any attention and Calmer waited patiently while he got up and brushed himself off, checking his behind from one side and then the other, like a woman in a dress shop. Then he pulled the table the rest of the way to the shade and Calmer set the ice bowl back on top of it, and if the ice had gotten cold or heavy against his arms or hands, he didn't let it show.

The aunts applauded his feat of strength, as by now they had been drinking half the afternoon, and Calmer smiled modestly and walked back into the house for more Ritz crackers and cheese spread, and the aunts commented to each other for the hundredth time what a godsend it was that he'd come along when he did, one of them even going so far as to call it proof that God existed, which surprised Spooner, because he had been thinking not exactly that but something like that himself.

And then if more proof of God were needed, a well-known mule belonging to Jaquith the one-armed attorney wandered up Spooner's driveway and went straight for the punch. Calmer was still inside the house. The mule had recently rolled in mud and was still wet, and the steam rose up off his back and the animal commenced licking the outside of the bowl with a tongue a foot long and a color Spooner recognized as the color of a skinned rabbit.

Uncle Arthur saw it first and laid his hand on Spooner's shoulder. "Hold on, old man," he said, "here we go." As if he'd been expecting something like this all along.

Aunt Violet noticed it next, the thing's awful blue tongue flattening itself against the edge of the ice, again and again, as if it meant to lick through to the flowers inside.

It is perhaps worth mentioning here that while Uncle Don had done quite well as a judge and before that as an attorney, and lived in a lakeside house and bought a new Cadillac every year just like Uncle Arthur except Uncle Arthur always bought convertibles—all this, by the way, and Violet still enjoyed torturing Spooner's mother by saying that she was on a budget too—Uncle Don was not and never had been in the legal profession for the money. It was love, pure and simple. Love of the law and, more than that, of the sound of his voice expounding on the law, which he still did at the slightest provocation, from the bench in his robes or a stool at the drug-store, to anybody who would listen, or had to, even sometimes to Spooner, although it was not clear that he knew exactly who Spooner was, and always ended with the pronouncement that the law alone stood between man and anarchy. And was at this moment making that very pronouncement to old man Stoppard, who'd wandered out of the house in sandals and underpants to see what was going on, but was interrupted by the shrieking of his wife. Uncle Don stopped midsentence—in fact the entire gathering stopped, even the mule. Aunt Violet pointed at the animal and called to her husband. "Don," she yelled, "for God's sake, Don . . ."

And Uncle Don looked up from his lecture on anarchy only to find himself staring it in the face. He was stunned at the size of this affront, not to mention the size of the beast—anarchy personified—not to men-tion the proximity of the beast's arrival to his discussion of the rule of law, and was momentarily at a loss for words. Which, as he would explain later in the evening, was the reason—not cowardice—he did not take matters into his own hands then and there. Pretty soon, though, he cleared his throat and made the sort of joke that had won Aunt Violet's heart in the first place. He said, "Heah now, this is private property."

Violet yelled at him again, apparently not having heard him. She said, "Damn it, Don, it's a darn mule in the punch bowl . . ."

Violet's hearing was not what it used to be, so he repeated it. "Heah now," he said, "this is a private party."

The oldest sister, Daisy—the only aunt Spooner had who could toler-ate him for longer than a few minutes at a time, and vice versa—stood up and went directly to the animal to give it a piece of her mind. She was the prettiest of the sisters, her hair prematurely gray and wrapped up into a bun. "You shoo," she said. "Shoo. Go back where you belong."

The mule was huge, almost the size of a horse. The steam still came up off its back, and flies circled the oozing spots of mange it had rubbed raw against a tree or a post, and it turned its head for a look-see at the source of the noise. The mule saw that Daisy did not have a stick to beat it over the head, and so it went back to the punch bowl without so much as lowering its ears, but then did a kind of double take just as Aunt Daisy, who was not used to being dismissed out of hand, stamped her foot. The mule reconsidered Daisy, and plucked the corsage off her blouse and ate it.

Uncle Don took another step closer, not wanting his wife's oldest sister to make him look like a sissy, but Violet called out to him to stop. "Don, don't be a darn fool," she said. "Let the police handle it."

Which was when the mule began to hum. It was, for reasons hard to explain, a disturbing noise coming from a mule, and even Daisy took a step back to reconsider.

"Here now," Uncle Don said, "that's enough out of you." He didn't mean anything in particular by that, and then he took another step forward, as if to handle the situation, and a quiver rippled over the animal's back, which was all Uncle Don had to see, and he retreated back into the adjoining yard.

Likewise all of Spooner's aunts except Daisy, who'd given as much ground as she intended to, and they picked up their plates and drinks and their youngest children and headed for safer ground. The older children, meanwhile, had begun darting in and out of range, touching the mule's hindquarters and tail, and one of them—Cousin Billy Damn— even pulled its ear, and the aunts yelled at them to stop.

The mule, meanwhile, continued to lick at the bowl with its awful, filthy tongue, teeth like Halloween corn, and then Violet's youngest girl lay down under the porch steps—right under Spooner and Uncle Arthur—covered her ears and issued a note so shrill that even Uncle Arthur, who was a professional musician, had never heard anything like it, and a minute later the Shakers' coonhound, perhaps fetched by the pitch of the little girl's scream, came loping into the party and began snapping at guests and mule alike, also urinating on Sibilski's card tables and the folding chairs Calmer had borrowed from the school.

This, then, was the scene as Calmer came out the screen door carrying a tray of crackers: Beneath his feet a child was making an unearthly noise, and ahead the Shakers' coonhound was snapping at anything that moved, and his sisters-in-law were huddled together with the smaller children in the next yard, where Uncle Don also was, explaining some fine point of property law to old man Stoppard, and Jaquith the one-armed attorney's mule was licking the ice bowl and humming.

Plus, Lily's brother Arthur seemed to have had a breakdown and was sitting on the steps helplessly weeping.

Calmer came down the stairs, turned, and set the tray on the step next to Uncle Arthur. "Excuse me," he said, and then he walked straight to the punch bowl, kicked the dog off and grabbed the mule roughly by the tongue, yanked it out and to one side of the animal's mouth for leverage, and led it in that fashion, making some unearthly noise, out of the yard and down the driveway in the direction of Jaquith's property, which lay beyond the top of the hill and across Macon Highway.

Uncle Arthur continued to weep from joy, and continued to drink champagne and smoke his black cigarettes even though his sisters wouldn't go near the ice bowl after seeing the thing's disgusting tongue all over it—the animal might as well have dry-humped it, as far as they were concerned—and from time to time the incident seemed to roll back over Uncle Arthur, and he dropped his head into his knees again and his back shook, and he had to wipe the tears out of his eyes to see.

Nobody said it then—it takes a little while for these things to settle out—but the truth was that for most of a week, Lily's relatives had been watching Calmer clean house and fetch drinks, remarking to each other on the miracle of his arrival, and his wonderful housekeeping, and his devotion to Lily and the kids, and how good he was with the children, especially Margaret, and referring to him generally as the godsend—all this noted with an unmistakable pleasure, Lily having settled on a eunuch—but into this picture had wandered Jaquith's mule, and half an hour later, with the size and smell and awfulness of that creature implanted forever in their memories, all matters of courage and manliness were taken off the table, and the sisters contented themselves with knowing how much a schoolteacher made.

SIXTEEN

Half a year after the break-in, Kenny Durkin's father still said he couldn't get a night's sleep until he shot a nigger to get even. "This heah has got implications," he said dangerously, and on that platform campaigned across Vincent Heights, usually on Friday afternoons, not that most of Vincent Heights needed to be campaigned to.

Outrages of this sort did not diminish with use and time, like tooth enamel or tire tread, and by now the story of the break-in at Mr. Durkin's house had grown and the coloreds had violated his home not once but three times, and not just pissed on his floor but stolen his toaster, the Hoover vacuum, his wristwatch, and the food right out of his icebox. Hearing this, some Vincent Heighters took to locking their doors at night and others, who knew Roger Durkin better, didn't. He had a flair for the dramatic, especially on Friday afternoons, although no one in the neighborhood doubted that given the chance he would for a fact plug one in the yard.

The only pluggable colored people who ever came through Vincent Heights, though, were the dollar-a-day house maids from down at the Bottoms and the toothless old vagrant who had skin speckled like the three-cent-a-pound bananas at the Piggly Wiggly, and some kind of table leg for a calf. He came around early in the afternoon, before the men got home from work, and went methodically through one garbage can after another, up one side of Vincent Heights and down the other, looking for something to eat. He had been bitten by half the dogs in Vincent Heights, and shot from ambush by children with BB guns, and chased off again and again by the police, but in spite of this he took his time and was neat and systematic about his work, picking up what he'd spilled, carefully replacing the garbage cans' lids.

The truth was, the possible shooting of the old colored man presented a dilemma. On one hand, he was a damn nuisance, and it was a known fact that where one of them found garbage today, twenty of them would come searching tomorrow, and the next thing you knew the whole place would be crawling with them, and nobody could get a night's sleep then. On the other hand, the Shakers' coonhound also went through garbage cans but left them tipped over in the driveway, so how could you logically shoot the one and not shoot the other?

There was also the fact that the old colored man's fingers were two times normal size, so stiff he had to use a stick to get the lids off and on the garbage cans. How was he going to break into somebody's house? Another thing was, he stayed down in the Bottoms with his sister, slept on the ground under her house, and had as much use for a vacuum cleaner as he did for roller skates.

In the end, the discussion came down more to Roger Durkin himself than if the old man had broken into his house.

Roger had been in the war and shot a hundred Japs, and times being what they were, people took his word for that, and times being what they were, they'd all heard stories about soldiers who had come home from the war and done crazy-mean things that would make shooting one old nigger seem like common sense.

For his part Spooner had a feeling of acquaintance with the old man and had occasionally followed him on his rounds through Vincent Heights, one garbage can to another, putting things in his mouth to consider if they were edible, spitting out what wasn't, like coffee grounds or steel wool, and he didn't see that Mr. Durkin shooting him would make it easier for anybody to sleep.

Five-thirty in the morning, half an hour before dawn. The pine needles were wet and stuck to Spooner's feet, and the sky was just beginning to show light over the sawmill. He hadn't planned anything, just woke up having to tinkle, and then padded right past the bathroom and out the back door. Just like that. He was barefoot and walked on his toes, and due to the excitement could barely hold off urinating on the way over.

The Durkins' screen door was locked and Spooner stepped back for a longer view. The frame had been painted earlier in the year, and even in the faint predawn light, Spooner could see bumps where the gnats had stuck as it dried.

Spooner broke a piece of the splintered wood off the bottom of the door, where it was warped and didn't close, and then climbed onto one of the empty paint cans that had been sitting in the Durkins' backyard all summer, and used the wood to lift the hook out of the eyehole. Except for the need to urinate, he had all the time in the world, and familiar early-morning noises came up out of the dark to him from the pasture.

He stepped off the paint can, set it to the side, and pulled open the screen. The back door was locked too. He looked around a moment and then went directly to Mrs. Durkin's flower box, nailed to the sill beneath the kitchen window, knowing somehow it was where she would put the key.

This brought Spooner back in front of Kenny Durkin's icebox, exactly the spot he'd been before, dancing slightly but pinching his pecker shut with his fingers, holding off the sweetness of letting go, picking the exact spot. Draining the lizard, he'd heard Mr. Durkin call it that.

As it had before, the bare bulb in the icebox threw a rectangle of light across the floor, and at the edge of the light just under the kitchen table, he saw Mr. Durkin's heavy black shoes. He picked them up and set them in the icebox, the only shoes he'd ever seen Mr. Durkin wear. He sprinkled them left to right, and some of the pleasure was in the relief of finally letting it go and some of it was in the tingle of apprehension in the room, and some of it in the sound itself, there in the silent house, a sound that pretty soon turned musical, like when a flower bed has taken as much water out of the hose as it can hold. He swung back and forth, evening the pitch, draining the lizard. And when he'd finished and shaken, he closed the refrigerator door and left, locked the back door behind him, and headed back as unhurried as if he was kicking a can home, the house key in the palm of his hand for later, and the sky had turned a little pink now over the sawmill and the Bottoms.

Spooner lay in bed unable to sleep, the greatness of what he'd done still fresh every time he went over it in his head, the picture of the shoes set neatly beside each other in the icebox—it just killed him, how perfect that looked—and then he finally slept, and then he woke up and ten minutes later was sitting in front of the same shredded wheat and milk that he'd been sitting in front of all his known life, and things were as ordinary as the hum of the day. And the feeling was lost.

Later that morning, Sergeant Audry of the Milledgeville Police Department pulled his patrol car into Kenny Durkin's driveway, blew the horn several times, and when nobody came out exited the vehicle with no small effort and went to the screen door, pounded on it twice, and then walked in.

Sergeant Audry lived in Vincent Heights, in a half-charred brick house up on the hill, across the street from the Shakers' place. He was the town of Milledgeville's most familiar policeman due to his size and a well-publicized shooting spree downtown earlier in the year in the height of the rabies epidemic, when he shot four mongrel dogs and then winged the Fuller boy Danny with a ricochet. A mitigating factor, offered at his administrative hearing, was that Sergeant Audry had recently been dog-bitten himself, and it had taken five stitches on his wrist to close the wound. On the other hand, this mitigation was somewhat mitigated itself with the subsequent disclosure that it was Audry's own dog that had bitten him, an incident that occurred in public during a scramble for a chicken leg that had fallen off the sergeant's plate during the town's annual police and fire department picnic dinner.

Still, the episode of the chicken leg had set him on edge, and then two weeks later came a failed arson attempt on the sergeant's house, which perhaps not coincidentally had been sitting around unsold in a depressed housing market for eighteen months. The job had been botched, though, and when Audry and his wife and his boy Junior returned from a long weekend at the beach in Brunswick, the façade of the place was singed black, and black water was still running off the roof into the missus's flower beds, and the fire department was still inside, hosing down the closets, and the whole place reeked of gasoline and yet miraculously, according to the insurance adjuster, was structurally intact, and off that news Sergeant Audry began shooting law-abiding dogs in the middle of downtown Milledgeville. The house still stank, even from the road, and the odor triggered the sergeant's allergies, and his eyes were always bloodshot these days, and his uniforms smelled like mildewed wool, and he hadn't been the best-smelling officer in the South to begin with, being of the old Saturday-night-bath school, and also the fattest man in Vincent Heights.

His son, Junior—his given name, Junior Audry—was thirteen and still in fifth grade (started late, and left behind twice) and the fattest *boy* in Vincent Heights, and had once made Spooner hold still while he drooled tobacco juice on his bare feet.

Spooner watched from his bedroom window now, and presently Sergeant Audry reemerged from the house with Mr. Durkin a step or two behind. Mr. Durkin was wearing long pants and suspenders, and a T-shirt without sleeves that revealed a tattoo of a grass-skirted girl who looked quite a bit like the grass-skirted doll on his dashboard. The screen door slammed behind them, and Mr. Durkin jumped at the noise and then hurried to catch up, and then walked alongside Sergeant Audry back to his cruiser, crablike, trying to keep up and plead his case at the same time, the case being that if this was what it finally come down to, the niggers was now pissing in white people's shoes, then it was war.

His voice carried over the neighborhood, and you could tell he'd cracked open the first beer quite a while ago, possibly when he got up that morning and found his shoes in the icebox. Mr. Durkin had his pistol stuck into the front of his pants and was gesturing with his right hand, pointing every direction except directly at Sergeant Audry. He used his left hand to hold the gun in place.

Sergeant Audry did not like to be called out to Vincent Heights in the first place—perhaps he resented being reminded of where he lived, or the fire, or his previous plans to move into town after he sold his house—and appeared to pay no attention to what Mr. Durkin was saying. Back at the police car, though, he stopped at the still-open door while Mr. Durkin continued to talk, and inspected his fingernails, as if he was about to say something logical. And when he did speak, it did sound logical, at least to Spooner. He didn't raise his voice or even turn in Mr. Durkin's direction, only said, "Lemme ast you somethin', Roger. You think I ain't got nothin' more impo'ent to have did at the end of the day but come out heah and lookit where somebody pissed in somebody's shoes?"

Mr. Durkin did not answer, and in a second Sergeant Audry wheeled on him, faster than you would have thought a fat man could wheel, and poked a finger that looked for all the world like a baby's leg into the middle of Mr. Durkin's narrow chest. Mr. Durkin was taken off balance and fell back a step.

"Lissen a me, cocksucker," Sergeant Audry said, and the logical part of it was over now, "I been on the police seventeen years, and I guess by now I can tell nigger crime from a domestic disturbance."

He backed himself into the front seat of the car and sat down and lifted his legs in after him, one at a time, grunting with the effort, and then slammed the door, and came close to running over Roger Durkin's feet on the way out.

Mr. Durkin stood in the driveway as Sergeant Audry drove off, stunned, his hand still on the pistol tucked into the front of his pants, like he might be thinking of shooting off his own pecker. His wife was watching from the front door, terrified, and Mr. Durkin looked down at his slippers—before this, he'd worn his black work shoes whenever he went outside, even if it was only to wash the car—and what he was thinking Spooner could not guess.

———

Spooner tried all day but could not get back to the feeling of standing in Kenny Durkin's refrigerator-lit kitchen and tinkling into Mr. Durkin's shoes. The feeling had been apart from and unconnected to the incident of the unshared cheese, or the fact that Kenny Durkin's mother would never give him a drink of ice water out of a glass, and always told him to use the hose instead. Or even, really, with the pleasant picture of Mr. Durkin taking his shoes out of the icebox and slipping his feet inside, then stopping cold in his tracks, as it were, knowing they weren't just cold but something worse, and waiting for his brain to tell him what it was.

In the end, this inability to reclaim the feeling of greatness would be a lifelong affliction. For all of Spooner's life, the only way back to the feeling was back to the icebox.

Sunday, after Sunday school, Spooner climbed the six steps out of the basement of the Methodist church, the clammiest place in Milledgeville, Georgia, and still in the wash of a crowded room of children who had to a person heard the word and felt Jesus in their hearts, heard something himself: *The world is full of shoes.*

Meaning it didn't have to be Kenny Durkin's daddy's.

And that same afternoon stepped over the Shakers' coonhound, who was asleep beneath Lance's bedroom window, and climbed through the window into the Shaker residence. Lance and his mother were in the backyard at the time with the maid, chopping the head off a chicken for supper. There was nothing young Lance—as his father called him—enjoyed better than chasing a just-decapitated chicken around the yard, whacking it with a switch.

The major himself was asleep on a chair in the living room, still in the uniform he wore to church, his lips loose and glistening with spit. The radio was on the table next to him, broadcasting Chicago Cubs baseball from Wrigley Field.

Spooner took his time. He picked up Major Shaker's shoes, which were set neatly together beside the foot stool, polished and shined. It was one of Lance's orders of the day to polish his and his daddy's shoes. Scuffed shoes meant demerits.

Spooner took the shoes to the bedroom and set them on the floor, cocking his head like a piano tuner as he went back and forth between them, evening the pitch, one shoe to the other.

On the way out, he noticed a small puddle on the floor at the foot of Lance's bed. Just a few drops, really, and he looked around for something to wipe it up, but now came a change in the sound of Major Shaker's breathing, and a moment later another sound as he got up off the chair, and Spooner was out the window.

All in all, a neat, well-timed job, but still, the puddle. It nagged at him all day, like a guilty conscience. He didn't know the word for the nagging then, but the nagging itself wasn't new and had bothered him one way or another for a long time. Which is all to say that on top of trespassing, spying on his mother from trees, lying, sneaking out of the house, and being sexually unfit for kindergarten, Spooner was, on top of everything else, a perfectionist.

Major Shaker called the police and again Sergeant Audry was sent to Vincent Heights. A reporter from the newspaper went through the neighborhood later that week, knocking on doors, interviewing housewives and the elderly in regard to the strange crime wave sweeping the area.

The story ran on the front page in Friday's paper, with a picture of old man Stoppard's house, which the newspaper identified as the residence of Roger Durkin. A fiend was loose in the community, the paper said, breaking in to homes and committing acts of an unprintable nature.

Margaret read the report to Spooner after supper, and he leaned in over her narrow arms and stared at the words he couldn't read for himself, and at the picture of old man Stoppard's place, glimpsing for the first time what newspapers did. The paper had most of it wrong, not just about old man Stoppard's house but the times and places the fiend had struck, and yet gradually, over the next day or two, he began to notice that to the citizens of Vincent Heights, the paper saying it that way made it so, even though they knew for a fact that it wasn't. Which kindled the theory that fibbing was only fibbing if you got caught by somebody more important, and if you became important enough—like the newspaper— you could get away with anything.

Thus Spooner's first interest in the printed word.

SEVENTEEN

They went shooting.

It had been a long time since they'd been alone with each other, and things had changed. Spooner was enrolled in first grade at Peabody Laboratory School and Calmer was buying Granny Otts's house next door, and there was a baby growing in Spooner's mother's stomach, and Calmer did not have to look for things to do these days, they were lined up in front of him the moment he got out of bed.

They drove out to the lake and parked; Calmer closed his eyes and leaned back against the seat, tired and thinking. They had not spoken much lately, even after Sergeant Audry had come to the door one Sunday and reported that Spooner had been seen climbing the Blakemans' roof out by the highway. Spooner had gotten the feeling lately that he was wearing Calmer out.

It was Spooner who broke the silence. "Should we shoot at something?" he said.

"Maybe just some bottles today," he said, and motioned toward the rotted fence posts still standing at various angles along the property line. Somehow Calmer seemed to know he had no heart for killing rabbits. The field had been a cow pasture once, and there were still cow pies the size of hubcaps all over the ground, dried out and picked over by crows for the corn.

Spooner set some bottles on the fence posts and plunked them off, hitting more than he missed. Afterwards, he looked back toward Calmer but already knew he wasn't paying attention. They hadn't come out here today to shoot. He opened the bolt to eject the shell, and a little circle of white smoke hung over the open breach. Calmer called him over.

He lit a cigarette and crossed his legs and looked out at the pine-tree horizon. "I don't know if I mentioned my cousin Arlo to you," he said after a while. "He lost three fingers at the polar bear exhibit at the zoo in Minneapolis." Spooner turned and squinted up at him, into the sun. He couldn't see much of Calmer's face from here, but there was something uncomfortable in his voice, as there usually was when he talked about his other family back in South Dakota.

Spooner said, "It bit off his fingers?"

Calmer shook his head. "No, from what he said, it just swiped them off with its claw."

Spooner tried to picture it that way, but it wouldn't come. "Did they shoot it?"

"No, they don't shoot bears for that. It was just being a bear. Arlo stuck his hand in the cage."

"Why?"

Calmer shrugged. "To scratch her ears, he said."

"It was a girl?"

Calmer looked out into the distance again, as if he was remembering. "He does things like that sometimes, but bears are bears and Arlo is Arlo. We all do things we regret . . ."

"But what happened?"

"That was it. They did what they could for him at the hospital and he went back home to the farm, and he learned to do as much work without his fingers as he did with them, and even though he'd done something foolish, everybody still loved him." He narrowed his eyes, remembering something. "I think the city put up a sign that said Do not place hands inside bear cage."

Calmer stood up and shook out his leg, which had gone to sleep. "I just thought you might be interested in that."

"Were they friends again, then?"

"Who?"

"Cousin Arlo and the bear."

"Probably not," Calmer said. "You can't be friends with a bear."

Spooner shot for a while longer and then they put the gun in its place in the trunk and got in the car. As they reached the highway a wasp flew in the window and moved across the windshield, rattling like death itself, points of color glistening in the black wings, and seeing Spooner draw back, Calmer leaned forward into the steering wheel and trapped it between the windshield and the back of his hand, held it there a moment, mashing it side to side, and then picked up the carcass off the dashboard and dropped it out the window like a cigarette butt. He gave no sign that he'd been stung, but when they got home and walked up the steps to the front door, his hand was so thick he couldn't get it in his pocket for the keys to the house.

The fiend had struck again recently, and Spooner's mother, like half the housewives in Vincent Heights, had taken to locking the front door.

Spooner was never sure what Calmer was thinking or what he knew. He was thinking something, though, Spooner could see that, and it was about him. Something that he hadn't told Spooner's mother.

Calmer bought Spooner and Margaret a puppy—a small, nervous Boston terrier, seven weeks old, that shook like change on top of the washing machine, a dog you could sneak up on and when you grabbed him he'd jump a foot off the ground. The dog would not come, or sit, or answer to his name, and sometimes Calmer sat holding it in the utility room—where they kept it at night—looking it over in the same peculiar way he sometimes looked at Spooner, when he thought Spooner wasn't watching.

Perhaps it was Spooner's attachment to Calmer, not wanting to disappoint him, or that being the Fiend of Vincent Heights itself had begun to feel ordinary—it had been a year now—whatever the reason, Spooner eased gradually into retirement. Thus, the idle mind being the devil's playground, as his grandmother would say when it was time to lick stamps, as if licking stamps was the next thing to algebra, he happened to find himself aimless one afternoon and wondering if he could throw an egg from Major Shaker's chicken coop across the road and into the always-open windows of Sergeant Audry's patrol car. Sergeant Audry reliably came home in the afternoon and parked the cruiser next to his house and slept in the front seat.

And so Spooner climbed to the roof of the Shakers' chicken coop, a fresh egg in each of his pants pockets, to wait for Sergeant Audry, and had heard the cruiser coming and then, not quite in time, saw that it was not Sergeant Audry but Major Shaker, pulling into his driveway, and Spooner—it was already too late to ask why—tossed the egg he had intended to pitch into Sergeant Audry's car window onto the hood of the major's car instead. Lance was in the car with Major Shaker, his head barely visible at the side window. Spooner froze a moment, amazed at what he'd done, envisioning a whole new career, and then, in an escape plan he had not completely thought out, climbed onto Major Shaker's roof and flattened himself against the shingles, breathing in the smell of the hot tar paper beneath his chin, and waited as Major Shaker first disappeared behind the dashboard and then sat back up and threw open the door, a pistol in his hand, and ran to the chicken coop and then circled the house.

Lance had gone into the windshield when the major hit the brakes, and was still back in the car, wailing like he'd been run over. The major went all the way round the house, keeping low and taking what cover he could, and then appeared again at the spot where he'd stopped the car.

He noticed young Lance crying then, and shouted, "Will you shut the hell up?" which only made him cry louder.

His voice was hoarse and, except for the fact that the words were from the English language, did not sound human. A neighbor came out her door to see what was going on. The neighbor had a clear view of Spooner on the roof, and she and the major's wife socialized together sometimes when their husbands went fishing. Lance was yowling like he was really hurt, but with Lance you could never tell. He cried all the time, and from what Spooner had seen had cried and tattled his way right to perfect grades in Miss Anderson's first-grade class at Peabody School, even though he copied off everybody, and everybody but Miss Anderson knew it. But then, giving him his due, he was the best speller in class, including the girls, and always won the Friday spelling bee.

All his life, Spooner would mistrust people who could spell.

Major Shaker did another, slower circuit of the house and young Lance continued to go at it in the afternoon air, and Spooner did not move from his spot on the roof, still in plain view of the neighbor and starting to bake. The neighbor had seen him, he knew that, but hadn't done anything about it yet, afraid maybe that Major Shaker would shoot him off the roof. He felt nauseated, but put it less to the heat than the strain of trying to come up with a story. Whatever story he told, he would have to tell it eventually to Calmer, who for all he knew could read his mind, and more and more lately gave him sudden, hard looks when he fibbed. He tried but all he could come up with was something he'd heard Calmer say: *Time waits for no man*. It sounded intelligent but as a story it had some holes.

The major went back to the car and pulled Lance out—he had seen his own blood and was crying more earnestly now—just as Mrs. Shaker came out the front door barefoot in a bathrobe, leaving wet footprints on the porch as she ran to him, her hair wrapped in a towel. She saw the gun in one of the major's hands and Lance in the other, and saw Lance was bleeding, and assumed the worst. Screaming at her husband that he'd shot their beautiful boy.

Spooner had an orderly, mathematical mind and fought down a wild, reckless impulse to climb down and straighten everything out.

———

Major Shaker left Lance on the walk holding on to his mother and went into the house. He was back out a minute later, no longer armed, and got in his car, which he'd left running, and blew gravel up against the undercarriage backing out of the driveway.

Spooner waited a few minutes after the major left, listening to Lance sobbing into his mother's titties, a come-and-go sound to it, wa-wa, like a trumpet, and then they went inside and he dropped down off the roof onto the chicken coop, making no sound at all as he landed, and climbed through the barbed-wire fence into the pasture and started home. Behind him, he could still hear Lance crying, but Lance was running out of juice, and couldn't keep it up.

———

He followed the fence line home. The sun was beginning to go down, and he ran at a few cows, bluffing them off their grazing spots, but his heart wasn't in it, and presently he came to a spot even with the back of his house, where the lowest strand of barbed wire sagged all the way to the ground. He usually ducked through to cross into his yard. From this same spot, though, he now saw Major Shaker's green Henry J parked in the driveway, directly behind Calmer's Ford. Major Shaker was standing to one side of the car with his arms folded across his chest, and Calmer was in the driveway with the hose, washing the dried egg off the Henry J hood.

Spooner turned and headed the other direction, downhill, toward the sawmill. The cattle had begun their regular evening ambulation to the swale in the pasture where the pond was, moving single file through the changing light, their shadows long and slow. They would spend the night at the pond, lying so close together that from the house they looked like a low black hill.

In front of Spooner lay the sawmill, quiet and empty. He stopped a moment and watched for the guard, who lived on-site in a tiny trailer between the sawmill and the Bottoms.

At the other end of the mill—the southern end—was a domed tin-roofed structure with an open door and a smokestack. Black smoke was floating up out of it, as it did night and day, every day of the year, giving Vincent Heights its peculiar sweet smell, like a dog passing air. Even on Sundays, the fire never went out, and sometimes after dark, when Spooner was sent outside to think over something he'd done, he could see fire glowing in the open door.

Spooner went under the fence at the bottom of the pasture, then crossed a plywood bridge over a creek and headed for the building, suddenly wanting to see the fire for himself.

He stopped a moment in the doorway, the heat nearly turning him around, but then went farther in. He thought his pants might catch fire. The floor of the building had been dug out, a crater almost as big as the building itself, and around the edge was an earthen path a yard wide. There was another open doorway on the opposite side, and a conveyor belt of some kind led from there into the building, and there were still pieces of lumber on it, the frayed ends sparking and rising with the heat to the roof. In the morning the belt would begin to move again, and these pieces would be the first to fall into the pit. Spooner now stared into the pit itself. The surface was dark but seemed to boil, and the smoke went up through the hole in the roof.

Spooner went farther in, stopping finally at a point where it seemed as far to one opening as the other, staring all the while into the pit, which was beginning to glow in the coming darkness. A moment passed, and he thought of the strangeness of the place, that you could step off the ledge and two minutes later be smoke yourself.

A figure appeared in the doorway, a small man with one hand in his pants pocket. He looked the pit over and then turned away and Spooner saw the empty sleeve. Spooner pressed himself back as far as he could go, remembering a story Kenny Durkin told him that during the war Jaquith cut off his own arm for something to eat and never lost the taste for human flesh, and now they let him eat dead people because he was a veteran and a lawyer.

Spooner felt his spine pressing into the hard inward slant of the wall.

Jaquith turned again and walked out of sight.

Time passed, and it was darker outside every time Spooner looked, and in the darkness the pit glowed and began to turn rosy. Spooner thought of Calmer washing the egg off Major Shaker's car.

He heard a starter weakly turning an engine. The engine coughed and then sighed, like somebody sick in bed, and then caught, and then the engine revved, again and again, until you could hear the insides hammering against the walls of the cylinders.

The headlights went on, and Spooner saw the beams in the dark, angled high and uneven, pointed like a blind man's eyes, and then he saw the car itself, moving slowly into view, mud-covered and dilapidated, the muffler dragging along the ground underneath. The car moved slowly past the opening and disappeared to the right, and a moment later Jaquith's mule appeared from the left. The mule was dead and, from what Spooner could see, attached to the car by a rope. The rope had pulled the animal's ears up against its head into a kind of bouquet, and it seemed to fight the rope, jerking and bouncing as it was dragged along slowly to the opening, losing ground all the time.

When the mule was even with the opening, the engine quit and popped once, and then Jaquith opened the door and got out. He stood for a moment, looking the situation over, and then went back to the car, leaned in to the trunk and came into sight again with an oar.

He pushed the oar deep under the mule, using his foot to drive it, as if he were spading the earth, and then set his shoulder under the oar and heaved up. The mule rocked and settled, perhaps a few inches closer to the fire. Jaquith went to the other end and stuck the oar beneath the animal's behind and lifted it again. He grunted under the strain, raising up on tiptoes to lift the oar as high as he could, then went back to the other end and started the process over again, making a similar noise, and in this way, the mule was gradually levered closer and closer to the fire, until finally, a point of balance was reached and the creature seemed to hang a moment on the edge, and then dropped in, the rear legs first, then the front. A puff of ash came up around the body, and a moment later it slid in farther and seemed to float for a few seconds, and then began to smoke, and then caught fire all at once, as if it had finally given in. There were popping noises at first, then a small explosion as the mule split wide open, and an instant later Spooner inhaled a putrefaction that engraved itself instantly and forever in his brain, and for as long as he lived, whenever he was truly scared—those times when he thought he was dead or as good as—he would catch a whiff of that exploded mule.

———

Jaquith stood at the edge after his mule was gone, still holding the oar, staring into the pit.

Daring himself, Spooner thought.

Then he turned and went back to his car and drove off, the rope bouncing along behind. Spooner started back to the opening, which seemed a long ways off. There was an unfamiliar weakness in his legs, and he reached out to touch the wall as he went, holding himself on the straight and narrow until he was safe. He stopped once, afraid he would fall, dizzy with the smell and the heat.

———

The moon was up when he finally crawled under the fence into his yard. He could see his shadow in the moonlight, and his face felt like frosting on a week-old cake. He circled the house before he went in, and it appeared that every light in the place was on, even the one in the bedroom where he and Margaret slept. Normally, Calmer would check the lights in the house all the time, turning off the ones no one was using. *Waste not, want not*; saying that out loud.

Spooner came in the back door, noticing the dog wasn't in his usual spot on the porch. The family was sitting at the kitchen table, eating; it seemed too late for supper. Chicken and dumplings. Nobody's face appeared to be a familiar color. The door closed behind Spooner and Calmer saw him and was over him a second later but then stopped, as if he'd forgotten what he'd gotten up to do. His mother was red-eyed and had been crying.

His grandmother continued to eat her supper. She did things one at a time, to the exclusion of everything else. On those frequent occasions when everything was going to hell in a handbasket, it seemed to cheer her up to remind them all of her simple rule of day-to-day living: *One thing at a time.*

Calmer grabbed Spooner by the elbow and lifted him up until Spooner could feel his shoulder pressing into his ear. It was the first time Calmer had ever put his hands on him without kind intentions, and as soon as he'd grabbed him, he seemed to realize what he had done and let go. His expression changed, and he stared down at Spooner, resigned, as if something had been dropped and broken that could not be fixed. They were all looking at him now, even his grandmother.

Then his mother said, "My God, Calmer, his eyebrows." And they all knew that tone of voice.

Calmer leaned over, staring hard at Spooner's face, then moved farther up, inspecting his scalp. He got a few inches closer and sniffed at his hair. Margaret's mouth had hinged open, and there was a piece of dumpling in the gap where she had lost her other front tooth.

"Have you been to the sawmill?" Calmer said, and he sniffed Spooner's head again. Not angry anymore, just sniffing.

Spooner said, "Jaquith's mule died and he pushed it into the pit."

A certain quiet was hanging in the room, even as he spoke. At the far end of the table Spooner's grandmother continued to eat. One thing at a time.

"I believe we take our fingers out of our mouth when we speak," she said without looking up from her plate. Spooner realized he was sucking his middle fingers again, something he'd quit about the time he turned into the Fiend of Vincent Heights. And in this moment he felt it all slipping away—the Fiend of Vincent Heights one minute, back to sucking his fingers the next.

Calmer was still puzzling over him, as if trying to see through a foggy window. "Sit down," he said softly, and Spooner could hear he was sorry for grabbing him by the elbow. He couldn't say the words themselves, especially not now, but he was sorry. "Eat some supper," he said, "and we'll put some butter on the burns later."

Spooner sat down and Calmer went to the stove and got him a plate of chicken and dumplings. Spooner's grandmother looked up and watched as Calmer picked out the wings, the part Spooner liked. She didn't approve of Calmer's child-rearing and didn't try to hide it. "When I was a little girl," she said, "children were on time for supper or they were sent to bed without."

The steam rose up from the plate and scalded Spooner's skin like he was back inside the burning shed.

Calmer got him a glass of milk and then returned to his own seat. Presently he said, "Major Shaker was over earlier. Someone threw an egg at his car."

Calmer had turned slightly away from Spooner's grandmother, as he often did when she stuck her nose into his business. Spooner nodded, as if the Shaker egging were an interesting development indeed. His fingers were in his mouth again, and he took them out and blew on a dumpling, thinking once it was in his mouth it was bad manners to speak. Not a great day in Spooner's life for long-range plans.

"He said it was you," Margaret said.

"The mule exploded," Spooner said. As if that superseded and explained everything else.

Spooner's grandmother affected a singsong quality to her voice sometimes, and did so now. She said, "Children who fib go to bed without their supper."

"I'm not a fibber," Spooner said.

"Of course you are," she said, and Calmer looked at her sharply but held what he was thinking to himself.

She caught the look, though. "It's my house," she said, "and I'll say what I want."

Another sort of look passed over Calmer's face, and Spooner realized that nobody had told Grandma yet that they were moving. Spooner had only found out himself that week, from Margaret. Calmer was buying Granny Otts's house next door, and Granny Otts and Marlis were selling their horses and going back to Arkansas, where they came from. Spooner pictured himself riding to school on Gypsy, tying her to the bicycle rack. He thought he might change her name to Brown Fury.

Margaret was getting her own room in the new house—Calmer was going to build it onto the back porch. She was at the age now when she needed her own room, and they all needed more space with the baby coming. And even though Granny Otts's house wasn't any bigger than the one they lived in now, it would seem bigger without Spooner's grandmother underfoot. How Margaret knew all this, Spooner never asked. She was only a year and a half older but so far ahead of him that she might as well have been a grown-up herself.

"We've all told fibs," Calmer said. And there he was, after everything that Spooner had done, still taking his side.

"Speak for yourself," his grandmother said.

Spooner's mother found her voice for the first time since she'd noticed his eyebrows were gone. She said, "Mother, would you please shut up for once?"

His grandmother was not used to being told to shut up. She got up out of her chair without another word, deposited her dishes in the sink, and walked out of the kitchen. Could have balanced a book on her head as she left, which was the way she said she learned to walk in charm school.

Spooner's mother dropped her face into her hands, and her shoulders shook, and before long she got up too, but went the other way—outside to have a cigarette. The rest of them sat for a while in silence, and finally Calmer got a stick of oleo out of the refrigerator and rubbed it on Spooner's face, and then patted him on the back of the head and began doing the dishes.

"Life goes on," he said, and the next morning the puppy was dead.

The puppy had been gone all night, but in all the things happening, the crying and singeing and the visit from Major Shaker, only Calmer had noticed he hadn't come home. They found him in the ditch at the bottom of the driveway where the wheel of Major Shaker's car had tossed him. Calmer picked Margaret up and held her while she cried.

"We should have been more careful because he was so little and deaf," she said.

"I know," Calmer said. "I shouldn't have let him out by himself until he was older."

Spooner said, "Deaf? It was deaf?"

EIGHTEEN

The baby's name was Darrow, after the lawyer. Calmer could not bring himself to call a child Clarence. From day one, he wanted to be carried upside down and would fuss when he was handled right side up. And would fuss if Calmer went anywhere without him. And so Calmer took him to the bathroom when he shaved, held him when he vacuumed the rug, carried him down to the road when he took out the garbage, and set him upside down in his lap when they went to the A&P.

For all signs, Darrow was born happy. He had a wide, pumpkin-shaped head that bounced and leaked saliva as he went about the world upside down, taking in the sights, and everything he saw seemed to strike him as humorous. He didn't cry much, only if he was hungry or hurt—nowhere near as much, for instance, as Lance Shaker.

Or Spooner's mother. She was crying pretty much every day now. According to Calmer, she was going through a certain sadness that mothers sometimes went through after they had babies. According to Calmer, it would pass, but then he wasn't the first to underestimate Lily Whitlowe.

Spooner didn't understand how having Darrow around could make anybody sad, being the baby was so happy himself, not to mention smart. Those two qualities were plain enough from the day they brought him home. It was there in the way he looked things over. He was barely in the house a month when Spooner caught him staring at him over breakfast one morning from his mother's opened robe—he was nursing and went after those things like the vacuum cleaner, and he had intelligent, clear eyes that got everything the first time around—and the baby not only saw Spooner, he flushed up a certain amount of bluish milk and smiled at him, or tried to, and then went back to nursing. Which to Spooner's mind was pretty advanced for only five weeks old.

Another five weeks found Spooner hanging his own head upside down off the davenport to see if it made him smarter. He had a certain curiosity about how that might feel, to be intelligent, but didn't dwell on it when it didn't come.

———

They took pictures at Christmas, the baby in Margaret's lap. The camera was on a tripod, and Calmer set the timer and hurried to the davenport to pose, sitting between Spooner's mother and Margaret, an arm around each of their shoulders, pulling them in to him until they wrinkled. Spooner was on the far right, sitting straight up. The Christmas tree was to the left, with a silver star Margaret had made at school wired to the top. Grandma was in her house next door, pouting, having said she couldn't be ready on such short notice to come over and be in the family picture, and wasn't really part of the family anyway. She was pretty good at this but not remotely in the class of Spooner's mother.

There was another picture that day, taken with Spooner holding his brother, but his mother was closing her eyes when the flashbulb went off so it wasn't a picture they saved, even though this was perhaps the only picture ever taken of Spooner holding his brother. He was not ordinarily allowed to pick him up. They told him it was because Darrow might twist out of his arms if Spooner weren't holding him the way he liked to be held, which, of course, was upside down. This rule was laid down the day Darrow arrived, and another rule—although no one called it a rule, or even mentioned it out loud—was that Spooner was never left alone with his brother, not for a minute. One of them was always there with them, watching and pretending not to watch.

And it might have been because of that, or it might have been something he heard or misunderstood, but whatever the reason, he began worrying that the baby would die. The worry grew in his imagination and lay there for him every night along the familiar circular route his mind took as he waited in the dark for sleep, and within a few weeks Spooner could reliably be found wide awake at two in the morning, imagining his brother strangled, imagining he was somehow the cause.

The worry came with a certain physical weight, at least at night, and he would feel it pressing onto his chest as soon as he lay still in bed, a feeling that in one way reminded him of being buried in the sand on the beach in Savannah, where the family had gone once on vacation—Margaret and Calmer had buried him, all but his head and toes, and then taken his picture—but in another way was nothing like that at all. It was always there, for one thing, waiting for him whenever he lay down, or sometimes if he was quiet for too long in a chair. He couldn't eat more than a few bites of breakfast and had to be shaken awake several times at Peabody Laboratory, asleep on his desk in the bend of his own arm.

His teacher came to the house one afternoon after school to talk over the problem with Calmer. This was Miss Bell, who was also a looker but no Miss Tuttle. Miss Bell was getting married in June and had invited the whole class to her wedding. They sent Spooner outside to play.

Spooner sat on the steps, pulling ticks the size of lima beans out of the Shakers' coon dog's ears, waiting for Calmer and Miss Bell to finish talking and tell him what they'd decided to tell him, and it was while he sat on the steps waiting that he began to wonder if something was wrong with him that the rest of them all knew about but hadn't said, like the puppy being deaf. Maybe they knew about the weight on his chest; maybe they knew that eventually it was going to press all the air out of his body.

The more Spooner thought about that, the more sense it made, and thinking about it had a certain beneficial effect in that he stopped worrying about his brother strangling at night and worried instead about himself. He was still afraid to go to sleep, and occasionally was so afraid at three or four o'clock in the morning that he whiffed the faint odor of Jaquith's mule splitting open in the burn pit.

A week passed, and then another, and nothing changed or got better, and he could not stop being afraid or thinking of being afraid, which were the same thing, and one day after school, without particularly even realizing what he was doing, Spooner walked out into the treeless empty lot that lay between his grandmother's house and the woods, carrying the pail and shovel he'd gotten when they'd gone to the beach in Savannah, and dug around in an anthill roughly the size of the back porch, stirring the nest into wildness, and then sat down in the middle of it, his arms around his legs, his chin resting on his knees, like some teenager dreaming of her true love.

———

The burning started inside his thigh, where he'd felt them crawling a few seconds earlier, tickling him, and then came rolling in like bad weather. The ants crawled into his underpants and up his back, and between his arms and his chest, and Spooner stayed where he was, lost at the center of a wild, live fire, in a place without order, or patterns, and a little later, he threw back his head and yelled.

———

Calmer had just seated himself in the kitchen to administer a bottle of formula. It was the baby's face that changed first—some shadow of worry passing over it—and then the sound came to Calmer too, faintly, nothing more really than a stir in the still kitchen air, and he looked again at the child, his beautiful, pale-haired son, and understood somehow something had happened.

He handed Darrow to Spooner's mother on the way out the door. Darrow loved to eat and fussed some at being taken away from the table empty. Lily and her mother were sitting in the front room, drinking iced tea—they were friendlier now that they weren't under the same roof—and he heard Lily's mother issue a particular snort that she often issued as he left the house, then heard her say, "He'll spoil that child rotten."

Calmer came down the steps sideways, like a dancer.

Spooner went loose with relief, knowing he was saved, and tried to stand to meet him, but his eyes were swollen nearly shut, and the day went light and dark, and he tipped and fell, landing on his face in the same spot where he had been sitting. His nose hit first and broke like an egg, and he lay stunned while the world passed over him, blistering everything it touched, blood and dirt in his teeth, the ants on his lips, his cheeks, his legs. Inside his ears. He felt them differently now, as something almost liquid, a slow, scalding wash that seemed to raise him up as if he were floating.

And then he was lifted up and was astonished at being airborne, at the feel of cool air moving across his face.

Calmer had him in his arms and against his chest, the way he would carry firewood, and he was running. It was strange to be held like this—it was so long since he had been held—and strange to feel the power loose in Calmer, to think this was what had been inside him all the time. He could feel Calmer's heart pounding, or perhaps hear it, and his fear, and in the next few moments, pounding for home, he knew Calmer as well as he ever would and was as close to him as he would ever be.

He tried to open his eyes, wanting to see Calmer's face, but his vision had been cropped by the swelling down to a narrow line, and someplace outside that line, the whole world was rolling and unattached. He thought of the baby and wondered if this was how Vincent Heights looked upside down. And then Calmer was running up the steps, eleven brick steps, Spooner had counted them a thousand times, and then they were through the door and out of the sun, and the air was cool and familiar.

He heard his mother somewhere in the distance, asking what was wrong, the old edge of tragedy in her voice, and that was familiar too.

Calmer took Spooner straight to the bathroom and holding him in one arm, leaned over to fill the tub. He brushed the ants off Spooner's arms and legs, roughly, as if he were angry, then pulled off Spooner's clothes, shirt and shorts and underpants, uncovering what looked like a whole new nest of them when his underpants came off, running around all over his pecker like it was recess. He felt them in his ears again, and his hair.

He glimpsed Margaret in the bathroom doorway, a hand faintly on Calmer's shoulder as she peeked around him to see what had happened, and as he watched, her face went colorless and slack, as if she'd been slapped and her cheek hadn't had time yet to begin to color. And in her reflection he saw the meaning of what was going on, and this was the thing he'd been afraid of when the weight pressed into him at night.

Calmer picked him up and set him in the bathtub, the spigot still running wide open, and laid him carefully in the cool water. When he looked again, Margaret had begun to cry, and Spooner tried crying too but somehow had forgotten how.

And now his mother was at the doorway behind Margaret, her fingers covering her mouth, and Calmer went over his scalp, scrubbing, and for a little while the air rained ants. He was still out of breath from the run, and knelt on one knee beside the tub, as if he were proposing marriage. He put his hand behind Spooner's head and lowered him farther into the water, and it came up around his face. "Easy does it," he said, "just take it easy."

What that meant, Spooner had no idea. He lifted his head and his ears unclogged and cleared, and he heard his mother. "Calmer?" she said. She was beginning to wheeze, the onset of an attack. He knew that sound like the first verse of "Dixie." She was trying to get closer to the tub, closer to the tragedy, but the bathroom was small, and Margaret wasn't giving up her spot.

"Just a minute," Calmer said without turning around, still catching his breath, almost like he didn't have time for her now. He would make his apologies later, but for now he had his fingers against a spot on Spooner's neck, counting his pulse, watching him breathe. Spooner had never heard him speak to her in that way before, or any of them, really. Calmer always paid attention.

"Should I call the doctor?" she said.

He nodded, still impatient. "Call the doctor," he said.

Spooner lifted his head and looked down toward his feet, and the surface of the water was a blanket of dark bodies, some of them crawling up the sides of the tub. There were also ants on Calmer's shirt and arms, and he noticed them at the same time Spooner did, and swept them off like crumbs, rolling their bodies into so many boogers before they dropped back into the water. He checked Spooner's hair, and then his ears, and then lifted him out of the tub.

Spooner began to slip, and Calmer moved him to the other arm.

From here Spooner caught his reflection in the mirror, his eyelids swollen into the shape of eyeballs themselves, red welts up and down his arms and legs, splayed across his chest and stomach.

Calmer wrapped him in a towel and pulled the plug on the ants.

Spooner was suddenly sweating hot, and just as suddenly shivering with cold. Calmer carried him past Margaret and his mother and laid him in bed, and the sheets were cool and soft. Calmer put a thermometer under his arm and felt again at the place on his neck.

He heard his mother again, the wheezing deep and pronounced.

"Calmer?" she said, but the control she had over him was gone, and he seemed not to have heard her voice.

———

Calmer came in later with some popcorn—white delicacies in a dishpan—and a stack of Spooner's comic books. He showed Spooner the bites on his own arms and neck and said that tomorrow they would look like they gave each other measles. Trying to pretend that by tomorrow it wouldn't matter.

———

Spooner slept.

He woke, and it seemed like a long time had passed, and then he heard Calmer and Margaret in the kitchen and knew it wasn't even her bedtime yet. His mother had gone to bed on Dr. Woods's advice, and Calmer had put Darrow down with a bottle before dark and was doing the dishes, listening as Margaret went over her multiplication tables. Not American numbers, she was practicing them in French. Spooner heard him close the cupboard and sweep the floor, and then he tucked Margaret in and checked on Spooner's mother. He was in there a little while, talking Shakespeare to her—*Wouldst have something to eat, my love?*—and then, much later, when the house was settled and quiet, Spooner's bedroom door cracked open and Calmer came in quietly, not to wake him up, and sat staring at him in the dark.

Calmer stayed a long time, just looking, and then softly sighed. One of his knees cracked as he stood up, or perhaps it was his back. He picked up the popcorn bowl and the pieces that had fallen on the sheets, and went out of the room, and half a lifetime later Spooner could still call up that night exactly. The man sitting in the dark on the chest beside the bed, helpless, and the child lying in the dark beneath him, pretending to sleep, also helpless. Strangely enough, Spooner would remember the scene not from the bed but from Calmer's spot on the chest, and would see himself as Calmer had seen him, through his eyes. A kamikaze aimed right at the middle of everything he had and loved. But more than that, the living evidence of the man who had been here first and who was more precious to Lily than Calmer ever was or ever would be.

———

Spooner was down three days with a fever. He scratched the bites until they bled and then picked at the scabs. The doctor came to the house again, looked him over, and left iodine to put on the sores and cough syrup to quiet the itching. Dr. Woods rarely saw a patient whose condition could not be improved with cough syrup.

Calmer was downhearted all week and barely spoke. On Dr. Woods's suggestion, they were putting mittens on Spooner's hands at night, but Spooner was a born picker and picked at his scabs anyway. He worked the scabs off carefully, taking his time, lifting one side a little and then the other, trying to take each one whole. Afterwards, he put the biggest ones on the windowsill and ate the rest, put the mittens back on and went to sleep. Why Spooner ate some and saved others, he didn't know. If you'd asked him, he could have said only that eating the perfect ones never entered his mind.

By morning, though, the scabs had dried and curled at the edges, and you could hardly tell them from dirt.

Each morning Calmer came into the bedroom before work and inspected Spooner's sores, which were concave to the skin and crusted at the edges—his arms resembled a battlefield—and cleaned out the infected ones with Mercurochrome, which stung less than iodine, and then he checked them again at night, when he oversaw Spooner's bath. Afterwards, he helped Spooner into his pajamas, trying every way he could to keep his mother from seeing the sores. *Warren eating his own flesh?* No, she wouldn't make much of that.

Calmer seemed confused when he first came on newly opened sores, as confused as he was by the idea of sitting down in an anthill in the first place, but kept it to himself. It seemed to Spooner that all that week Calmer kept everything he thought to himself.

On Friday, nine days after the incident, Spooner returned to Peabody School and saw the look on Miss Bell's face, perhaps imagining what this human scab would look like at her wedding.

———

Friday supper: fish sticks, macaroni and cheese, frozen peas. They always had fish sticks on Friday, just like the Catholics. Better safe than sorry. Spooner had gone to sleep on the cool kitchen floor when he got home from school, and in his sleep felt his mother stepping over him half a dozen times, going from the icebox or the sink to the oven. He got up with no feeling at all in one of his arms, and everything else itched.

Calmer got home just before they ate, carrying a brown and black puppy. It was bigger than the Boston terrier and had long hair that stuck straight out as if it had been recently vacuumed. Clumps of it came out at the least tugging. He set the animal carefully into Spooner's arms, and it had only been there a second when it squirmed out, trailing dog hair, and then stepped onto the table and, passing on the fish sticks, went straight for the macaroni and cheese, skidding over the table toward Margaret, and Spooner's mother fell back into her default setting, a spontaneous attack of asthma.

They named the animal Fuzzy, although Spooner wanted to call him Brown Fury, and put him in the tiny utility room with the washing machine. Then they put some of the dog food left over from the Boston terrier into a pie tin and poured milk over it, and Fuzzy/Brown Fury stepped into the middle of it to eat, and when he'd finished and stepped out, the surface behind him was matted thick with his hair.

Spooner's mother disappeared into her bedroom, breathing impaired. Asthma, fish sticks, the puppy, the baby, Spooner—it was all too much. Supper reconvened without her, however, after Calmer had fixed her a plate of food and picked as much of the dog's hair out of it as he could, and Spooner had taken it back to her bedroom, and when he returned to the table Calmer, who had been quiet all week, was suddenly animated again, as if the puppy had cheered him up even if it was strangling Spooner's mother. He leaned in on Margaret and said, "So, my dear, how goeth the struggle?"

"What struggle, my dear?" she said. Everything came to her so easily.

Calmer was holding Darrow with one hand, eating with the other, and now he dropped his eating hand under the table and grabbed her bare foot. "The struggle for civilization, my dear," he said, "for shoes . . ." And like that he was back with them again, back to being Calmer.

———

Weeks passed. "When I was your age," Calmer said one night, talking just above a whisper because it was late, "there was no one to play with, and sometimes after church . . ." He took a moment, as if he wasn't sure if he should go ahead, "after church, I used to sit out in the middle of a field we left fallow that year—*fallow*, that means it's not growing anything on it, giving it a rest—and shoot my gun into the air just to see how close I could come"—Spooner didn't understand at first—"to getting one to fall right back on top of my noggin."

Spooner saw what he was talking about, and the scene opened up for him like the start of a Technicolor movie. "I had my dad's helmet from the war," Calmer was saying, "and I'd shoot up into the air and then put the helmet on and wait to see where it landed. You could see the little puffs of dust."

"Did you?"

Calmer shook his head. "Close a few times, though," he said. He put his hand on Spooner's head and rubbed his hair, setting off a wild itching. It was the first time he'd put his hand on Spooner in a friendly way since he'd sat in the anthill. But then Calmer was never much of a toucher. He stood up to leave, his bedtime too. "Moderation, man," he said—called him *man*—"that's the key. Men of our ilk, we have to practice moderation."

Spooner dropped off to sleep happy and woke up early in the morning thinking of being in a field with a gun and a helmet and a hard wind, and bringing one in right on top of his noggin.

NINETEEN

During the family's last spring in Georgia, Calmer took Spooner for a walk one morning in the woods at the edge of Vincent Heights. They were moving to Illinois at the end of the school year—everybody but Spooner's grandmother, who said she thought she'd just as soon stay there alone in Vincent Heights and die.

Earlier that day, Calmer had tied a chain to the dog's collar, to get him used to his new life in Illinois. The dog had fought the chain until he foamed at the mouth and bled, biting into it.

"It's a brand-new place," Calmer said, meaning Illinois, "a fresh start for everybody." It did not have to be explained to him whose fresh start Calmer was talking about. After quitting cold for a long time, Spooner was back breaking into houses and pissing in shoes, although not with the old enthusiasm. He hadn't been caught yet, or even seen in the vicinity, but he'd heard Kenny Durkin's father talking about him one afternoon to his wife:

"Well, the boy ain't his, so he's afraid to touch him. It's a manner of pussy-whipped."

"Well, I wisht somebody would whip him," she said.

The newspaper was running stories again, "The Fiend of Vincent Heights Returns," and a policeman Spooner had never seen before came to the door one afternoon and talked to Calmer down on the road in front of the house. Still, Calmer had never asked him about it directly, and if he did, Spooner didn't know what he would say. Lying to Calmer was harder for him all the time.

And so—maybe instead of asking him directly—Calmer took him for a walk in the woods and talked about starting fresh and wiping the slate clean, and Spooner, who had not believed before that such a thing was possible, found himself weeping, and bore down on it and promised himself to change then and there, and that same afternoon, unaccountably, Calmer's car rolled down the hill in front of the house.

Spooner and Margaret were outside when it happened; Margaret was playing with the Ennis girls, Spooner in the yard with the dog, peeling scabs off the animal's head from where he'd been kicked two weeks previous by one of the garbagemen riding the back end of the city garbage truck. The dog had the instinct to chase cars—cars, cats, deer, anything that was moving away—which was one of the reasons he had to be chained up when they moved north. That and the Village of Prairie Glen had rules and dog laws.

The old black Ford was perched in its usual spot in front of the house at the top of the hill, and suddenly, slowly, of its own volition, began to roll, and in that same instant the dog was gone, as if something had torn him out of Spooner's arms.

Margaret looked up and saw the car had got loose, and she was off running too, crossing the dirt road going one way while the dog and then Spooner crossed it going the other. They almost touched, Spooner and his sister, and then she was taking the front steps two at a time to report what had happened.

Spooner continued after the runaway car and the runaway dog, down the hill, and then stopped in his tracks when the car veered left off the road and into Mr. Ennis's briar patch. Spooner and Margaret had picked wild plums around the edge of this same patch every summer of their lives. The car tilted up and rolled briefly on two wheels, then fell over and came to rest on its roof and was immediately attacked by the dog, who'd apparently had something like this in mind ever since he'd started chasing automobiles.

Spooner looked back toward the house just as Calmer came out of the front door and stood for a moment with his hands on Margaret's shoulders. Spooner estimated the car was barely visible from there, upside down and a yard deep into Mr. Ennis's briars, the tires still spinning, and he waved to show Calmer where it was. The dog was biting the tailpipe and appeared to have gone crazy with the lust to kill.

Calmer came down the steps calmly and walked to Spooner, who was standing barefoot, on the exact spot where the tire tracks left the road.

Calmer looked him over, and Spooner put his fingers in his mouth. Margaret had come back down out of the house, following Calmer, but he turned to her now and said, "You better go inside and tell your mother everybody's all right."

Calmer walked past Spooner and followed the car tracks through the crushed plum bushes. Spooner hurried to catch up. When he had, Calmer said, "I want us to be sure about this, man to man. Were you playing in the car?"

Spooner shook his head. "No, sir," he said. He did not usually call Calmer *sir*, it sounded to his ear like Lance Shaker talking to his father.

Calmer closed his eyes a moment and seemed to shake beneath the surface, but he held the shaking inside, the same way he had the time he'd smashed his thumb with the hammer fixing the back steps. Spooner remembered now that the thumbnail had split and then turned black the next day and fallen off a week later, in two parts, and he gave them to Spooner. He thought of himself and Calmer together that morning in the woods.

Without another word, Calmer set off through the thorns and briars, Spooner following along, the stickers grabbing at his legs and ankles. Ahead of him, Calmer reached the small clearing the car had made skidding on its roof to a stop. Spooner came beside him, almost reached for his hand.

"Go on. Get out of the way," Calmer said.

Spooner took a step back, and Calmer took a step forward and, without even removing the dog, took the running board in his hands and rocked the car until it tipped, then rolled over onto its side. That was as

far as he could get it, though, and he opened the trunk and pulled out the
three pieces of the jack, then slammed the trunk lid shut.

He put a rotted two-by-four, crawling with pale insect life, between
the jack and the edge of the window, and in this way jacked the Ford two
feet off the ground, enough room to get his back under it, then bent at the
knees and slowly stood up under the weight. His face went red with the
strain, and then dark red, and the car rose steadily, a foot and then another
half, and Calmer's legs, not quite straightened, began to tremble, and then
the car stopped rising. Calmer couldn't move now, either farther under
it for a better angle, or out from under it entirely, and his whole body
began to shudder beneath the weight, not just his legs, and in that moment
Spooner saw Mr. Ennis come out of his house and begin to run, cutting
through the thorns as if they weren't there, shouting *Good Christ*, and when
he got to the car he dropped next to Calmer and got hold in the open
window frame, and his face gradually went red also, but then the car began
to rise again, barely moving at first, then reached a counterpoise, paused,
and then the two men seemed to heave together, and the car fell away from
Calmer and Mr. Ennis, bouncing back onto its tires.

The dog attacked it all over again, and Calmer stumbled and sat on
the ground, his arms bleeding from the thorns and briars, and he sat still
for a moment, spent, his face gone white as the moon.

Mr. Ennis was standing with his hands on his knees, trying to catch
his breath. "That right there," he said, "is the damnedest crazy thing I
ever hope to see an educated man do." He leaned over and threw up, then
took a pack of cigarettes out of his pocket and lit one up, offered another
one to Calmer. "If you'll pardon my saying so."

Calmer waved to show no offense taken, and smiled in a good-natured
way, but he'd been scared. He got back on his feet, his legs still not right
underneath him, never looking once at Spooner, and patted Mr. Ennis on
the back to thank him for his help. And then he got in the car and started
the engine and backed out of the patch of wild plums, leaving Spooner
where he was.

Spooner watched Calmer drive the car back up the hill. It was coated in orange dust, and dirt of the same color was packed into the door handles and wheel wells.

Leaving him behind.

And Spooner knew that something terrible had happened, or nearly happened, not because the Ford had rolled down the hill but because Calmer had gone crazy inside, not knowing what to do about him.

PART THREE

Prairie Glen

TWENTY

The family loaded up at daybreak, Calmer's ancient V-8 Ford shining with dew, some of it pooling on the flat part of the roof where the car had rolled through Mr. Ennis's plum bushes, lending it the old *something not quite right there* look—which was a pronouncement Spooner's mother was apt to make on unfortunates she saw along the road—and headed north to the Village of Prairie Glen. That was the town's official title, the Village of Prairie Glen.

Nine hundred and forty miles, four breakdowns, asthma attacks every two or three hours; six hard days in the saddle.

Vacation rules went into effect for the trip, and Spooner was assigned to the back seat, behind his mother, where Calmer could keep an eye on him in the rearview mirror. He was not allowed to open his window wide enough to hang an arm out or, more to the point, drop anything out of it that could blow out the tires or windshields of the cars coming up behind. He was not allowed in motel rooms by himself, or allowed in restaurants by himself, or to take matches or sugar or toothpicks off the table, even though they were free and obviously there to be taken. He could not touch the telephones in motel rooms, or the room keys, or lock bathroom doors.

Margaret was not subject to any particular rules except as to seating. She had the spot behind the driver and from there rested her cheek against the window, her head bouncing with the movement of the car, as if it was percolating with ideas. The dog lay on the floor between them, and from time to time Margaret would reach down and play with his ears. It was supposed to be Spooner's dog, but like everybody else it preferred Margaret's company and faced in her direction all the way to Illinois.

Darrow, a toddler now, was in front between Calmer and Spooner's mother, fussing not at all, tilting out of the car seat Calmer had designed and built for the trip far enough to see the landscape sideways, more or less, as he was unable to arrange himself to see it upside down.

Some days Spooner's mother drove an hour or two after lunch, shifting too late or too soon and lugging the engine, plugging along twenty miles an hour slower than traffic, muttering under her breath, such as it was, at drivers who pulled out and passed. She called them *darn fools*.

It made Calmer edgy when she drove, and to hide it he would take Darrow into his lap and point out the colors of license plates from different states. The game was too easy though, and pretty soon Calmer was using the plate numbers to teach him poker hands, explaining which ones beat others, and Darrow picked that up as fast as he'd picked up the colors, and then somewhere near the Kentucky state line, Calmer realized that in addition to learning to play poker, Darrow was remembering all the plate numbers that Calmer had pointed out since they left Milledgeville, and could recite them like his ABCs.

The dog, for his part, was depressed and uninterested in life, and threw up what he ate, and seemed somehow to have fathomed what suburbia meant for his kind, and if in fact something like that was on the animal's mind, he was right on the money.

The Village of Prairie Glen was not a prairie, and not a glen, and no place for a dog. Eight years previous, it had been farmland, corn and hogs, but the hog farmers sold out to the developers and the developers hired city planners, and in no time to speak of the hog farms were laid out as a village. The village, in turn, was assembled all at once—houses, apartments, stores, the fire department, city hall, schools, even a historical society, which did not change the fact that the town had no history, except the histories of pigs and pig farmers, and there wasn't a tree anywhere you couldn't take down accidentally with a gas-powered lawn mower. But then there are some things that can be put up overnight, and there are some things that can't.

Thinking this brought Spooner back now and then to his last conversation with Kenny Durkin's father. Mr. Durkin had been fired from the sawmill right before the move and was staging a kind of vigil for the common man all week, out on the porch drinking beer morning to night, one after another, sucking them down to the foam, sitting in his underwear and black work shoes, his feet propped against the railing, looking out at the world like he was seeing it for the first time for the stab-in-the-back place that it was. The belches that rolled out of him echoed to the far ends of Vincent Heights, and sometimes when he pissed he got up and pissed off the porch, into Mrs. Durkin's flower box, and when he pissed he sometimes lifted up his shirt and rubbed his stomach and even by Vincent Heights standards it was pretty uncouth. By now the ladies of the neighborhood avoided looking anywhere in the vicinity of Mr. Durkin's porch, and tried not to listen, and said to each other that it was a pity for Mrs. Durkin and the little boy but it was no wonder that man was fired.

Spooner himself had forgotten Mr. Durkin was on the porch and passed beneath it that last Friday in Georgia and was stopped cold at the sound of pissing behind him, close behind—if he knew anything by sound, it was the sound of urination—and turned and saw the sun sparkling in the colorless arc that at one end was eating a small hole in Mrs. Durkin's bed of petunias. He followed the arc back to its origin, back to Mr. Durkin, who was leaning out over the porch railing, murderous, holding on to his pecker with his fist, like he had his nigger by the neck at last.

"Hey you, Wendell," he said—on those rare occasions Mr. Durkin called him by name, he always called him Wendell—"Kenny repo'ts you-all is gone up north to live in the cold with the coons." He continued to gaze at Spooner and the gaze turned black and then clouded over, as if he were looking at something else. He put away his pecker and went for another beer, and Spooner walked away.

Spooner recalled Mr. Durkin's remark these days, wishing he'd turned out to be right, but there weren't any colored people in Prairie Glen, which was part of the strangeness of the place, and he felt their absence, and the absence of trains coming through, and train tracks, and high-tension wires and pine trees, and the smell of the old men who sat in chairs outside the feed store spitting lines of tobacco between their shoes, and the smell of the sawmill and even the air itself—hot summer air, full of insects, humming with appointments. They didn't have air like that in Prairie Glen.

What they did have were sidewalks and Little League fields. The streets and schools and parks were named for Indian tribes. Dogs and bicycles had to have licenses—you were required to pass a written test and turn it in to the police department, signed by your parent or legal guardian, to prove that you knew the proper hand signals—and the stores were all packed into one place, like a cluster headache, and dogs were not allowed in there, even on leashes, and bicycles had to be dismounted and walked.

According to ordinances posted at every entrance, you could be jailed for littering, a word that Spooner understood only in the context of puppies and kittens.

The houses were all constructed from three basic blueprints and laid next to each other, eight to an acre, with square, flat lawns and ordinances spelling out the covenants and required maintenance of property.

Spooner's grandmother, as promised, stayed back in Milledgeville to die. To live and die in Dixie, just like the song, and carry on the family name in the town where she and the Whitlowes had once been important, intending to battle feral cats to the bitter end and save the native song-birds of Georgia.

Pretty soon, as if she were already dead, she began to fade away from Spooner, she and the house and the pasture, the sawmill—everything faded but the various aromas of the place and a few scenes caught like snapshots in his head: the surface of the bathtub water alive with ants, Jaquith's mule igniting in the burn pit like a piece of the newspaper thrown in the fireplace, Mr. Durkin's shoes side by side in the refrigerator, loaded with piss—these things were cut deeper into the stone and were indelible.

That house that Calmer and Spooner's mother bought was gray shingled and less than a block from the new high school where Calmer oversaw the departments of science and math. The street in front of the house was named Shabbona Drive. Twice a week Spooner delivered the town's morning newspapers, beginning two hours before school and in the winter it was often still dark when he finished. Once in a while a garage door would open as he walked past, and he would stop and watch as the car slowly emerged, the wife behind the wheel usually, still in curlers and a housecoat, her face puffy and creased with sleep, driving the breadwinner off to the train station. Most everybody worked in Chicago, twenty-odd miles to the northeast.

The husbands, from what Spooner saw, were partial to fur hats in the winter and wore parkas over their suits and ties, and galoshes over their shoes; they smoked cigarettes and stared poker-faced out the car windows as their wives backed out of the driveway, expressions deadened into some joyless exhaustion, the same look Spooner saw these days in poor old Fuzz, as if the world had been drained of taste and color and even the notion of escape.

The dog himself was clearly ruined. He'd come a thousand miles on the floor of Calmer's old Ford, lying half over the driveshaft hump, panting the whole way, scolded when he moved because of the hair that came up off him like his aroma and rode the currents into the front seat where Spooner's mother sat, allergic to the entire world but especially to dog hair, fighting for every breath. And the chain. Always attached to his chain, which he still fought and did not understand.

In Prairie Glen, Calmer built the dog a doghouse and the chain was fastened to a stake a few feet from the open doorway, the entire living quarters just outside the kitchen window, where the breeze carried his hair into Spooner's mother's lungs as she cooked or washed the breakfast dishes. And this was where the old boy spent the rest of his life, lying in the backyard all day, lying in the garage all night. Once a day, after school, Spooner took him across Saulk Trail Road to a derelict old Catholic church and cemetery, and allowed him to dig holes in the churchyard and sniff gravestones and urinate on the ones where other dogs had urinated, names cut into granite a hundred years earlier and already half erased by time and weather. And dog piss, of course.

A fat man and a bulldog came into the cemetery once, the man dropping the leash once they had crossed Saulk Trail, and then he watched as the dog raced across the field for them, the leash bouncing behind him, and Spooner saw the animal's intentions and then saw the look in his own dog's eyes and took the chain off Fuzz's collar too and let them fight, and by the time the fat man arrived, old Fuzz was crazy with lust, punctured and bleeding a dozen places and missing half an ear—just having a wonderful time of it—and the bulldog, who was bred for this, had also lost an ear and was bleeding at the throat and a back leg and there was a long, wide gash in the folds of flesh below his neck, and the fat man began to yell at Spooner as he arrived—or maybe at old Fuzz, it was hard to say because he was out of breath—and then kicked at Fuzz as he continued to maul the bulldog, not that Fuzz minded being kicked at such times, or even noticed, and continued on until the bulldog had lost another ear, and the fat man was screaming as he kicked, screaming at the dog that he intended to sue him, and at that point Spooner lifted old Fuzz off the bulldog—both animals coming a foot or two off the ground before Fuzzy let go of the bulldog's throat and dropped him on the ground— and left, putting the dog back on his chain and jogging away, ignoring the fat man who was now demanding to speak to Spooner's parents.

As far as recreation went, that was about it for old Fuzz. One attempted murder. Maybe twice a year the animal slipped his collar or uprooted the chain and chased cars or a bicycle up Shabbona Drive, or snapped teeth through a chain-link fence with a German shepherd who lived on Marquette Place, or dry-humped some child's leg, but in the end the old dog was not a suburban sort of dog and would have been just as happy back in Georgia with Spooner's grandmother, licking stamps. Spooner fed him at bedtime, a can of Rival dog food that slid out whole on its own grease and was eaten whole the second it landed, maybe without changing shape.

That was pretty much it for the dog and Prairie Glen, and pretty much it for Spooner. Watching the animal eat, Spooner would sometimes think of the way he'd fought when Calmer first put him on the chain, and wonder if he'd somehow known what was coming.

It was dark outside, a Wednesday night during that first winter in Prairie Glen. Supper was over, the dishes washed and dried and put away, and Calmer was smoking a cigarette, looking over the *Sun-Times*. They took the *Sun-Times* even though Calmer preferred the *Tribune*, which was the better paper, but the *Tribune* was owned and run by Republicans, and Lily would not put a cent of honest money into a Republican's pocket. Darrow was next to Calmer at the kitchen table, having milk and crackers before bed, staring at the back of the paper as Calmer read the front. It was the first breather Calmer had had all day.

"Cubs drop two more to Pirates," said Darrow.

Calmer lowered the paper and looked at his son, unsure what he'd said. Then, still watching him, he turned the paper around and stared at the headline across the top of the sports section. And while he was staring at that, Darrow said, "Cops nab rape suspect in Calumet City."

So, just like that. First poker, now reading. And not only a word here and there, like Spooner, but whole sentences. How long he'd been able to read or how he'd learned, nobody knew. Spooner for once was not suspected of involvement.

Later that month, early on a Saturday morning, Calmer took Darrow via commuter train to the University of Chicago's Department of Child Development for testing. One test and then another and another, the scientists giving each other certain rolling-eyed looks at first, as if this were a trick they had seen before, and then as morning changed to afternoon, the expressions gradually changed too, and they realized they hadn't seen this before after all. In the end they kept him all day—nine until six-thirty at night—and one of them, a young white-haired man with a foreign accent, asked Calmer if he might bring the little fellow back the following Saturday for more tests and perhaps also to discuss designing a program of study for him there at the school.

Calmer said he would think it over—the tests—but was not sending his three-year-old son off to the University of Chicago.

Still, it was a festive mood at 308 Shabbona that night when Calmer and Darrow got home from the university, especially for Spooner, who loved celebrations, although not being much of a test taker himself didn't quite get the nuts and bolts of what this one was about. For Spooner, it was like being in the audience after Uncle Arthur had polished off Tchaikovsky and everyone around him stood up and applauded and yelled *Bravo!* and Spooner would stand with everyone else and clap like a wild man and yell *Bravo!* until the other people in the crowd began to look at him like he'd robbed the collection plate. He enjoyed his uncle's concerts, except for the music, and wondered sometimes what the tunes would have sounded like in English.

Tonight they all sat at the kitchen table until midnight, Calmer looking as optimistic as Spooner ever saw him, drinking Scotch, smiling in a contented, satisfied way that infected the whole house, and bedtimes were forgotten and ice cream came out of the freezer, but then about twelve-thirty something about all the happiness got on Spooner's mother's nerves—most likely just the look on Calmer's face; he'd been sitting there for hours by now, smiling like he had all the luck in the world—and she turned cross and likely wanted to slap him across the head with the *Sun-Times* to bring him back to his senses.

Yet even as Calmer bathed in contentment at the kitchen table, three blocks from the table, his friend Metcalf, his first friend in Prairie Glen and his truest friend, was up late too, sitting with his wife at their kitchen table, drawing outlines on table napkins, little square pictures that for Calmer might as well have been mushroom clouds.

Metcalf was assistant principal of the high school, five years younger than Calmer, energetic, bursting with decency and honesty and compassion, yet all in some strange combination that did not make you hate his guts. He made eleven hundred dollars a year more than Calmer made, and drove a two-year-old Ford instead of a twelve-year-old Ford, but in spite of all that, even Spooner's mother did not pine for his destruction. The reason for this was as simple as niceness itself. You peeled back layer after layer, and Metcalf was nice all the way through. His clothes were nice, his voice was nice; he probably had a nice pancreas. And his wife was nice, and they lived in a single-story, pigeon-gray shingled house with bad plumbing that wasn't big enough for the family, a carbon copy of the house on Shabbona Drive right down to the floor plan, and the Metcalfs also had three children and a dog—a pure-bred beagle that didn't shed—and the children were all clean and polite and together did not get into as much trouble in a year as Spooner could on a weekend, but on the other hand, none of them was as smart or pretty as Margaret, and none of them was busting up high school IQ tests when they were three years old. And if Metcalf exuded an unmistakable aroma of success, he showed deference to Calmer, and to Lily, even if he was technically Calmer's boss. All to say, again, Metcalf was nice. Enthusiasm unbounded and good intentions, a man who read the books Calmer recommended and believed in the Democratic Party and in education, and laughed easily and knew the principal—a gray-toothed politico named Baber—for what he was, and knew the board of education for what it was too. Somehow all these things together evened out in Lily's books; in her book she and Mrs. Metcalf were even-steven.

And then, out of the blue, this likable Metcalf with his easy smile and good intentions lobbed a grenade right into Calmer's lap. This nice, decent, fucking Metcalf with his three polite children and his beagle decided to build his wife an addition to the house.

The Metcalfs were going to have a den.

———

The news hit without warning, and for weeks the occupants of Spooner's home treaded lightly indeed around his mother, while three blocks away at the Metcalfs' birds chirped and flowers bloomed and optimism was in the air. Plans were drawn and bids offered and accepted, and permits were issued, and construction itself was begun. All in six weeks. And while it was generally accepted in the Village of Prairie Glen that such a project would take six months to get under way, no one was much surprised at how quickly Metcalf had gotten his paperwork done. He was the sort of person you just wanted to help.

On the day construction began, Lily woke to the distant sounds of heavy machinery, something vaguely poisonous in the air, like mildew or cat dander or ragweed, sounds so faint that no one else in the house could hear. Calmer was in the kitchen eating breakfast with Darrow; Margaret was showering.

Spooner was dressed for school but back in bed, in his shoes, whacking off as he thought of Mrs. Metcalf, who struck him as something of a looker. Thinking of her lipstick.

Spooner's mother walked into the kitchen in her robe, her hand cupped over her mouth because she hadn't brushed her teeth.

"That noise is driving me crazy," she told Calmer.

Which was a perfect example, if anyone needed one, of putting the horse before the cart, but was also in its way true. On the other hand, the sounds of construction drew her, and for that month and then the next, every morning—rain or shine, asthma or clear pipes—she walked the three short blocks to Mohawk Street to check on the progress of the addition, and often ended up sitting in Mrs. Metcalf's kitchen over a cup of coffee, watching the construction workers through the window over the sink. In this way Lily became familiar with the job, with the problems that always came up when you were building an addition, unexpected delays, cost overruns, sloppy workmanship. There were four workers on the job, five if you counted the boss, but the boss was overseeing two other job sites and the workers took breaks every hour when he was away, standing together smoking cigarettes and drinking coffee, shooting the breeze, and took their sweet time getting back at it, nobody moving until the last cigarette had been finished, the last lid screwed back on the last thermos. These workers were what was called semi-skilled labor and made six dollars an hour—more than a starting schoolteacher—and Lily watched the four men sitting together smoking, and thought, *twenty-four dollars an hour.* More than four starting schoolteachers.

She reported on the addition's progress nightly over supper. It would drive you crazy, she said, trying to keep track of four of them at once, making sure they were all working.

Strangely enough, Mrs. Metcalf was not bothered by the slacking or the cost. As impossible as it was to Spooner's mother, Mrs. Metcalf apparently had decided to whistle her way through life and ignore the hosing she was taking along the way. And as Lily made her evening reports, it began to sound almost as if she were glad not to be getting an addition herself, glad for once not to be the one getting hosed.

Still, before she'd finished, she would gaze wistfully out the window over the kitchen sink and say, "It must be nice."

———

Calmer did what he could to divert her attention. He bought the family a television set and got her pregnant again. Even so, she continued to follow the construction like it was the pennant race, up there every day even though it was November now and getting cold, and the cold air set off her asthma attacks. On days she was too sick to get out of bed, Mrs. Metcalf came over in the afternoon, after she'd finished her own work, to see if there was something she could do to help. Sometimes she brought dinner. Spooner could walk in the door and tell from the aroma if Mrs. Metcalf had been in the house. As a rule Mrs. Metcalf herself smelled good enough to eat, although the food she brought over, as a rule, didn't.

––––––––––––

The new baby was called Phillip Whitlowe, after Spooner's mother's father, and was born without any ordeal to speak of, leaving Spooner the undisputed champion of nearly killing his mother in childbirth. In a family of exceptional children, Spooner had that to hold on to, and his throwing arm.

The same year Phillip was born, the sixth-grade guidance counselor at Mohawk Elementary counseled Spooner to begin thinking about trade school. Refrigeration and plumbing in particular paid well. The counselor made this suggestion sounding not a little bitter and in fact spent the rest of Spooner's hour—each student was required to go through an hour of counseling before starting junior high school, so he would know what to do with his life—listing many different kinds of manual labor that paid better than teaching.

"A *garbage man* makes more than a starting teacher," he said at the end. They always closed the show with that one, the garbage man being the final word in any discussion of the comparative esteem that society held for its educators.

The counselor was apparently unaware that Spooner himself came from a teacher's family and had heard all this before, mostly from his mother, and knew it by heart. "No, sir," the counselor said, and leaned across his desk to feel Spooner's bicep, "there's nothing wrong with making a living with your hands." Somehow by now the counselor had gotten the idea that Spooner's dad was in the building trades, possibly a plumber.

And in fact the house, like all the houses in Prairie Glen, was cheaply built, and something was always up with the pipes. Calmer would spend one weekend replacing faucets, the next underneath the sink, the next caulking around the bathtub. On weekends when nothing was wrong with the plumbing, he undertook *projects*—built bookshelves or a kitchen cabinet, or rewired the bathroom, or repainted it and the kitchen to cover water marks.

He was tired at times but never complained of having too much work—it seemed to relax him, fixing things that had broken or worn out.

Whatever the project, it was stop-and-go—diapers to change, lunches to fix, Margaret's piano lessons, Darrow's piano lessons, checking in on Lily every thirty minutes when she was in bed with asthma—and then back to wiring the kitchen.

Then the workweek itself would begin, and he went to work, and at night he checked homework, and changed diapers, and made dinner if Lily was feeling punk. He changed tubes in the television set; he powdered the baby's rash. But where Darrow was the spitting image, the baby resembled the Whitlowe side of the family, and did not like to be held upside down and in other ways was not such a happy little crapper as had been Darrow.

And while Calmer worked—what he sometimes called making a *joyful noise unto the Lord* (Spooner never knew or asked exactly where Calmer stood on the matter of religion)—Spooner's mother lay in bed with her atomizer, pining for a den like the Metcalfs'.

In that entire first year in Prairie Glen, Spooner never saw Calmer sit down with a drink or a smoke before eight o'clock at night. The second year, one afternoon in April, Calmer built an awning over the doghouse door, to provide old Fuzz some shade for the summer ahead, and at dinner asked if anyone had noticed the new addition, and for a little while the table went quiet as Stonehenge and Spooner sat speculating that Calmer had gone nuts, or that it was a dare, something he'd dared himself to do. And he wondered if he and Calmer were secretly connected after all.

———

Phillip Whitlowe turned a year old and was obviously going to be ahead of his age group all his life. From all the early signs, he was as smart as Margaret and Darrow. He was a touchy child, though, given to tantrums, and not much interested in Spooner. You could say that from the very first he preferred being with his own kind.

TWENTY-ONE

The grass grew, Spooner mowed it. Every Saturday, year after year. In winter, he shoveled the snow. On days he forgot, he would come home and find Calmer doing the job.

TWENTY-TWO

It was summer and Margaret was headed off to Harvard
in the fall. She'd been the homecoming queen in high school, a cheer-
leader, perfect grades, on and on—if they'd stayed in Georgia somebody
would have built her a statue.

This particular morning, as they crossed the state line into Iowa, she'd
turned to Spooner and said, "If I wanted to, I could just open the door
and jump out of the car." Spooner didn't make much of that—the family
was on vacation, and who hadn't thought of jumping out of the car?—but
then a few hours later, as if continuing the same sentence, she dropped
this in his lap too: "And then I'd be dead and rotting too."

It was two-thirty in the afternoon, and those were the first words she'd
spoken to him since the remark about exiting the vehicle. The family, as
mentioned, was on vacation, a merciless trip they took every August from
Prairie Glen to Conde, South Dakota, to visit Cousin Arlo and the rest of
Calmer's more or less living relatives. The old Ford had progressed to the
city limits of Boone, Iowa, and was sitting at the pump in a Sinclair gas
station, the regularly scheduled two-thirty break. Spooner had returned
from the men's room, where Calmer had walked in five seconds too late to
catch him pissing in the sink, and was alone with Margaret in the backseat. She hadn't gone to the bathroom since they hit the state line, or eaten
anything for breakfast.

Spooner for once did not have to ask what she was talking about,
which was their dead father. Spooner had imagined until now that she
pictured him in heaven. Regarding that matter, Spooner had told enough

lies of his own to recognize one when he heard it (and likewise had begun to recognize a certain accidental quality in things that were true), and this particular story—robes and sandals and angels and harps—was so obviously a string of lies, one after another, each one made up to cover the last one, that it would have embarrassed him to tell it. He wondered now why he'd assumed all this time that Margaret couldn't see that for herself.

She turned away and stared at a silo standing in the farm yard across the highway. "He's rotting," she said slowly, as if she could see it happening, as if the silo were his headstone. "They just bury you, and you rot."

There is something in sports called refusing the gate; the horse comes to the fence and slams on the brakes and the man in the lawn-jockey outfit floats on over by himself. Spooner sat in the backseat with Margaret, refusing the gate, unable to engage the idea that roaming around inside his sister's brain were thoughts of rotting in the grave. It had been his understanding from the beginning that he was the one who would think about rotting, etc., leaving Margaret and his brothers free to cogitate on Voltaire and Tchaikovsky and Calculus, and people of that general ilk.

Calmer came back to the car then with Darrow in one hand—Darrow was getting too heavy for this but still liked being toted upside down, Calmer holding him by a foot, the way you carry a chicken—and two small bottles of Coke in the other, which he had by the necks, and handed them through the open window. Spooner took them awkwardly—he had sore fingers—and gave one to his sister.

Calmer placed Darrow in the front seat and then got in behind the wheel and turned to look at them. "Why so quiet?" he said.

There was no answer, and presently, Calmer laid one of his thick forearms across the seat back and turned to them further, smiling, vaguely worried, sweat in his hairline. "Make a joyful noise unto the Lord . . ."

Spooner sat still, holding his Coke bottle in the palm of his hand to protect the tips of his fingers. Normally, he would have come up with something to say to hide what they'd been talking about, but the revelation of what was going on with Margaret was skipping through him like a current—a sensation he'd been introduced to only the evening before when he'd tried to blow the fuses at the Dude Ranch Motel in Davenport by sticking a paper clip into the wall socket. The tips of his fingers had blistered and hurt now when he even brushed them against his shorts.

"We were talking about dying," Margaret said.

Just like that.

Calmer nodded, still smiling, no idea what to say. A minute or two later Spooner's mother emerged from the ladies' room with Phillip. He was a strange, lonely sort of kid, Phillip, as precocious in his way as Margaret or Darrow had been but more aware of the spotlight, a three-year-old who preferred the company of adults to other children, wanting to show off his brain where it would be appreciated. And you had to admit it was some brain. Privately, Spooner worried he was using it too much, putting all his eggs in one basket.

Calmer saw them coming and turned back to Spooner and Margaret, still smiling, but close to desperate. "Let's not mention this to your mother," he said. "It's her vacation."

TWENTY-THREE

And time went by; the grass grew and Spooner mowed it.

Old Fuzz turned gray in the muzzle but even in old age still got loose every few months, and Prairie Glen being the sort of place it was, there were always calls to the police department reporting him for chasing cars. Once a policeman came to the door and issued Spooner's mother a five-dollar ticket for not keeping a domesticated animal under control.

This constituted a very bad afternoon for the policeman, who came away from 308 Shabbona Drive with a new understanding of how hard it was raising a family on the little money that teachers in the public schools make.

Spooner played football three of his four years in high school. He had no talent for the game except a certain craving for collisions, which the coach, a tree stump of a human being named Evelyn Tinker, took for a sign of good character. Always on the outlook for character was Coach Tinker, and on those occasions when he remembered who Spooner was, he was not reluctant to predict that the boy would go a long way in life. Tinker wore football pants all year long and was never seen without his whistle, which he was inclined to blow indoors, the smaller the room, the better.

Tinker's salary had been published in the *Prairie Glen Mercury-News* that spring, three hundred a year less than Metcalf's, eight hundred more than Calmer's, which was also published, and seeing these figures side by side in the newspaper was an outrage and an embarrassment that

Spooner's mother would not forgive. Not the newspaper, not Tinker, not Calmer.

Coach Tinker was a lover of noise and also a man consumed with numbers, hell-bent to translate all human experience into percentages, and each long, hot meeting of the two-a-day August practices was called together first by the sound of his whistle, which he would blow as hard as a whistle can be blown and still whistle, and then with a short discussion of the day's mathematics. Tinker and his assistants would wait while the players assembled around them—"take a knee, gentlemen, take a knee"—and then, slowly, one by one, he would inspect them for signs of character.

"What am I willing to give?" he would say, and you could almost picture him at the pulpit over at Faith United Protestant Church, beginning a sermon. "It's hotter than heck, and I'm tired, can I get by with ninety percent? It isn't a game, it's only practice." About here Spooner would find himself nodding along, as these were probably the most reasonable and intelligent words Tinker would speak all year, but no, it was a trick question, and a moment later the coach, finding Spooner or someone else in the crowd nodding along, was red-faced and screaming.

"No, goddamn it! No! What I demand from every individual is one hundred percent, every minute you're out here. That and hit the books. I want you guys going home and hitting the books."

Some years before Tinker had lost the most vicious player he'd ever coached to bad grades—a kid named Gerald Tonkoo who was from some island out in the middle of the Pacific Ocean where all they had for a language was vowels, and who moved to America and failed English, music appreciation, and shop class all the same semester—and thereafter the coach took a personal interest in his players' academic progress, sometimes, if the player was important enough, even visiting a teacher to explain how a passing grade could be the difference in the young man's life. Tinker did not enjoy these visits into the regions of the school where no one else wore whistles, and he often came away with the uncomfortable feeling that he'd been laughed at, and he never ended football practice without reminding his players to hit the books when they got home. It was still August, and nobody had found the right moment yet to tell him that school hadn't started.

By the time school had started, Tinker was asking for 110 percent, and two weeks after that it was 120. Injuries were not allowed at practice, nor drinking water—not a coddler, Evelyn Tinker. There was also a rule against the removal of helmets. The helmets had a swampy smell, and the rubber padding was always slick with sweat and grime, and Spooner expected that if his head was ever stuck in a pussy, it would feel something like a football helmet in August.

Currently the most vicious player on Tinker's squad was a kid named Russell Hodge, a three-sport hero who once had kept his helmet on all practice even though a yellow jacket crawled into the ear hole and eventually stung him deaf in one ear. Tinker submitted an essay on the incident to the editorial page of the *Prairie Glen Mercury-News*, ending with this prediction: *Russell Hodge is a individual who will go a lot further in life with one ear than most of his generation will with the traditional number of two!*

When the time comes, he wrote, *Hodge will be ready!!! He will know what it is like to give and take no quarters from the enemy!!!*

The coach wrote the way he spoke, a machine gun of exclamation points, a lover of noise. The louder a thing was, the more important. In Spooner's experience, Tinker lowered his voice only to pray before football games and once in a while to comment on the half-dozen geezers who assembled every day on a mound at the far side of the practice field and chewed on weeds and smoked cigarettes while they watched practice. For reasons that were never clear to Spooner, Tinker did not like the spectators, although he was unfailingly polite to their faces. "When the time comes," he would say, his hushed voice scraping like a tailpipe across the garage floor, "you won't have to sit out here and watch high school football practice, because you'll know you gave it a hundred and twenty percent when you had the chance."

As if an adult human being ought to be ashamed of having nothing better to do with a weekday afternoon than watch high school football practice. As if nobody had told Tinker yet what he did for a living.

TWENTY-FOUR

There was in every sport Spooner ever played, on every team he ever joined, an outcast. Some kid who had been plucked from the safety of home and homeroom and tossed, often at the insistence of his own father, out into the world. Unprotected. Often this kid was the fattest, dopiest kid in school, someone who had been *it* every day of his life on the playgrounds, shunned or insulted one day, beaten up the next, and was now introduced to the rest of his life, which was more of the same except better organized, with the degree of abuse he suffered depending mostly on the mercies of the adults in charge.

In the case of the 1973 Golden Streaks football squad, the adult in charge was the coach, Evelyn Tinker, and the outcast was a short, fat kid named Francis Lemonkatz, who had body hair, front and back, like some hibernating animal, and legs so short as to remind you of such an animal coached up onto his hind limbs to walk.

Tinker had ignored young Lemonkatz in the beginning, assuming he would quit along with the rest of the momma's boys and softies who came out every year thinking football would be fun, and who didn't usually last even to the end of the first morning of the two-a-day August practices.

Lemonkatz, however, did not quit. He had not come out thinking football would be fun, but instead was one of those kids you run into now and then who seem to have been born without a sense of what fun was, or what it was for, who arrived at puberty already resigned to the world as a trap, as miserable one place as another. And in this posture of resignation Lemonkatz came gradually into Tinker's world, something fat out on the edges, a whining, slovenly presence at the periphery of team meetings, hiding among the practice dummies at practice, a kid unable to do a single push-up or sit-up, or even hold on to the chinning bar long enough to try a chin-up, who cheated on all his calisthenics, jumping jacks to six-count burpies, was dead last in wind sprints and shied from physical contact.

And would not quit.

Tinker, who valued practice time like a conjugal visit, was not inclined to waste it on rehabilitating the likes of Francis Lemonkatz, or even getting his name right—always called him Lemonstick—and instead went about finding him a use. Once, for instance, at the end of an afternoon's practice, Tinker called the team together—"take a knee, gentlemen, take a knee"—and then called Lemonkatz up to the front. He held him by the arm with one hand, pointing at him with the other. There was a long silence, and then Coach Tinker yelled, "IS THIS HOW YOU WANT TO END UP?"

The response was an explosion, *"No, sir!"* the collective voice deeper than any single voice in the bunch. And unmistakably one of those voices was Lemonkatz's.

For his part, Spooner was unmoved by threats of ending up like Lemonkatz. He didn't think far enough ahead to worry about how he would end up, for one thing, and for another thing had his own Lemonkatz problem to worry about, the more and more frequent occasions when he found himself centered in the boy's piteous, needy gaze, which was no different for Spooner than eating a ham sandwich in front of old Fuzz. Or in front of Lemonkatz, for that matter. And as the weeks went on and Lemonkatz suffered more and more piteously at the hands of his teammates and Coach Tinker, Spooner was more and more often drawn into these awful glimpses of Lemonkatz's situation. It didn't only happen at football practice; it was just as likely in English class or Spanish, or in the hallways between classes, or in locker rooms or buses, or sitting on the bench during games. Spooner would come back after a kickoff—he did not get to play much but was on the kickoff teams due to his willingness to throw his head in front of things moving in the other direction—and sometimes, if he'd gotten his head into things just right, the world would seem slightly unfamiliar for a while afterwards, and by the time he got back to the present, his eyes, without Spooner's even knowing it had happened, would be settled on Lemonkatz, who was always there waiting for him, silently begging him for something, and what that was, Spooner could not even guess.

Lemonkatz's hair oozed oil and was infested with dandruff the size of cereal flakes. He had been shaving since sixth grade and since that time had been coming to school reeking of aftershave but something else too, like he was carrying cheese in his pocket. He never showered in the locker room shower, but would stand naked in a corner instead, away from the water, covering his genitalia with his hands and hiding as well as he could in the noise and steam until a whistle blew and it was time to dress for class.

Worse than matters of personal hygiene though was the distinctive nasal puling that came out of Lemonkatz whenever his class was assigned to write an essay or read a chapter of a book, or even when Señor Rosenstein addressed the Spanish class in Spanish. Spooner suspected the noise was involuntary, as it occurred in spite of the fact that Lemonkatz had never done a homework assignment in his life. It takes one to know one, as they say.

But then the puling wasn't the worst of it either. The worst of it was that Spooner understood the puling, understood the feeling of knowing that every time things changed, everything got worse. And understood that the sound coming out of Lemonkatz was the sound of being torn, a kid afraid to let go of what he had, no matter how awful it was, and at the same time afraid of being left behind.

He also puled during football practice, issuing that familiar, unmanly sound sometimes even at the announcement of plays in the huddle. Why some plays and not others? Who could say? Every play was the same for Lemonkatz—the ball would be snapped, the lineman across the line would run over him on his way to the ball carrier. Sometimes a linebacker would come in behind the lineman and also run over Lemonkatz. Sometimes a linebacker and then a safety. Lemonkatz would lie still, waiting for it to stop, resembling some dead pigeon out along U.S. 30, feathers ruffling in the wind as the traffic blew past.

Spooner had heard that Lemonkatz's father had been a football player back in college, but you could never tell about those things, if the fathers were really what they said they had been. Spooner had also heard that he taped his son's ankles and fed him T-bone steaks for breakfast on game days—this in spite of the fact that Lemonkatz would never in his football career play a single down in a game against another team—a regular reminder of the disappointment Lemonkatz was to them both.

———————

Then came an afternoon about halfway through October when Tinker gathered his players at the beginning of practice and announced that he intended to make Lemonkatz into a football player. The reason for the announcement was anybody's guess. Possibly Lemonkatz's father had called him, asking him to make his boy a man—Spooner had heard of things like that, throwing the child into the river to teach him to swim—or maybe it had nothing to do with Lemonkatz; maybe Mrs. Tinker hadn't been giving Coach 100 percent on the home front. Whatever the cause, something had changed, and as always for Lemonkatz, the change was not good.

Fifteen minutes after the announcement was made, Tinker caught Lemonkatz cheating on his six-count burpies and sent him twice around the goalposts carrying a tackling dummy, then brought him up from the back of the line six times in a row to face Russell Hodge in agility drills.

Russell Hodge was an invulnerable, unapproachable knot of muscle and hostility—invulnerable from the left, at least; you could sneak up on him from the right where the yellow jacket had stung him deaf—a consensus all-conference linebacker for three straight years, second-team All-State in his junior year. Or had been until the afternoon he tossed Miss Degruso the music teacher into an open locker and slammed the door shut on her fingers and knee. Miss Degruso suffered two broken metacarpals and a cracked femur in the attack, and Russell was suspended not only from school but, several days later, in spite of Tinker's calling in favors from his friends on the school board, from the football team. Miss Degruso was a tiny thing—had fit nearly entirely into the locker—and until this incident, had been quite a cellist.

Tinker called a special meeting of the squad to break the news. There had been only one other special meeting that year, when a kid named Neal Meredith was killed crossing the train tracks on his way home. Tinker said now what he'd said then, that *setback* was only another word for *opportunity*.

In spite of that speech, the Golden Streaks lost 33–20 in a game that was not as close as the score. Leaving Coach Tinker 8-1 for the second year in a row, so close and yet so far, and nothing for comfort but the bitter satisfaction that Miss Degruso's string quartet had canceled its annual Thanksgiving recital because her left leg couldn't comfortably accommodate her instrument. *Comfortably*, he loved that. In the end, you always found out who wanted it bad enough and who didn't.

The struggle to change Lemonkatz continued through the long last month of the season. Week after week, Tinker screamed and blew his whistle, and week after week Lemonkatz dropped the dummies when he held them in blocking practice or turned away from other linemen in the agility drills, sometimes even covering his head. He feigned new injuries and once was discovered lying among the blocking dummies—it was uncanny how a human of his amplitude could disappear into a horizon of smaller objects—eating a whole box of Baby Ruth candy bars that he'd smuggled into practice under his jersey.

Tinker grabbed him from behind and dragged him back to practice, candy bars falling out here and there like pieces of Lemonkatz himself. Later half a dozen of his teammates tied him to the bicycle rack, and the following day they threw him into the bleak, icy waters of the school lagoon, where he clutched his heart and screamed that he couldn't swim. And through all this, he cowered and puled and sometimes cried, but he would not be moved from the place he occupied in his life and had decided was his.

At every practice a time would come when Tinker seemed to remember that day with the candy bars and stopped whatever he was doing, the afternoon suddenly quiet, and called for Lemonkatz, and eventually that singular, awful, puling noise would be heard in the silence and Lemonkatz would appear from his hiding place behind the rest of the players and get into his lineman's stance, his behind too high in the air, the hip pads coming out of his pants and all his weight on the back of his feet—almost like a circus act, that moment Spooner could never stand to watch before the elephant or the bear was forced up onto its hind legs—and wait in that posture for the whistle that would signal Russell Hodge or Ken Jonny or one of the others that it was all right to maim him. It was like a reward to be given Lemonkatz in this way, and depending on Tinker's mood it could go on for ten straight minutes, sometimes five turns for two or three different players in a row.

Afterwards, when it was over for the day, Lemonkatz would collect himself slowly, limping or holding his stomach or his wrist or his groin, and go back to his spot at the end of the line.

The day came, inevitably, when Lemonkatz would not get up. When he lay in the dirt and wouldn't move, even with Tinker kneeling next to him, blowing his whistle into Lemonkatz's earhole and screaming that he wasn't giving even 10 percent.

Tinker assumed—the truth was, everybody assumed—that Lemonkatz was pretending again that he was hurt, and Tinker threw down his clipboard and picked him up as if he weighed no more than the uniform itself, just lifted him up off the ground and set him on his feet and began to scream in his bleeding-voice-box voice that if Lemonkatz didn't fire up now, he would be lying in the dirt for the rest of his life. At least that was what he seemed to be saying. The words were unintelligible, lost in the spit and noise Tinker made getting them out, a noise, it seemed to Spooner, that might have been around back when language was first invented, when all of us had pelts like Lemonkatz's and our most artistic ancestors first felt the urge to articulate their cravings to eat or murder or fuck something squirmy, and it all came out of Tinker at once, in one long, horrible howl.

Even under this remarkable assault, Lemonkatz remained Lemonkatz. He dropped back onto the ground as soon as Tinker let go of him, nursing his leg. Tinker picked him up again and head-butted him—this while Lemonkatz was still inside his helmet—opening a gash on Tinker's forehead so wide that it seemed to have lips.

The blood blossomed up and then ran like a leak in the bathroom pipes over Tinker's face and shirt, and when he blew his whistle again little bits of blood-covered spit came out of the top and blew into Lemonkatz's face too. And he screamed, "Run it off, Lemonstick! Run it off," and then he turned Lemonkatz around and punted him, lifting him slightly off the ground. Lemonkatz started for the far goalpost, limping badly, weeping. It took the rest of the afternoon for him to finish four laps, which was the standard distance for running it off.

Tinker's blood dripped steadily off his head as Lemonkatz did his laps, and various members of the team were inspired by this bloodletting into murderous acts of their own, which set off murderous acts of retaliation, and by the time practice ended, half a dozen players required stitches and fingers were bitten and broken and there was hardly an unbloodied face on the team and Tinker was joyous with the afternoon's work and with life itself, and jogged in happily with his players, not noticing that Lemonkatz had stayed behind, collapsed beside a blocking dummy. And was still out there five hours later, ten o'clock at night, weeping, when his mother and father found him and took him to the hospital in Chicago Heights.

Russell Hodge, it developed, had broken Lemonkatz's femur,

coincidentally in the same spot he had broken Miss Degruso's, four inches above the knee. Lawsuits were filed, legal depositions taken, state-mandated student-injury reports filled out. Tinker himself filled out one of these reports, taking full responsibility for what had happened, although noting in the *additional comments* section that in fairness to all concerned, Lemonstick had NOT specifically notified anyone that his leg was broken.

In football you have injuries, he wrote, *and if anyone was to blame, it was the inventors of the Game of Football and those like myself, committed in the effort of molding today's youth!*

The team went 8–I, again, and as an addendum to his financial settlement with the school district, Lemonkatz was given a varsity letter and allowed to ride on the team bus to the last two away games. He sat alone, still the outcast, and still there.

A month later the school board issued its findings in the matter, mildly remanding Coach Tinker for leaving Lemonkatz among the blocking dummies but also noting that due to the darkness of the hour, it was an understandable error to have made.

Spooner's mother read the school board's findings in the paper and swooned at the injustice.

But not only that.

That same week—the week after the season ended—the Lions Club threw a standing-room-only luncheon on Coach Tinker's behalf at the VFW meeting hall and presented him with a five-hundred-dollar gift certificate from Goldblatt's department store.

And Spooner's mother counted the days until some Lions Club do-gooder wandered up Shabbona Drive and tried to sell *her* raffle tickets. It is probably unnecessary by now to point out that she took these things personally, but it was strange even to Spooner that of all the people she talked to about it, she seemed angriest when she brought the matter up with Calmer.

———

But that wasn't all of it either.

Early in the spring, at the end of wrestling season, Coach Tinker was given a weekly column in the sports pages of the *Prairie Glen Mercury-News*, making, if you can believe this, an extra forty dollars a week, and when the first column appeared and the evidence was there in front of Lily, in black and white, the absolute confirmation of who was getting ahead in the world, she closed shop and more or less quit breathing for three days. Back open for business, her first act was to call the *Prairie Glen Mercury-News* and cancel her subscription. She wasn't going to pay good money to read a rambling illiterate, she said, and hung up before anybody could give her any lip. She spent the rest of that afternoon and most of the evening trying to start a boycott of the paper, a stand against throwing away good money to read a rambling illiterate. All this talk about illiterates, by the way, went on as if Spooner weren't sitting right there at the kitchen table listening.

Over time Calmer tried—gently, gently—to persuade her that the situation had a humorous side, there in the columns themselves. If a fair world was what you were looking for, he said, you had to appreciate irony. And their own time, he reminded her—Calmer and Lily's time— was coming. Dr. Baber was retiring, Metcalf had taken another job, and Calmer had been informally notified that he would be the next principal. There would be money then for the addition.

And to a degree this mollified Lily and to a degree it didn't, and she was not slow to remind him that she had learned the hard way not to count her chickens before the eggs hatched.

TWENTY-FIVE

Later that year Spooner began his career in organized baseball. The coach of the baseball team was Evelyn Tinker, who in addition to being held almost blameless in the Lemonkatz boy's injury was now rumored to be collecting sixty bucks a week for the newspaper column, this in spite of Lily's public campaign to have him fired, and being as Spooner was not old enough yet to have voted for Richard Nixon, this joining of Tinker's team constituted the single most disloyal thing a child of Lily Whitlowe Ottosson's had ever done.

How could he?

The question hung in the air at 308 Shabbona Drive, unspoken, like another dead father.

The answer—not that the answer mattered—was that Spooner had stopped at the baseball diamond on the way to the shopping center after school, and watched through the fence as Russell Hodge pitched four innings of a practice game against Crete-Monee, striking out twelve of the thirteen batters he faced. It was a tiny school, Crete-Monee, six hundred students, kindergarten through twelfth grade, and two of the players were only thirteen years old. The smallest one—who wore number thirteen, and was the only batter Russell Hodge did not strike out—was plunked between the shoulder blades as he turned away from an inside fastball, and cried.

Half a dozen times Spooner started to leave but couldn't, waiting around to see one more pitch, and in the end hung on the wire fence more than an hour, leaving diamond-shaped imprints on the underside of his forearms, wrists to elbows, taking the measure of Russell Hodge's throws.

It came to him as he watched that Russell Hodge pitched in much the way he played linebacker, which is to say blind with rage. But it was more difficult in baseball, a game that had very little maiming, to sustain a murderous rage than it was in football, even for Russell Hodge, and after an inning or two Spooner thought he saw him working to conjure it up, sucking from the air every bit of resentment he could find. Giving Russell Hodge his due, even in a practice game against little Crete-Monee, he brought himself again and again to a state just short of foaming at the mouth—furious at the batter, at his own catcher, the umpire, who, behind the mask and protective vest was only Mr. Kopex the math teacher, furious even at the ball itself—and by the end appeared to have lost all his stuff.

Monday afternoon, Spooner showed up at the practice field in tennis shoes and shorts. He didn't have a glove—he'd taken the one he had out of his closet, but it was a toy and he could barely get his hand inside, and if he'd brought that along, he might as well have worn his old cowboy hat too.

The players were already scattered in the outfield when he arrived, loosening up their arms or throwing each other grounders or fly balls. The student manager was chalking the batters' boxes. Spooner stood behind the fence, unsure how to announce himself.

Presently, Tinker materialized and blew his whistle, and players jogged in and players jogged out, and pretty soon Mr. Kopex took the mound and threw a few tepid fast balls in the direction of the plate, and the star players took turns and took their cuts, and the players who were not stars chased the balls they hit.

Russell Hodge put one over the fence marking school property boundaries, fouled the next one off, and then lined a screamer back up the middle, catching Mr. Kopex, who'd given him a D in slow-track Introduction to Algebra, in the foot. Mr. Kopex was a large, fleshy fellow and he made one complete turn on the way down, 360 degrees, then lay on his back a long moment, getting his bearings. Here and there were scattered his glasses, his glove, and his cap. Presently he sat up and took off his shoe and sock, revealing a tiny, bone-white, misshapen foot, and lifted it up like a contortionist, cradling it, pulling it up almost to his mouth, and rocked slightly back and forth, staring at Russell Hodge, hoping, Spooner imagined, to get one more shot at him in slow-track algebra.

Coach Tinker went to the mound in a concerned jog but did not tell Mr. Kopex to run it off. Thanks perhaps to young Lemonkatz, Tinker had tamed his wild impulse to make the injured run.

Meanwhile, Russell Hodge was still at the plate, stamping his feet, stoking the fire.

Coach Tinker studied the problem, which in essence was that Mr. Kopex was holding up practice, and pushed back his cap to scratch his head. There was a scar there the shape of a smile from butting Lemonkatz. He nodded to Mr. Kopex and then turned and yelled, "We need a pitcher."

The other assistant coach, Mr. Speers, the typing teacher, was also a large, fleshy man and, like Mr. Kopex, pigeon-shaped and had seen the line drive hit Mr. Kopex and was coming in from the field, walking at what appeared to be emergency walking speed. Mr. Speers and Mr. Kopex were bachelors and best friends and had volunteered together to coach baseball, thinking they could use the extra $250 the school district paid toward a European trip they hoped to take next summer. They were much alike physically, although Mr. Kopex belted his pants beneath his stomach and Mr. Speers hitched his together just below the nipples. They enjoyed exercise, that is, what they had considered exercise, the outdoors and fresh air and all that, hiking together in the forest preserve, but coaching base-ball for Tinker had turned out to be nothing like exercise as they had known it before. On top of that the season was less than two weeks old and Mr. Speers had discovered he was allergic to dust and was runny-eyed and sneezing all the time. For his part, Mr. Kopex had developed hammer toes over the years and worried constantly about someone in spikes stepping on his feet. Unlike Mr. Speers, who wore black high-topped Converse sneakers, Mr. Kopex had played Little League ball in his youth and, as a matter of dignity, spent the money for a new glove and spikes of his own, and had, a few days earlier, admitted to Mr. Speers to a certain stirring at the sound they made as he walked over gravel.

Mr. Speers stood hesitantly over Mr. Kopex now, unsure if it was against the rules to help him up. "Get us off the field, Frank," Mr. Kopex said, and Mr. Speers nodded at his friend and then bent down and rooted his head through his armpit, and tried to lift him up. Mr. Kopex was a loose handful though, slippery with sweat and pretty soon Mr. Speers gave up his hold on the armpit and fastened on to whatever parts he could fasten on to, and before they had cleared the practice field the two men had more or less reversed positions, with Mr. Kopex in a kind of headlock and making strangling noises as Mr. Speers dragged him off.

Spooner had stopped cold at the sight of Mr. Kopex's misshapen foot—had the man been tortured in Korea?—and now he also saw Mr. Kopex's glove, which lay brand-new and halfway open behind the pitching mound, where the imprint of the accident itself could still be seen in the dirt. Spooner thought he could smell the leather.

Tinker called again for a new pitcher, and Spooner walked onto the field, just like he belonged there, straight to Mr. Kopex's glove. He picked up the glove as if it were his own and retrieved the same ball that had bounced off Mr. Kopex's ankle. There were another fifty or sixty balls in a basket behind the mound, all of them scuffed and brown with dirt. The glove was still damp from Mr. Kopex's hand, and Spooner remembered being introduced to him a long time ago at a faculty Christmas party. Spooner might have been eleven or twelve, and Mr. Kopex's hand was no bigger than his own. He conjured up the feel of that hand exactly, it was like someone had passed him one of Phillip's wet diapers.

Russell Hodge pounded the plate.

On the sidelines, Mr. Speers eased Mr. Kopex to the ground—not that he had been so far off the ground—and Tinker bent down in front of him with his hands on his knees and proceeded to scruff his hair playfully and compliment him on giving 120 percent, which was all that anybody could ask. Tinker was not easy with those sorts of compliments—for instance, Spooner couldn't imagine poor stubby-legged Mrs. Tinker getting even an 85 or 90, even if she fucked him on a trapeze.

A certain look came over Mr. Kopex's face. This was the third day of the second week of practice, meaning Mr. Kopex had been hearing Tinker's percentages tossed around for nine days, and now, removed from the business of assistant coaching and back on his home turf, he returned fire.

"A hundred and twenty percent of what?" he said.

"A hundred and twenty percent," Tinker said, as if percentages were self-evident, like your won-lost record.

Mr. Kopex, who was still sitting on the ground and in pain, nevertheless picked up a small stick and drew a circle. "Show me," he said, and handed him the stick.

Spooner felt a stillness in his heart, waiting to hear Mr. Kopex discuss percentages with Coach Tinker, and likewise could barely breathe in anticipation of pitching to Russell Hodge.

"Let's say this is the whole," Mr. Kopex was saying.

Spooner decided to let Russell Hodge wait.

Coach Tinker set his cap back a little on his forehead again—this was his thinking mode—and said, "The whole what?"

"The whole whatever. The whole pie. And what you're trying to say is that you want it all. You want a hundred percent."

"It's not for me," Tinker said. "It's for the youth. I want them to learn to give more than a hundred percent."

Back in the other direction, Russell Hodge was pounding the plate again with his bat.

"Ah, but that's just the point," Mr. Kopex said. "One hundred percent is all there is. That is the whole. That is the definition of the whole."

"The whole what?"

"The pie. The world. Everything. Where is the extra twenty percent?"

Mr. Speers was nodding along as Mr. Kopex spoke, and Coach Tinker was staring at the circle Mr. Kopex had drawn in the dirt, also nodding, as if he saw what Mr. Kopex was getting at too.

Coach Tinker said, "What I'm trying to instill in these individuals is to want a bigger pie," and he leaned in even closer and looked at Mr. Kopex's foot, which had blossomed like an orchid. "You might want to tape that," he said. "Keep moving it around so it doesn't stiffen up on you."

Presently Mr. Speers and the student trainer eased themselves under Mr. Kopex's arms and began to walk him very slowly back in the direction of school.

Tinker had another quick look at the circle Mr. Kopex had drawn in the dirt, then scrubbed it out with his shoe and turned away from the world of geometry and all its inhabitants. He clapped his hands and blew his whistle. "Let's go, let's go, move it . . ."

Tinker could not stand to waste practice time.

And all around Spooner the throwing and catching resumed, and Russell Hodge pounded the plate again and cocked the bat and waited for Spooner to feed him the ball.

He had never pitched from a mound before—even the roof of Major Shaker's chicken house was flat—and as he threw he experienced a sensation like stepping into an unseen swale in the road.

The baseball headed east, just missing the wire backstop, passed a foot over Tinker's head, curving slightly to the north, and vectored on out in the direction of Mr. Kopex, who was holding his injured foot behind him and a few inches off the ground and using Mr. Speers and the student manager as crutches. It hit him, of course, as Spooner already knew it would, struck him exactly on the knob of the heel of the hammer-toed, orchid-blossomed bare foot that Russell Hodge had just mangled with his line drive.

Mr. Kopex dropped to the ground again, bringing the student manager down with him. He cried out, "Oh, for the love of Christ," and it sounded like he was begging for mercy, but of course if what you are looking for is mercy, high school isn't the place for you anyway.

Tinker stared at Spooner, trying to remember who he was, then turned to the outfield and called for a new pitcher. And then headed out to tend to Mr. Kopex again.

One of the second stringers fielding balls in the outfield jogged in to throw batting practice. Spooner watched the kid coming, realizing he'd just gone through all the chances he was ever going to get.

He picked a ball out of the basket and motioned Russell Hodge back to the plate. When he looked again, trying to judge how much time he had left until Tinker returned, Mr. Kopex was writhing in the dirt, in a circular motion around his foot, which seemed strangely fixed to one point, as if somebody had pinned it to the ground with a compass from geometry class.

Russell Hodge pounded the plate and stepped in, pointed his bat at Spooner, aiming at him down the barrel. Spooner laid his fingers carefully across the stitches before he threw, putting a little extra pressure on the middle finger so that the ball would tail to the right, and as a result, the pitch hit Russell Hodge in his deaf ear instead of the mouth.

The sound was like breaking the seal on a pickle jar. Russell Hodge curled on the ground, holding both ears, as if the volume of the world was suddenly turned way too high. The thought passed at a strange, leisurely pace through Spooner's brain that he'd killed Russell Hodge.

His first whiff of celebrity.

He stayed where he was, looking for signs of life, not really sure if he wanted to see any or not, not even sure if he'd hit him on purpose—if the thought had been there before he let the ball go or if his arm had just taken over. It hadn't been an accident the way hitting Mr. Kopex was an accident, though. Spooner had known when the ball left his hand where it was headed.

What had Margaret said? "I think they just put you in the ground and you rot"?

———

Tinker knelt beside Russell Hodge and gently rolled him onto his back. "Everybody get back," he yelled. "Give him air."

But there wasn't anybody close enough to suck up Russell Hodge's air. Most of the players took one look and were inching as far away as they could get. Russell Hodge lay cockeyed in the dust with his eyelids half open, staring off into the blue.

Tinker looked around, frightened. He lifted one of Hodge's eyelids, stared for a moment and then let it go. He took Hodge's mouth in his hand, puckering the boy's lips, and moved his head slowly back and forth. "All right, Hodge," he said, "let's shake it off." But even Tinker—who privately was still of the opinion that running a few laps on a broken femur wasn't as bad as it looked on paper—even he knew better than that.

He rocked back on his heels, looking at Russell Hodge, and then went forward again and gently fitted his hands under the body—two hundred pounds if he weighed an ounce—and took him up in his arms and stood, and then walked slowly east, back in the direction of school, casting a surprisingly long shadow for a fellow of his height.

———————

Tuesday morning Dr. Baber came on the loudspeaker to announce that Russell Hodge was still in the hospital with a brain injury, but doing well and expected to make a full recovery. A cluster of troublemakers booed from the back of Señor Rosenstein's second-year Spanish class, where Spooner was at the time, and were sent to Dr. Baber's office for detention slips. The two cheerleaders in the class both wept in gratitude, and one later claimed to have prayed for his recovery.

Tinker had spent all night and most of the day at Russell's bedside, and, in the way these things sometimes turn out, news of this simple act of concern went a long way toward repairing his reputation among those who had criticized him after the Lemonkatz affair, and also served as a cooling-off period in another matter, as only last Friday Tinker had caught a student named Richard D. Peck lying under the bleachers reading *Othello* when he was supposed to be taking the sit-ups portion of his national youth fitness test, and threatened to kill him.

Peck's family had already notified the school board of its intention to sue.

———

That afternoon found Spooner standing alone as warm-ups began, Mr. Kopex's glove curled under his chin like a baby's head. He felt no guilt about stealing the glove, which he viewed as no worse than grave robbing—*grave robbing* being one of the terms Spooner still misunderstood at this stage of his matriculation, thinking it meant taking something old or unwanted. Kopex had been in the hallway on crutches when Spooner saw him earlier that day between classes, overwhelmed by the movement and jostling and noise, fighting for breath, sweat soaked and old overnight. No, Kopex wouldn't want the glove anymore, wouldn't even want it around the house where it could fall out of the closet and remind him of what had happened.

Spooner was thinking of Mr. Kopex and the glove—grave robbing wasn't stealing, but it must have been something because he kept thinking about it—when Coach Tinker appeared at his side. "Spoonerman," he said, and Spooner jumped at the sound of his voice, "I know you're worried about Hodge."

Spooner nodded, although the only specific worrying he'd done about Russell Hodge was that he would get out of the hospital and kill him.

"The best thing you can do," Tinker said, "is go out there and give it a hundred and twenty percent. That's what he'd want."

Two questions at once: Did this mean Hodge was dead, and was Tinker, after everything that had happened, still going to let him pitch? Spooner hadn't expected another chance. He was now two pitches into his career in organized baseball, after all, and one had taken out the heart of the school's math department—Mr. Kopex's heel was cracked, while the roof of the foot, where Hodge's line drive had drilled him, was only bruised—and the other had possibly killed the greatest all-around athlete in the history of the Prairie Glen High Golden Streaks.

"How is he?" Spooner said. The truth was Hodge dying still didn't strike him as the worst way this could end.

"Who?"

"Hodge. Is he dead?"

Tinker gave Spooner a little elbow in the ribs, as if he had just told him a joke or wanted to point out a set of tits. It left Spooner's ribs tender all week. "Don't worry about old Hodgie," he said, "he'll shake it off. You just throw the baseball. Keep us in it until he gets back."

———

Tinker divided his players into two teams that afternoon and put Spooner on the mound to pitch to both sides.

They played three innings before it rained, Spooner getting used to the mound, to the movement of a new unscuffed baseball, to the sense of the players behind him in the field, depending on what he did. The center of attention. He walked two batters and struck out the other eighteen he faced. No hits, no runs, nobody hurt except the catcher, Ken Jonny, a perfect toad of a kid who, although apparently designed without a neck, was in fact hit twice in the neck when balls skipped over his mitt and under his face mask.

TWENTY-SIX

Russell Hodge came back to school on Friday morning, looking like he'd been lifting weights in the hospital. He was wearing a yellow dress shirt, open to the waist. Spooner was sitting in the hallway beside his locker with one foot bare, attaching a Band-aid to a toe blister, when he apprehended a certain menace in the milieu, as Calmer might say, and looked up to find Russell Hodge standing over him, looming up there in the hallway's artificial light, and experienced in that moment a clear perception of himself as a lawn mower and Russell Hodge as a mower of lawns, about to set his boot on his chest to hold him in place while he grabbed the starter cord and yanked off his head.

Spooner put his shoe back on and got to his feet and, possibly making a bad situation worse, found himself staring at the spot where the baseball had broken through Russell's cranium and momentarily entered his brain. Not that there was much to see, really, at least no imprint of the ball. Only a short line of thick black stitching farther back on his head where they'd gone in to ease the pressure and swelling.

Spooner realized now that he was still holding his sock, and realized he'd been staring at Russell Hodge's head a long time. Safety-wise, this was like napping on the highway, but he found himself unable to look away, and wondered idly if Coach Tinker would visit him in the hospital too. He ruminated awhile, there under the gaze of Russell Hodge, coming eventually to the realization that beyond pain and mortification, what was about to happen would embarrass Calmer and mortify his mother, who still worked that pump like a spare lung—the disgrace waiting for them all if he was ever in trouble at school. Public humiliation, a ruinous effect on Calmer's career, especially now that he was going to be principal. And the newspapers. The newspapers would have a field day.

Spooner's mother lived her life with the certain knowledge that the whole thing—cradle to grave—was an ambush. Spooner didn't necessarily disagree with that, but had never seen any reason to take it personally. The incident about to occur, for instance, would end up in the archives as one more piece of evidence that the world was out to ruin *her*.

But even as these things floated through Spooner's brain, some other information was coming in right behind it. As impossible as it seemed, Russell Hodge appeared at this moment to be having misgivings, that or had forgotten who Spooner was, or couldn't make up his mind how he wanted to kill him.

But wait, it was dread. Spooner saw dread in Russell Hodge, and he knew dread when he saw it like the palm of his hand. These two things, by the way, dread and masturbation, went together all of Spooner's life once the reproductive system checked in, initially preparing him perhaps for all the dilemmas and complexities that would mark the affairs of the heart all his life.

Right now, for instance, he faced the following choice every afternoon between fourth and fifth period: He could step into a bathroom stall and quiet his reproductive system or take his chances on being caught with an erection in music appreciation. Damned if you do, damned if you don't, which—no happy coincidence—was what the reproductive system was all about. Meaning the fear of being caught—he himself had been in the bathroom when Mr. Craddock, the dean of boys, had stormed in and broken through a stall door trying to catch a kid named Wendell Jeeter smoking, and instead found him in the act of spilling his seed—had to be weighed against the possibility of being called to the chalkboard by Miss Degruso. The problem with music appreciation was that Spooner's seat was directly in back of the smoldering figure of Dee Dee Victor, at whose back he stared all period long, studying her details through the sometimes translucent shirts she wore, in love with her shoulders, her shoulder blades, her blood pressure, every little pebble of her spine. And when she leaned forward to take notes, a narrow space would open along the line of her skirt, and he would lean forward too, inhaling the air like it was loaded with roast beef, thinking that what he was breathing that instant had just floated out from under her skirt. And then old Peckenpaw would float out too, like a piece of driftwood, and begin to leak, and what if at this critical, boned, leaking, helpless moment Miss Degruso asked him to come to the front and distinguish a piccolo from a fife? It was possible. In fact, that was what she'd asked Russell Hodge to do on the day he'd broken her leg in the storage locker.

Now, however, as he and Russell Hodge continued to stare at each other in the hallway, Russell's expression continued to change, dread to misgivings, misgivings to confusion, and settling finally almost on the same empty look he'd had lying on the dirt next to home plate after Spooner had plunked him in the head.

The fire alarm rang—one of the Ploof twins at it again probably—and Hodge jumped at the sudden noise, and then, regaining himself, turned and looked up the wall to the spot where the bell was installed, and, finding the source of the noise, he smiled. One of his front teeth had grown in crooked, and while Spooner watched, a line of saliva dropped half a foot from his lip and then held, dancing in the eerie, artificial light, and then broke off and landed on his shirt.

Which was when Spooner noticed that Russell had his shirt on inside out.

———

Spooner next saw Russell Hodge half an hour before baseball practice. Hodge was sitting on a wooden bench in the caged locker room area where the team dressed, naked except for his socks and cleats, studying a piece of stiff, crumpled gauze about the size of a finch. He turned it one way and another, trying to place what it was. The gauze was crusted with dried blood, and he abruptly shook it, and then held it up to his good ear to hear if it was ticking.

TWENTY-SEVEN

Spooner did not like to be told how to throw a baseball, much less where to throw it. The throwing came from a thousand afternoons outside his grandmother's house back in Georgia, alone, with his mother inside, crying or sick, and it was secret then, the things he did to get away from her, and somehow secret to him now.

Besides, everything that could be said about throwing a ball had already been said a thousand times, and he understood he was exceptional at this one thing in his life and was chary of talking about it, of even thinking about it too much, afraid of losing the sensation, afraid the happiness of it would dissolve. That was usually the story when he went over a thing too much, began thinking about what he'd done or hadn't done or should have done instead, or could have done if he'd only done it better. Which is to say that before he'd finished chewing a thing over, it was tasteless.

Least of all was he inclined to discuss throwing with Tinker, but Tinker—who hadn't got where he was by worrying if he was wanted—continued to come to Spooner again and again, making sure, as he put it, that they were on the same page.

And Spooner continued to throw the ball where he wanted to throw it, and the local papers wrote their headlines, and then one of the Chicago newspapers noticed the local papers and sent a stringer around, who wrote his own stories and pretty soon even the first-string big-city reporters came around to look for themselves, some of them famous, and as the story gained impetus Tinker pressed all the harder to be included.

Not long after the big-city reporters showed up, there were scouts, two of them, sitting behind the screen in hats and short sleeves and ties, charting every pitch Spooner threw, and always Tinker would find a reason to call time-out when they were in the seats, to walk slowly to the mound, put his arm around Spooner's shoulder, and turn him away from the stands—the way you might create a bit of privacy to tell someone bad news. He would say, "Let's make sure we're on the same page with this guy, Spoonerman," or simply, "Let's move this guy off the plate." Sometimes delivering this message in the middle of a string of perfect innings.

After the game, on the bus ride home, he would drop into the seat next to Spooner—the seat next to Spooner was pretty much always empty—and try to insinuate himself into the matter of Spooner's throwing again. Always pushing him to throw more inside. "What are you *afraid* of, Spoonerman? That's what it looks like. It looks like you're afraid."

Which was not exactly it, but it was clearer to Spooner all the time that Russell Hodge was no longer Russell Hodge. He was now timid at the plate, unable to find the strike zone on the occasions he was allowed to pitch and, more worrisome, seemed to be taken over by an unnatural sweetness of disposition, and was often distracted as he stood out in his new position of center field by some small creature or plant, and often was watching it or smelling it when fly balls were hit his way, and only his great natural speed, unaffected by the beaning, had saved him from half a dozen embarrassing errors. Russell Hodge was taking time to smell the roses, and it was a pitiful thing to watch, and it would have taken a colder heart than Spooner's not to regret being the cause.

And so he held Tinker off, one advance after another, like a girl in the backseat who didn't want to be felt up.

The truth was, Tinker did not much understand baseball, a sport in which no one was doing anything 90 percent of the time. To Tinker, it was more like a *student activity* than a sport, and he had taken over as the head baseball coach only after hearing the manager Billy Martin on television one day saying that baseball was a contest of wills over who owned the inside part of the plate. Tinker, who had trained himself to think in these terms, saw immediately that life was also a contest of wills over who owned the inside of the plate. He coached it and wrote it in his column and used it in public appearances.

By now the whole Village of Prairie Glen hung on every word he said and still this kid Spoonerman wouldn't listen.

His fee for public speaking these days was one hundred and fifty dollars, and you can imagine what she said when she heard about that.

———

Nine games into the season, a columnist showed up from the *Chicago Tribune*, arrived late and watched only the last inning of a rain-shortened game, and wrote that an instant before Spooner's slider reached the plate, an intervention seemed to take place, and a pitch would dance out like a fish hitting the lure, and predicting its movement was like predicting the thoughts of a rainbow trout on the hook.

It was about this time that Spooner began to understand that newspaper writers were going to write what they were going to write no matter what they saw when they arrived on the scene.

TWENTY-EIGHT

And so it happened that Calmer looked up from his desk one afternoon and saw Evelyn Tinker standing in the doorway, the ceiling lights reflecting off his skull, which had been shorn of hair down to maybe a sixteenth of an inch.

"Welcome, pilgrim," Calmer said.

There was a yellowed black-and-white picture on the wall of a professor out somewhere on the prairie, with a dozen students before him on their knees, pressing their ears against a railroad track. The professor was holding a sledgehammer. Tinker knew it was a professor because he had glasses and a beard. He stared at the picture a long time.

Calmer's tie was loose and his sleeves were rolled up to the elbows, and when Tinker finally turned away from the picture, he noticed Calmer's forearms and wondered if he'd played ball in high school. He wondered if in some way Ottosson's forearms might explain how Spooner could throw a baseball.

Calmer motioned to the empty chair on the other side of his desk. Tinker took it and rolled up onto one hip to cross his legs. There was something discordant about Tinker with crossed legs, like a cowboy riding into town sidesaddle. The legs themselves were thickened, and perhaps shortened, by years of four-hundred-pound squats in the weight room, and his forward foot protruded like the beginnings of an erection.

Tinker had another look at the picture. "I like that," he said. "I could use it myself to help motivate some of these kids I've got."

Calmer smiled and waited. The coach continued to stare at the picture.

"So, Evelyn, what can I do for you?"

Tinker turned back to Calmer, not much caring for the familiar use of his first name by an ordinary member of the faculty. He liked to be called *coach*. Even Mrs. Tinker called him Coach.

He said, "It's about our boy," and realized that he'd just at that moment forgotten Spooner's name, although now that he thought about it, he wasn't sure he'd known it in the first place. It wasn't Ottosson, that much he knew.

"Warren?"

It didn't sound right, but Tinker nodded along, thinking Ottosson should know. He said, "See, Warren seems to be one of these kids that come along now and then that you can't coach. That isn't coachable, if you follow what I mean."

Calmer nodded as if he had some idea of what Tinker was talking about. "In what way?" he said.

"Well, you know, you coach him, but he doesn't listen."

A fire alarm went off in the hallway, the Ploof twins strike again. Every time one of them pulled the alarm, the whole school had to exit in an orderly manner, single file, and stand in the parking lot until the fire department got there and shut off the alarm. The Ploofs themselves were untouchable. Even if an eyewitness saw one of them do it, each of them would only blame the other.

Tinker turned in his chair and stared as the students in the hallway filed out. Smoking, horsing around, dancing—not orderly and single-file at all. "Right there," he said, "that's exactly what I mean."

Calmer got up and closed the door against the sound of the alarm, and when he sat down again it was on the edge of his desk. "You were talking about Warren . . ."

"Let's just say I'm not sure he follows everything, if you get my meaning. I thought maybe it was something you'd run into with him at home." There was a pause, Tinker beginning to feel uncomfortable, like somehow it was his fault the kid was slow. "But the important thing now is the scouts. They're out there every day, and they're interested, I can tell you that. This could be the chance of a lifetime."

"Scouts?"

"Big-league scouts. They're required by the state to notify me before they can make contact with the student; it's a state law." There had been only the two scouts, and one of them had only stayed a few days and left. The other one was still hanging around.

Tinker turned for another look at the picture on the wall, feeling Calmer watching. He wished he could tell him to sit back down behind his desk where he belonged.

"And what is it again that you want him to listen to?"

"To coaching."

"About what?"

"About playing ball. That's what we're talking about. This could be his chance."

The talk wasn't going the way Tinker had thought it would. For one thing, there was no sign of appreciation from Ottosson yet that Tinker had taken the time to come over and talk. He wasn't even sure they were having a talk; it felt like he was confessing. He found himself wondering if he could take Calmer in a fight.

"You never know about these things," Tinker said.

"He's seventeen," Calmer said. "He hasn't finished high school. He hasn't even read any books yet."

Books? Yeah, he could take him.

"Don't get me wrong," Tinker said, "I'm all for higher education. All I'm saying is he could get injured tomorrow. He could reach into a lawn mower and cut a tendon." He told Calmer about a Negro boy he'd played with back at Normal who reached under a running mower with his bare hand and after that it was nothing but fumbles.

The fire bell went quiet, and the room went quiet with it.

Calmer sat on the corner of his desk, remembering how the world outside had looked to him from the farm, when he was sixteen and ready to leave. He'd known things, though, how to work, how to keep what he had, how engines ran, how things were put together, how to fix them when they broke. He wondered sometimes if he should do less of the work around the house, let the boys figure things out more for themselves.

"I just wanted to check he doesn't have any problems at home that we should know about," Tinker said. "Family history, things like that. Hearing problems, trouble hitting the books, if he took a whack on the head . . ."

Calmer continued to stare, stared right through him.

"He has to claim the inside of the plate," Tinker said. "He's got to make the batter aware that the inside of the plate is his. That's the whole psychology of the game. Of life, when you think about it. Life is a contest of wills for the inside of the plate. And all these scouts, they aren't just looking for an arm, they're looking for the maturity to go with it."

"He's seventeen," Calmer said again.

"There's still time," Tinker said, and when there was no reply to that, he stood up to leave. He looked at the picture again and smiled. "There's an old saying," he said, "that a picture's worth a thousand words, and you know, if you really think about that, it's true."

TWENTY-NINE

Calmer left school early, right after fifth period, and drove the Ford to Chicago Heights, where that afternoon the baseball team was scheduled to play Bloom Township. It was six miles and twice that many railroad crossings, and on the way over the muffler dropped off.

He continued on, though, ignored the noise and the looks from the street, imagining what it would be like telling Lily that Warren was going to play baseball instead of going to college. In Lily's family, a child who didn't go to college might as well go to prison.

The team was on the field warming up when Calmer arrived, the coaches hitting grounders and fly balls, the infielders turning double plays. A pretty fair sampling of adults sat in the stands along with some students, but baseball didn't matter in high school the way football did.

Calmer stood off to the side at first, studying the bleachers, and immediately spotted the overweight, middle-aged man sitting alone, smoking Pall Mall cigarettes, making notes on a small pad. He had a permanent-looking tan that he had not acquired around here and the skin at the edges of his ears was crusted. He looked comfortable even with his back pressed into the edge of the bleachers, using his knees to hold his notepad while he wrote. He looked like someone who would be comfortable sitting on a pail or a train track: a man born to sit.

Calmer had no idea how to begin the conversation, if this would be another version of his talk with Coach Tinker, or something different, or worse.

"One of them yours?" the scout said.

Calmer was sitting a few feet away. The scout pulled on the Pall Mall and the smoke went in deep and only began leaking out as he spoke.

Calmer pointed toward Spooner. "Over there," he said, "the pitcher."

The scout nodded. "Well, he's the one, all right. He's got the live arm."

A kid came by selling hot dogs, and the scout bought two of them and asked for a receipt. Out on the field, a boy with an enormous head was laying a fresh chalk line up the first base side, smiling out from under the awning of his baseball cap, pushing a one-wheeled barrow, and the line behind him was perfect and straight. Calmer thought it wouldn't be such a bad thing to lay chalk lines. He was catching himself at this all the time lately, picturing himself trading jobs, usually for some kind of work that would be finished for the day when it was finished for the day, that would leave him time to rest and read. Other jobs, other lives. It was strange how often it came up.

The boy with the chalk marker moved at a slow, even pace out into the grass of the outfield, passing within a few yards of the place where Spooner was warming up, throwing effortlessly to a fat kid named Ken Jonny. Ken Jonny had been failing biology last fall when Tinker sent an assistant around to see Calmer about it, pressing him to use his influence with the teacher to get the boy a passing grade. Calmer had waited until Tinker's assistant finished and then went to his bookshelf, picked out *Introduction to Biology*, handed him the book without a word and showed him out the door.

Spooner seemed to be throwing a little harder now, and the scout watched him throw and set the cigarette next to him on the bleacher and began to eat a hot dog. Then he stopped, maybe the second bite still in his mouth, and set the hot dogs aside, on top of his notepad and, using the napkin, took out his upper plate and inspected it for some bit of hot dog bone that had gotten between it and his gums. He blew on the plate to clean it and then used the teeth to indicate Spooner. "Any ways you look at it, that's damn unusual stuff," he said. Then had one more look at his teeth and set them back in his mouth.

Calmer watched, and presently, without any appreciable difference in effort, there was a change in the sound as the ball arrived into the catcher's mitt. A cracking noise one time, a popping noise the next—you could almost think of firewood. And then the ball began to rise and dive and jag sideways, as if one side were heavier than the other, and Calmer sat in the stands—a physicist, a mathematician, a pilot, a man who knew and understood the principles of flight—trying to conceive what spin would account for the sudden movement of the ball as it reached the plate.

The scout had taken his teeth out again and spoke as if he were reading Calmer's mind. "That poop at the end of them pitches," he said, "it's something like a knuckler, but it don't look like a knuckler coming to the plate onaccount of the ball gets to you so fast."

A hundred feet beyond Spooner, the kid with the chalk marker had come to the fence and turned around and was standing in the sunshine, smiling, looking something like an angel, waiting for someone to tell him what to do next. Calmer stretched in the sun and then thought again of telling Lily about Spooner, and that prospect rolled in on him like low, boiling clouds over the old trailer park, and scared the sun out of the sky.

Calmer sat with the scout most of the afternoon, stunned at what he was seeing—nobody from Bloom Township could touch Spooner's pitching—and at what he was thinking. Then the rain started, and then the lightning, and finally the umpire called the game.

The storm blew over trees and street signs, and there were sightings of funnel clouds all over northern Illinois and Indiana. Calmer drove back to Shabbona Drive, oblivious of the weather.

———

Lily was in the kitchen, waiting for him. It was still blowing outside, and a piece of hail the size of a baby's fist had come through the utility room window and lay on the linoleum floor where it had landed, melting, and there were shards of glass all over the room. It looked like a migraine headache in there.

"I thought something had happened," she said, indicating that he was late.

He heard echoes of old abandonments in her voice, of the death of her first husband, her father, Spooner's twin brother. All of that wrapped up like a sandwich in waxed paper. Five ordinary words. How did she do it? He supposed you might as well ask Picasso the same question, or Sophia Loren, or that kid with Down syndrome laying down his perfect chalk lines to mark the field.

"I was in Chicago Heights watching Warren," Calmer said. "He's quite a baseball player."

She was fixing a meat loaf for tomorrow's dinner—it was Friday, so it would be fish sticks tonight—and at the mention of baseball, she dove bare-handed into the bowl of raw meat and raw eggs and onions as if she'd glimpsed Coach Tinker hiding at the bottom and meant to strangle him. Calmer waited, dripping rain on the kitchen floor, but she did not look up from her business. The storm blew and the curtains billowed over the broken window.

"There was a fellow at the game," Calmer said. "A baseball scout."

Now she did look up, daring him to say another word.

"Apparently, he's got unusual . . ."—he reached around for the word the scout used and found it—"poop. Quite unusual poop." It was a satisfying word, *poop*, and he said it and waited, and in the quiet that followed, his thoughts went to a caving expedition a long time ago in the Black Hills, of that certain, dark stillness and sensing the presence of other living things.

He waited for the air to explode in bats.

He and Lily had arrived here at the old bat cave before, of course, and usually it was over Spooner. It was never said in exactly these words, but Spooner was hers, not theirs. Strangely, there was no such undercurrent when it came to Margaret, and had never been, but then, it was a different thing, worrying if Radcliffe would be a better school than Swarthmore or

Stanford, and having to figure out what to do when your kid gives everybody Christmas presents stolen from Massey's Hardware.

"You know that I don't think he should be playing baseball," she said,
and seemed to be talking more to the meat loaf than to him. "How is he
going to get in to a decent school?"

Calmer thought of having a Scotch but reconsidered—afraid it might
be perceived as indifference. He sat down across from her at the table. She
took her hands out of the bowl, bits of onion glistening like diamonds in
the ground meat. And now he was thinking of a summer day not so long
ago, the year Spooner began seventh grade and Calmer had gotten him a
job mowing lawns at the high school, and they'd walked down a hallway
after lunch, Spooner stopping a few seconds here, a few seconds there,
still keeping up, and when Calmer turned to see what he was doing, the
kid had opened half a dozen combination locks in the hallway lockers,
apparently as easily as untying his shoes.

"Next year he'll be on his own," she was saying, "and he can barely
read. Did you see his report card?"

Calmer had seen the report card, D in English, but it was only a midterm card and the D had been dropped on him by Miss Ethel Sandway,
who was as crazy as a loon. Miss Sandway was an enormous woman
with a master's degree in education from Normal—what was it about
that place, anyway?—who was working even now toward a doctorate. He
trembled to think of what she might be planning to do with that.

Lily wiped her hands on her apron and took the atomizer out of her
pocket and squeezed two quick hits into her tonsils. All these years, and
it still tore him to pieces to watch her fighting to breathe.

"I'll talk to Miss Sandway," he said, "see what the problem is."

They had talked once before, Calmer and Miss Sandway. Miss Sandway had assigned a freshman class to memorize the poem "Trees" by
Robert Frost. Margaret was in the class and told him what she'd given
them to do, and Calmer went to the woman, thinking she'd probably
been in a hurry, or preoccupied, or had a mouthful of potato chips at the
time, and found himself shortly in a pitched battle over the authorship

of "Trees," which Miss Sandway said she'd been teaching for twenty years and imagined she could continue to teach without interference from the science department. Calmer politely held his ground, as he always did, always would, and they walked to the school library together and looked the poem up, and seeing that the author was not Robert Frost, Miss Sandway slammed shut the book and poked a finger in his chest. "The whole point, Ottosson," she said, "is the trees. He writes about the beauty of trees."

And Calmer—who admired Robert Frost above all other poets, and had fixed broken things all his life, making do with what was on hand, who had once landed an airplane using the wind against his open door to steer after the ailerons cable broke, who had delivered a dozen breech babies from the wombs of the animals on his father's farm, and who had undertaken to mend the life of a woman for whom misery itself was a comfort—Calmer looked at the hulking figure of Miss Sandway and punted. Some things could be fixed, some things couldn't.

These days Miss Sandway kept an office on the second floor that smelled strongly of canned fish, even from the hallway. She maintained her person like some contented hobo, folds of fat sacked into her worn, unwashed print dresses, old sweat lines stained into the armpits like age rings in trees, and was defiant of all authority save Dr. Baber himself. She had intimated to colleagues that she had been told she was in the running for his job.

Calmer sat a moment, ruminating on the oddness of it, the unwanted people who found their way into your kitchen, into your life. He got up, went into the utility room, and began sweeping up the glass, and tried but could not quite remember how the ball had moved when Spooner threw it.

———

At dinner, before a single fish stick had been poked, Spooner's mother announced that there would be no more baseball this year because of Spooner's D in English. The rules, she said, were the rules. Spooner looked up briefly, then back at his plate, feeling, among other things, a strange relief.

The fish sticks lay on a plate on the table, cooling, glistening, limper by the second, as appetizing as a pile of dicks. Moments passed, and in the end it was Phillip who spoke up. "That's ex post facto," he said.

Spooner looked up, thinking for a moment that his little brother had developed a speech impediment.

Spooner's mother had not come unprepared for arguments. "We all have to live by rules," she said. "What if your father decided he just didn't want to go to work? What if I decided I didn't feel like making dinner?"

Spooner looked at the fish sticks, considering that.

Phillip was five years old, always trying out something he'd just read. Now he said, "It's ex post facto if it wasn't against the law at the time." He looked up at Calmer, expecting to see him tickled to death, as he normally was when Phillip was showing it off. But Calmer hadn't seemed to hear what he said.

"It is not ex post facto," Spooner's mother said. "I studied Latin too, mister. We have to live in this community."

He said, "We can't live here if Warren plays baseball?" He was just learning sarcasm, and the tone was purely hers.

Then, even before she could warn him not to take that tone of voice with her, they all seemed to look across the table at once, and there was Darrow, his eyes brimming over with tears. Spooner looked at his brother and thought of all the little tortures he'd inflicted on this kid over the years. Thinking he couldn't remember the last time he'd seen him cry.

Calmer sat motionless and stunned. He had thought she'd agreed to let him talk it over with Sandway, to find out what had happened, and for a little while there was no sound in the kitchen save the scraping of Phillip's silverware against the plate. He had begun to eat after he'd staked his ex post facto claim. Five years old and ready for the debate team tomorrow.

Spooner's mother abruptly stood up. "Well," she said, "I don't seem to have much of an appetite," possibly laying the blame for the stricken

mood on those who might feel like eating, and headed off into the back
of the house, where all the years had come and gone and there was still
no addition.

And later that night—as Lily slept and Calmer, as always when these
things happened, could not sleep—later that night, it all came back to
him, Spooner taking in what she'd said almost as if it didn't matter, then
silence, then Phillip and his Latin—where had he picked that up?—and
then Darrow, Calmer's spitting image, sitting across the table, blinking
tears.

His spitting image.

———

Saturday broke clear and warm, a beautiful day for baseball, and without Spooner, the Golden Streaks lost to Thornton 19–1. The second loss
of the year.

THIRTY

No one but the participants themselves knows exactly what went on the next afternoon in the small office Miss Sandway shared these days—technically—with a mouse-gray chemistry teacher named Mr. Hinter.

Hinter was seventy-one years old and a groper of female students for as long as anybody at the school could remember. Complaints were first filed in the late 1960s, back when women's liberation started to catch on, and were handled quietly by Dr. Baber, who issued Hinter warnings and at the same time just managed to hide a smile at the old guy's spunk. Finally, after the lawyers took over the world and every other time the phone rang it was somebody threatening to sue the school district, Baber issued orders barring Mr. Hinter from entering the supply room with female students and, as further precaution, assigned him to share an office with Miss Sandway.

Miss Sandway had previously had the office to herself and resented the intrusion, and seeing Hinter's various bottles of cologne as he was moving in, threatened on the spot to break his fingers in the desk drawer if he ever even thought of getting frisky with her. Hinter, who did not know exactly what sort of behavior constituted friskiness, thereafter kept himself scarce.

Meaning that when Coach Tinker, still smarting from the beating the Golden Streaks had taken Saturday from Thornton High, called on Miss Sandway Monday afternoon to discuss Spooner's midterm grade, there were no eyewitnesses to what happened. Hinter was outside the office, waiting for her to leave so he could go in and retrieve his nasal spray, which he kept in his desk.

It was commonly known that Miss Sandway used this period after lunch to grade papers and polish off whatever was left of the package of Oreo cookies she bought each morning on the way to school, and it is easy to imagine the cookies were lying out in the open, exposed and vulnerable, when Tinker blundered in, uninvited, and might even have closed the door behind him. Not realizing perhaps that he'd just closed off the avenue of escape. This is a familiar and tragic pattern, of course, to forest rangers who investigate the killing of tourists by bears.

So the door closed and a moment later Hinter, who was waiting in the hallway, heard growling inside, distinctly heard growling, and then voices were raised, and there was crashing into walls, and glass broke and then the door flew open again and Tinker, red-faced and bleeding from scratch marks across his forehead, cords as thick as your fingers standing up in his neck, pointed back into the office and screamed, "If you were a man, I'd beat the hell out of you, buddy!"

———

Calmer came into the bedroom early that morning, before daybreak, and when Spooner first opened his eyes and saw him, knowing it was too early to get up, he thought for a moment that someone had died. Calmer was wearing the same expression last year, after the news arrived that one of his uncles had been killed trying to put his little Cessna down in the cow pasture at night.

Spooner sat up and Calmer touched his lips, not wanting to wake up Darrow, asleep in the upper bunk bed. He started to say something and then stopped. He hadn't shaved, which was the first thing he did in the morning, and it didn't look like he'd slept. He sat down on the foot of the bed a moment and gathered his thoughts. Then he patted Spooner's foot. "You go ahead and play baseball," he said.

Just those words, and then he got up and left. And Jesus knew what that cost him with her.

In the end, a letter was put in Miss Sandway's file, noting the assault on Coach Tinker, and Spooner got out of her survey of American
literature course with a C-plus, and graduated from high school with a
1.9 GPA and a 0.24 ERA, and was offered signing bonuses by both the
Cubs and the Cincinnati Reds. There were more spectators at the last
game he pitched than would show up later that month for graduation.
People filled the stands and sat five deep on blankets and lawn chairs
along both foul lines all the way to the fence. Behind the blankets, they
sat in their cars and on their cars, and they crowded next to each other
along the fence in the outfield, some waving school banners, some with
homemade signs, and cheered every pitch Spooner threw until he finally
gave up a hit, a cheap, soft liner over the shortstop's glove to start the
fifth inning.

Lemonkatz and his friends were there too, and pretty soon had an
area all to themselves near the left-field foul pole, and played their car
radios so loud nobody near them could hear the public address system,
and blew their horns and passed quart bottles of beer back and forth in
brown paper sacks.

The police were called, but Lemonkatz's father appeared from the
stands when they showed up and gave each of the officers his business
card and threatened to sue them personally for harassment.

There was some applause in the stands for that, and then Russell
Hodge fouled a liner right into the policemen's parked cruiser, and dented
the door, and the whole place went crazy.

A moment later Russell delivered one of his Howitzer shots reminis-
cent of the old Russell Hodge before he himself got dented, and it landed
fifty feet beyond all the cars and spectators and then disappeared into a
pile of pipes left over from the irrigation system the school had installed
the year before, and in the end that was all the Golden Streaks needed
and they won their twenty-second game of the season, 2–0, and a spot in
the regional finals.

As his last official act as principal, Dr. Baber presented Coach Evelyn Tinker with the Teacher of the Year Award during graduation.

"Coach Tinker has given our students and staff a transfusion of new school spirit and pride into the entire student body, encouraging even some of our marginal citizens into a healthy interest and respect for athletics . . ." And he continued on from there until half the place had dozed off.

The same wording showed up again later that summer, word for word, in the school board's press release announcing Coach Tinker's promotion to the position formerly held by Dr. Dean Baber, principal of Prairie Glen High.

The board hadn't told Calmer of Tinker's promotion ahead of time, had let him think it was his right up until the announcement in the *Mercury-News*, and a week or two later when the president of the board thought he'd had enough time to cool off, he called Calmer one evening to say that he knew he could count on him to continue his excellent work for the district and for the community. "As you know," he said, reading perhaps from a prepared text, "you, Calmer, are irreplaceable to us. And between you and I, this thing was a very close call. I want you to know—"

"Between you and me . . ." Calmer said.

The line went quiet. "Calmer?" Stallings said. "You still there, buddy?"

"Where else?"

"You were saying something, between you and I—"

"Me," Calmer said. "I said between you and me."

"Yes?"

"That's it. You and me."

The connection was broken and the president of the school board looked at the phone and then at his wife, who drank a little bit herself.

He said, "That was strange."

Four days later, there was a call from another school board, this one in a place called Falling Rapids, South Dakota, about a new high school, just under construction. Calmer had been there twice in the last eighteen months for interviews.

"The only stipulation we'd have," the man said, "is we'd need you as soon as possible."

The bonus offers Spooner got were all for more money than Calmer made in a year. Thirty-eight thousand dollars was the one he took, from the Cincinnati Reds. Spooner's mother was stunned at the figure and wandered around the house feeling purposeless for days, having hated rich people—all except the Kennedys—all her life. Spooner himself had a different feeling, as if he were being watched like a mouse in those first moments in the terrarium, before it sees the snake.

The check arrived special delivery, and Spooner opened the envelope and looked at the amount, thirty-eight thousand dollars and no cents, and was suddenly visited with the old feeling that he had been caught, and was suddenly and strangely reluctant to even touch it, did not want to accept the largest amount of money he'd ever seen or heard of, and tried handing it over to Calmer instead.

"Here," he said, "I don't need this."

Calmer said, "You hold on to your money. You can never tell when you might need it," and patted his hand, a strange gesture to interpret.

Still, Spooner could hear the South Dakota farmer in Calmer's words and remembered sitting with him at a gas station back in Milledgeville one cold January day on the way to school—Calmer had been out in the driveway in the dark at five-thirty that morning with a flashlight, still in his robe and slippers, trying to fix the car's heater and two hours later he sat behind the steering wheel in his uniform, his fingernails on one hand still black with crescents of grease, the windshield fogged over, sealing

them in, and stared at the coins in the palm of his hand, trying to decide if he should go back into the station over a nickel. Shortchanged a
nickel.

You can never tell when you might need it.

———————

In September Calmer and Spooner's mother and his two younger
brothers moved to South Dakota, and Spooner bought a three-year-old
Jeep and drove to Wichita, Kansas, to join the Reds' AA club, the Wing-
nuts. Early the following spring, he was sent to the Billings Mustangs to
work on his control, and there, six months shy of his nineteenth birthday
and demoted to the bullpen, he picked up a baseball one afternoon to
loosen his arm, and with that first easy toss, the most familiar and natural
motion of his life, shattered his elbow like so much glass. He heard it before he felt it, and when the feeling came, it came first as an instant of bewilderment, and then he saw what he felt, looked down at the underside
of the elbow where a shard of bone pressed up into his skin like a tent
pole and then, at the softest possible touch, the skin tore and the shard
sprung up, white and jagged, as if it were raising a point of order.

Calmer was there with him when he woke up after the first surgery.
There would be eight more surgeries before they gave up on making an
elbow of it again, and Calmer was always there when he woke up.

"It's good news," he said. "It was benign." And an instant later remembered himself and said, "Your momma sends her love."

PART FOUR

Philadelphia

THIRTY-ONE

Spooner came to the city on a train, in a snowstorm, a week before Christmas. He'd spent half his money on the one-way ticket from Florida, where everything he had except the dog and the clothes in the washing machine had gone up in fire. Regardless of all the places he'd been and was no longer welcome, and all the chances he'd had and blown, he was still surprised at these glimpses into the way things worked, at how little forgiveness was built in to the plans.

———

He had been sitting on the floor barefoot and naked on the afternoon of the fire, unemployed, on the outs with his wife, talking about the weather with his mongrel Harry. Harry had just come in out of the rain, as wet as new born and smelling like an army blanket, and they were watching the end of the storm through a screen door on the east side of a one-car garage that had been converted into a laundry room.

"Well, they say we need the rain," Spooner said.

Spooner would turn thirty later that fall; the dog would be three the same day. Gonad-wise, neither had been altered, although there had been attempts on them both. More than Spooner, Harry was streetwise, and could see trouble coming a mile away.

Just now he laid back his ears and slightly lifted the flaps covering his teeth. You could almost think he was smiling.

———

The tow truck driver appeared as a shadow in the screen door, shading his eyes as he leaned in to it to look inside. Spooner saw the hands first and thought of bat wings, of the possibility that he'd just stumbled across the greatest bat in the history of the South. Capture the bat, and the world will beat a path to your door.

Finally, a plan.

A face appeared, but Spooner couldn't tell that it was a face yet, at this point could only say in regard to what was on the other side of the screen that even if it wasn't a bat, it appeared to be carrying diseases.

"Mr. Spooner?"

The laundry room and the attached house belonged to the only friend Spooner had left in Florida in those days, with the exception of the mongrel next to him on the floor. Ever since the marriage broke up, the dog never left him alone more than a few minutes at a time. The friend came from eastern Tennessee and had once had a hillbilly band called Melancholy Panties, and a hit song the band was named for about going through a drawer full of heartbreaking panties, and in those days it seemed like every girl in the South wanted a ride on his bus. Now he was a newspaperman, and a good one, not bitter or used up, but he'd had his own band when he was twenty years old and the truth was that nothing since had much caught his attention.

How the friend had gotten here from there was a long story, and mostly about his wife. She had been one of the girls who took a ride on the bus but when the ride was over she'd refused to get off. Sometimes that's how it happens—one of them refuses to leave. Her name was Honey, and she was a woman now, and like so many women of Spooner's acquaintance, she'd looked at him one day and seemed to come all at once to her senses. It was always the same, like they'd wandered into a pet store and almost bought a monkey. There had been a load of them by now, these wives of his friends, women who gave off a certain playful, warm tenderness in his direction at first, as if Spooner were something she and her husband might share, and then one day froze over, with the smile still intact, and began watching every move he made and making notes for later, thinking perhaps that itemizing his faults would somehow arrest the Spoonerly leanings of her own husband. What button in them he pushed, Spooner never knew. It had been going on a long time, though. In Minneapolis, his own cousin's wife once broke into tears at the sight of him on the front porch.

Spooner got up, wrapped a towel around his waist, and stepped to the door. He didn't put on his tennis shoes because that was where his wallet and his money were stashed, and beyond that, both pairs of his socks were in the washer, and as far as the shoes themselves were concerned, he would as soon stick his bare feet in the septic tank.

These days the tennis shoes were it, vis-à-vis footwear.

"Good afternoon, sir," the driver said. He had a practiced bad-news voice that Spooner had heard before. "Conforming to state law, I am required to inform you of your rights."

Spooner waited to hear his rights, not optimistic. But now the man paused and seemed to lose his place, staring at the two raised, rootlike scars that grew in opposite directions from Spooner's elbow, a reminder of his career as a hurler of balls and eggs and rocks.

"You are entitled," he said, and tried to remember where he was, "you are entitled to remove any and all of your personal belongings from the impounded vehicle." Twice in his life Spooner had been given his Miranda rights, and both times it was a better reading than this. This was just words.

Spooner waited, but he and the repossessor of cars seemed to have hit an impasse.

"That's it?" Spooner said.

"Sir," the man said, "I'm just a cog in the machine." He was distracted by the scars, and trying not to stare. Spooner turned his palm right side up to give him a better look.

"It was a lightning strike," Spooner said.

The driver leaned closer. When you looked at the scars closely they were jagged, like the surgeon had used pinking shears, and you could see they didn't just meet at the elbow but crossed and then headed off in altered directions for half an inch or so, the skid left from a collision of slugs maybe. Spooner rarely looked at his elbow these days unless he was drinking, and then he would imagine the squeal of tiny suction cups, the little wet mouths forming horrified O's as the distance closed . . .

The driver's hands were enormous and hung a little low for a human, and there was more hair on either one than Spooner had left on his head. Seeing these hands, Spooner realized that the driver never could have played any musical instrument that required fingering. He didn't look like he could even play pool, unless there was someone else there to fish the balls out of the pockets. *You wonder how people end up in a job like this*, Spooner thought; *there is always a reason.* Spooner had empathy to a fault, perhaps had learned it from Calmer.

He followed the driver around to the front of the house, where his car and all his personal belongings were being repossessed, a particularly public repossession, it seemed to him, the butt end of his old Wankel-engine Mazda hanging from the cable at the end of the tow truck. The house address was 419 Palm Tree Way, and the smell of gasoline was everywhere.

"I would offer to assist you," the driver said, "but under state law, I cannot touch anything you own. Technically speaking, if you were to make a complaint, Tallahassee could pull my license."

Spooner did not move, except to retuck the towel around his waist. He was considering what things weighed, what could be carried. There was an ancient Underwood typewriter in the trunk and fifty pages of a story he was trying to write about a showdown back in Prairie Glen between his mother and Coach Tinker. He'd stalled on it after she'd given the coach until noon to pack up and leave. There was also a basketball and a box of books, and a few of the books mattered to him, and most of them didn't. The truth was, Spooner still wasn't much of a reader. There was also a high school yearbook from his sophomore year, with pictures of Margaret as homecoming queen and Dee Dee Victor as Miss Pep. For reasons he couldn't remember, he'd gone through it with scissors a long time ago and cut out all the pictures of himself, removing the evidence that he'd been there at all.

In the backseat were Coleman coolers of several different sizes and a

Sunbeam steam iron he had claimed from the big split-up, and nothing in the entire spectacle of his life—including standing barefoot and toweled in this patch of clover watching most of it being repossessed—was as ridiculous to him at this moment as carrying an iron around in his car all this time to impress her somehow that he had plans too. That this time he was going out into the world pressed.

"Sir?" the driver said. "Could we stay focused here?"

He was already running out of patience.

"I'm trying," Spooner said, "but it's not that easy."

The driver lifted his hand to look at his watch, which lay half buried in the hair of his wrist. And his *thumbs*. Had he been able to suck his thumb as a child? Had he choked up hairballs?

"Look," he said, "I'm trying to be polite, but I've got a pretty full day." It occurred to Spooner that the man might be angling for a tip. "So, cut to the chase. Do you want a hand getting your stuff out of there or not?"

Spooner spotted a pool of liquid beneath the car, winking blue and green with the changing light. The car had a leak somewhere in the gas tank that showed up at about six gallons, and instead of having it fixed he'd just gotten in the habit of putting in only a dollar's worth at a time. Spooner pointed at the puddle. "You know, that's coming from the car," he said.

But the driver wanted to cut to the chase, and knew a stall when he heard one. "The car is no longer your problem, sir," he said. "It is that simple. The only question is this: Do you or do you not want to remove your possessions?"

But it wasn't as simple as that. For one thing, the car also had mice. A litter had been born under the passenger seat sometime earlier in the week; the mother was nursing the babies and living herself off the spillage of Spooner and Harry's one meal of the day in the parking lot of Hamburger Heaven, a restaurant about a mile from the flophouse where they currently resided. Who would feed her if they took the car? Hamburger Heaven sat beneath a blue neon halo that was turned off every night exactly at ten. At ten-fifteen, a kid in a chef's hat and blue jeans would come out the back door and throw everything they hadn't sold that day into the dumpster, and every night Spooner and Harry ate there in the parking lot, in the quiet of the front seat, the food leaking out of both sides of the animal's mouth. He'd clean it up, though, even the crumbs, before he started on the next one. Once Harry had gagged, trying to swallow too much at once, and Spooner had ended up giving him a Heimlich maneuver to clean his air passage, and afterwards Harry cleaned up what he'd choked up, and then went back for another cheeseburger.

Spooner was living closer to the vest these days, now that he had no standing in the outside world, and looked forward all day to watching the dog eat. Harry preferred cheeseburgers to hamburgers but didn't care for pickles. Even swallowing the cheeseburgers whole—as he would the first two or three—even swallowing the wrapping paper, he would somehow sort out the pickles and leave them beside him on the seat, as whole and shiny as they'd come out of the jar.

Spooner had been hearing peeping noises for days whenever he started the engine. He supposed the babies connected the shaking to being nursed.

"You don't mind me offering a word of advice," the driver said, "from my experience? What gets people into this situation in the first place is indecision. Indecision and procrastination, those are the big two."

"What do you get for this, anyway?" Spooner said. "For repossessing a car." The driver looked at him in a different way but didn't answer the question. Spooner said, "I mean, do you work for the finance company, or do they hire you by the job?"

"I don't see where that's relevant to the situation." The repo man got his back up at the thought of somebody like Spooner poking around in his private business.

Spooner said, "I mean, if you got paid by the job, you might make more money just putting the car back on the ground and saying you couldn't find it." This was the wildest sort of bluff. Spooner had twenty-eight dollars lying in his tennis shoes on top of the washer. That and a

check for ninety-nine dollars from the gas station where he'd been working until last Tuesday was it. Net worth.

The driver shook his head as if he pitied Spooner, as if there was
no hope for him at all. "Jesus H. Christ," he said. "What world do you
people live in? You think I happened to be just driving by today and saw
your car? You think I keep some list of them in my head?"

Spooner glanced back at the house, noticing for the first time that
Honey's car was gone from the driveway. Realizing what had happened.
He didn't take it personally, although he did wonder if they paid her a
finding fee, or if it was only that she didn't want Spooner using her washer
and dryer anymore. He could understand that. She'd been referring to her
house as the commune in front of him quite a bit lately.

"It's out of my hands," the driver said. "Ethically, from the moment I
winch the wheels off the ground, it's out of my hands. Now, I repeat, do
you or do you not wish to unload your personal belongings?"

And that was the question, all right, and had been for eighteen months.
Spooner stood thinking it over. The driver gave up on him and climbed
into the cab of his truck. He started the engine and then edged forward,
over the curb, and as the car came over that same curb the undercarriage
scraped the cement, and then there was a sound like someone blowing
out a candle, and before the tow truck made the first cross street, the
Japanese-engineered, Wankel-engine Mazda had lit up like homecoming
at Texas A&M.

Spooner stood in his towel, watching, aware suddenly of the coolness
of the wet clover between his toes. The driver stopped beneath some palm
trees and jumped out of the cab, leaving his door open, and ran to the
back to unfasten the winch, and Spooner guessed that the truck belonged
to him and not the towing company.

Either way it was a kind of heroism you didn't see much anymore.

The fire was already too hot, though, and drove the driver back, and
he appeared from the dense black smoke with his arms clearly smoking
themselves and rubbed at the singed hair with his hands, oblivious to the
possibility of setting them on fire too, and above and behind him the

smoke rose into the palm trees that lined Palm Tree Way. Something was oozing up out of the car's trunk, about the consistency of pancake batter. The heat was amazing. Spooner thought of the mice—he thought for a moment he heard little cries from inside—and then a tree was on fire too. The driver was screaming at him—probably at him, he couldn't be sure—and from what Spooner could make of it, he wanted Spooner to call the fire department. It was almost as if he'd changed his mind about the car not being Spooner's concern.

Spooner and Harry stayed where they were, though, barefoot in the clover, spectators, like a couple of New Yorkers watching a mugging. Spooner in his towel, Harry looking like he'd just stepped out of the shower, and presently they turned away from the heat and looked at each other, wondering what they were going to do about supper.

THIRTY-TWO

Spooner by now was a newspaperman too. Not a good one, like his friend, or employed, like his friend, but still a newspaperman. It was not his most recent job—he had only that week turned in his dipstick rag at Ron's Belvedere Standard—but it had a more dignified sound than *gas pumper*, or for that matter *baby-picture salesman*, or *mail sorter* or *beer truck driver* (the stint as a beer truck driver in particular had not ended well), or anything else he'd done since he left baseball.

He'd begun his newspaper career walking home one day in August from his job in sales and he happened to pass the combined offices of the *Ft. Lauderdale News* and the *Sun-Sentinel* and saw what looked like a prairie of women in shallow skirts through the darkened window, many of them wearing white boots, and, reminded of the prairie, was strangely beckoned inside. Spooner had been to the prairie many times by now, on family vacations to Conde, South Dakota, and once had stepped through a cattle guard and broken his ankle, and afterwards would never understand how a whole herd of cattle could walk around all day without stepping into a cow guard or even a cow pie when he'd done both of those things in about fifteen minutes. He'd asked one of Calmer's uncles about it after they all got back from the hospital, a joyless old farmer sitting in a hundred-year-old chair next to the family organ, in a living room with as much stir to it as the attic except Spooner was sitting there right in the middle of things, disturbing the gloom with his new blinding-white cast. For Calmer's relations, dropping through a cattle guard and breaking a bone was no better than wasting food, and most of them had gone to bed right after supper, as if Spooner's carelessness were a personal affront.

The uncle looked over Spooner and his cast, perhaps estimating the lost days of work the injury represented—or would have represented if the boy had been his boy and known how to work.

He said, "Common sense, I expect."

And years passed by, and Spooner got taller and older and smarter but showed no improvement in regard to common sense and watching where he stepped, but every dog has his day, and on this day he stepped into the editorial offices of the *Ft. Lauderdale Sun-Sentinel* and fifteen minutes later he was a reporter.

———

The job at the *Sun-Sentinel* lasted two years. The managing editor had been a baseball player too, and a bonus baby, and had played seven years in the minor leagues. His name was Sloan, and he brought Spooner on board under the misapprehension that Spooner shared his love for the game.

The city editor was named Jerry Bunns and he had never played baseball and had no misapprehensions about Spooner at all. Very likely he recognized a natural enemy. Spooner was assigned to cover tomatoes, juvenile crime, the health department, the hospital district and all the county agencies receiving monies from the federal government to improve the plight of the poor, which the newspaper railed against on its editorial pages about three times a week. The city editor was perhaps already planning to have Spooner fired—nobody lasted long on the poverty beat, as the powerful voices at the newspaper were prone to confuse the messenger with the message—but had completely underestimated Spooner's ineptitude as a reporter of poverty programs, and mistaken his long, unbarbered hair for his politics, and Spooner's colossal indifference to both progressive politics and poverty programs shone through his prose like headlights in the fog, and the powerful voices of the newspaper mistook this indifference for subtle contempt, and in this way Spooner became, fleetingly, the darling of the staff.

In spite of that, nothing Spooner learned in Fort Lauderdale was what you could call useful in later life, even in regards to his continuing career in newspapers, although he did feel a certain prick of interest in the number of reporters who took offense at being called reporters, and insisted on being identified as staff writers or senior writers instead. From what Spooner could see, most of them were pretty good reporters—at least better reporters than he was—and from what he could see, none of them could be trusted in the vicinity of a thesaurus, especially when they were trying to flower things up. Some of them drank too much after work and threatened to write books.

The stranger thing, though, was that even those without ambitions to write for the ages were savagely protective of their prose. They were something like the parents of ugly babies in this respect and gathered nightly in a bar across the street to complain to each other about editors and editing, and could recite word for word changes in their lead paragraphs from six months past. In the way these things often went, changes were perceived as insults, and unlike everything else about newspapering, insults did not go out with tomorrow's trash but were stored and allowed to fester. Spooner sensed a story in all this festering, maybe even some recasting of his own story about Coach Tinker and his mother, but couldn't put his finger on where it would naturally lead.

As for ugly babies, Spooner could put his finger on that exactly. On the day he had passed the newspaper building and glanced inside, in fact, he was employed selling baby pictures door-to-door. Spooner's boss in the baby-portrait business was a clean-cut, low-living sort of human outcast named Stroop, who had found his niche in the world selling door-to-door, an occupation that not coincidentally limited his exposure to the outside world to thirty minutes or less per inhabitant. In the art of selling, Stroop often said, timing was everything, and in baby pictures the timed thirty-minute visit was the ticket to success. This was probably true—mothers with new babies are often on tight schedules—and especially true in Stroop's case, as at the moment one of these new mothers let him in the house, something was already stirring awake behind his dark, oddly-fitting sunglasses, and even as the cowhide brochures came out of the briefcase, the thing would be there in the room, a leering, foul, breathing presence that perhaps wanted breast milk too. Wanted its turn at the titty.

In half an hour mom would be looking around the room for a weapon.

Spooner had met Stroop in a conference room at the Holiday Inn on Flagler, where Spooner and two dozen other applicants who had answered a newspaper advertisement for a rewarding but unspecified career in sales had come for orientation. Stroop sat on a desk at the front of the room, wearing a suit and a nicely starched shirt, smiling confidently and saying not a single word until the whole room had fallen quiet. It was one of his selling techniques, possibly left over from his previous career at a company called Dare to be Great, where he often spoke to large groups of prospective employee/investors.

The room gradually settled into quiet, and then Stroop stood up, walked to the window, and pointed like somebody in a play out into the parking lot.

"That car," he said, "that white Lincoln Mark III out there is brand-new. I bought it last week. I'm not sure I like the color yet, but if I don't, I'll go get me another one next week."

Somebody said, "Fuck me," and got up and left, and this applicant was followed out two minutes later by another applicant, and then another, and another, then two at once, and exactly thirty minutes after Stroop had begun speaking, he and Spooner were the only people left in the conference room.

"You think I'm discouraged?" Stroop said after the last nine applicants had walked out together. "Not in the least."

The final exodus had come when he'd broken the news that it was baby pictures. Spooner did not comment on what Stroop said about not being discouraged, but he couldn't see any reason why he shouldn't be. Spooner himself was still here only out of habit. In theaters and airplanes and church—not that he had been on any planes lately, or in church since he left home—he always waited until the aisle cleared before he got up to leave.

Stroop said, "Can you guess *why* I'm not discouraged? Let's call this an aptitude test for the job."

Spooner saw this was probably an old habit, giving tests, laying traps. Holding out the carrot. They waited each other out a little while, and it was Stroop who finally broke.

"They're losers!" he said happily, as if Spooner himself had guessed the right answer. "I've got a new Lincoln to pay for; they're looking for jobs. I've got a blond girlfriend and a color television set and a dozen suits just like the one I'm wearing, and I didn't get all this wasting my time on losers."

Spooner had his doubts about the woman, but he was married to one and by now nothing that any of them took into her heart or head surprised him completely.

Presently, Stroop pulled some album brochures out of a worn leather briefcase and gave them to Spooner to take home and study. He also gave him a pamphlet, which he referred to repeatedly as the bible of the baby-picture industry. Stroop had apparently written and illustrated the pamphlet himself, a seven-page, stapled, mimeographed instruction sheet that included crudely drawn pictures of top-heavy young mothers with squalling babies. Spooner noticed the breasts first, which were disproportionately large and leaking milk, but on closer review saw that they were not in fact as disproportionately large as the young mothers' calves. All the mothers had massive, muscular calves.

Beneath the drawings were instructions: what to wear, when to smile, what to say when you first saw the baby, tricks to get in the door without seeming to come in the door. There was a set of responses he was supposed to memorize to overcome buyer reluctance. There was another set of responses—Stroop called them *bailouts*—if things were going badly. If, for instance, the person who answered the door was black, or if the baby had died. "You *will* run into that," Stroop said, loving the craziness of it all. "In this business you run into everything."

The next meeting Spooner had with Stroop was in the Lincoln, and the one after that was in Stroop's house, which was in a run-down section of Pompano Beach out near the racetrack. This was before Spooner had a car of his own, so he'd taken the bus. The baby-picture business wasn't going well, although by now Spooner was addicted to the smell of their heads.

Stroop answered the door smelling of sour milk, although Spooner hardly noticed, accustomed as he was by now to dairy-based odors at the front door. He took a seat at the table near the only window in the place. It was June in South Florida, and the plastic chair cover stuck against all the places it touched his skin.

Stroop got them iced tea out of the refrigerator—Spooner could see from where he sat that there was nothing else in it—and began to quiz him on situations presented in the bible of the baby-picture industry, reminding him again and again of his motto, which was *Buyers are liars*. Trying to figure out why Spooner wasn't closing any sales.

"What do you do, you're setting there, the baby goes red-faced and messes his diaper?" he asked. Spooner did not answer, and Stroop said, "Too late, it's got to be second nature. The answer is, you offer to change it yourself. They won't let you, you don't have to worry about that, but you make the offer."

Spooner stared at him and offered nothing back. He noticed that Stroop had tied knots in his shoelaces when they'd broken. The shoes themselves were wingtips, black and freshly shined.

"Let me tell you a story," Stroop said. "A true story. One of my salesmen went to a lady's house Thursday morning and sold her the whole package—a twenty-four-month contract with bimonthly sittings and the cowhide leather album—in fifteen minutes. How do you think he did that?"

"No idea." Spooner did not believe for a minute that Stroop had other salesmen.

"Concentrate. How did he do it?"

"No," Spooner said. "This isn't something I should concentrate on."

But Stroop hadn't gotten into a brand-new Lincoln by taking no for an answer. Persistence, as he said again and again, was what separated the winners from the losers. That and timing. Timing was everything, but then, so was persistence. It was how you made it in the world. Not just baby pictures, everything. And anyone could do it, that's what people didn't understand. They could be like Stroop himself if they'd just have persistence.

"He went to that baby like he couldn't help himself," Stroop said. "Picked it up, told the mother that when his associates saw the negatives of that child, they'd want to use it as a model for the company brochure. That she probably wouldn't have to pay for a thing, because this baby, her little baby, was so perfect. The company might even end up paying her."

Spooner had no more intention of telling anyone a story like that than of changing a stranger's diapers.

"It always works," Stroop said. "Sixty, seventy percent of the time. My salesman made two hundred and seventy dollars on that sale, and it could of been you."

Spooner did not react, but he pictured the look on Priscilla's face if he came in the door with two hundred and seventy dollars in his pocket. He was always picturing the look on Priscilla's face. He did not know yet that she had other plans.

"This girl had huge legs," Stroop said, polishing it a little. "Not fat, just muscular. Great big calves, the kind that can just crush your head." He made a crushing motion with his hands, as if this were a naturally appealing thing.

Spooner, it should be said, did not lack for sexual imagination, starting with his expulsion from kindergarten, but until he'd met Stroop the baby-picture salesman he had never thought in a sexual way of having his head crushed by a lactating woman with muscular calves. Stroop, he noticed, seemed to be working himself into a sweat as he continued the story. And then something strange. As Stroop spoke, he walked out of the kitchen and returned a few seconds later holding a cattle prod. A casual sort of thing, like he'd just picked up the cat. He pressed a button and the appliance made a purring sound, never interrupting the story of his salesman and the woman with the head-crushing calves.

Spooner was sure now of a few things. He was sure that Stroop didn't have any blond girlfriend. The Lincoln was a fact, the suits were still a possibility, although every time he'd seen Stroop, he was in the same one—he was wearing the pants with a T-shirt today—but there was no girlfriend, blond or otherwise. That much he knew.

Stroop looked fondly at the cattle prod. "What is the most money that you can imagine making?" he said. This was the same question he'd asked the assembled job applicants back at the Holiday Inn. Spooner guessed it might be something he also asked himself, to keep on track. "In one day," he said. "What's the most money you can imagine making in a day? The perfect day."

Spooner thought he was about to hear again about the time Stroop sold half a dozen twenty-four-month contracts in one afternoon. That was a story he loved so much that he told it pretty much every day, the way lovebirds were always telling each other they're in love.

"Perfect days," Spooner said, "I don't work."

"You know, I suppose I could let you have your weekly draw early," Stroop said. "I'm not supposed to; I'm supposed to hold it back four weeks."

Spooner was pretty sure by now he would never make a baby-picture sale, and the weekly draw only seemed fair. He'd been knocking on doors for two weeks and the closest he'd come was a woman sitting in a cloud of marijuana smoke who thought he was her dealer and tried to give him a twenty-dollar bill.

"Take your wife out to dinner," Stroop was saying, "come home and get a little of that pussy."

Spooner nodded, not liking the direction the conversation had taken, but at the same time not wanting Stroop to change his mind about the money. It was strange to be so hungry for seventy dollars. He never thought these days of his signing bonus or of where all that money had gone.

"You ever felt one of these?" Stroop said, turning the cattle prod off and then on again. And although he had been to South Dakota at least ten times, ridden a horse, fed chickens, picked flowers, and broken his ankle in a cattle grate, when it came to cattle themselves, Spooner had never touched one, much less a cow prod.

"It makes you feel sort of frisky," Stroop said.

THIRTY-THREE

He went back to Priscilla that night with seventy dollars in his pocket, a little queasy at the way Stroop's mouth came slightly open when Spooner allowed him to touch the cattle prod against the side of his neck. Spooner had the distinct feeling that he'd sold his body.

"You let him stick you with a cattle prod?" she said. "For seventy dollars?" All her worst suspicions confirmed.

Priscilla had been a nursing student when he met her. The meeting place was the emergency room at Deaconess Hospital in Billings, and he was still in his baseball uniform at the time, in spectacular pain, and she was standing right over his head, at the very edge of his vision, and was there as they examined his elbow, and was still there watching while the technicians maneuvered the arm for the first set of X-rays. The maneuvering for the X-rays caused the exposed bones to move, and brought forth soft, broken noises from inside the joint, and even in all this discomfort Spooner could see that he cut a pretty romantic figure, the young athlete maimed in his prime—not that he'd had a prime, but she didn't know that. The point was that right from the start she was attracted to pathos—you didn't become a nursing student for no reason at all—and of which he had been a prime example. He had thrown up the three helpings of Chinese noodles he had for breakfast and something that might have been a silverfish, although he'd have to check back with the restaurant about that, and without being instructed to by the real nurses, Priscilla took a cool washcloth and laid it on his forehead. Later, she would say it was love at first sight.

Still later, she would say it was no such thing.

She was there in the room the next day, along with Calmer, when Spooner woke from the first surgery, and there again after the second surgery, and the third.

But all that was old news now, and pathos and broken bones can take you only so far in a marriage, and then you have to do something to re-kindle the flame, and the truth was that Spooner wasn't sure he was up to it anymore. To get her back now he'd have to end up in a body cast.

———

In the end, she left him the same week of the cattle-prod incident—actually she told him he had to leave, since the house they were renting belonged to her cousin—and called it a trial separation. She got a job holding Slow, Men at Work signs at highway construction sites.

For his part, after the split-up Spooner found that he lacked whatever small confidence around women he'd previously enjoyed, and now was occasionally unable to even speak to them, thinking somehow that they'd all heard of his cattle prodding, or could sense it there in his character, and while this perhaps did not bode well for a door-to-door baby-picture salesman, it had no effect at all on his career in newspapers.

He hired on at the *Sun-Sentinel* and rented a tiny apartment across the street from a city park, and he and Harry moved in, sleeping together on a cot, and the refrigerator made a noise like he had a maid in the kitchen humming, and a month later Priscilla came over with a heavy-equipment operator she introduced as Garth Hodge, and told him that she and Garth were headed out West and she wanted to say good-bye to Harry.

Spooner said, "There's a coincidence. I once beaned a kid named Hodge," but there was no family connection.

Garth was also a sign holder, and even Spooner had to admit a fine-looking one, sign-holding muscles just popping out from under his shirt. They were both the color of Hawaiians. They were going to Texas, she said, where the highways were crumbling due to the corruption in the prison labor system, and between the corruption and theft and the pris-oner escapes, the legislature had voted to quit using prison labor entirely, and now the state had to replace all those murderers and rapists with civilians, so if Spooner wanted anything from the house, he had until the end of the week to get it.

Priscilla laid it all out in one long, breathless sentence, as if once the potholes started showing up in Texas the rest of it was inevitable. And even as she told Spooner that she was leaving, she absently draped her hand through Garth's forearm. Spooner noticed his tattoo, a purple likeness of himself, and beneath it his name, written in script: *Garth*.

Later, thinking of the visit, what Spooner always remembered first was that small, familiar gesture, her hand going through his arm. And he remembered the excitement. *Going to Texas.* Garth the sign holder was smiling but had his eye on Spooner every second. Spooner guessed that no matter what she'd told him about the seventy-dollar cattle prodding, that no matter how big his arms and shoulders and muscles were, he understood that you were never in control when somebody in the room had nothing to lose.

In the end, though, all Spooner did was pick up his basketball when she began to talk again and start to dribble, a slow, rhythmical dribbling on the carpet, and pretty soon, between the dribbling and the refrigerator noise, she couldn't hear herself think, and as she raised her voice to talk over the dribbling, he dribbled his way out the front door, down the wooden steps to the lawn, then onto the gravel driveway—you had to really pound the ball down to get it to come back to you in gravel—and then across the street to the park.

Before he'd crossed the street, he heard her inside talking to Garth. She said, "Now do you see what I mean?"

The dog went with Spooner, but he stayed in there with her a little while first, making up his mind. Spooner didn't know what he'd do if Harry decided to go to Texas too, and when he finally heard the animal coming, he stopped and looked back, tears welling up in his eyes, and there were clouds of dust hanging in the air about every four feet, everywhere the basketball had bounced. It had been a dry summer, if you didn't count humidity, none of the usual squalls or thunderstorms, and everywhere you went somebody was saying we needed rain. He thought he heard her laugh, but it could have been his own stomach, or the birds.

He shot baskets until it was too dark to see the rim, Harry running down the ball and trying to fuck it whenever Spooner missed, and Priscilla and her boyfriend were gone when he got back to his place. Two days later he went to the house and picked up his books, his Underwood typewriter, and the steam iron. Making sure she saw him take the iron. He told her good-bye, and then said good-bye to their other dog, the one she was taking with her to Texas—a sweet little terrier named Pork who had a taste for lizards.

Spooner didn't know himself very well yet and did not expect to recover.

THIRTY-FOUR

Philadelphia.

Spooner got off the train at the Thirtieth Street station and walked outside into twenty inches of snow. He was wearing tennis shoes and jeans and carrying two Winn-Dixie shopping bags full of clothing. He set the bags down in the parking lot and put on an extra shirt. The wind came up Market Street blowing newspapers and taco wrappings in front of it, and he thought of Harry, back in Florida with his friend and his friend's wife Honey until Spooner got himself established. He and the dog had been sleeping in the same bed for two years, and every time he'd jerked awake on the train, heading farther north, Spooner longed for the animal's smell and the feel of his bones.

He rented a room for twenty dollars a week on the third floor of a small, windy hotel at the corner of Nineteenth and Race. The shower was at the end of the hall, and the linoleum floor was warped where it met the walls and stuck to his bare feet when he made his way down the hall to shower and shave before work. Sometimes he found awful things in the toilet, and once one of the whores walked into his room while he was in the shower, tied his old tennis shoes together and dropped them over the telephone wires under Spooner's window. That morning he stuck his socks into his pants pocket and went shoe shopping barefoot.

On the good side, the place was as quiet as the Library of Congress in the morning—the hotel did its business at night, renting rooms by the hour—and he never had to wait to use the shower. The hardest thing was the morning cold. The building was owned by a family of Koreans who alternated shifts in the chair behind the front counter, night and day, sharing the same parka, and the Koreans did not turn on the heat until evening, when the girls began bringing in their dates.

———————

Spooner spent his evening hours those first few weeks in the bars along Pine Street—warm, crowded neighborhood bars, staying in the background and the smoke where no one would notice he wasn't buying anything to drink, watching the locals fall in love or break it off, sometimes disappearing hand in hand into the bathrooms. A drunk, weeping lawyer came in at the same time every evening and took the same stool at the bar, weeping, as far as Spooner could tell, because he was a drunk lawyer, and on the next stool was always the same frail hypochondriac giving the lawyer daily updates on her various conditions. It was possible she and the lawyer never heard a word each other said. Everywhere Spooner looked stories were playing out, and lives were reeling out and in, and even on the happiest, loudest nights, a quiet malignancy hung in the smoke and reminded him of family get-togethers back in Vincent Heights. The bars closed at two a.m., and he would walk back to the hotel in the cold, and by then business would be dropping off for the evening.

Once, reaching the third floor of the hotel at two-thirty in the morning, he encountered a handcuffed man in horn-rimmed glasses and diapers standing in the hallway, begging to be let back into the room. Spooner nodded as he went by and the man nodded back, as if they'd just passed in the street, and a moment later the man was back at the door but whispering now. "Please, Adrianna, this is too long. It's not funny anymore." And then Spooner heard her voice from the other side of the door, as cold as an empty fireplace, laughing.

The girls who used the hotel knew Spooner but also knew that anybody who had any money wouldn't be staying there longer than an hour and on the whole ignored him when they passed on the staircase. Still, Spooner thought about them constantly, ranking them sometimes, other times putting them into a sort of batting order in case they all came in at once to wish him Merry Christmas, but he kept these feelings to himself and never said much to any of them beyond hello and wouldn't have even if he'd had enough money to afford them. For reasons that made no sense, he was as married now as he'd been before his wife went off to Texas with the sign holder. Dear Jesus, the hours he spent trying to imagine why somebody would tattoo his name and face on his own arm.

Sex and warmth were constantly in his thoughts—he found himself thinking quite a bit these days that he'd like to take a shot at Fran of *Kukla, Fran and Ollie*—and once in a while when he was thinking of Fran, a sudden warm push of air came back to him, like a blown kiss, and then he would remember what it was, the Mazda going up in flames.

———

Philadelphia Newspapers, Inc. published two papers in the city and occupied most of the 400 block of North Broad Street, nine blocks from Spooner's hotel. He worked for the smaller paper, the *Daily News*, and arrived at the office on the seventh floor every morning in one of the three or four shirts he owned, all of them short-sleeved. When a comment was made on his clothes he would say that he was still cooling off from all those years in Florida. Sometimes he even opened the window near his desk.

These were the sorts of lies Spooner would tell all his life. He would as soon be caught naked in the hallway in handcuffs and a diaper as have anybody know that he didn't have enough money yet to buy a coat.

———

The paper itself was nothing like the paper he'd worked for in Florida, but editors were the same everywhere he went. They were all like his friends' wives: They liked him a little bit at first and then wanted him to go away. He had no way of knowing what he'd stumbled onto at the time—he was not a student of newspapers, had never been an intern or a copyboy or a city kid who grew up dreaming of his own byline—and there had even been a moment on the train ride up from Florida when he realized that this was how it could all end up for him, making his living as a spectator, and he'd come pretty close to getting off at the next stop and going back.

But then, in the way these things happen, one morning in that first spring in Philadelphia the elevator for reasons of its own ran past his regular floor and did not stop until it reached the fourteenth, opening into the waiting room of the complex of offices used by the paper's columnists, and onto the spectacle of Jimmy Lester, the *Daily News's* asthmatic gossip columnist, passed out and drooling on the waiting room couch, making rooting noises in his sleep, dressed in monogrammed silk pajamas and Italian loafers, his tiny plump hand wrapped around the handle of a machete. Jimmy had once attended a reception for Princess Grace of Monaco, gotten drunk and stepped on her dress—white dress, mud-ringed Italian loafers—as she stood in the reception line, and rebuked by the princess herself, remarked that back in the days when she was a movie star, Her Highness had blown everybody in Hollywood to get good parts, and moments later, as the princess's private security force was dragging him out, Jimmy had yelled words across the ballroom that would always strike Spooner as pretty much immortal: "Gracie, you've got no class and you never did." And even though Spooner still knew next to nothing about newspapers, and less than that about being a reporter, he had experienced a strange summoning when he heard that story, maybe what a homing pigeon feels on the way home, and now, presented with the legend in the flesh, the chubby, wet cheek pressed flat against the machete blade, he knew for the first time in his life that he was in the right place.

———

Spooner had been getting paid now regularly for several months and had moved out of the hotel into an apartment on Eighth Street just off Pine. The apartment had a fireplace and kitchen appliances. Spooner had brought in a mattress, a telephone, a boning knife with an eight-inch serrated blade, and a chair. He checked out a company car over the weekend and drove it to Florida, eighty miles an hour, down and back, and collected his dog. In Spooner's life, no human had ever been as glad to see him.

It was a homey spot, Harry and Spooner, the fireplace and the mattress, the telephone, but sometimes, particularly in the morning, Spooner was lonely. He brought women up once in a while, but it was harder getting them out than getting them in and he couldn't make up his mind what he wanted from them anyway. On the weekends there were calls from Priscilla, usually about money, and lately he couldn't make up his mind about what he wanted from her either. She'd gotten tired of holding road signs in Texas and was back in Florida these days, living with a tax lawyer, and off this news, he woke up one morning with his mouth full of dog hair, hungover and smelling of a different kind of smoke than he usually smelled of in the morning—which is to say real smoke, not barroom smoke—and, looking around, saw that he'd burned the chair in the fireplace, which more or less cut his furniture in half.

For a while Priscilla called every weekend, usually at night, always about money and divorce. The tax lawyer was under the impression that Spooner had accumulated some wealth during the trial separation, and wanted an inventory of his assets—Spooner at least, was giving her the benefit of the doubt regarding whose idea it was.

It was fifteen minutes into one of these calls when Spooner, trying to change the subject, said, "How's Pork?" and there followed a silence at the other end as she covered the receiver, presumably consulting the tax lawyer before she answered.

Presently she came back with a flattened tone that was familiar to him from the years they'd lived together. "We had to get rid of her," she said. Just like that. The next moment, strangely, Spooner couldn't hear. He wasn't deaf—the words were clear enough—but something had disconnected, and there was a sound in his head like breaking waves and then he looked around the apartment and couldn't remember the word for the refrigerator. "We're moving into a new place," she was saying, "and they don't take pets."

The line went quiet, and when he got himself back together he said,

"Where is she?" Thinking he could drive down again and pick her up too.

Pork, if you are interested in family sagas, was Harry's mother. She bore him no resemblance, though, and was almost perfectly round, a little balloon of an animal, which Spooner hoped had nothing to do with why Harry was always trying to fuck the basketball. He'd bought her for five dollars when he and Priscilla were first married and living on St. Ann's Street in New Orleans, brought her home on a bus under his shirt, no more than a pound or two, feeling her shaking the whole way.

"This is the part you aren't going to like," she said.

"I already don't like it."

"Well, I couldn't actually do it. We were taking her to the animal shelter, but I couldn't do it, so we just stopped and let her out beside the road."

Spooner hung up without another word, still unable to match the refrigerator to the word *refrigerator*, and the next day sent Priscilla a check for a few hundred dollars, which was all he had, all there was in his account, and then later that morning, gathering clothes for his regular visit to the laundromat, came across his boning knife in the sheets. The knife had been missing for a couple of weeks and presumed lost. It was the only utensil in the place and the only tool, and he used it to open cans and tighten screws and pick gravel out of the tread of his tennis shoes and cut the knots out of Harry's coat, and he held the knife in his hand a moment, as if he were sensing the balance, and then, glancing at the refrigerator and again unable to think of what it was called, he stabbed it. Stabbed the refrigerator and left the knife there, buried to the hilt, as a reminder.

Not that he needed one. For the rest of his life every time Spooner smelled Freon—an odor which you run into more frequently than you might imagine—he thought of the round little dog standing along some two-lane county highway, watching the car disappear. Other changes were that he could no longer keep ice cream in the apartment, and he quit thinking of himself as married.

THIRTY-FIVE

A woman came along now who was not the kind of woman who could be talked into leaving an old dog out beside the road. She showed up late one afternoon at the newspaper office, emerging from the elevator in jeans and a clean white shirt, talking apparently to someone still on the elevator, and while strangers wandered through the place all the time holding conversations with unseen parties, they were not ordinarily in clean shirts. Ordinarily when the elevator opened what came out was someone tilted way off the here and now—addicts of one kind or another, schizophrenics, community activists—some of them still without the laces that were taken from their shoes at the Round House. Murderers, as a class, were overrepresented—one visitor in thirty, forty?—and often came directly from the scene of the crime looking for the paper's famous columnist of African extraction, who would accompany them to the police station. At this time in Philadelphia, at least in certain neighborhoods of Philadelphia, there was a certain cachet to having this columnist walk you into the Round House after you had killed someone, and beyond the prestige there was the practical consideration that showing up with the press pretty much immunized you against a thumping at the hands of the police, at least any thumping that would show.

Which is all to say that every time the elevator stopped at floor number seven and the bell rang and the doors opened, an entire city room raised its eyes, all holding the same question: Is this person armed?

The woman who came off the elevator wasn't armed—this Spooner knew instinctively, just as he knew she could not be talked into abandoning an old dog by the side of the road. He would wonder later if these sorts of insights counted as love at first sight.

He gaped openly at the woman from his desk—he was on the telephone at the time or he would have gotten up and found some excuse to move close enough to sniff her—and not only wasn't she packing, her shoelaces were tied and she had hair that shone and an elegant bottom he could not stop picturing bouncing in a saddle, and in fact one evening twenty-five years later, sitting in a pretty good restaurant, he would fall out of his chair trying to kiss it as she walked by on her way to the bathroom.

But that is further down the road. For now, a summary of the romance: Spooner became habitual with the woman with the elegant bottom and took her out on romantic dates and one night set his hair on fire as he leaned over the candle on the table of another pretty good restaurant to kiss her, and she said she thought it would be all right if they skipped the flammable parts of the romance now and moved in together. Next they bought a little house on a shallow, clear lake in the New Jersey Pine Barrens, and got married in a bank and had a baby girl.

For the first time in his life Spooner found himself content to be where he was, although over time this would come at a price, the earliest sign being that sometimes he would catch some glimpse of Mrs. Spooner and the baby together and find himself barely able to move, at the fear of losing what he had. The truth was, Spooner wasn't wired much for getting what he wanted, and had never given a thought to protecting what he had, in fact had never considered that any of it could be protected or that it was even in his hands. Until the woman came along, and then the baby, he had always taken it for granted that anything that fell into his lap would also fall through his lap, sooner or later.

———

Jobs, for instance. Spooner ran again and again into the same problem at the places he worked, connected in some way to the matter of natural selection. That is to say that even though he was frequently willing to do his work and even sometimes to follow instructions, he had no idea how to go about behaving as if a supervisor's claim—not on his time, but on his person—did not run uphill of human nature. Which over the years had led to the loss of a dozen jobs or so—in and out of newspapers—all on the grounds of insubordination.

In Philadelphia, though, there were labor unions, and they were serious business here, and it was no easy matter to get rid of a reporter, particularly on the grounds of insubordination, which, aside from a broken typewriter, a few dents in company cars, and an incident at a staff chili party thrown to improve office morale, was really all management ever had to work with. And which wasn't nearly enough to fire him. In Philadelphia a formal case had to be presented, evidence gathered, files kept, written warnings issued, and in the first twenty-four months Spooner was in town, none of the three city editors who had set him in their sights had lasted long enough to do the job. Bitter world that it is, there was no union for city editors, and firing one of them was the easiest thing in the world.

Strangely, it never occurred to any of them simply to ask him to leave.

Further evidence that the world had swung Spooner's way: A new boss took over, and not only was the new boss unthreatened by Spooner, he didn't particularly want Spooner to go away. The man's name was Gilman, and he came in, looked around, and immediately took to bed—more accurately, took to the davenport that sat against the rear wall of his office. He was a tall, elegant, accident-prone man—each of these traits unusual in newspaper editors who make it to the top—whose small physical calamities (Spooner had never seen an adult actually kick over and then step into a trash can before) perhaps hinted at the arguments he had going on all the time in his head. Gilman liked a cool, wet towel over his eyes when he argued with himself, and an ashtray on his stomach so that he could chain-smoke in the dark, lighting one cigarette off the stub of the other, although in this configuration he occasionally set fire to himself or his couch.

But then the man had a lot on his mind. Gilman was a gentle, instinctively reasonable human being who one day of his own free will gave up a comfortable, respected, midsized newspaper in New Jersey to take over what was probably the least comfortable newspaper in the world, at least for the editor who had to run it. On his arrival, half the city room was planning mutiny. There were late-night raids into management files in which letters warning and reprimanding the reporting staff disappeared, and embarrassing evaluations of various middle management showed up in the morning on bulletin boards all over the building. There were daily shouting matches in the city room and threats, one day a fistfight, the next day an eighty-five-year-old staff photographer showing up at a national convention of inner-city housing directors, asking if this was the place he was supposed to come to take pictures of the *jitterbugs*.

Six calendar days after Gilman's arrival, the grandson and namesake of the owner of the newspaper chain that owned the *Daily News*, the heir apparent who had been sent to Philadelphia for seasoning, was shot in the gizzard with his own spear gun during a one-night romance with a boy whore and died on the floor of his elegant Rittenhouse Square apartment. A week after that, two of the paper's columnists—one of whom had a short-lived radio show—got drunk on the air and welcomed Gilman to Philadelphia, assuring him that the time he'd served at Joliet state prison for child molestation would not be held against him by the staff. Another columnist lent a company car to a woman he met in a stripper's bar, who lent it to her boyfriend, who used the automobile, a four-door Chevy Citation, in a series of convenience store robberies over the following week, at least some of which were recorded—robber, vehicle, and license plates—by security cameras. "Vehicle in 7-Eleven Robberies Traced to *Daily News*," ran the headlines in the *Evening Bulletin*.

The incidents kept rolling in endlessly, like the tide. New problems, old problems, a catastrophe a day, and Gilman would fix one and a new one would take its place, and all the while a line formed outside his office door—copyboys on up—waiting to make some pitch for attention, to get in on the bottom floor with the new boss. At the front of this line was Howard Buckle, the city editor and Spooner's direct supervisor, the giver of chili parties to improve staff morale.

At this time Buckle was still operating under a management system called specific performance incentives, and one of his specific performances was supposed to be the removal of Spooner from the *Daily News*. Buckle was not the first city editor who'd been given this incentive, but he worked at it harder than the other ones had, and over time the resulting frustration brought out a certain pettiness in him—perhaps in them both—that turned more bitter and personal by the day. Buckle now kept notes on everything from Spooner's messy desk to his unusual work habits to his abuse of company cars to his acts of disrespect and, yes, naked insubordination. And yes, there was the night of the chili scare, but before that there had been the alleged death threat, which occurred after Buckle inserted a readers' poll into a maudlin piece Spooner was assigned to write about a comatose young skateboarder in suburban New Jersey asking readers to vote on pulling the plug on the respirator that was keeping him alive. Yes, no, undecided.

This being very close to the smarmiest thing he'd seen Buckle do yet, Spooner went to the city editor and congratulated him on his neat desk, and in the course of this conversation said, "If anybody should get his plug pulled around here, it's not the kid who fell off his skateboard." Which Buckle interpreted as a threat to his life.

Then Spooner, whose name was attached to the story and the poll, walked into the city room and picked up the first typewriter he saw, which as it happened was being used by poor Delores Schultz to take notes from the Round House, and threw it at the floor—not out the window, as it is often claimed—loosing a pain in his throwing arm the likes of which he had not felt since the night in Billings, Montana, when he allowed X-ray technicians to manipulate it back and forth to take its picture. Certain factions in the city room stood and applauded, but Delores fell to pieces, bending over into her handkerchief making terrible squealing noises, and then turned violently on Spooner, baring teeth and nails and a hideously runny nose when he tried to touch her shoulder to assure her that he would take the blame.

Spooner backed away from her slowly, fascinated at the transformation, and a day later found her sitting back at her desk near the door, still crying. In the end, it developed that she'd snapped, and afterwards, even after she was given the city hall beat, which, with the exception of an occasional fistfight in city council meetings, was rarely violent, she would still sit at her desk and sob. Much later, Spooner heard that the sobbing went on twenty years, right up to and then through her retirement party.

The typewriter incident did not just go away, of course. Howard Buckle put another letter of reprimand in Spooner's file, and for his part, Spooner filed a letter of complaint to company headquarters in Miami, accusing the city editor of molesting comatose children. Everyone except Delores had a wonderful time, and grudges were set in cement.

So it surprised nobody when, only ten days after Gilman arrived in Philadelphia and on the day of the heir-apparent's funeral, Howard Buckle went into Gilman's office to engineer Spooner's departure. Ordering the hit, as they called it in the newsroom. By now, the city editor's file on Spooner weighed several pounds, and he took it with him, perhaps, in addition to getting rid of Spooner, to impress Gilman with his own work ethic, as the managing editor Gilman had inherited from the previous regime—this being the job just above city editor—had been invited to leave almost as soon as Gilman arrived.

And now Gilman sat quietly as Buckle described Spooner's poor work habits, his abuse of company cars, his disrespectful manner, the broken typewriter—leaving out the part about the kid who fell off his skateboard—his cheekiness, his negative influence on office morale . . .

"Wait a minute," Gilman said. "Cheekiness?"

"Ask anybody of his supervisors, they'll all tell you the same thing."

Gilman nodded and Howard Buckle picked up where he'd left off. Presently, Gilman put a cool washcloth over his eyes and lay down, and taking this signal the wrong way, Buckle ventured into practical problems of firing a member of the Newspaper Guild, and the tactics he was employing to get around the rules. And Gilman lay on his davenport, listening, thinking, his feet hanging off the far armrest, smoking Virginia Slim cigarettes, and when Buckle finally stopped, Gilman thanked him for coming in and told him he was fired.

The new boss, it developed, detested stoolies, which as far as Spooner knew was not only unusual but unprecedented in the history of bosses, particularly the bosses of newspapers.

THIRTY-SIX

Gilman picked his new city editor from the ranks, a city hall reporter named Stradivarius, and a month later promoted him again, this time to managing editor, and soon came to depend on and love this Stradivarius like his own son, and for that reason more than any other reason also promoted Spooner, giving him a column and an office on the fourteenth floor, where he would not be in Stradivarius's hair or even his line of sight.

Gilman was lying on the davenport with his eyes covered when he called Spooner in to inform him of the change. A cigarette was going in the ashtray on his stomach. "Nine hundred words," he said, "three times a week. That's it." Yes, Gilman loved the lost causes, and yes, Spooner saw the connection, but took no offense. You might even say that he loved Gilman back.

"Now," he said to Spooner, not unkindly but pointing in the direction of the window (had he meant to point toward the door?), "please get the fuck out of my office."

In the years ahead, as they grew more and more familiar, this phrase would become a kind of code between Gilman and Spooner, meaning more or less that Spooner should get the fuck out of Gilman's office, and Spooner, for reasons unknown, never received these words without a feeling of wild affection for his boss, and never left the man's office without thinking that someday, when he had the money, he would find a way to repay Gilman, maybe buy him his own jockey.

Much later on the day of the promotion there was a phone call from

South Dakota. Ten minutes before Spooner and the dog and the woman with the elegant behind had returned home from a remote spot in the Pine Barrens where they'd drunk several bottles of iced Boone's Farm apple wine to celebrate Spooner's new column, and by now had showered and put calamine lotion on the two hundred or so chigger bites they'd collected rolling around in the grass and pine needles, and Spooner picked up the phone, still naked, as the calamine hadn't dried yet, catching his reflection in the big window at the back of the house, and stared at the image a moment—he did not look good freshly plucked—and even as he stared his mother's voice was in his ear, telling him that Calmer had just gotten himself fired.

That was how she put it, *gotten himself fired.*

THIRTY-SEVEN

He was not so much fired, though, as demoted. Calmer had been principal of the new high school in Falling Rapids, South Dakota, for six years and then was asked to take over as assistant superintendent, a step away from running the whole show. The man he was asked to replace, out of jail on his own recognizance, had disappeared a month before his trial and was never caught, taking at least four hundred and ten thousand dollars of the school district's money with him.

In Falling Rapids the wiseacres said, *And they say there's no money in teaching,* and voters swore that no bond issue for the schools would pass till pigs flew and hell froze over, which in Falling Rapids meant a long time.

The house they bought sat on a homey little street canopied with elm trees, a block from the oldest park in the city, and was roomy enough so there wasn't any more talk about additions. When Spooner's mother complained about the house these days, it was in regard to how she was supposed to keep it all clean. She wanted a part-time maid.

The woman directly across the street had a maid, possibly the only black face ever seen on Ninth Avenue in Falling Rapids. The woman's house was bigger than Lily's, with a bigger lawn and bigger trees, and her husband was the superintendent of schools, the man who had set Calmer up and demoted him to a classroom at Toebox Junior High, which is what Spooner's mother had meant when she said Calmer had gotten himself fired.

Dr. C. Merle Cowhurl, Ed.D.

Can the world ever have enough doctors of education?

Spooner flew out to South Dakota and stopped at a store on the way from the airport for a bottle of Johnnie Walker Black. Calmer would never buy good Scotch for himself, and they put away most of the bottle that night, sitting at the kitchen table, and Spooner's mother came out of the bedroom at hourly intervals to fill her water glass and then squint at the clock. She wore an old robe with Kleenex stuffed into the pockets, and covered her mouth with her hand, not to offend anyone with her sleep breath. All her sisters did that, one of the tricks of the trade they'd picked up learning to be ladies in the grand old house in Milledgeville.

"Are you two going to stay up all night?"

"I'll be in in a little while, my love," he said. He'd called her *my love* since the day she accepted his proposal of marriage, all those years ago, and all those years ago she had stopped hearing it.

Around midnight, Calmer went to the sink and made drinks—he used a shot glass to measure, something in his nature wanting the exact amount—and with his back turned, affording him at least that bit of privacy, Spooner asked what had happened.

Calmer didn't answer at first. He brought the drinks back to the table and sat down. Spooner saw that the whole thing was too big for Calmer to get hold of now, that he didn't know where to start. Spooner was familiar with the feeling.

Calmer rubbed his eyes and considered his drink. He remembered something then and reached over the drink for an old copy of the *New Yorker* magazine lying behind the salt and pepper shakers, and the heel of his hand bumped the rim of the glass and spilled it over. Calmer made no move to catch the glass, did not even set it upright on the table. He did pick up the magazine to keep it from getting soaked, and watched the ice cubes drop off the table one by one, and pretty soon what was left of the drink pooled and began to drip through the crack where the two sides of the table fit together.

He smiled at Spooner and shrugged, as if the spill were the explanation. Spooner got up and made another drink and then looked out the kitchen window and thought of Calmer stepping out his front door every morning to pick up the newspaper, and every morning glancing across the street at the house where Cowhurl lived.

"You know," Spooner said, "if you ever needed help . . ." and then stopped, not knowing how to finish it.

Calmer continued to look at the spilled drink, or perhaps at his hands, one closed and resting in the palm of the other. "We're all right," he said. "You hold on to your money; you've got a family of your own now." Although at this point, the baby was still on the way.

Calmer hadn't mentioned it at home yet, but he'd taken a second job, common labor on a construction site, starting Monday. A man at the very end of middle age, headed out into the heat of a South Dakota summer.

Spooner set the drink on the table and sat back down. He felt unconnected to the years he had spent poor—could not quite remember what it was like to let a man touch his neck with a cattle prod for seventy dollars, or the feel of the flophouses he had lived in, in cities all over the country, the winter he'd spent in Minneapolis pushing cars up the hill outside his rooming house for tips when it snowed, and the week it didn't snow and there was nothing to eat—seven days without even a piece of gum—all that could have been someone else. With one exception, now that he thought about it. There was a morning in New Orleans when he'd killed a pigeon in Jackson Square, chased it down and squashed it with a brick in front of a tour group of Orientals, some of whom had taken photographs, and carried it back to his rooming house to eat. He cleaned the bird and plucked it and boiled what was left, feet and all. He expected there was more meat on a human head.

Even now the picture of that gray, naked, waterlogged creature steaming on a paper plate floated up to him at unexpected times, still sporting little patches of feathers—like someone who'd shaved in a hurry—still attached to its feet.

Across the table Calmer smiled at nothing in particular and said, "We'll be fine. Onward and upward."

Onward and upward, he had been saying that a long time too, as long as Spooner could remember.

Spooner's mother came into the kitchen a little before two, checking the clock, holding her hand over her mouth. Calmer got up when he heard her in the hallway and began cleaning up the spilled drink. "We were just talking about the addition to Warren's family," he said.

But even with all the years that had passed since Prairie Glen, *addition* was not a safe word to use around Spooner's mother.

She looked at Calmer more closely and saw that he wasn't feeling as bad about being fired as he had been before, which wasn't what she'd come out into the kitchen expecting to see. Not at two o'clock in the morning. She eyed the drinks next and said, "Well, I just hope you're both around long enough to see it graduate from high school."

The house creaked and settled, and in a little while Calmer opened the *New Yorker* to the story he'd been meaning to point out, a pitch-perfect John Cheever story about a man who decides to swim home one night to his house in the suburbs, one neighbor's pool after another.

Calmer pushed the open magazine across the table and stood up, stared a moment toward the back of the house, collecting himself, and hitched up his pajama bottoms and headed back in there to meet his fate. Yes, the man would face the music.

THIRTY-EIGHT

When Spooner came home to South Dakota again, it was late September, and Calmer was helpless.

"I don't know what's going on with him now," she'd said on the phone. As if a breakdown were some harebrained idea he'd read about in the paper and decided to try for himself.

Spooner found him in the bedroom, still in his pajamas, pressed into the wall at the far side of the bed. Embarrassed to be seen in this condition; barely able to talk. He smiled, trying to get something out. "Everything just stopped," he said.

Spooner went upstairs to shower. His brothers were already home, their suitcases lying on top of the bunk beds in the larger bedroom. Darrow had come from Chicago, Phillip from New Haven, where he was starting his second year at Yale.

The upstairs bedrooms were full of trophies. Phillip was the defending chess champion of the five-state region, a title he'd held since sixth grade. In high school he'd been captain of the state-champion debate team. There was a picture of the debate team from his senior year on the wall, and the coach had written, *For Phillip, the <u>best</u> debater I ever had. Good luck at Yale! Mr. Heater.*

Spooner hadn't kept anything like that himself—now that he thought about it, he didn't have anything like that to keep—but had never been much for trophies anyway. He imagined one for trespassing and wondered if he'd been as good at that as Phillip was at chess or debate. As Calmer said, each to his own.

It was warm for late September, and after dinner Spooner and his brothers sat outside in the driveway on lawn chairs and Spooner made them fresh screwdrivers. Spooner's mother had gone to bed with the sun still in the sky. Asthma.

Presently he felt the beginnings of a cramp crawling up the inside of his thigh and realized he'd been sitting quietly for some time, holding the frost-cold bottle of vodka between his thighs, gradually drifting off to a slightly less conscious state of consciousness, imagining Dr. Cowhurl coming out of his house and crossing the street to express his concern and best wishes. It rang true, exactly the sort of thing that this sort of big wheel did, on a whim, subsequent to squashing an underling. Maybe offer to shake hands, tell the boys it was never personal, or that he hoped there were no hard feelings. The South Dakota version of Chicken Man Testa's appearance at Angelo Bruno's funeral, everybody in South Philadelphia knowing who ordered the hit.

Spooner got up and stamped his foot, trying to stretch the muscle before it knotted up, and the story started over with Cowhurl crossing the street again, and he was suddenly disgusted with himself, knowing that all he would do if Cowhurl came over was send him home. He set the vodka bottle down on the driveway and went in the house for an egg.

It was the first thing he'd thrown in maybe fifteen years, and the elbow began to tear at the instant his hand began to move forward. There was a small noise, about like the first kernel of popcorn popping in a covered pan, and a moment later the egg lay wet and glistening in the grass—it had not even made it to the street—and Spooner lay in the grass too, glistening with sweat, wondering if the whole mechanism they'd assembled in his elbow had come apart.

Presently he looked at the elbow, tried opening and closing the hinge. It was already swelling but nothing rattled inside and nothing poked

through the skin, and he sat up in the grass, wondering if time had completely passed him by. Not just the elbow but Spooner himself, the whole
idea of Spooner. If the whole idea of throwing an egg at your neighbor's
house had no meaning anymore, even if you still had the arm to get it
there. He wondered if the injury might at least in some way demonstrate
to Calmer how much he loved him.

And then realized, suddenly, that Calmer was watching. The sun was
murder at this time of the afternoon, blinding Spooner as he looked
up toward the kitchen window, which he could see was open behind the
screen. There was a slightly darker shape toward the middle of the screen,
indistinct; it could have been a stain. Calmer standing at the sink behind
the open window.

"The plan," Spooner said to Darrow, "was I throw eggs at his house
to lure him over, and then you make him feel academically inadequate."
When cornered, Darrow had in the past left the occasional academic
wishing he'd inflicted his advanced mind on a different dinner table.

Spooner looked at Phillip then and saw that he'd left him out of the
plan. Phillip had been out in the world a year or so and was still getting
used to it, an insult at a time. Spooner didn't know but thought that
Yale was probably a place where nobody cared that you had been a child
prodigy. Likely the school was full of those, children of *singular intelligence*—as they used to call it back when Spooner was in school and they
were talking about Margaret—who showed up at Yale or Harvard and
overnight weren't singular anymore at all. Disarmed prodigies, you might
say, left to fend for themselves, to find something besides their brains to
set them apart, which would be Phillip's situation more than most. He'd
never spent any time with people his own age; how was he supposed to
know where he fit?

Spooner turned to him now, as if Phillip had been the key to the plan
all along. "And in the meantime," he said, "you run across the street and
fuck his wife."

Phillip was quiet a moment. Had Spooner insulted him?

"You know," Phillip said finally, thoughtfully—and who could say if this was something he'd picked up in his years as a champion debater or something he'd picked up from Calmer?—"we haven't heard both sides of the story yet. We haven't heard the other side of it at all."

And Spooner looked back up at the kitchen window, but the dark shape in the screen was gone.

THIRTY-NINE

Four years after Spooner arrived in Philadelphia, cold and hungry and broke, another pilgrim from the southern climes got off the train at the Thirtieth Street station in much the same condition. His name, unfortunately enough, was Stanley Faint, and he was in many ways even more out of place in the city than Spooner had been.

Then again, in other ways he was already at home. Stanley Faint was a prizefighter, and Philadelphia was the place for that. There were hundreds of boxing gyms in the city's neighborhoods, and even winos brawling in the street threw jabs and hooks and butted each other in the clinches. Stanley loved the gyms and the streets and the winos. He loved hitting and being hit, he loved public adoration.

And loved his public. The adoration was not a one-way street, at least, and his fans became his friends, and he often took some miserable example of the human race under wing and set him up in business. As a heavyweight contender, he made money suddenly and in huge amounts, and financed more bars, quarter horses, dojos, dancing halls, pool halls, churches and hardware stores than he could keep track of, and if the money he lent never came back to him, which it did not, nothing about that surprised him at all. To Stanley such was the nature of business and money, and nothing about it mattered to him anyway.

In spite of this monumental indifference to matters of finance, however, Stanley was regarded in the boxing world as *hungry*, a quality familiar among young fighters making their way up out of poverty. Stanley Faint was hungry another way, something like the way you are hungry when you first step into the street after a month in the hospital, when you want to see and smell and taste the world again all at once. There was no greediness about him, no hint of the meanness that usually went with being *hungry*, even in the ring, and in this way he was more like an old fighter than the young fighter he was, the old ones—most of them anyway—having achieved a certain serenity that comes in life when there is nothing left to prove.

Which is all to say that Stanley was a complicated human being, and for that reason Spooner was a long time coming to understand that he did not fight for complicated reasons. Oh, they talked it over, but it wasn't about growing up without a father—like Spooner's father, Stanley's had died early on—or some mystical awareness of who he was coming over him in the ring, nothing like that at all. The reason Stanley fought was that it was easier than working for a living and so far it was what he did best.

Even at this early stage of his career, Stanley had been hit quite a bit, although he'd never been tipped over. But even Spooner, his greatest supporter, admitted that for a practitioner of the art of self-defense, Stanley had a curious indifference to the subject of defense. Until now, he'd fought his fights in states like New Mexico and Oklahoma and Arkansas, against the kind of fighters that came from places like that, which is to say fighters who couldn't fight much, but were still big, rough, scary-looking people with scars and missing teeth—no one whose usage you might correct in a barroom—and most of them were low hitters and head-butters and not disinclined to use their thumbs and elbows, as fighters who can't fight much often are. Stanley did not hold bad sportsmanship against them though, understanding, as he put it, that we all do the best we can with the tools we are given to work with. And he knocked them out, one after another, beginning with an eighteen-second, one-punch dusting of a 280-pound Mexican oil rigger, for which Stanley and the Mexican made a hundred dollars each, and spent together that night in a bar. But the opponents, like the money, were in some way beside the point.

The point was simply that Stanley woke up one day with an egg in his nest—an egg in his nest as opposed to a nest egg—and determined to sit on it for as long as it took to hatch. This required a kind of faith that someone like Spooner, full of self-doubt, both admired and could not begin to understand. It was in some way the underpinning of the friendship—Spooner not only unsure of himself as a novelist, but at the bottom of things not even sure he was good enough to write a column for the *Daily News*, and Stanley believing heart and soul that he was the next heavyweight champion of the world. It struck them both as humorous.

Previous to departing Texas, Stanley had signed a contract with a third-rank fight promoter who paid for his ticket north and gave him a few hundred dollars a month toward living expenses. It wasn't much of a contract, but from the beginning Stanley signed contracts the way movie stars signed autographs, paying exactly that much attention to what was on the paper. He contemplated no trouble when it was time to go another way, as they said in the business world, and smiled tolerantly at his pro bono lawyer's warning that the pen was mightier than the sword.

He settled in to a section of town with a depressed housing market, as he called it, and socialized at night in the local clubs and ran for an hour or two in the morning and trained in the afternoon at Joe Frazier's gym on North Broad Street, where five or six world-ranked heavyweights were also in residence. Stanley was thrown in with these fighters from the first day, and it is possible that in the history of the democracy no citizen has ever had his nose broken by so many different people in one week. He ate dinner in those early days with cotton packed into his nostrils, and leaked blood as he ate, and occasionally shot a blood-soaked ball of gauze across the table when he brayed, a terrifying noise to the uninitiated which, perhaps due to Stanley's peculiar wiring and social skills, did not always seem to fit the situation.

A month or two after he arrived, word made its way back to Texas that Stanley's progress had slowed owing to his not being able to breathe, and the promoter himself flew up to supervise his medical treatment, taking

him to a friend in West Philadelphia who happened to be a veterinarian—
not the last time Stanley would be worked on by a vet—and who removed
all the various pieces of broken cartilage from his nose, filled the cavities
with gauze, and had him back in the gym the next afternoon.

It was Stanley's slant on the human condition that a visit to the veterinarian for a nose job was an amusement, and likewise living in an apartment without heat or a lock on the front door was an amusement, as
were the needles and syringes and scalded spoons, ladies' dainties, used
condoms, etc. that he sometimes found in and around his kitchen sink.
It was a mystery to him, what sort of people would come into a strange
house and fuck in a kitchen sink—not to mention what sort of people
could fuck in a kitchen sink—and even tried it himself once or twice, but
more comfortable than that was being punched in the face back at Joe
Frazier's gym.

Strangely enough, especially considering the jaded nature of the fighting public in general and in Philadelphia in particular, Stanley developed
a following in the city very early in his career. The following was an odd
collection of women, some of whom would happily try it in the sink,
and an odd collection of friends. He was never short of friends and
women, except at Frazier's gym, where there were no women, and his
peers—as Stanley referred to the other fighters—had begun to sense that
the poundings he was taking were not discouraging him, as they were
intended to, but were, like everything else at the time, amusements. And
in this happy frame of mind, Stanley was learning, and slowly narrowing
the gap. Understandably, the peers found this insulting.

FORTY

It is not a well-known fact, but the last time anybody remembers seeing her upright and under her own power, Margaret Truman was in the vicinity of Spooner and Stanley Faint. It could be said that this was the day they all met, except Margaret did not say as much as howdy-do to Spooner and left without exchanging a single pleasantry with Stanley. This in spite of the fact that Stanley and Spooner had both rearranged their social schedules to fit her in.

Still, it could be said that Margaret Truman brought them together— Spooner and Stanley Faint—and this meeting occurred not in some bar or after Stanley had flattened someone in Atlantic City or Las Vegas, but at a fifty-dollar-a-plate literary luncheon sponsored annually by the *Philadelphia Inquirer* and held in the grand ballroom of the Sheridan Hotel on Market Street in Center City. A frontal system had moved in that morning from the south, and the grand ballroom was standing-room-only and smelled like a Mississippi terrarium—a certain sweet mildew that Spooner had noticed before at gatherings of aged women. Chairs were set up for a thousand of them that day, fourteen to a table, and every seat was taken, with the exception of a single table on the left side down in front, which was surrounded by chairs recently vacated, left out of true with the table settings, napkins tossed into plates or on the floor, a few glasses of water with lipstick-blotted rims, all emanating a feeling to Spooner, sitting above the table at the dais at the end of the room, of a bird nest ravaged by a cat.

Sitting alone in this nest was a large, freely perspiring man in jogging pants and a sweatshirt that read I'M ON THE RAG, but who somehow, in spite of the jogging shoes and the jogging togs, didn't look like a jogger.

But live and learn. Until fifteen minutes before, the specimen at the otherwise-empty table had in fact been jogging, or at least running at some mingling speed through Center City, and had rounded the corner on Market Street and spotted the sign on the hotel marquee.

Thus Spooner first laid eyes on Stanley Faint from the dais that he— Spooner—was sharing with Margaret Truman, waiting his turn to read. Spooner had taken pain medication as he entered the hotel, correctly anticipating an uncomfortable afternoon, and under the medication's flush of generosity was at this moment feeling like Clarence Darrow and experiencing a terrible urge to take Miss Truman's case, to somehow defend her against her own prose. She was at the lectern now, reading from her new mystery novel to a throng of citizens who had by this time begun to look to him more like a choir than a jury. Dropped mouths, slack jaws, and double chins. Miss Truman was doing very well with the audience, which was clearly attached to her and perhaps even loved her, but the words, the words. What could these people be hearing?

The sentences rolled out of Miss Truman, bloodless and arthritic, one after another, more dangling fancies stuck to the ends than a French tickler.

At this point in the story, Spooner had written two novels of his own, which is what he was doing at a *Philadelphia Inquirer* literary luncheon in the first place. He had been the subject of a dozen magazine stories that year, and he'd had invitations to speak at universities that until recently wouldn't have allowed him on campus to cut the grass. There had even been invitations to teach. More important to Spooner, the books had pleased Calmer, who could not have been more surprised if he'd found a couple of manuscripts in the doghouse after old Fuzzy died.

For Spooner, though, the novelty of being a novelist had already begun to wear off, and he'd been turning down invitations to speak, but in the end, like Stanley Faint, he could not pass up a shot at Margaret

Truman, and was sitting behind her now, waiting for her to polish off the English language for good, and trying to imagine what it would be like to be Harry Truman's only child, to wake up on that first morning that FDR didn't and find yourself suddenly insulated and protected for every minute of the rest of your stay here on earth. A whole life ahead of you with no one to suggest, for instance, that you might want to rethink singing in public, or writing books under your own name. Or even that you might want to choose a different fragrance or go easy on the lipstick. The thought had occurred to Spooner previously, usually sitting around some anonymous newspaper bar, listening to reporters grumbling over a changed word or phrase in a lead paragraph, that what the world needed these days was more discouragement than it was getting at home.

He thought of example after example, could even remember some of the leads themselves, and occupied in this way, his mind wandered out of the yard, as they say, which could only be a bad thing when he was waiting to speak in public. For public speaking, it was vital to have Spooner focused on the matter at hand. Vital. Passing through his head just now, for instance, was the idea of following Miss Truman's act with a few impressions. He did a pretty good seagull, if he said so himself, and if they liked that and warmed up to him a little, he did an excellent pussy.

Margaret Truman was coming to the end now, and although he was trying, Spooner could not unfasten himself from the notion of at least doing the seagull. Of the pussy business—or snatch, as it was called in less refined circles—he was still calculating the pluses and minuses. The problem with doing the pussy was that it was a visual sort of impression, and you needed pretty good vision to appreciate it. He glanced again at the audience, the vast, milky-eyed public. How to make them love him? He was nervous—he was always nervous before he spoke publicly—but calmed himself with the knowledge that in a hundred days the ones who weren't dead would have forgotten him anyway.

On the table in front of Spooner was a microphone, a glass of water, and a copy of his own new book, a story wrapped around the town of Deadwood in the last days of Bill Hickok. He reconsidered his plans, deciding to read a little of it, and then, if it wasn't going well, to do the seagull to wake everybody up.

Presently Margaret Truman wandered out to the end of one of her sentences and stopped, as if she'd moseyed off into the wrong wing of the White House and gotten lost. A sporadic applause began, and blossomed into the real thing and she closed the book, and then held it up for the crowd, like the executioner holding up the queen's head, and as the applause finally died away she stepped back from the microphone, and then, even as Spooner was being introduced, collected her things and headed for the door. Not even a glance in his direction.

Spooner stood to very modest applause and approached the lectern, which was still slightly ripe with Miss Truman's gardenia scent, and noticed for the first time that half of the women in the audience had gotten up when Margaret did and were following her out. She was signing autographs on the fly, left and right, all the time heading for the exit signs at the far end of the hall, and Spooner stood briefly dumbfounded, watching her work the crowd. Thinking back on it later, he supposed that he could have yelled at her to stop—*Margaret, wait, I can do a pussy*—but he was embarrassed and was no good at thinking on his feet in emergencies (that was Calmer's gift, not Spooner's, always clear and collected in a crisis) and so he opened *Deadwood* and, as if by some miracle, found himself staring at a passage in which a character named Charley Utter and a young whore named Lurline were looking at some semen recently spilled on a hotel floor, peering into it for signs of life, and opening up to this scene, Spooner took it as a signal to proceed, realizing that the lovers of Margaret Truman mysteries in the room most likely had never been introduced to the use of erotica in western fiction and therefore couldn't be blamed for having no taste in literature. It was one of those moments in Spooner's life when things fell into place and life made sense.

And so he began reading:

. . . and then the jizzom was running out of him and down both sides of her mouth and dropping on the floor. When she had let him go, he sat back in the chair

with his pants still around his ankles and studied the little puddles. "There is
something alive in that," he said. She had wiped her mouth on a pink towel and
sat down on the bed. She stared at the floor too. "I never thought of that," she said.
"It's dying now," he said, and took another drink. "Similar to a polliwog, removed
from the pond before it had time to grow lungs." Lurline leaned closer to the floor.
"I never liked to see nothing suffer," she said.

He could not say later exactly when the stampede began, but it was
early in the paragraph, either on the word *jizzom*, or an instant later, when
the man in the jogging outfit broke into his amazing bray. This braying—it cannot be overemphasized—was a phenomenal noise to come out
of a human, and surely had a hundred uses back in the dark, mossy caves
where it was programmed into the gene pool, but was never designed to
quell herds of the elderly. And so one moment the aisles were packed
with ancient women looking for some contact, however fleeting, with the
president's daughter, and a moment later the remaining, more gracious
faction of the audience, women who although similarly ancient hadn't
initially gotten up to follow Margaret Truman out, rose up all at once and
flooded into the already occupied spaces between the tables, running for
their lives.

Those already standing, meanwhile, heard the braying and surged
ahead, the noise perhaps awakening some long-dormant instinct for sur-
vival, and at the same time the women who had initially stayed seated for
Spooner's reading tried to push through the Margaret Truman faction,
and this being Philadelphia, the Margaret Truman faction pushed back.
It mattered not a smidgen in Philadelphia if you were a frail, deaf elderly
lady growing a beard, you still had to be ready to brandish your cojones
at the drop of a hat.

Spooner saw the flash of an umbrella, and a moment later one of
them was down. It looked like a sucker punch, launched from behind. But
his attention was immediately pulled away to an angry, collective noise
rising from the exit, where a living aneurism had formed as the lines from
the aisles billowed out in front of the three double exit doors, and the

noise in the place grew not really louder but shriller by the minute, and even so certain voices, certain individual words, could be heard over the continued braying from the front of the room.

Spooner spotted the woman on the floor again, and as he watched she rolled over beneath a table, a spot that sheltered her head but at the same time provided Spooner an open view of much of her underrigging. The old woman covered her head with her arms and lay where she was, kicking occasionally at the women coming up from behind. Her own legs were trampled but sprung back, like tree branches in a wind, and the meat of her legs hung off the bones like snow melting off the branches, and the bones were narrow and long, and the joints that connected them looked huge, like coconuts—and yes, Spooner understood as well as you do that coconut trees didn't have branches that looked like that, and if they did, there wouldn't be any snow melting off them. This was the problem with the literary theory that your first thought was your best thought, and maybe the problem with the theory of literary lunches: Sometimes it all came out plumb-bobbed and perfect, and sometimes it was a coconut tree in Vermont.

Meanwhile, the annual *Philadelphia Inquirer* Literary Luncheon was now conclusively over, and in the way of a historical footnote, there was never another one. By and by Stanley and Spooner and the old woman were the only humans left in the grand ballroom of the Sheridan Hotel, unless you count the organizer of the event, who was walking aimlessly through the rows of empty tables and spilled chairs, touching an occasional chair seat for warmth, perhaps to verify that it had only recently held a body.

The woman suggested that they all repair to a bar she knew and have a drink, and the organizer approached Stanley and for some unknown reason began explaining to him that he'd had nothing to do with picking the speakers.

And so when it seemed safe to leave the hotel, Stanley and Spooner and the old woman went to the bar on Rittenhouse Square where the drinks were strong enough to satisfy Stanley that adequate damage was being done to his person to make up for missing the day's sparring in North Philadelphia.

Spooner politely listened to the old woman, who craved celebrity and spoke of the odd friendship—the elderly but still attractive bookstore owner, the city columnist, the heavyweight fighter—as if the friendship already existed and were already some interesting quirk of the city. Her stories were practiced but not remotely true, a peek at the merciless heart that lay in that sweet old manipulator's breast. It was interesting enough but Spooner, for his part, was more interested in the details of how the veterinarian had repaired Stanley's nose, and as the afternoon wore on and then disappeared and Spooner and Stanley Faint got better acquainted, Spooner was allowed to squeeze the nose freely anytime he forgot how it felt.

FORTY-ONE

Losing your marbles was an expression pleasing to Spooner's ear from the first time he heard it, back in Vincent Heights. Early in life, he'd liked the idea of a head full of marbles, like a gumball machine, and later, after he'd had time to look around a little bit and meet a few psychologists, the expression seemed to put exactly the right timbre on the study of mental health.

Not that he dismissed mental health entirely. He knew from experience that it could be disorienting, walking around without your ordinary number of marbles and trying to put your finger on where you lost the ones that were missing. The key, therefore, from early on, had been not to get so attached to your marbles that you would miss a few if they escaped. Thus Spooner's excellent mental health.

He wondered now when things had begun to change.

Looking back, he supposed it might have been an afternoon in Philadelphia, not just inside the city limits of Philadelphia but also inside the soon-to-be Mrs. Spooner, as they were lying perfectly still—he loved those first few moments most of all, just lying quietly, enjoying the ooze—and she looked up at him and smiled and tightened down at the same time, and thus having his complete attention, dropped into the afternoon's gaiety the results of her appointment that morning with the gynecologist. He was never sure if the soon-to-be chose this moment to illustrate cause and effect, that life is a trade-off, in which case it was unneeded, or if it was a *Cosmopolitan* magazine he was pretty sure he'd seen lying around the living room with a cover story entitled "Ten Little Things to Whisper That Will Drive Him Crazy in Bed."

Later, he couldn't even remember exactly how she'd put it, and wished he'd written it down when it was fresh.

This much he did remember: About fifteen minutes later, after the oozing stage gave way to the yodeling stage, and the yodeling had yodeled and died and given way to the looking at the ceiling and drying off stage, he in fact lay looking at the ceiling, still slightly tacky, about like paint an hour from dry, and realized that marble-wise, he was no longer intact.

Yes, that was probably where it started.

He set out to think less, to occupy his mind. He worked harder, bent into the new novel. His columns provoked a demonstration outside the paper. The Margaret Truman incident came and went, he befriended Stanley, the *Inquirer* terminated its annual literary luncheon, and for a while Stanley endeavored to teach him to box, so that Spooner would know what they were talking about when they talked about boxing. Not at Joe Frazier's gym, where he surely would have been molested the moment Stanley took his eye off him, but a quiet little place over a car repair shop off Chadwick Street in South Philadelphia. And pretty soon Spooner loved the gym's proprietor and his son like his own family.

He enjoyed the boxing more than he'd expected. He hadn't minded being hit, knowing that Stanley and the gym's owner and his son were being careful not to kill him, and all day he would look forward to the three or four rounds he got in every afternoon. And yet the familiar unease was there in the gym too, and even as he boxed himself happily into nausea he felt it waiting. But now it took another form, a kind of panic while he waited for someone to unbuckle the headgear and pull off his gloves, a fear that he couldn't get enough air into his lungs. That he was being smothered.

He tried boxing without the headgear, but the unease had taken root. He tried not to think so much but would find himself thinking about not thinking, often sitting in the car outside the gym, amazed at some dangling nine-inch night crawler of a blood clot he'd pulled out of his nose.

It wasn't claustrophobia; he would have noticed before. It seemed somehow to come back to Mrs. Spooner and the baby. To the fear of losing what he had.

———

Came a cold Friday night, dead of winter, heading home from the bars where nothing much mattered to the house in the Pine Barrens, where everything mattered, crossing the Walt Whitman Bridge, late, and he was all at once swallowed up in the smell of Jaquith's mule, so fresh that he thought he might vomit right there in the front seat. Which wasn't as awful as you might picture it, by the way; it was a company car. He opened his window and a moment later, still not halfway across the bridge, he heard a distinct popping noise in the backseat, followed by a tinkling of glass. The tinkling was too high-pitched to be beer bottles rolling into one another on the floor, more like wind chimes, and he thought it over and then reached tentatively into the back, where his fingers came to rest on the soft, wet lips and nostrils of a human being.

This would mark the closest Spooner ever came to driving a company car into the Delaware River.

He stood up on the brakes and the wheels locked and the car skidded across two of the three eastbound lanes and bumped solidly into the curb. He opened the door and in the candlelike shine of the overhead light, he turned and had a look. A man in a filthy, torn-up parka was lying on the backseat. The parka suggested a dog attack, and Spooner saw that the pockets were stuffed with lightbulbs. The man squinted up into the light and rolled slightly away, casting about for a more comfortable position, and more of the bulbs popped in his pockets.

Again he opened his eyes, for just a moment, and one of them was as cloudy as the shards of glass that had spilled out over the cloth upholstery.

And Spooner was running.

He ran east, uphill, running for home. He passed over the crest of the bridge and in the overhead lights his shadow doubled and grew more distinct, and presently there were other lights and other shadows and the long arm of the law drew up close behind and put on the red and blue. The lights worked on Spooner like a cattle prod—at this point in his life, of course, he knew what that was—and he sprinted another quarter mile, downhill now, making a small note that all the work at the gym had left him in remarkable shape. Presently, another Port Authority police car appeared, this one from the other direction, the New Jersey side of the river, and pulled sideways and directly into Spooner's path and also began blinking its lights. The door swung open and a policeman got out holding a nightstick. He was younger than Spooner and anxious to whack him and threw his hat back into the seat as he got out, not wanting it in his way when the whacking began.

"Halt," the policeman said.

But Spooner already had.

"Put your hands where I can see them," the policeman said.

Spooner looked at his hands, wondering why the officer couldn't see them where they were. He was coming back to his senses now, realizing where he was. The cop moved a step closer, a certain look of anticipation rising in his eyes. The Port Authority police did not get to whack as many citizens as the city police did, and some of them never got over the unfairness of it. But now the other cop stepped out of his cruiser too, and he was older and not so anxious to hit Spooner over the head.

"What's the trouble?" the second policeman said. He was looking at Spooner carefully, trying to place him. "Hey, you're that newspaper reporter, right?" he said.

Spooner's picture by this time was hanging fifty feet wide in the subway stations and riding the side of city buses. It was a feeling he never got used to, seeing himself rolling past on the street.

Spooner did not answer right away, not wanting to embarrass himself further than he was already embarrassed.

"What's going on?" the first cop asked. He could have been talking to Spooner, or he could have been talking to the other cop.

"Spooner," the second cop said. "That's who you are, right? Spooner?" He made some motion to the other cop, who stepped away.

"What are you doing out here, pal?" the second policeman said, and glanced out over the bridge. "You're not despondent or nothing . . ."

Spooner had no idea. "There's something in the car," he said.

The second, older cop patted him on the shoulder. "Let's see what we got," he said, and this unexpected kindness touched Spooner, very nearly brought him to tears.

The second policeman held the door of his own car for Spooner, and Spooner got in, went quietly, as they say. They drove the seven or eight hundred yards back to the company car, which was still angled against the bridge walkway, the front door still open, the headlights shining off into the darkness over the Delaware River. Spooner's shirt was soaked through with sweat.

"You been tootin' the horn a little this evening, Warren?" the cop said. But Spooner was safe. What was after him tonight was not the criminal justice system.

They stopped and got out and approached Spooner's car from behind, the younger cop holding his flashlight in one hand and resting the other hand on the butt of his pistol. He pointed the flashlight into the back and then, without saying a word, set it on the roof of the car, opened the door and yanked the man out by the feet. The man's head bounced once on the running board and then hit the cement. More lightbulbs broke. One of the man's shoes came off, and the policeman who'd pulled it off dropped it and stepped back, repulsed, as if the foot were still inside it. Spooner edged closer and looked. There was frost in the man's beard, and little bubbles in the corner of his mouth. The bubbles popped and were replaced by other bubbles; the rest of the package was calm water. Spooner could not see him breathing, but bubbles didn't just bubble up out of the dead. Or maybe they did. The man was wearing an argyle sock on the foot without the shoe, oily black with dirt at the bottom, and all his toes stuck through. The toes were swollen and some color of dark red approaching black, and all in all Spooner had seen better-looking toenails on chickens.

"Jesus," the older cop said, "how long's this guy been in the backseat? He's practically froze."

Spooner tried to remember the last time he'd looked in the backseat. "I don't know," he said. "I think they vacuum the cars once a week, when they wash them." He supposed the man could have been back there a long time.

The other cop headed back to his cruiser, lights still blinking on and off, and Spooner heard him on the radio, calling for an ambulance.

"Ten minutes," he said when he came back.

It was quiet a moment, Spooner studying the man's foot. "You think we should put him back in the car?" he said to the older cop.

The older cop looked at him a moment, then scratched the back of his head. "No, you don't want to do that. My advice is, you find somebody lying out on the bridge like this, you don't touch nothing. You never know what happened, what kind of internal injuries he might have." He looked at the body again. "He might of got hit by a truck before you found him and called for help." He looked at Spooner and winked.

Spooner stood still, and the cop looked back over the bridge toward the city. "Why don't you go home, leave this one to us?" he said. "You look like you could use some sleep."

FORTY-TWO

Spooner headed home to the little house in the Pine Barrens. Back to his wife and daughter, safe and warm. He pictured them curled in bed, each into her own familiar curl, and then, against his will, thought again of the sound the man's head had made when the cop pulled him out by the feet. The shoe that had come off; the hole in the end of the man's sock. The toes. He could not stop picturing the toes.

―――――

Three hours later—it was now five o'clock in the morning—Spooner got quietly out of bed, walked outside and pried the lid off the septic tank.

Due to the unusually wet winter, not to mention the lake, the water table on Spooner's lot was only about thirty inches beneath the ground, and things had been backing up septic-wise pretty much ever since October. You flushed and shapes blossomed up to you from the toilet bowl like nightmares.

He lifted the septic tank cover, dropping it an inch or two onto his fingernail, crushing it, spilling blood into the septic system and possibly vice versa, and then picked up the whole lid—the heaviest thing he'd picked up since Mrs. Spooner quit insisting on live Christmas trees—and threw it violently and as far as he could throw it, which was just barely far enough to clear his feet, and then stood slightly out of breath, beholding the proof that he was and had been for some time alive and functioning here on Earth.

He continued to behold the proof a moment longer, swaying over the open tank, trying to divine some solution for a moody septic system. Spooner squinted the way he had seen Calmer squint, trying to force into himself some mechanical intuitiveness, but just as well could have been trying to invent internal combustion. In the end his best idea was to run the garden hose from the tank across the road into the woods on the other side, and siphon it over there, the way you siphoned gas out of the car tank when you didn't have enough to get the lawn mower started.

He stood thinking about that plan a moment longer, his thoughts coming to rest finally on the lawn mower.

The lawn mower.

———————

Mrs. Spooner climbed half asleep out of her marital bed that morning to administer the five-thirty feeding to baby Spooner, so sleep-deprived as to not even notice Spooner's absence at first, but did gradually notice a noise out front, then saw that the front door itself was open and, holding baby Spooner close to her chest against the cold, walked out the door and stood transfixed in the light of the moon as her husband mowed the front yard.

Spooner looked up from the mowing and saw his wife crossing the lawn, wrapped in a blanket and holding the baby. She appeared to be hurrying and appeared to be thinking the same thing she'd been thinking that afternoon last summer when he'd set the porch on fire, and he was momentarily paralyzed with dread, knowing there was something going on that he was supposed to have seen for himself.

She had to yell because the lawn mower had no muffler. "What in the world are you doing?" she said. The words fogged in the morning air, and now baby Spooner turned in her arms and was looking at him, smiling. The baby, only a couple of months old, already got him completely, understood everything that mattered. He looked from one of them to the other, and the expressions on their faces could have been bookends for the entire encyclopedia of human experience.

Wrapped in her blanket, Mrs. Spooner appeared faintly biblical this morning, and he was struck by her purity. In answer to her question, he indicated the part of the lawn that he had finished mowing, as if it spoke for itself. Which, in fact, it did. Her gaze moved to the open septic tank and the garden hose leading across the street into the trees. She reached down and disconnected the cable from the lawn mower's spark plug, and the morning turned eerily quiet.

"You're going to wake up Lou and Penny," she said. Lou and Penny Harker were the people next door, and as she said that, the lights in fact went on over there, and a moment later the front door opened and there they were, both of them wearing what looked like sleeping bonnets. They were good, frugal people, Lou and Penny, and kept the house cold at night.

"Everything okay?" Lou called over.

Except for no neighbors at all, Lou and Penny Harker were the best neighbors Spooner could imagine. They were quiet and loved their dog, and in the summer they liked to sit in the lawn chairs out by the lake and drink martinis, and kept their yard so clean that Spooner wiped his feet before he stepped over the short fence that served as the property line. Twice a week Mrs. Harker hung her astonishing lingerie out on the clothesline, where it lifted and fell in the wind along with Lou's checkered shirts and blue jeans.

Spooner waved at Lou, thinking how lucky he was to have good neighbors. "I'm mowing the lawn, Lou," he called.

Lou nodded, as if that was pretty much in line with how things looked to him too. Then he looked out over his own lawn, white with frost, and called out, "It's pretty early in the year; don't cut too close or you'll damage the roots." He waved and closed the door.

Mrs. Spooner considered him closely. "What is it?" she said.

He shrugged. "The water table, I guess," he said. She was still staring, perhaps looking for some sign that he was pulling her chain, which he did quite a bit when they were courting and was one of those qualities about him that she liked better later on, after he didn't do it so much. "Look," he said, "I don't want my daughter growing up thinking she has to watch what's in the toilet to make sure it flushes."

"You're mowing the grass," she said.

"I was waiting to see if I'd fixed the septic system, and thought, Why waste the whole morning?"

She eyed the open septic tank and turned the baby's face away, as if she were too young to know these kinds of things went on. "Come inside," she said. "It's cold out here."

"And then the lawn looks like hell," he said.

"Nobody can see the lawn," she said, "it's still night, and it's probably going to snow again anyway."

Not wanting to start an argument, Spooner put the lawn mower back in the shed and came inside. Mrs. Spooner was feeding the baby, and Spooner lay on the floor at her feet a little while, looking up, trying to see her from the baby's perspective. Then he got up and began washing the dishes.

The dishes were already washed and sitting in the dish rack—Mrs. Spooner spent much of her life in those days trying to stay ahead of the mess, but might as well have been trying to drain the septic tank with the garden hose—but he did them anyway. And then took out all the dishes in the cabinets and washed them too. The feel of the water was somehow reassuring, hot enough to sting, and he was pleased to note that his fingertips had turned pink and wrinkled. Spooner's plan was to keep doing dishes until daylight, and then take it from there.

"Why don't you try lying down?" she said.

———

Spooner went back to bed. His wife finished the feeding and lay down behind him, curled into his back and holding on, and was asleep again in half a minute. She was tired; she slept. She was so pure, so purely what she was. If nothing else, he could have loved her just for that. Forget her bottom; he could love her for purity alone. It was how you came to love someone in the first place, he was thinking, you notice something pure. Thus the popularity of dogs and babies.

You had to admit that philosophically he was on a roll.

———

Unease was all over him these days and there was also a feeling of absence, something like living in the third person instead of the first. He hid this from Mrs. Spooner, and went through the motions, week after week. She would never guess that he had lost touch. He lay with her at night until she fell asleep, and then he quietly rose from bed and stayed up most of the night, counting every pill in the medicine cabinet, reciting the presidents of the United States, the states of the United States, teaching himself Christmas songs on the touch-tone telephone, putting the dog in the crib with baby Spooner to watch them sleep together—a sight that made him weep. He wept more in six weeks than he had in the previous thirty years.

He went to the gym, exhausting himself every afternoon, trying to empty himself so completely that what was wrong would empty out with the rest of it, and wrote his columns at the paper and was eerily absent from them too, and his own writing, which began to sound to him like the hushed conversations you hear in emergency rooms—*we can order out for pizza when we get home*—while some other, more important issue, the reason for being here, was being decided out of sight, and it was during this third-person period of absence that he wrote the column about the dead boy.

FORTY-THREE

The dead boy was a kid from South Philadelphia, a pipe fitter at the naval yard who'd gotten himself killed in the course of some small drug transaction, hit from behind with a pipe or a bat. An eye had been knocked out of the boy's head. Spooner had been in Philadelphia five years now, which wasn't long enough to know the city, but he had spent his share of time in the neighborhoods, especially in South Philadelphia, and had glimpsed the rules that held the place together. Which is to say that he should have seen the column for the intrusion it was.

Still, it looked harmless enough. He represented the kid in the way the kid was represented to him. Likable, not a bum or a thief, a kid who could have had a whole life but who lately had struck various citizens of the neighborhood as a little loopy on the street.

Spooner wrote the column as if the kid mattered to him, and he didn't. The truth was that he couldn't picture the dead boy, and picturing him was the ground-floor requisite for this sort of newspaper column. Without it the column came out of Spooner's typewriter as dead as the boy himself, as ordinary as a box of cereal. There were two things Spooner absolutely knew about writing, and the first one was that you can't get away with pretending to care. The other one, if you're interested, is that nobody wants to hear what you dreamed about last night.

But live and learn. Spooner did what he did, and should have seen the insult in it but didn't, and should have left it alone until he could picture the kid and get some piece of who he was into the story, and some piece of what he meant to the people who loved him. But he didn't.

There were a dozen messages waiting when he got to the office, about average the day after a column, but six were from the same number. The first few from a woman, then some from a man with the same last name. It came to him slowly whose last name it was.

Spooner sat down at his desk, reread the column, took a minute to cringe and then picked up the telephone. The woman was the dead boy's mother, and she undertook wailing the instant Spooner spoke his name. The conversation went downhill. He understood very little of what the mother was saying, but the nub of it was clear enough, that Spooner had brought back all her shock and grief, and, in spite of the way he'd died, had gotten her boy all wrong.

That he had missed the kid entirely was probably true. Part of this was inevitable—even on a good day, the best you could hope for was a glimpse—and part of it was Spooner's strange disappearance from the first person. The volume seemed to fade then, like a train gone past, and another voice came on the line, the other son.

The other son made several points, building his argument logically, from the ground up. Spooner was a motherfucker. The drug deal could only have been a first-time experiment because the kid had been a pipe fitter at the navy yard, and pipe fitters had to be alert. Spooner had ruined his mother's life all over again, just when she was beginning to get over the shock. Spooner was a motherfucker. Spooner was a motherfucker's motherfucker. On and on. Spooner guessed that the other son was saying this more for the mother than for Spooner, and that he did not believe the part about this being the kid's first time with drugs any more than Spooner did. The rest of it, though, seemed sincere enough. Spooner heard the mother moving away, maybe back to her bedroom, wailing, the train gone round the bend.

Now, in a quieter voice that she wouldn't hear, the other son began telling Spooner all the ways he was going to get even: broken legs, broken arms, broken fingers so Spooner could never write again. Spooner waited him out, trying to listen but paying less and less attention, and presently he found himself trying to remember the anatomical names of the bones the dead boy's brother was threatening to break. Ulnas, femurs, carpals—or were those metacarpals? Or were metacarpals toes? Maybe it was phalanges. *Christ, don't break my toes.* There could be a poem in the names of bones.

Finally the other son stopped, or at least ran out of bones he intended to break, then began on how he planned to hunt Spooner down. He knew where Spooner worked, where he went at night, where he lived.

Spooner excused himself and interrupted. "Where are you?" he said.

The question stopped the other son a second, and then he gave Spooner the name of a bar in Devil's Pocket, six till two, five nights a week.

"I don't mean that," Spooner said. "I mean where you are now. Maybe I could come over and talk to your mother." Realizing what he'd just offered to do, picturing the scene at the dead boy's house, Spooner was washed in the odor of Jaquith's mule, and could no longer get enough air into his lungs.

"My mother don't wanna fucking talk to you," the other son said, and slammed down the phone. Spooner felt a tremendous wave of relief, the first one in quite a while.

"My mother don't wanna fucking talk to you," he said out loud, liking the sound, wondering if that could be the last line of the poem about the bones. Hoping she wouldn't change her mind. Thinking that was the end of that.

———

It wasn't, of course. Too late to picture the dead kid himself, Spooner began to picture the brother, to see how privileged his—Spooner's—life must look to the other son, the dead boy's brother, whose own privileges were most likely only what he could negotiate on the street.

Why this came into his head, why he should care about it, Spooner couldn't say, except he was still barely removed from all those years when he had no say in things himself.

It had stayed cold and wet all winter, and now, early in February, it rained and then turned cold again and the rain froze and left the sidewalks and streets slick, with victims piling up in emergency rooms everywhere in the city.

He found a legal parking spot in front of Dirty Frank's at Thirteenth and Pine, an event so rare that after he tucked his company car into the spot he sat still a little while trying to enjoy it, and a little time passed and the space wasn't more fun than anyplace else, but still, it was a rare thing, a legal spot in front of Dirty Frank's, and he took it for an omen.

In spite of the slick sidewalks, he walked to the place he was going. No traction at all under his feet. It was only a mile or so but a walk that ordinary citizens did not often undertake, even when the pavement was dry. Like most of the neighborhoods on the edges of Center City, Devil's Pocket was in a process of gentrification—Gilman's own house was only a block from the understood boundaries of the neighborhood—but civilization was slow in coming to the Pocket, and in spite of its proximity to Center City and all its cultural advantages (this was a phrase that often came up when Spooner's mother was talking about places she didn't live) the area was still among the most dangerous neighborhoods in the city, at least to outsiders. There were parts of Kensington and North Philadelphia and West Philadelphia where they killed more of their own, but for maltreatment of outsiders, you could hardly beat the Pocket.

Spooner walked past a corner where a sweet-natured, gentle soul, a man everyone called Pally, had made his stand the previous year. One o'clock in the morning, the witnesses reported two black men in a car. The car slowed, a window went down. Strangers talking to strangers, words that meant nothing, and could change nothing, except in the moment. Pally was eleven days on a respirator, and then he died.

Spooner stopped at the spot where Pally's head had hit the curb, and wondered what he had been thinking when the car slowed, what he'd thought was at stake. Or if that night he had just been throwing it all away. In spite of where he was and what he was about to do, nothing in the way of similarities came into Spooner's mind.

He crossed the line into the Pocket a few minutes later.

———

Spooner stopped again before he went in, thinking there was something he'd forgotten, or forgotten to do, and stood kitty-corner from the spot a minute or two, shaking in the cold, thinking, but couldn't remember what it was.

The main entrance was on the corner; there was a side door farther down the street. He could see inside—a fat boy with red hair sitting slump-shouldered at the bar, staring at the beer bottle like a picture of his own true love. At the far end of the bar there were two other customers and the bartender—four citizens in all, grazing their way through life in the Pocket. Twenty, twenty-five years old, and nothing new left in the world, and the smoke rose up through the artificial light and softened the scene, as American as the cover of the *Saturday Evening Post*.

Spooner noticed the bar itself, a beautiful old U-shaped bar that obviously had a rosier future than its inhabitants. The gentrifiers would surely hang on to it even as they tore up everything else and disposed of it, along with the locals.

He opened the door and some of the bar napkins blew off a stack of napkins and floated a little ways and settled on the floor. The bartender's face washed in surprise, and in that same moment Spooner realized his mistake, what he couldn't remember when he'd been standing across the street looking in. It wasn't that he shouldn't have come—although looking back on it, he could have given that possibility more consideration—but that he'd made no allowance for an audience, and the audience changed everything. There were only four of them in all—three spectators—but it was still an audience: the fat boy alone and gazing at his bottle, and two stinky-looking kids sitting together at the other end of the bar, looking him over. Without them—if it had been only Spooner and the dead boy's brother—the place would have been as safe as a nursery.

Spooner walked farther in and took a seat. No introductions, everybody there already knew more or less who everybody was. The three kids picked up their beers and headed in his direction, one of them covering the side door so Spooner couldn't get out. The bartender made a small, *don't kill him yet* gesture, and the others slightly relaxed. The fat boy stirred, and Spooner guessed he was the one who had to be watched.

"Well, here we are," Spooner said.

And ten minutes later, he came out of the place with most of his upper teeth sheared off at the gum.

FORTY-FOUR

It was Stanley Faint's twenty-sixth birthday. He was living these days in a little place in New Jersey where the front door locked and nobody was fucking anybody in his sink. He'd confided to Spooner that it was a nice enough place but it felt empty. Tonight, though, he was throwing a party.

Spooner showed up about eleven, pretty much unkissable, with blood-crusted lips split open like the top of the pumpkin pies his mother always made at Thanksgiving—he hated pumpkin pie—and half his teeth, and had a drink. The ice did not feel good on the places his teeth were broken off.

"You look like somebody broke your heart," Stanley said.

Spooner smiled but his lips didn't feel like his lips anymore, and the gum line where his teeth had been sheared felt strange and sharp, like the mouth of a fish, and he couldn't stop running over it with his tongue.

"Things have been strange lately," he said. He thought of telling Stanley about the panic and the feeling of living in the third person, and oddly enough, Stanley, alone among his friends, would have understood what he was talking about. But this was Stanley's birthday, and his party, and there were a hundred people in the little house, all of them wanting to tell him stories and hear him bray, and be his amigo. And Spooner, who had never been a line-cutter, only recapped the evening's highlights so far.

Hearing the story, Stanley did bray, and a hundred people stopped what they were doing and turned to look.

The point here being that life had kicked Stanley Faint around as much as it could, and for him it was still no end of merriment, and for Spooner it wasn't. Spooner had tried optimism for an hour or so one morning—this was months ago, before he started thinking of himself in the third person—and it exhausted him, physically exhausted him, and by the time he sat down to work that afternoon he couldn't write a line.

Stanley asked if he needed to tie up loose ends.

Stanley watched him, waiting for an answer, and Spooner tried to decide if he needed to tie up the loose ends. Shortly, he found himself wondering where the expression *loose ends* came from, and what sort of loose ends they had been, back in the days when tying them up was important. And if they were supposed to be tied to something else or to each other. This was all familiar territory—one question mutating into a dozen other questions, each one a step more removed from the question on the table.

"I guess so," he said, and it was in fact a guess.

———

Stanley and Spooner got in Spooner's company car. Behind the company car were two other cars carrying the following occupants: an emergency medic/ambulance driver for the city fire department, a trombonist from the Philadelphia Symphony, a judo player of self-inflated local reputation, Stanley's pro bono lawyer, and the woman who owned the bookstore in Center City. The little procession headed back over the Ben Franklin Bridge to Philadelphia and the Pocket. It was midnight and snowing now, and Spooner sensed his lack of traction with the earth all the way there.

They parked across the street from the bar. There was no one on the street except a man who came out of his row house to move his car, leaving it double-parked at the end of the block. If the snow kept up, the only cars moving tomorrow would be the ones that were double-parked tonight.

Stanley said, "Well, Sunshine?"

"Here's something I hadn't thought of," Spooner said. "There might be a gun behind the bar."

"That's a thought, all right," Stanley said, and got out of the car any-

way. Once Stanley decided to do something, it was at that moment of-
ficially too late to reconsider, especially over something like the possibility
of a pistol or a shotgun behind a bar. Not a tortured life of second guessing was Stanley Faint's.

They crossed the street and went into the bar. Spooner, Stanley, the
trombonist, the judo guy, the emergency medic, Stanley's pro bono attorney. The streets here looked meaner than they had from New Jersey, and
the woman from the bookstore reconsidered and decided to wait in the
car. Still, not an unformidable collection of humanity, although Spooner
was already squashed, and the attorney was in his late fifties, a happy,
agreeable man of pale, freckled skin who resembled a dumpling.

The bartender and the same three inhabitants were still at their stations. The bartender saw Spooner and then saw that he was not alone.
He was surprised again, and also afraid, and the moment Spooner saw his
face he knew there was no shotgun behind the bar and felt better than he
had all night. It was surprising to him how good it felt, knowing he was
not about to be shot.

Stanley and Spooner walked directly to the bartender, who at first said
he had nothing to say and then began to plead his case, telling Stanley
about his brother and his mother and the newspaper and what Spooner
had written. The bartender did not know that Stanley was at the time the
fourth-ranked heavyweight prizefighter in the World Boxing Association,
but there are certain people in this life who explain themselves simply by
walking in a door, and the bartender seemed to realize the gist of Stanley
Faint immediately, and also came to see that violence was not the answer
to the world's problems after all.

Stanley listened to the bartender without comment. The bartender
took this for a bad signal, although the truth was that Stanley was listening, that Stanley listened to everything and everybody—except the few
people left in his world who still tried to tell him what to do. And he
was not unsympathetic. Stanley had seen firsthand that newspapers were
a flawed source of information. Beyond that, he had a mother of his own,
and several brothers.

When the bartender ran out of things to say Stanley turned to Spooner. "What do you want to do?" he said.

It was another crucial moment in Spooner's personal history, and he had nothing short and to the point to say, not even a sense of how he would like the place to look when he left. His mouth still hurt when he swallowed, but he could already see that it was no better to walk into a bar with Stanley and the medic and the judo player and the trombonist and turn the place into a parking lot than it was for the citizens of Devil's Pocket to have sheared off his teeth when he'd come in alone earlier. That was where his mind was now, ethics.

"What do you want to do?" Stanley said again, slower this time, and perhaps a little impatient—not unlike the repo man back in Florida who'd come for the Mazda. The bartender looked at Spooner and waited to see if he was going to be thrown through a window, or perhaps the wall, and as this was going on, the fat boy with the red hair, the one Spooner had liked the looks of even less than the others during his earlier visit, got up from the bar and skipped right past Stanley's pro bono attorney and out the side door.

Meanwhile, Spooner and the bartender looked each other over. What Spooner wanted, he decided, was for the bartender to understand that safety was relative. That even here, nestled in with all his bar-rag friends and neighbors, he couldn't shear off Spooner's teeth with immunity.

"It's not the same now, is it?" Spooner said.

By way of answer, the bartender glanced at the door where the fat boy with rotten teeth had disappeared. A minute or two had passed, no more.

"Is it possible," Stanley said to Spooner, "that sometime this evening you could get to the point?" He seemed edgy, which, if Spooner had not been absorbed in questions of ethics, he might have correctly seen as a clearer omen to the evening than finding an open parking space in front of Dirty Frank's. Stanley was never edgy about the ordinary things that put humans on edge.

Spooner noticed the snow when the fat boy appeared in the side door again. It was coming down in big, wet flakes, and it was beautiful falling through the headlights of the two cars parked on the sidewalk just outside. The fat boy came in and stopped, smiling in some anticipation, and behind him an army of local inhabitants poured through the door, each one carrying a bat or a tire iron or a taped piece of reinforced steel stolen from some construction site. The establishment's other door opened then, and the second wave came in, similarly outfitted, and then for a while this little piece of the Pocket was a wonderful place to be from, if not to visit.

The little party from New Jersey made its way to the door, and then out the door, and then Spooner and Stanley were somehow alone among the horde of locals. Where everyone had gone Spooner never knew, but you couldn't blame anybody for leaving.

Stanley was hit first, one of them sneaking up from behind, the black tire iron in perfect focus even in the night. Stanley dropped where he stood, and seeing this amazing sight, which no one in Texas or Philadelphia or any of the places in between had ever seen before, Spooner spotted the flaw in his exit strategy, as they say at congressional hearings, realized that there was no contingency plan for Stanley's dying first, and determined that as a gesture he would at least try to make his way to the boy with the crowbar and bite off his cheek. He took a step or two in that direction, but again there was no traction, and then he was distracted by the barrel of a ball bat homing in, not a foot away—he could read the label. *Louisville*, it said—and in that same moment, still before the bat arrived, there was a noise from behind, nothing monumental, about like the snapping of a pencil in half.

So that was it, the way things end. No thoughts of his wife or his child, no settling up accounts, no thoughts at all actually beyond the desire to bite off that fucker's cheek. If it had been like this for Pally, he thought, it wasn't too bad.

All these thoughts came later, of course, after he'd been brought back to the here and now and the ice-covered sidewalk of Devil's Pocket. A different kind of noise had revived him, something from hell itself. It said—distinctly said—"If he's dead, so is every one of you. Every one of you motherfuckers is dead."

You may notice the use of the word *is*. In times of stress, Stanley Faint often reverted to correct grammar, which indicated to Spooner that he—Stanley—wasn't dead, which further indicated that neither was Spooner. In fact, it turned out that Stanley was barely scathed, relatively speaking, suffering only what looked like an inconsequential break of the ulna of his left arm. The tire iron hadn't knocked him out, or even down; he'd slipped.

To Spooner's huge relief, he looked up into the night sky, and found it full of Stanley's remarkable face. That boneless nose. "Another night in the life of a big-city columnist," Stanley said, and picked Spooner up off the street with his good right arm. Spooner achieved verticality, but noticed that one of his legs had ceased to function. Absolutely would not move.

"We've got to go," Stanley said.

Spooner tried to walk with him back in the direction of the car they'd driven over in, but the leg stayed where it was. "My leg won't move," Spooner said. He tried again, but the leg might as well have been cut off and lying in the street for all the attention it was paying to Spooner.

Stanley looked down the expanse of row houses where the locals had run—somewhere out there they were regrouping. "We don't have time for your leg not to move, Sunshine," he said.

Spooner stared down at the leg again, trying to see what was wrong with it, and pretty soon the blood that was running from his scalp found its way through his eyebrows and into his eyes, and his vision blurred. "You think it's serious?" he said.

"It could be if we don't get out of here," Stanley said.

"I know how odd this sounds to you, but it just won't move."

Without another word, Stanley put his head under Spooner's arm and walked him/carried him back to the company car, then deposited him in the front seat and got in the other side and started the engine.

"So where are we going?" Spooner said a little later.

Stanley checked the rearview mirror. "The hospital, unless there's some place you've got to be."

"You think it's that bad?"

And Stanley looked at him again and began to bray, and it was good to hear that noise again, although here in the confines of the company car, it set off a ringing, like standing in the street when the fire engine blows by.

FORTY-FIVE

Stanley pulled Spooner out of the car and carried him through the doors to the emergency room at Hahnemann Hospital, where he was taken right to the front of the line—some of the other victims of the night complaining that they were there first—and before long an emergency room doctor came in and began sewing Spooner's scalp and lips back together, and then an orthopedic surgeon came in to look at his leg, and a brain surgeon came in to look at his brain.

Pictures were taken of everything and two shots of Spooner's brain were fastened onto a lighted viewing board where the brain surgeon studied them, back and forth, apparently disapproving of everything he saw. Spooner tried to engage the doctor, asking if one of the pictures might show why he'd been living in the third person lately, but it was two-thirty in the morning now, and Spooner's mouth was swollen snug against his gums, affecting his speech, and the doctor was in no mood for Spooner even if he could have understood what he was saying.

The emergency room doctor was finishing up sewing pieces of his lip back into place.

Would this embarrass the family? How much school would he miss?

There were hints now that Spooner was in the wrong time zone. He thought it over and was pretty sure that he'd graduated from high school.

"How old am I, anyway?" he said, and at the sound of his voice the emergency room doctor spooked and his hands jumped, and a piece of Spooner's lip dropped onto his teeth.

"Quietly, please," the doctor said, "I am working on these lips." He was a high-strung fellow, a native of some country where the people were small and brown.

Up at the X-ray board, the brain doctor turned away from the pictures of Spooner's brain and gazed down upon the real thing. "You were a very lucky young man," he said, words that took Spooner back even further than high school, all the way back to Georgia. And even then he'd known this remark was ridiculous. The lucky people were home in their beds or fucking in their sinks; luckier people than Spooner were outdoors in the snowstorm cutting their grass.

The bone doctor came back through the swinging doors, rolling like a bear—when had he left?—and asked the brain doctor a question that Spooner could not follow. The brain doctor showed the bone doctor the pictures of Spooner's skull, and they both bent in closer to look, one and then the other, making little circles over this gray area or that gray area as they talked. Spooner lay waiting for a pronouncement of some kind but at the same time sensed that the doctors were unsure, leaning too much on each other. He had an acquaintance with the medical world by now, and these were not first-string doctors.

"Well, the next couple of days will tell the story," the brain doctor said finally, and everybody seemed satisfied with that. Spooner only closed his eyes and began the long process of waiting it out. He didn't know much, but he knew the story would not be told in any couple of days.

FORTY-SIX

It developed that the bone doctor worked for the city, a medical practice devoted almost entirely to keeping city employees off disability. He set broken bones for firemen and police and garbage collectors, and did all the surgeries associated with all kinds of fractures, dislocations, torn cartilage and ligaments. He drew a yearly retainer for this work and received an additional flat fee for each consultation and surgery, regardless of outcome, and also picked up a few dollars now and then at Hahnemann Hospital operating on the indigent. Or the comatose, or people who'd had their eggs scrambled so badly they didn't care who was cutting them open.

Spooner fell into the egg-scrambled category, or at least had enough else on his mind not to care much who was cutting him open. Under ordinary circumstances, he would have asked for his own bone doctor, who was on staff over at the University of Pennsylvania and had not gotten his job by way of having a cousin on the city council, or, for that matter, gotten into medical school the same way.

The reason Spooner happened to have a bone doctor of his own was that he'd broken the same leg twice in the last four years and also broken the ankle of the other leg, and a collarbone. The ankle and the second leg fracture had required surgeries, and there were screws and bolts and wire now holding him together inside, and he could feel the bolts beneath his skin when he was putting on his socks. Luckily these screws and bolts were not magnetic, or he supposed he would be waking up every morning of his life with his legs stuck together.

Which is only mentioned here to reemphasize that Spooner knew his way around the orthopedic community, and knew that as a rule, the old-school bone doctors like this one had been the bottom of the barrel back in medical school. More recently, of course, with the dawn of artificial knees and hips and surgeons making dancers out of gimps—and rich men out of orthopods—they weren't the bottom of the barrel anymore, and once you knew what to look for, it didn't take a brain surgeon to tell which was which.

Arriving as he had, however, in the middle of the night without an appointment, Spooner had fallen victim to the orthopod's code—finders keepers—and never had a chance.

———

As mentioned, there were things besides bone doctors on Spooner's mind, first among them Mrs. Spooner, at home in bed, presumably wide awake now and possibly at the end of her wits. It was hard to say what reserves she had left, but this incident, which she would very likely view as preventable, would not be well received. He wondered if it had been the smart thing, asking the nurse to make the phone call. On the other hand, who else to ask? Stanley?

The ER doctor puzzled one last piece of Spooner's lip into place and commenced sewing, and the room began to empty out. There were suture threads hanging off Spooner's lips and lying against his gums and in his mustache, and the feeling in his mouth reminded him of a backlash in a fishing reel.

They wheeled Spooner up to a room in the intensive care unit, where he spent the next few days in the company of an elderly black man named Sylvester Graves who had been run over by his wife in a parking accident. Mr. Graves was suspended from a scaffold near the ceiling, and moaning in his sleep.

"Well," Spooner said to the nurse who tucked him in, "they say the next couple of days will tell the story."

Mr. Graves moaned in his sleep.

The nurse patted Spooner on the hand. "Don't worry about him," she said. "He can't feel a thing."

———————

The down-state returns were not in yet, but unofficially Sylvester Graves had even more broken bones than Spooner. His wife was named Betty, and a month or so previous they had purchased a new car, a dark green Pontiac Bonneville. Mr. Graves had been out in the street every day since, washing and waxing, some days just sitting in his chair watching it shine, keeping the neighborhood children with their skates and twirling batons away, not allowing Mrs. Graves herself inside it without taking off her shoes. And in the way these things sometimes happen, the first time Mrs. Graves was allowed behind the wheel, she scratched the bumper, not incidentally pinning Mr. Graves against the brick wall of a parking lot. They had been visiting Mrs. Graves's family out in West Philadelphia, and he was taking no chances on the Bonneville's bumper even touching the wall, and was out of the car guiding her, like a signalman on an aircraft carrier. He'd just given her his first signal, in fact, motioning the car back toward himself, when she drove it into the wall, the impact modified only slightly by Mr. Graves himself, who was still there in between, motioning *come to me* with his hands.

Then, unbelievably, she'd panicked and done it again, the first time crushing both his femurs, the second time breaking his pelvis and dislocating his hips.

Mrs. Graves hadn't wanted any part of it from the start—it made her nervous even getting into the passenger seat, afraid she'd do something wrong, and even when she'd heard the first scream she wasn't sure of what had happened, except she was pretty sure from the noise he made afterwards that she'd scratched the car.

———————

Suspended as he was from the scaffolding, the old man was unable to move much and perhaps due to this unnatural positioning, was visited by strange dreams night and day, whenever he slept. Falling dog dreams, it looked like, as he twitched violently and made yipping noises and grabbed at the bed rails as he came awake to break his fall. Awakened in this way, he was often out of his head with pain, pleading with the nurses somewhere in the maze of hallways outside for his shot.

It was always half an hour before someone answered, or an hour, and then one of them would come in, taking her time, and would remind Mr. Graves as she administered the injection that she had other patients to take care of and that he should learn to wait his turn. Then the nurse would leave and a few minutes later Mr. Graves would sag into the straps holding him up, and then for a while he was content enough to hang from the ceiling and talk about women drivers and common sense, and a couple of hours would pass—pleasantly, considering the man was hanging from the ceiling—and then he would sense the drug beginning to leave his system and he would start watching the clock.

Spooner was much in sympathy with Mr. Graves, and grateful that his own injuries didn't require being hung from the ceiling. On the other hand, he—Spooner—was not allowed to have morphine or anything else for the pain, and every move he made was instinctively countered by an opposite and corresponding part of his body, which set off the same pain again, but headed in the other direction. He had a broken femur of his own, and a broken rib and torn connective tissue in his rib cage and nerve damage in both hands. His cheek was also broken, and his eardrum, and one of his eyebrows apparently had been sanded off against the sidewalk. His back was fractured, although nobody had noticed it yet. The thing that bothered Spooner most those first days, though, was not a specific injury, or being unable to move, but a feeling of riding a cold, violent wash down into the vortex of an eddy. He was being flushed. The floor of the world dropped away and everything moved clockwise and down, and he panicked again and again and grabbed for the sides, but there was nothing to hold on to because it was all going down with him.

Without moving his head, he asked Mr. Graves if he also had feelings of being flushed.

Mr. Graves said, "None I noticed; they just got me spunned up here like a spiderweb is all I know." He thought a little while and said, "That woman come after me out of nowhere. They wasn't no common sense in it, she just do."

They brought breakfast at dawn and gave Mr. Graves another shot of morphine and fed him quivering eggs. Spooner stared at his own pile of eggs and felt it staring back.

A technician arrived and took blood from them both, and a little later a nurse came in and changed the dressing that covered Spooner's skull, and cleaned dried blood out of his hair and his remaining eyebrow and his mustache. The strokes she used were short and punishing, as if she were angry. He asked the nurse if head injuries commonly made accident patients feel as if they were being flushed down a toilet. He had begun to suspect a connection between the tunnel that near-death-experience experiencers often reported and the eddy at the bottom of the whirlpool, beginning to see the pure, bitter genius behind everything if the act of dying turned out to be flushing the toilet.

———

The first call came in about seven-thirty from the Associated Press. Spooner hung up.

He wasn't angry—how many times had he made the same kind of call when he'd worked for the city desk? Or knocked on somebody's door? Granted, he'd usually gone to a movie instead, but there had been times back when he was a reporter when he'd done what a city editor told him to do. And now, a few years later, and the tables turned, Spooner the newspaperman was refusing to talk to the press. It struck him somehow as a pure distillation of the human condition.

But then, what didn't?

The next call was the woman from the bookstore, asking if there was anything she could do.

Spooner knew the woman by now though and knew she was not calling to offer help. "Not a thing," he said.

"I'd come over in person, but I was thinking it might be better if I didn't have any public connection to this. You know, with the store and all . . ."

Spooner didn't answer.

"I mean, it might be best for everyone if I weren't there at all last night, if you follow my meaning."

"Of course," he said.

And now she thought of it, it might be best for everyone if Stanley's attorney wasn't there either.

"You know what I'm thinking?" Spooner said. "It might be best for everyone if none of us were there." And in the quiet that followed, the floor spun and dropped out of the world.

It was a day for visitors. Just before lunch Stanley came in with his arm in a cast, and was hugely amused at the gauze cap covering the top of Spooner's head. His left arm was broken below the elbow, and even though the ulna was the smaller of the two bones connecting his hand to his elbow, it was the slower and more difficult bone to heal. It was strange talking about bones with Stanley Faint, strange to think of his having bones with the same names as everybody else's.

Stanley had dropped Spooner off last night and then, possibly in some bit of instinctive misdirection, gone to a different emergency room to have his own arm set. Spooner often wondered at the variant things they saw, looking at the same world, and wondered how it might have looked to Stanley last night when the bar filled up with bats and tire irons and sociopaths. What was it he'd said? *I hope that's the softball team?* Or had Spooner said that himself? Had he—Stanley—even been afraid?

"This is Mr. Graves," Spooner said, indicating Sylvester, suspended as always from the ceiling.

"What's happening?" Stanley said.

"Oh, everything lovely here," Mr. Graves said.

"In a way he was in a car accident," Spooner said.

"You that fighter, aren't you?" Mr. Graves said. "What you gone done to your arm?"

Stanley shook his head. "I wouldn't know where to start," he said.

"You two boys concoct this all up?" Mr. Graves said.

"That's the sorry truth," Stanley said.

A little later Stanley signed an autograph for Mr. Graves and posed with him for a picture when his wife came in with her Instamatic camera. Mr. Graves told Stanley the story of how he had been crushed, and while Stanley's braying was rattling the china everywhere in the hospital, Spooner considered the cast covering his left forearm. In Spooner's view Stanley's one great asset in the ring was that quality which in the boxing world was called the intangibles. The problem was that at Stanley's present level of competition his opponents had all the *tangibles*—i.e., speed, reflexes, power, most of all power—in the world and these had to be worn out and used up before Stanley could narrow the matter to a contest of hearts. Which is to say he got hit too much—you didn't have to know anything about boxing to see that—but until now at least nobody had ever walked through his left hand to do it. What would happen now if he couldn't jab?

Spooner gagged and leaned over the lunch tray sitting beside his bed. Nothing came up, but the gauze cap fell off his head, and Stanley borrowed Mrs. Graves's camera to get the picture.

———

Stanley was still there when Mrs. Spooner arrived. Mrs. Graves had left—it was time to change some of Mr. Graves's dressings, and she could not stand to watch or hear him moan when they moved him around. For all his good qualities, Mr. Graves did not suffer quietly.

Stanley got up from his chair, making elaborate room for Spooner's wife to attend his bedside. She did not speak to Stanley, did not so much as acknowledge that he was there. Instead, she delivered the news that Calmer was due in later that afternoon, and then sat down quietly and stared across the way at Spooner's roommate, suspended from the ceiling.

"He gagged a little bit ago," Stanley said, "but don't worry, I got pic-

tures." He laughed again, filling the room and the hall outside with the
great sound, but the room had changed moods. Mr. Graves had gotten his
shot of morphine and was beginning to drift, and Spooner's pulse and his
various miseries had slowed to one and the same thing. And Mrs. Spooner
sat in a knot, faintly vibrating—nothing audible, like a snake, just a faint,
steady vibration—and, like some post office clerk who notices the package is ticking, finally Stanley felt it too and moved carefully away, trying
not to even stir the air, and vacated the premises. He'd looked vaguely
hurt that Mrs. Spooner hadn't said hello, but then he was not used to
being unloved.

It was a strange thing to watch. The man had recently boxed Early
Shavers—his given name—who was the most powerful and feared heavyweight of his era, absorbing a quantity of blows that would have knocked
out all the other heavyweights who ever lived, and in the end had exhausted him, worn him out, then knocked him out, and Mrs. Spooner
had just run him out of the room.

Spooner touched her hand. She did not pull away but continued to
vibrate, and did not touch him back. A candy striper came through the
door carrying two bouquets of flowers. All day long, candy stripers would
be delivering flowers to Spooner's room. When she had gone, Spooner
touched his wife again.

"He stayed there with me when he could have run off," he said, meaning Stanley. "It's why I'm here."

"That is exactly why you're here," she said, which should not be
taken to mean that she agreed with what he'd just said. Still, she knew
as well as Spooner that he hadn't been led anywhere by Stanley Faint;
that wasn't how it worked between them. More to the point, Spooner
had been getting himself into one scrape or another ever since he could
walk. Even more to the point than that, Mrs. Spooner was not only
aware of the spontaneous aspect of Spooner's personality but back in
the day had been tacitly drawn to it. But that, of course, was back in
the day, before they had a baby to think about, and a house and a lawn
and a septic tank.

She closed her eyes and the vibrating turned into shaking, and then a pretty good imitation of herself beginning to come, but he did not see how it would do anybody any good to bring it up.

Instead, trying to maneuver the conversation away from Stanley, he said, "It's not as bad as it looks."

Mrs. Spooner opened her eyes now and slowly beheld what lay on the bed in front of her, beheld Spooner until he realized the terrible mistake he'd made, bringing his physical appearance into it.

"Have you *seen* yourself?" she said.

Which, now that she mentioned it, he hadn't, and the next time a candy striper came in with flowers, he asked for a mirror and began to appreciate the extent of the damage. He tried imagining that he and his wife were in each other's places, that she'd walked into a bar in the Pocket and been beaten with crowbars and bats. That thought—Mrs. Spooner bruised and broken and sewn together—led to nausea, then to half a dozen cold-wash flushings, which came one after another, with the new flushing beginning even before the last flushing stopped. Like airport toilets.

He put the mirror down and picked up his lunch plate—meat loaf, macaroni and cheese, cling peaches, each set into its own little quadrant with raised boundaries to keep it apart from the rest—and spewed a small helping of green beans more or less back into the quadrant they had come from. Mrs. Spooner looked away, offering him what privacy she could while it came up, and then got a washcloth and a plastic bowl from the bathroom and carefully cleaned off his mouth, a touch so light he barely felt it. He saw that she liked him better now that there was something she could do to help.

And while Mrs. Spooner was tidying him up, a nurse appeared and took his vital signs and his temperature, and then noticed his lunch tray, sitting just as it had been delivered. Except the beans didn't look as good as they used to.

"We aren't hungry this afternoon?" she said.

FORTY-SEVEN

There was no ultimatum. All she said was "You can't do this to us," and he knew that was true even if he didn't know which *us* she meant—Spooner and her, or the baby and her, or maybe all three of them together. She said that—whispered it, really—and then got up and kissed him on the forehead and left.

Spooner turned his head and saw that Mr. Graves was asleep, twitching his dog-like twitches as he dreamed. He envied Mr. Graves not just his morphine but his situation. No questions lingered over that broken body, no guilt, nothing of that sort in his head at all, only an inexhaustible disbelief at what Mrs. Graves had done to his person and his new car. Also, he was apparently free of the sensation of being flushed down a toilet.

Spooner had begun to think that the sensation of flushing was brought on by too much introspection. It was, in a way, what had gotten him into this mess in the first place, and now, unable to get to a septic tank or a lawn mower or a typewriter, there was nothing he could do to make it stop.

Later in the day, two heavies from the X-ray department came in and moved him onto a cart for the ride down to the second floor for more pictures of his various broken bones, and then to the first floor for pictures of his brain.

The X-ray department boys bounced Spooner going onto the elevator and again coming off. They said, "Sorry, Mr. Spooner," but they were furniture movers at heart, and if they'd dropped Spooner down a flight of stairs or even the elevator shaft, they would have just collected him from the bottom and said, "Sorry, Mr. Spooner," in that same tone, and delivered him to the X-ray station as if nothing had happened.

And if anybody asked, he'd been like this when they picked him up.

———

Mrs. Graves was back in her regular spot when Spooner was wheeled back into the room. She was sobbing quietly into her handkerchief, which by now was more or less regular too. Mr. Graves was overdue for morphine again and in no mood for the Gospel or taking pictures, which was all she had at the moment to offer. It appeared to Spooner that the lateness of Mr. Graves's morphine deliveries was deliberate; the nurses seemed to have decided that he was spoiled, and even when one of them finally showed up with the juice it was always administered as if it was against her better judgment, the way you finally give in and cork the baby with a pacifier to shut it up.

And so Spooner returned and Mrs. Graves was weeping, and Mr. Graves was going over the details of the accident again, how she had to go and squashed him twice and there was something comforting in the sounds of their voices by now, and he fell off into a jumpy half sleep.

———

Calmer came to the hospital right from the airport. His pants were wrinkled and he was still carrying his suitcase. The suitcase had been in Calmer's family fifty years, and the leather was soft and worn, like an old, favorite baseball glove. He set it down inside the door, and the weight of the thing was there in the way he stood up.

He looked at Spooner from the doorway, worn out in much the same way he'd been the last time Spooner saw him, after he'd lost his job and, as he'd put it then, things just stopped. He smiled hesitantly, taking stock, and Spooner saw that he wasn't sure he was in the right room.

Spooner said, "It's me, all right."

Calmer came farther in and was again momentarily arrested, this time by the sight of Mr. Graves, as everyone was on first entering the room, and then took the chair where Mrs. Spooner had been sitting earlier and crossed his legs. He began to speak but didn't. Spent beyond words.

"It isn't as bad as it looks," Spooner said, and remembered that he'd provoked Mrs. Spooner with exactly those words. "It's just the stitches . . ."

Again Calmer seemed about to speak and nothing came out.

"This here the newspaper boss?" Mr. Graves said. "Man, you somethin', ain't you? You got fighters and reporters and flowers comin' in here like you was big britches." He'd finally gotten a shot of morphine while Spooner slept, and was floating as high and happy as the Goodyear blimp.

Calmer looked across Spooner's body at the man suspended from the ceiling and then stood up to introduce himself.

"This is my father, Calmer Ottosson," Spooner said. "Calmer, this is Sylvester Graves."

"Howdy-do."

Calmer nodded politely and said, "Good to meet you."

"They got us in here all fucked up together on the nurse schedule," Mr. Graves said, "but your boy Spooner ain't complained once. And he don't even get nothin' to make the time pass."

"He means morphine," Spooner said. "I don't get morphine."

Calmer nodded as if he understood, but in some way the information wasn't getting all the way through. A minute passed and he got to his feet and gently fingered the bandages perched on Spooner's head, like a blind man picking out a melon, then squeezed his shoulder—as much intimacy as men ever showed one another back in the place he'd come from—and stood over him awhile, his head bowed in reflection, or exhaustion. And as small as the gesture had been—Calmer putting his hand on Spooner's shoulder—it choked Spooner, and for a little while he did not trust himself to talk.

Calmer continued to watch him, and then he finally found the words. He said, "Why this?"

Why this?

Spooner tried to think but nothing came. "It's just the way things turned out," he said.

"That's God's truth," Mr. Graves said. "You go to park the car and the missus run over you twice. What is a man to do? You buy the car, somebody got to park it. Cain't just drive it around in circles."

Calmer had turned to Mr. Graves to listen to what he said, and now he looked back at Spooner for a translation.

"Mr. Graves was in a car accident in a parking lot," Spooner said.

"Yeah, that's what they callin' it now," Sylvester said. "But how you gone run over somebody twiced by accident? How you did that without malice? That's what we been trying to get to the bottom of here. You an educated man, sir, what would be your opinion in regard to the matter, if you was in my place, that is."

Calmer said, "Well, I like to give a person the benefit of the doubt."

"Oh, I agree wit that. I agree you there, yessir. But I already married the girl. That's benefit of the doubt right there."

"Oh, it was your wife."

"Yessir, thirty-some years. She keep sayin' she never done nothin' like this before, but then again, how long it been festering around in her to do it? You see what I mean? Her mother like that too, she hit the old man in the head with a car battery, him asleep in the bed."

Calmer nodded, considering Mr. Graves's family situation from one side and then another. Even engaging a stranger, he was careless with nothing.

"But it was only this once," Calmer said.

"Once and twiced both," Mr. Graves said. "All the same time."

Calmer said, "But it's not a pattern of behavior."

"How many times you think I'm gone stand back there while she park the damn car after this?"

"Still," Calmer said, "it's not a pattern."

Mr. Graves said, "That car got six hundred miles on the clock. The first new car I ever drove."

Perhaps thinking of the Bonneville on the street, perfect and shining, Mr. Graves closed his eyes and dozed off into the morphine, and Calmer sat back down in the chair next to Spooner, possibly thinking of what he would tell Lily when he called home.

And Spooner slept.

Having Calmer there in the room, knowing he was there with him, Spooner was finally able to sleep.

FORTY-EIGHT

Calmer carried his suitcase down Market Street toward the train stop that would take him to New Jersey, to wait with Spooner's wife until the situation settled out into whatever it would be. He still ached to have somehow been there with her when the news came in.

It was almost dark and beginning to snow. A freezing wind had come up from the east while he was inside with Spooner, and people made their way into it sideways or backwards, some of them lifting their spectacles to dab at their eyes with Kleenex. The bag was heavy and bounced into his legs, and he stumbled as he walked. Inside it, along with his clothes, were some pages from his journal.

Calmer himself had been hospitalized only once, an infection during his last year at the academy. He'd kept a diary in those days—two diaries if you counted the one he kept for the goat—as he'd been doing pretty much since he'd learned to read and write. He'd begun feeding the chickens when he was four and half a century later, if he wanted to do it, he could look up the name of any hen in his father's henhouse and the hiding places she used for her eggs. He'd only quit the journal after he got married and realized that nothing was his own anymore, no place, no time of day, not even for that.

Oddly enough, the same week Calmer came down with his infection, Bill got sick too. The notations from those days included Bill's temperature, heart rate, appetite, urination frequency, general alertness, stomach softness, and a certain melancholy that Calmer had noticed even before the goat's fever began to spike. These notes ran side by side with Calmer's own symptoms, filling a whole sheet of notepaper at the end of each day's entry, with Calmer's numbers growing progressively worse until he was hospitalized, delusional, with a temperature of 105.

He'd found his journals in the basement and brought this part of it along, thinking that, passive as it was, what he'd done—not reporting to the infirmary until the infection nearly killed him—might bear some resemblance to whatever it was that led Spooner out to the very edge, and always had. Thinking he might show him the notes, and that Spooner would see it for himself. But see what? That he'd been in a hospital? That the goat's heartbeat topped out at 192? That once he almost died himself?

No. He'd left the pages in the suitcase, and here he was again, helpless and uneasy and mostly useless, he supposed, as he'd been all the boy's life, and even now, with Spooner lying in the hospital beaten half to death and Calmer fighting his way down Market Street into the howl of the storm, he felt a quiet strum of apprehension simply at the thought of trying to approach him on the subject again.

And thinking of how he might go about it this time, he realized that if what he was looking for was a parallel with Spooner, it was the night he'd finally gone drinking with his classmates from the academy and got up the next morning with a tattoo:

$$E = mc^2$$

high on his shoulder.

It wasn't much, but it was as much damage as he'd ever inflicted on himself intentionally.

Or maybe not. Considering where he was, who he was, how he'd gotten here, maybe not.

FORTY-NINE

They came for him at fifteen minutes before six in the morning. Spooner had seen his X-rays and knew the femur had to be realigned, but he couldn't remember anybody telling him this was the morning they meant to do it.

He said good-bye to Mr. Graves, who was scheduled for his own surgery in the afternoon—the sixth in three weeks—and then was rolled off into the cold. He'd become attached to the old man and imagined himself dropping in to visit him after they both got out.

The hallway outside the operating room smelled like meat.

FIFTY

He came awake the first time seemingly an instant after he'd gone to sleep, paralyzed. He remembered the shot of Valium, then something else, and being asked to count backwards. And an instant later here he was—there is no sense of time passing under anesthesia; what it imitates is not sleep but death—awake, unable to draw breath or open his eyes. Above him somewhere he heard the bone doctor giving orders—he wanted this, he wanted that, no, not that, that—and felt an occasional dull tugging in the area of his hip, and there was no air to breathe, and it reminded him of times when he'd stayed down too long underwater, of that last ten or fifteen feet to the surface.

Why this?

And he lay on the table, waiting to break back into the breathing world, and then went beyond that into new territory, passing through random passing thoughts, and then came a certain reflexive panic, and presently the panic dimmed with everything else, and in the place where it had been was something strangely familiar, the process of dying.

Then the bone doctor's voice: "What the hell's going on over there?"

Into the random thoughts a series of hallucinations: he was locked in a box, in a closet, and finally in the trunk of a car. There was a kid back in Vincent Heights named John Arthur Ramsey whose daddy took him fishing one Sunday morning, locked him in the trunk, and shot himself in the ear.

Was that Calmer he heard looking for him somewhere outside?

He thought of causing some sound, some tiny movement, but what that might be he didn't know. He could cause nothing in this world.

And life moved away a little at a time. It seemed to Spooner that a long time ago the bone doctor had asked an excellent question—*What the hell's going on over there?*—but there had been no answer. Had he meant something else? Was someone masturbating in the corner?

He heard a faint whistle as breath went in and out of someone's nose, and dropped further away, so far away, he realized, that Calmer would never find him now, and then abruptly a tube of some sort was being forced roughly into his throat—gouging the sides as it went down, he thought, like picking your nose with a hangnail—and a moment later, unexpectedly, he felt his lungs fill with air, and Spooner, mute and helpless, dead meat, came fully alive again without moving a muscle.

He heard the bone doctor again, perhaps speaking to the anesthesiologist—not a nurse, anyway, to someone of his own station. He said, "Imagine the fucking tap dance we'd have to do if we lost this one."

Someone laughed—a man's voice—and then abruptly stopped when nobody laughed with him.

That was all Spooner heard. Someone laughed alone, and then Spooner went back into the dark.

———

What now?

He felt the tugging at his hip more distinctly than before, and a moment later a feeling rose through his body at amazing speed, and nothing had moved through him like that since he'd tried to short out all the lights in that motel in Iowa on the family's annual trip to Conde, South Dakota, and blown himself halfway across the room instead.

There was a pause, and things settled and went still. He thought about his grandmother, wondering if she was still alive. He couldn't remember her now, what she looked like.

And oh, lord, it came through him again, and the sound and the feeling converged into one thing, and then it was quiet again, and in the

quiet he realized what it was. A drill. They were using an electric drill
to screw home the bolts and screws into his bone, and it came again and
stopped again and the elements of the thing, the pain and the noise and
the electricity, settled out during the quiet, one from another, and then
rose together in an instant, and Christ in heaven he was not supposed to
be feeling this, was not supposed to know something like this existed, and
he lay helpless to open his eyes, to move even the smallest muscle.

Then it was quiet, and then it coursed through him again, and again,
and another screw went home into the bone.

Why this?

He could taste something burning. The screws went in and he tasted
the burning and then they paused and there was the tugging again as they
pulled aside muscle or tendons to clear a section of the bone for the next
screw, or manipulated the bone itself into a new position, and then would
come the stillness and quiet, a kind of blessing before it washed through
him again. He thought of his wife and could not remember her name.

The bone doctor was five screws into the job before he looked over at
the heart monitor and noticed Spooner's vital signs. "Now what?" he said. As
if a child were tugging at his pants leg, nagging him while he tried to work.

And then mercifully the world went black and dead, and Spooner
went with it.

How long had it gone on?

He couldn't say.

Fifteen minutes?

A voice in it now, whose he didn't know.

*Look, time's got nothing to do with it. Try buying your dog a wristwatch; see how
much time means to him.*

———

Still, time had passed somewhere, and when Spooner and the world
reconvened on the other side of it, Spooner found it—the world—subtly
distorted, and realized a little at a time that he hadn't quite made it all
the way back.

FIFTY-ONE

The nurse was too loud.

He was in the recovery room, he knew that. And she was a nurse, he saw the uniform, an angry nurse. Wait, not exactly angry, *querulous*. She was talking to him in a certain *querulous* tone taken by adult children when the old deaf codger tries to walk out of the house without his pants on.

"Warren? Wake up, Warren. Warren, do you know where you are, Warren?"

Spooner didn't mind short, simple sentences and had no real objection to being watched to make sure he had his pants on before he went outside. The volume, though. The volume was unnecessary. He touched his index finger to his lips and tried to make the shush sound, but with his teeth sheared and his finger splinted, nothing came out, and the stitches tickled his lips.

The nurse left for a few moments, and then she was back. "Warren," she said, "wake up, Warren. Do you know where you're at?"

"Why do you have to say *at*?" he said. "Why can't you say, 'Do you know where you are?'"

He slept.

The surgeon appeared late in the afternoon, carrying the X-rays under his arm, affecting the appearance of someone interested in Spooner's condition. Spooner was awake again, sucking on ice, disinclined to conversation until he was surer about where he'd been dropped off on the way home.

The surgeon opened the envelopes and took out the X-rays, fitted them into the light box and turned it on. He leaned in for a closer look at his work.

"Perfect," he said, tracing his work, "great. Great, perfect." He ran a finger along the picture of Spooner's femur as if he were checking it for splinters. "See?" he said. "It's perfect."

The bone, Spooner saw, had been screwed together in seven places and then baled together in a haphazard way with wire. At least he'd missed the baling.

"What do you think?" the surgeon said, assuming the unmistakable pitch of a salesman, but to what purpose? Was Spooner being sold his own leg? Were they negotiating a price?

Spooner felt the familiar, cold wash that announced that he was again spinning down the shithouse walls, and even as the bottom dropped out of the world, he realized he had lost interest in his recovery, would as soon look at pictures from the bone doctor's family reunion (hairy, monkeylike little children all making faces for the camera) as X-rays of his femur. Then again, at the present moment, he couldn't think of anything he was interested in. Food, sex, sleep—what else did he like? Nothing came to mind. Boxing? Worse yet, it seemed the bone doctor, having ignored him the last three days, now craved his company and goodwill.

"So?" said the bone doctor. "You're thinking, *Where am I at in all this?*"

Spooner looked but did not answer.

"You want to know how long it's going to be, right?"

"Something happened," Spooner said, although he had no inclination to get into it now.

He saw that he'd hurt the bone doctor's feelings. Perhaps this was the moment, walking in with the X-rays, when the doctor customarily accepted thanks and congratulations. "What do you mean?" the doctor said. Yes, it was hurt feelings. A moment passed. "It went perfect," he said, and referred again to the X-rays, as if they were the proof. "Everything went perfect."

"I was awake," Spooner said. "I felt you putting in the screws."

The doctor smiled at that as if he were relieved and sat down on the side of the bed. To Spooner's horror, the orthopod wanted to be pals. Maybe somebody had finally broken the news to him regarding Spooner's identity, possibly even passing along the thought that a man who'd written openly of his wife's menstrual cycle (*In the morning, there were bears in the yard . . .*) would have no qualms about violating whatever patient/doctor confidentiality was ordinarily in effect when a doctor drilled five of seven screws into a fully awake patient on the operating table.

Not that the true nature of Spooner's aversion to the surgeon was medical incompetence. Spooner had a tolerance for incompetence of all kinds, which was clearly tied to ambition, which was the main thing, along with opposable thumbs, that separated humans from the rest of the creatures of the forest in the first place. No, what Spooner couldn't abide in regard to the bone doctor was the ooze. The man was all ooze, too sure of himself by half, too comfortable in his own skin. Too comfortable in the world.

He was looking at Spooner now in a pitiful way, and there were flakes of dandruff in his eyebrows. "You had a dream," the bone doctor said. "It's a very common phenomenon for patients to dream as they come out of anesthesia."

"You sometimes put them to sleep, then."

The surgeon chose not to hear that. "The important thing," he said, indicating the X-rays, "is the procedure. The procedure went perfectly." He watched Spooner closely to see if he was making any headway.

And they sat there a little while, the bone doctor nodding away, encouraging Spooner to nod along with him.

Spooner would not nod, though, and when quite a bit of time had passed with nothing else coming out of the bone doctor, Spooner looked down and considered his leg from one side and then the other and said, "Image the fucking tap dance if you'd lost this one."

The bone doctor chose a look of hurt and bewilderment, as if Spooner were making no sense to him at all, and a minute or two passed and he got up off the bed and left the room, which was all Spooner had wanted him to do in the first place.

FIFTY-TWO

Weeks passed. Spooner went home to the little lake in New Jersey, to his wife and daughter and his dog.

Recovery, though, was slower than he'd expected, and injuries began to show up that nobody had noticed until the bigger, more obvious injuries began to heal. It was two months before he found out he'd fractured his spine—two fractures, actually, one about midpoint, the other at the base of his neck, and a month after that his own doctor noticed that a tendon had split in Spooner's forearm and rolled up like a snapped piano string into his elbow, and was the reason he couldn't close his hand. The pain in his hands gradually went away but was replaced with numbness, especially when he sat at the typewriter and tried to work. The feeling of being flushed gave way to a quieter, more horizontal disorder that felt to him like his body had washed up on a beach, the ocean sliding in underneath, his head bobbing in it like a cork.

More troubling than all that, something was between them now, Spooner and his wife. He'd been home only a couple of days when he found her on her knees in the corner of their bedroom, sorting baby clothes in a bottom drawer so that he wouldn't see that she was crying.

She never said it out loud. She did all the things she'd done before—took care of him in all the ways he could be taken care of, cooked, shopped, took their daughter to preschool, fucked him all the time and so carefully it never hurt him at all (and he was still colorfully bruised in places and tender all over), and held him afterwards. It was in this holding afterwards that he saw it most clearly, the damage that he'd done. Not that she would leave him——he never thought that——only that she had gone sad, and he had lived around sad women all his life and couldn't stand to think of her like that too.

He knew what she was thinking, that she had only a little time with him left. That she and then the baby had come along and interrupted him while he was in the process of killing himself, and now he was back on schedule. That nothing had changed.

It had, though. Not on the night itself, or the operating table, but in the aftermath, watching her, seeing what it had done. Yes, he was different, but there was no talking it over, because what he and Mrs. Spooner had together also depended on her believing that he had come through this whole. Which is to say, she not only wanted him changed; she also wanted him back the way he'd been.

Not for the first time Spooner was reminded that marriage was not the straightforward assembly the instruction book led you to believe.

He remembered now that on the operating table, dancing along the very edges of his life, he hadn't been able to remember her name. That one especially he thought he might keep to himself.

So he held her and pretended the healing was all on track, and she held him and pretended that she wasn't thinking that he was still trying to get himself killed.

FIFTY-THREE

The cast came off Stanley's arm in early April, and a couple of times a week Spooner, usually after his regular dental appointment, drove up to Frazier's gym in North Philadelphia to watch him spar. Spooner was still on crutches, and jumpy, and in this condition no longer felt safe in North Philly.

On one hand, it was probably true that no major racial healing had occurred in the city while Spooner had been laid up, but on the other hand, no one of color had ever done him any harm whatsoever, and he was nervous about things these days that he had never thought about before. The sun would be low in the sky when he went in, and the streets were always dark when he left. Sometimes with Stanley, sometimes alone.

And either way, he always felt worse when he left than he had coming in. And looked worse too. Not that somebody walking around—if *walking* was the word—on crutches, with temporary teeth, swollen lips, head scars still showing through a two-month growth of hair and nerve damage everywhere in his body looked like springtime in the Rockies to begin with. But what was ruining Spooner's looks was worry.

The bone was the ulna, a word Stanley had at first insisted was associated with the female reproductive apparatus, but which in the fact of the matter was one of the two bones connecting wrist to elbow, and thereby a fundamental connection between Stanley's brain and his hand. At least the part of his brain that wanted to fight. And as it became clearer—to everyone but Stanley—that this ulna business had not mended the way it was supposed to, Spooner's thoughts returned again and again to the night in Devil's Pocket, wishing he'd had the sense to take his sheared teeth home to bed after visit number one.

The damage he'd done was there in front of him every day. Mrs. Spooner continued remote and resigned, as if she were already left alone with her child, to fend for herself, and Stanley, without his jab to hold the other fighters off, was eating punches in the gym that he hadn't eaten since those first months in Philadelphia. He must notice, Spooner thought, but Stanley persisted in the view that the punches of other heavyweights were amusements, this in spite of the sure knowledge that a total was being kept somewhere. No one, of course, knew what that number was, or what number was possible, or what happened when the number was reached.

As for Spooner himself, nothing tasted the way it had before, particularly alcohol, and he was not sleeping much, and more and more it seemed to him that going back to Devil's Pocket had left them all sitting ducks in the world.

But it was more complicated than that too. Mrs. Spooner was certain that in Stanley Faint, Spooner had found someone trying to kill himself even faster than Spooner was, and their continued connection—Spooner and Stanley's—served to reinforce the picture of sitting in some hospital waiting room all her life, waiting for the days to pass that would tell the story on Spooner's brain. It always came back to that, to the idea he was only comfortable leaning out a little too far over the railing.

He wondered sometimes why all the people he loved were so sure of what they knew.

———

Spooner had resumed his duties at the newspaper the week after he left the hospital. He wrote his columns from home at first, and there was something between himself and his stories now too, and nothing came to him easily. His sense of taste was ruined, and he gave up on drinking. He didn't miss the bars—he was soon hearing better stories at the little gym in South Philadelphia, and once he was off crutches, he was at the gym every afternoon, working himself back into shape, exhausting himself before he went home. He loved the man and his son and the place in its way became another home, and he worried about it and them accordingly.

He followed Stanley to Las Vegas and Texas and Atlantic City for fights that were always close and increasingly awful to watch. And he saw more clearly all the time that Stanley was a diminished prizefighter.

And on the night Stanley finally got his chance, when he fought for the championship and lost every round, Spooner went into the dressing room afterward and waited while Stanley urinated into a cup for the Texas State Athletic Commission. "Lookit here, Sunshine," Stanley said, and Spooner looked at Stanley Faint's urine, and it was the color of coffee.

Over in the other tent, the champion could barely move his hands. As Stanley would tell a couple of hundred reporters later that night at the press conference, he could fuck up a pair of hands like nobody's business. "Van Cliburn, Tchaikovsky, Rubinstein, we've got offers on the table to all the piano players."

From all accounts, it was one of Stanley's greatest press conferences, but even if he'd known Stanley was going to call out Tchaikovsky, Spooner still wouldn't have gone. He went back to his hotel room instead and called Mrs. Spooner. "It was awful," he said. "I don't know what kept him up." She was quiet, and he pictured her at home, not knowing what to say.

"Is it over, then?" she said finally.

Spooner said, "Yeah, I think it is."

Hours later, three or four in the morning, Stanley knocked on Spooner's door. The excitement was gone; Stanley had left everything he had in the ring and in the hours that had gone by since the thing ended. They sat at a window, keeping the lights in the room off, and Stanley drank half a gallon of orange juice while he tried to get some hold on the meaning of what had happened.

He seemed to want Spooner to explain it, how he'd lost fifteen straight rounds on the night he'd been pointing to all his adult life. He was more confused than embarrassed, which isn't to say he wasn't embarrassed, and more embarrassed than hurt. Which isn't to say he wasn't hurt. His eyes lay small and blue in the swelling, like glimpses of clear sky in a storm, and his lips were cracked open in half a dozen places they were not already stitched, and there were lumps all over his face, particularly the forehead, like he'd gotten into a nest of wasps. What Spooner could not take his own eyes off, though, was a small, jagged cut an inch below one of his eyes, about the shape of a fingernail, that had somehow gone so deep as to sever a tear duct, and as they sat talking and thinking the tear duct leaked and the fluid ran down his cheek, and the lights of Houston blinked on and off in the window, and it looked for all the world like Stanley Faint was crying blood.

PART FIVE

Falling Rapids

FIFTY-FOUR

A week before she died, Spooner's mother wrote him a letter. She didn't know she was out of time, it wasn't about that, although the letter was melancholy enough to make him wonder later on if she'd had a premonition. But probably not. Probably, in her own way, she was apologizing, and, also in her own way, it was to the wrong person.

The letter began in an ordinary enough way, a description of the new Oldsmobile 98 convertible that Superintendent Cowhurl had bought his wife and that was parked, even as she wrote, red as a fire engine in his driveway directly across the street. It had a standard opening; a cheerful reminder of the unfairness of life, which took only about the same amount of space and time as Spooner's other correspondents' reports on the weather. Just running a few scales, clearing the pipes before the start of the opera.

Superintendent Cowhurl bought his wife a convertible every other autumn, just before the new models came out and the prices for the current year's models went down. There had been an incident four years previous when Cowhurl's wife had been stopped by the city police driving around the perimeter of the park in another new convertible with the top down—but, as Spooner's mother always pointed out, with the heated seats heating away (*it must be nice*)—sobbing, naked, and drunk on New Year's day, but that little incident, as Spooner's mother called it, hadn't ever made the paper, even after, to her certain knowledge, an anonymous caller had made the editors aware of the story, and the school board hadn't brought the matter up either, much less fired Cowhurl, or demoted *him* to teaching English.

So now the Cowhurls had three cars—the old convertible had been handed down to their youngest son, who had just turned sixteen—and Spooner's mother and Calmer were still driving the old stick-shift Buick, white with black seats, as unadorned as any car ever made, and Calmer was still working two jobs to make ends meet, and beyond that, Mrs. Cowhurl, currently visiting the manic phase of her manic depression, was tooting the horn whenever she left home for a ride, and tooting again as she pulled into the driveway on the way back. That was what Spooner's mother had to wake up to every morning, the prospect of tooting.

Spooner pictured his mother at the kitchen table, composing this letter in a decaying bathrobe, the pockets stuffed with damp Kleenex, keeping an eye on Cowhurl's house from the window over the sink, waiting for some sign that calamity had finally struck over there, waiting for the Cowhurls to find out what it was like. Waiting for things to even out.

The woman had spent her life waiting for things to even out. The thought that she could be ahead in the game never entered her head.

By now—only two-thirds of the way down the first page—Spooner knew what was coming. The letter wasn't about Mrs. Cowhurl or the new convertible or the unfairness of life, which was old news; it was about her own behavior the week before, when Spooner and Darrow and Cousin Bill Damn from Beaver Island, Michigan, had come to Falling Rapids for the opening of pheasant season, and spent a Sunday afternoon road-hunting with Calmer. This is not to say that any of them came halfway across the country to kill a pheasant, or, with the exception of Cousin Bill—who occasionally, from his second-floor bathroom window, picked off the woodchucks that were undermining his foundation—had any particular inclination to kill anything at all; it was only about getting into a car with loaded shotguns and cold beer and Cousin Bill, who was a piece of work by anyone's estimation, to see what would happen.

And what happened was that for a little while Calmer ran loose. Spooner and Darrow and Cousin Bill drank Falstaff beer until their feet could not touch the car floor for the empty bottles, and along the way

Calmer decided he wouldn't mind having one or two himself, even though he was at the wheel, and they drove all over the dirt roads of eastern South Dakota all afternoon, the back roads of Calmer's childhood, stopping for warm nuts and beer at the little stores where the dirt roads crossed, talking to the locals—although this appealed more to Spooner and Darrow than to Cousin Bill, who had not ended up on an island in the middle of Lake Michigan because he craved the company of strangers—then back in the car, speculating on the sex peculiarities of the family's cousins and aunts and uncles.

It was a wonderful hunt, nobody so much as winged or deafened; in fact no shotgun was even discharged within the confines of the car. For all Spooner knew, it was the safest hunt in the history of the Whitlowe family, and half an hour into it Calmer was himself again, almost the way he'd been in the years before he was ruined professionally, moving in and out of the car like a dancer, as if there was nothing in the world he dreaded, and then, too soon, they seemed to notice all at once that the sun was going down, and it was time to head home. Spooner's mother was fixing a roast.

They were an hour out of Falling Rapids when the sun set, and as the dark closed over the prairie it closed over Calmer too. Late for supper. Spooner watched his old man's afternoon grace disappear into worry. Calmer stopped once to call home, but there was no answer. After that he held on to the steering wheel as if someone were trying to pull it away from him, and changed gears by rote, without regard to speed, and the engine coughed and bucked. A man who had landed planes on the decks of aircraft carriers driving like an eight-year-old farm boy having his first turn behind the wheel.

They hit the city limits right at seven o'clock. Darrow and Cousin Bill in the backseat, Spooner up front with Calmer, all of them except Calmer still drinking, but quietly now; Calmer focused a long way down the road, no longer with them at all. Little cracks of worry everywhere in his face. They drove along the northern boundary of Kissler Park, past the brick mansions that stood facing it—car dealers, doctors, attorneys; Spooner's mother had once claimed she could smell the Republican money—and then onto a street canopied in elm trees where the houses were not so big but were still a long ways up from Milledgeville and Prairie Glen, and drove another half block and stopped in front of the gray, two-story house that was the net financial return thus far into the life of Calmer Ottosson. Not much for what he had put into it; not even a farm, and most of it still belonged to the bank. The car was quiet a moment, then someone in the backseat moved and the beer bottles rattled. Seven-fifteen p.m., pitch dark, eerie as a pasture of blind cows.

It was Cousin Bill who finally broke the silence. "Oh, boy," he said, "the missus has turned out the lights."

Even his critics had to admit that Cousin Bill had an uncanny insight into the workings of human intercourse. In fact, it was one of the great mysteries of the Whitlowe family how, with this uncanny insight and his willingness to blurt it into the public arena, he'd managed his own human intercourse so well, or had ever gotten laid at all. But there he was, successful in business, lucky in love, beloved by his wife, who looked like more fun than the circus, and a large family—for all Spooner knew, the greatest man in Michigan.

Calmer pulled the old Buick into the driveway, past the house to the garage. From there, they could see the back of the house, which was as dark as the front. It didn't have the look of abandonment—the paint was fresh, there were no weeds in the yard—but at the same time it was a shade too quiet for a place just shut down for the night; what it really looked like was one of those farmhouses out in the country where the old farmer dies and the widow stuffs corncobs into the light fixtures to save on the electric bill.

They went into the house through the side door and found her sitting in her bathrobe at the kitchen table, in the dark. Her atomizer was on the table, next to a glass of tap water, and when they walked in she gave herself a couple of hits off the atomizer, making sure that everyone understood the situation. Not only was the roast ruined, so was her ability to draw oxygen.

They had all seen this kind of behavior before, of course, even Cousin Bill. It was the way generations of the Whitlowe women, one of whom, after all, was Cousin Bill's mother, kept blood relatives in line.

"The roast is ruined," she said, as if the cow itself had died of inconsideration. She took another shot off the atomizer and pulled it deep into her chest. She had the humidifier on and the air in the room was as wet as fog. Spooner's mother fought for every breath, and Spooner was suddenly conscious of his own breathing, and soon found that he could not clear his head of its mechanics, the in and out. When Spooner's mother was on her game, she was as good as there was, or ever had been.

Calmer appeared pole-axed but calm, at least not monitoring the workings of his own lungs.

"Well, there's still beer left," Cousin Bill said, and he turned on the kitchen lights. Everyone squinted. Beyond his uncanny insight, Cousin Bill had another quality unique to the Whitlowe family; he could *recover*, could overlook the scene just presented, for instance, as if it had never happened. "There's nourishment in beer," he said. "Quite a few vitamins, actually."

Spooner's mother said, "I'm afraid I don't feel well." Impenetrable even to the charms of Cousin Bill. She turned away from them, walking right past Calmer, moving like a much older woman would move, and disappeared into the bedroom.

Calmer thought about it for only a second or two and then went in after her, and Spooner and his brother and his cousin did not see either of them again all night.

They found the roast in the garbage under the sink, and it wasn't bad, although Cousin Bill would remark the next morning that he thought it could have used a little more time in the oven. But then, his branch of the family liked their beef well done.

And that was really all that happened. Five humans of various blood relations got together for a weekend, four of them drank beer and went hunting, three ate some beef out of the garbage. In the morning Calmer went back to work and Spooner's mother came out of her bedroom and sliced cantaloupe for the boys without mentioning the previous evening, and in the afternoon the boys all started home, and a week after that, the letter arrived with Spooner's morning mail.

———

When Spooner thought about it later, it seemed to him that the letter was the closest thing to an apology his mother ever issued.

Not that she specifically said she was sorry—not in this life—but she did offer an explanation for what happened, which went like this: Her father died, then Spooner's twin brother died, then her first husband died, then the ruination of the roast beef.

But it was more than that. Things happen, after all, in a context. The Whitlowes had once been wealthy and prominent in Milledgeville, only to be ruined during the Depression. Her father, who was dead years before Spooner hit the ground, had been a famous football player at Brown University, then a famous coach at the state university, then a state senator, and then a businessman of sorts, part owner of a lumberyard, and then the Depression hit, and, like most people who went into business for themselves, he didn't know what he was doing and went broke.

Spooner's grandfather was a legend now, a man's man and the relative whom Spooner was supposed to favor most, although it was Spooner's brother Phillip who resembled all the pictures of him that Spooner had seen. But then, Spooner was no good at matching faces with pictures and by now had lost even the sense of what he himself looked like, and often caught himself glancing at his own reflection in windows, like some dog sticking his nose into his own rectum every ten minutes to remind himself who he is.

FIFTY-FIVE

By his own estimate, it was now the second half of Spooner's life, which was not some actuarial calculation of middle age but the hard fact that his point of view had been altered, and there was no going back to the way things had looked before, when he was closer to the ground.

He hadn't come gradually into his second half, but all at once, in those minutes he'd been left awake on the operating table, and afterwards, as evidence of the change, his body, which did not care for the new perch, began a sort of food strike, regularly tossing whatever arrived into his stomach back out into the world. This was now his body's answer to miseries of all kinds—worry, torn knees, torn nails, broken bones, form letters from the IRS, Mrs. Spooner's PMS, other people's vomit, dead pets—whatever it was, he'd blow lunch. Afterwards, perhaps not so strangely, he would feel lighter, and often relieved.

Thus, the minute Spooner saw his mother's handwriting on the envelope from South Dakota, his stomach stirred, and he took the letter into the bathroom and sat on the edge of the tub to read it. Forewarned is forearmed. Due to his mother's penmanship and the length of the manuscript, it took him half an hour to finish. But he did finish, every line right down to *Love, Your Mother*, and then had to move only a step or two to reach the toilet, where he chipped a tooth—one of his replacements from the evening in Devil's Pocket—on the bowl. It was a small chip, but felt strange to his tongue.

He put the letter on his desk, waiting to feel lighter and relieved, but another half hour passed and he didn't feel relieved at all, and the letter was still there, nine pages long, folded into thirds, lying face-up in a shaft of sunlight from the window, opening on its own like some poisonous flower. Spooner didn't want to read it again—he didn't want to touch it again—but he would, he knew, and he did. Twice that week, and then again, after she died. But never after meals.

For Spooner, the worst of it was a single line at the bottom of page six: . . . *and then Calmer came along, and you two kids needed a father, and so that was that.*

There were other parts that were not good—after all, it was a nine-pager—but that line, that single line. Spooner would always wonder what she expected him to think when he read it, and he was reminded again that he'd grown up under strange rules. The strangest of these rules, of course, erased the fact of Spooner and Margaret's father from history, but this was barely stranger perhaps than the apparent understanding between Lily and Calmer never to have cross words with each other in front of the children. Somewhere, somehow, it had been decided that parental conflict wasn't good for children's development. How exactly this conflict avoidance was supposed to groom Spooner and his sister and brothers for adult life was never clear, and when Spooner's first marriage began to fall apart, they might as well have put him in a room with a screwdriver and a hammer and told him to fix the television. Spooner sometimes wondered if the whole family wouldn't have been better off if they'd all just blown lunch when they were miserable, like he did.

Or, absent that, if his mother could have brought herself to get it out of her system some other way, to scream at them—*You drunk bastards ruined the roast!*—and throw a pan at Calmer's head, or at Spooner's head (he wouldn't have minded) and then a week or two later drop him a post card saying *Sorry about your head,* instead of a nine-pager containing the story of her life. The difference being that Spooner would never hold a lump on the head against anyone. That was miles from unforgivable, and who was he, after all, to cast stones? Still, there was a line somewhere, and the letter from his mother crossed it and somehow obliged him to declare where he stood.

And Jesus, did he not want to get into that.

And because he didn't want to get into it, the letter was still lying open and unanswered on his desk the night Calmer called with the news that she was gone. While they were still on the phone, Spooner imagined him going through her things and finding the letter he would have written, slowly realizing what it was about. And Spooner, who had never experienced writer's block before in his life, realized that this one occurrence had saved his neck.

FIFTY-SIX

The details: Spooner's mother had died during a regular meeting of the Greater Falling Rapids Great Books Club, the first fatality in the club's history. The meetings were held once a month in the living rooms of alternating members, and this month's host, who had joined the group only the month before and had suggested they take on *Swann's Way*, was a retired admiral, a Democrat, who lived in a big new house on the fourth hole of the country club with a snow-white, asthmatic bulldog named Silly.

Spooner's mind wandered even as Calmer told him the story. How many people in South Dakota had read *Swann's Way*? How many dogs were named Silly? How many Democrats lived out at the country club? What were the odds, what were the odds?

Spooner's mother hadn't known there was a dog in the house, or she wouldn't have come. Dogs set off her asthma. As did cats, dust, mold, smoke from Morrell's meat plant at the edge of the city, cigarette smoke, and mammal dander of every kind she had been tested for. Beyond that, she secretly didn't think the great books were so hot, and most likely she hadn't read *Swann's Way*, which was no mark against her as far as Spooner was concerned. He'd tried a couple of pages of it himself once and failed to find a pulse.

It wasn't the Proust that finished her off, though, it was the dog. The navy man, it developed, had given Silly a tranquilizer and put her in a back room, where she would not bother or be bothered by his guests. The animal, it further developed, could match Spooner's mother allergy for allergy, and was particularly prone to asthma attacks and hysteria whenever strangers came to the door.

Spooner's mother had been in the house about ten minutes when she asked Calmer to get her atomizer, the little one she kept in the glove compartment of the Buick. The group was having refreshments—cocktails, wine, peanuts, crackers, pâté—and had not yet begun to discuss Marcel Proust.

Calmer asked if she thought they should leave, but no, she would be all right. It was probably just autumn pollen. "I'm just a little tight in the chest," she said.

He got her atomizer. The evening grew longer and the refreshments kept coming, and the members of the Great Books Club drank quite a bit of alcohol, and some of them confessed that they hadn't read *Swann's Way*, and others had read a page or two and quit, and Spooner's mother disappeared into the bathroom more and more often to discreetly inhale from her inhaler.

Calmer offered again to take her home, but she was having a good time now—the discussion had moved off literature and on to politics—and didn't want to leave.

Then, a little after nine, one of the other guests, a professor in the math department at Augustana College who had food and wine stains in his beard, reeled down the hallway to use the admiral's toilet but opened the wrong door and roused the beast.

Tranquilized or not, Silly tore into the living room like Christmas morning, her nails clicking and scratching across the oak floor, and there confronted the entire Greater Falling Rapids Great Books Club, the force of her barking lifting her front paws off the floor, backing away from one guest and into another, wheezing and making terrible wet guttural noises, and then began to sneeze, and mists of dog snot blew across the room, settling Jesus knew where.

And now the animal's breathing shortened, and you could see her ribs as she worked to pull oxygen into her trembling body. The admiral tried to coax her back into the bedroom, but the dog was too upset. She backed away, bumping into one guest and then another, whirling to cover her flank, wheezing, drooling, growling, violently sneezing, and eventually bumped into Spooner's mother, who had ducked her nose and mouth into her blouse, filtering out as much of the air with its microscopic dander and dog snot as she could, and now leaned back into the sofa and picked up her feet.

From there, they both went downhill fast.

The dog collapsed shortly, her breathing shallow and strangled, rattling. It was hard for the many animal lovers among the club's membership to listen to her struggling to hang on to life.

Calmer took Spooner's mother out of the house, but she did not think she could make it to the car and they sat down on the steps, she and Calmer, and then she lay down, trying to get some air into her lungs. Panic was everywhere, and feeding on itself. Calmer made a pillow of his coat, and called inside for someone to call an ambulance.

Inside, the bulldog had gone into shock. The retired admiral sat with her on the floor, weeping, holding her head in his lap, running his hand over her coat while fifteen feet away, on the other side of the living room wall, Calmer, absent the weeping, did the same for Lily.

And in the end, neither of them made it.

Spooner's mother died on the way to Falling Rapids Memorial Hospital and Silly was likewise DOA at the vet.

Spooner and Calmer were on the phone most of an hour that night, all the sounds still fresh in Calmer's mind, the clatter of the animal's claws as she ran up the hall toward the living room, the rattle as she tried to breathe, the strange noise in Spooner's mother's chest outside on the porch steps, and then at the end, in the ambulance, a different, draining-sink note in her chest after she'd sighed and stopped breathing.

Calmer finished the story and stopped, and in the silence that followed added, "At least she didn't suffer," which, Christ knows, was not the way she would have told it.

When he hung up Mrs. Spooner was standing in the half-light of the bedroom door. He was sitting at his desk.

"What's wrong?" she said. She had been a good sleeper when they met, but not so much these days, even though she still dropped off half a minute after the lights went off. These days she woke up at the smallest noise, frightened; these days she was always expecting bad news.

"Mom's dead," he said. He saw her watching him to see how he was.

"An accident?"

"No, it was a bulldog. She had an asthma attack. She went to a meeting of the Great Books Club, and there was a bulldog there. It had asthma too . . ."

He had to stop before he lost control. She came to him and put her arms around his head and held him against her stomach, and he hiccuped, once and then again, and she held him tighter, and they stayed together like that a pretty long time, Spooner allowing her to think whatever she was thinking, and then he stood up and she noticed his erection.

FIFTY-SEVEN

Spooner arrived in Falling Rapids, having changed planes in Chicago and Omaha and then been re-routed to Sioux City, and headed to the liquor store before he even thought about going home. He had intended to buy Scotch but ended up instead with two cases of Beefeater gin, twenty-four bottles of it, imagining the sight of a whole shelf of the stuff—a shining red-coated guard on label after label, quiet, orderly, there to do his job—every time Calmer opened the cupboard to get a plate or a glass. Calmer was not anybody's idea of a big drinker, and under torture Spooner could not have explained why he'd bought so much of the stuff.

Relatives had begun to filter into town, and the neighbors brought over hams and macaroni salads, and Calmer sat at the kitchen table, not so much bereaved as distracted. By now he'd quit trying to keep track of the growing loads of food and relatives being dropped off at the door. He didn't seem pestered in the least by all the movement and attention, although to Spooner the place felt like it was being ransacked.

The doorbell rang again, and Calmer came back into the kitchen carrying a ham the size of a pygmy.

—

They went to the funeral home in the morning to see her, in two cars: Darrow and Phillip and Calmer in the Buick, Margaret and her husband and Spooner in the rental Spooner had picked up at the airport.

Spooner had taken a pain pill when he woke up in his old bedroom that morning, then had another one when he heard they were going to the funeral home. But even drugged and sweet, he did not want to see his mother. The rest of them did, though, as Spooner had known they would.

Spooner could not predict what note the sight of their mother's body might sound in his sister or brothers, except that Darrow, who was born wise and calm in that same familiar way Calmer was, could be counted on to keep his head and conduct business. To take that weight at least off Calmer's shoulders. He was younger than Spooner, but in a world that made any sense would have been the older brother.

The leadership of the expedition having been conceded to Darrow, Spooner envisioned his own function as the muscle, like one of those fellows standing behind the president in sunglasses with that doohickey in his ear, there just in case. If something happened, he would be the one to throw himself on the grenade, which, everything considered, was not such a bad way to go, a painless death plus you got to miss the funeral.

———

Margaret rode with Spooner in the front seat of the rented car. Her husband was in back, reading the obituary that had run that morning in the newspaper, the stem of his unlit pipe clamped into his mouth all the way back to the molars. Calmer and Phillip and Darrow had left ten minutes ahead of them in the old Buick.

Spooner looked over at Margaret now, gazing through the passenger window at the town. She'd left home for college before Calmer took the job in South Dakota, and although she came home most summers to visit, the place was never the place you come back to for her, the way Prairie Glen might have been if they'd stayed there. And even though Spooner was no more tied to Falling Rapids than she was, he found himself sorry that Margaret had no connection to the place. She was hungry for these things, and for as long as he could remember she had tried to hold on to whatever small pieces of the past she could. He supposed it was the difference in their ages. It was only eighteen months but in some way she'd known their father and lost him, while for Spooner he was missing from the start. And out of this difference came her hard claims on the things she had left, while Spooner lived more or less on the other side of the mirror, never believing anything was his for good until it was so generally worthless that nobody else would want it.

The dog, for instance. The dog was definitely his.

Harry was deaf and blind and brittle now, horrible to smell, always gnawing away at some part of his body, a leg or his tail or his pecker, apparently trying to whittle himself out of this world. He still occasionally wandered the small dirt road along the south shore of the little lake where they lived, yearning perhaps for one last feel of some fluffy white poodle's throat in his jaws, but mostly these days he just stayed home, gnawing.

Doing all this chewing on his person, he would, by evening each day, have accumulated long, crescent-shaped glops of hair behind his lower front teeth, soaked in the saliva of his poor infected gums, and every night while Mrs. Spooner warmed his—Spooner's—dinner, Spooner would sit on the floor with the dog, pry open his mouth and pick out the day's accumulation of hair. Usually it came out all at once, like a dentist's impression of your teeth, and lately on occasion one of his teeth came out with it.

Yes, Harry was all his.

No one would take his dog.

FIFTY-EIGHT

Spooner walked behind his sister and her husband toward the funeral home. Calmer, Darrow, and Phillip were up ahead, waiting near the door. Another family was emptying out of the place, happy to be loose again and free, nobody exactly skipping, but no dawdlers either, about like the unloading of an airliner.

Some of the mourners in this group nodded to Spooner as they passed, a few even stepping off the sidewalk into the grass to let him by, perhaps an acknowledgment that they'd made it out and Spooner was just going in. Or that they were all in the same boat. For whatever reasons, half a dozen small connections were struck and extinguished, all in the same moment.

The business office was small and warm and smelled of the press of flesh, not as neatly kept as Spooner would have predicted—an ashtray had been left on a chair, and there were others here and there around the room, half full of ashes and gum wrappers and ground-out cigarette butts, some blotted with exotic shades of lipstick, and the trash can beside the old man's desk was stuffed full with papers—but remarkable in its size and seating capacity. There was a sofa, a love seat, nine leather chairs; fifteen people could be right at home. Sixteen, if you moved the ashtray.

"Please," the old man said, "make yourself comfortable. Call me Junior."

Now that Spooner looked, the old man was a very old man, and small; the desk was enormous. An old man in an old suit, a freshly cut flower in one of his lapels. Junior's suit appeared to be four sizes larger than Junior, but he was old, and Spooner supposed he might have shrunk.

"May I begin," Junior said, "by offering my deepest condolences." He distributed business cards, looking from one member of the family to the next expectantly, as if he'd offered to fight anyone in the bar.

The card identified Al Hershey, Jr., co-owner of Hershey's Funeral Home with Ralph Hershey, Jr., serving the needs of Falling Rapids since 1939. Dignity at Reasonable Prices. Two Hersheys and each of them a junior. Cousins?

It was hard to say how long ago Al Hershey, Jr., might have been born—eighty-five, ninety-five years—his head was strangely shaped, disproportionately large on top, like a muffin. And lying sideways across this muffinlike head was a patch of hair as black as the Bible but apparently constructed for someone with a narrower pate than the old man's. It lay up there like a house cat, and gradually an unthinkable thought slinked into Spooner's consciousness, and once that thought rolled in, Spooner speculated that Junior might have gotten the suit the same way. And the shoes! Nobody of Junior's stature had feet big enough to fill the shiny new wing tips he was wearing.

Junior was talking business; bereavement, respect, sacred memory, comfort, dignity, waterproofing for the ages. Spooner wondered if words like these had the same meaning for the old man as they did for everybody else, or if they lost their meaning over the years, or had come to mean something else. And if that were true, he wondered how the two undertakers, Junior and Junior, would comfort each other when the time came.

Junior said, "A viewing in the chapel is always nice. It's a little extra but it gives everyone a chance to say good-bye to . . ."—and now he ran a shaking finger down a sheet of paper, finding her name—"a chance for all of Lily's friends to say good-bye in a religious setting, which was so important to her during her stay here on earth."

He stopped abruptly, as if he sensed he'd said the wrong thing, and then rechecked his paperwork. For the few seconds the name checking required no one spoke or moved, and then, satisfied, Junior simply stood up and headed for the door, motioning them with a wobbly roll of his head to follow along. Another eight ounces of weight up there, and his neck would have snapped like a pencil.

The display room seemed to be a place full of good memories for the old man. Around the perimeter were ten demonstrator caskets in an assortment of models and colors, and at the center of the room was the crown jewel, a box that seemed in the half-lit room to glow.

The old man entered first, finding the light switch. The lights were dim and fluorescent, and the boxes lay tall, dark, and handsome all over the room. The room had four windows, hidden from view by heavy off-red curtains, and Junior went to the curtains now, taking his time, and drew them open one after another, and a layer of foreboding and mystery dropped away from the caskets as each new wide shaft of light fell across the wooden floor.

When the last curtain was opened, he paused a moment to look over the room in its new, brighter mood, and smiled with the morning sunshine at his back, and his teeth were huge and as white as wet paint, seeming almost to spill out of his mouth—whose teeth could they have been?—and the cuffs of his trousers lay on the carpet around his feet, as if he were sitting on the commode. It gave Spooner pause, imagining the old fellow looting Lily.

Now Junior moved from one casket to the next, opening the lids. Most of them caught some glint of the light coming in through the room's southern windows. A small satin pillow had been placed inside each box, and across each pillow was a small white tag, where the price was written in elegant script.

Spooner had not been in the room a minute before fixating on the most luxurious model—the Eternity—and was now peering down into its green velvet bed. The sides of the casket were heavily cushioned and had the billowy look of clouds, and pockets had been sewn here and there so that small objects could be stowed for later on.

"You're looking at the very finest casket ever made," Junior said. He reached up and took Spooner's bad elbow, and the grip was sharp and unbalanced, like a parrot had landed on his arm. "In my opinion, there is no finer tribute to the person who brought you into the world."

Spooner continued to stare, and now Calmer walked to the foot of the casket and stared in too.

Behind them Darrow said, "We were looking for something modest. It would be more in line with her wishes."

The old man pretended not to hear him and continued on with Spooner. "Totally watertight," he said. "Comfort for the ages, and you can see the craftsmanship for yourself. Classic lines."

Calmer leaned into the box and sniffed, and then he patted the floor and the sides. The casket was narrow and steep, much deeper than it looked from the door, and Calmer leaned so far in as to nearly disappear.

"Don't worry," the old man said to Calmer, "it doesn't look so lonesome once the body's inside." A moment passed and brought Margaret to the edge of the coffin too.

"A thousand years will go by," the mortician said, "and this casket won't leak a drop. Guaranteed. No water, no rodents, no roots. Roots grow around this casket, not through it. All money-back guaranteed. A redwood will not grow through this casket. Think of it, these trees have been out in the forest since the time of Christ, and the Eternity will outlast them all."

There was another long moment of silence, which the undertaker, thinking the deal was now as good as closed, completely misunderstood. "Of course, it's your loved one—"

Which was when Calmer climbed in and lay down. He turned sideways, away from them, and fluffed the pillow and lay his cheek against it and closed his eyes. And for a long time he simply lay still.

Looks passed, one of them to another, some uneasy current in the room, nobody knowing what Calmer intended. Or if he'd broken down for good. He issued a noise that could have been a sigh of contentment, or could have been the last straw.

"Sir?" Junior said. "Your shoes, sir?"

FIFTY-NINE

Margaret was quiet most of the way home. After Calmer had climbed out of the casket ("It's a little hard on the back," he'd said), she and Darrow and Phillip had gone into the back to see the body while Spooner sat in the waiting area with Calmer, reading a six-month-old copy of *Sports Afield* magazine. It wasn't clear what was going on with Calmer, but something had changed and as far as Spooner could tell, it was all for the good.

"If that was supposed to be funny," Spooner had said to Calmer, speaking of his climb into the Eternity, "it was."

And Calmer had smiled and leaned back until his head touched the wall and hadn't said a word.

Now Spooner slowed the car and pulled to the curb, leaned out, and vomited. "You know," he said to his sister, when he was back inside, "it's strange, but I never threw up that night when Calmer called to say Mother was dead." She looked at him a little oddly, and he wiped at his mouth and said, "Usually I would. That or go outside and cut the grass in the middle of the night. I don't handle stress well anymore."

Margaret studied him a little longer and said, "Have you ever thought about therapy?"

And like that Spooner was braying like Stanley Faint. Therapy! Had he thought about therapy? It was the idea of bringing a psychologist into it now, at this stage in the game, that had set him off. It would be like picking up a hitchhiker out on the interstate without slowing down.

He looked at his sister, who had been seeing psychiatrists since college, hoping he hadn't insulted her. "It's just that every time I bust up a knee or an elbow or something, I have to see a therapist." Which sounded lame even to him. "You know, just a different use of the term."

Worse and worse.

That night, back at the house, some of the cousins were sitting in the living room, talking about Aunt Lily. Getting their stories together, things to tell their children when they returned home. The children, of course, wouldn't care if their Aunt Lily could tinkle and play the harmonica at the same time; it was nothing to them.

Later on, seven relatives from Calmer's side of the family arrived from Conde in two Ford pickups, each truck with extra wheels on the back axle to accommodate heavy loads. The men carried the suitcases and clothes for the funeral and Arlo's wife brought in a keg of beer that must have weighed a hundred pounds. The other woman was holding six dead pheasants by the feet. Gutted and partially plucked.

Spooner picked out Arlo right away, just the way he'd pictured him; gone were the index finger, the middle finger, and the pinky, right down to the knuckles. Unaccountably, the bear had left the ring finger intact.

Arlo had picked off the pheasants on the way to Falling Rapids, and the woman who brought them in had gone right to the kitchen sink to finish cleaning them. Arlo's dog Dick was in the bed of the truck outside. The pickup belonged to Arlo's wife, Arlene, who hugged Calmer, lifted him off the floor, pumped herself a beer and sat down. She pointed at Arlo. "I'll tell you this much, none of you characters are driving home. Not my rig. You want to hunt pheasants, use your own truck from now on."

Arlo moved behind her and stuck the remaining finger of his left hand into his mouth all the way to the ring, wetting it so that a little line of spit hung between the tip of his finger and his lips as he took it out, and then moved up on her from behind and screwed it into her ear.

"God*damn* it, Arlo," she said, and pulled loose from him and grabbed

the Minnesota Twins baseball cap off his head and used it to scour out
her ear, using that same twisting motion that he'd used to befoul her.
Then she spit into the cap and set it back on his head.

He said to Calmer, "She just loves that."

It wasn't pheasant season, as one of the Whitlowes—an environmen-
talist, it developed—pointed out, and Arlo patiently explained that he
wasn't shooting pheasants, he was killing them with the truck.

The pheasants came up to the road at dusk to eat gravel, and Arlo
bore down on them at seventy, eighty miles an hour, sometimes catching
two at a time as they scattered and ran or tried to fly. Hearing the thump
or thumps, Arlo would slam on the brakes, putting the truck into a slide,
and then his dog Dick—who went with him everywhere—would be out
of the truck bed even before they'd stopped, and back thirty seconds later
with the bird.

Hearing this so repulsed the environmentalists of the Whitlowe side
of the family that half a dozen of them or so went into the living room
and discussed turning him in.

Arlo looked at Calmer, shaking his head. He said, "What you got
yourself into now, Calmer?"

Spooner saw the play in Calmer's eyes, and thought for a moment that
they might have lost him back to the other side.

The day after the funeral, Spooner found Calmer sitting alone in the
garage. The Ottossons had gotten up at dawn to go home to their farms,
but there were still Whitlowes all over the house, and Calmer was out
there reading the *Minneapolis Tribune* by the light of the single bare bulb
that hung from the ceiling. Sitting in a lawn chair, a glass and a bottle
of the Beefeater on the cement floor next to him, a lit cigarette tipped
into the ashtray in his lap. The line of smoke came up like he'd been shot
in the balls with a Roman candle.

Spooner took a chair from a stack of chairs against the wall and wiped
off the spiderwebs. He sat down a few feet from Calmer. It was cool in

here and smelled of gasoline and cut grass. Spooner wondered if Calmer had come to the garage out of habit—he couldn't smoke in the house because of her asthma—or if he'd just wanted to get away from all the random noise and movement inside.

They sat together a little while, neither of them talking, and Calmer handed him the sports section of the paper and nodded in the direction of the gin bottle on the floor. Spooner spotted a paper cup on a cross beam, emptied the nails inside into a coffee can, then cleaned out the cup with his T-shirt and poured himself a little straight gin. He took a seat and presently lay the newspaper in his lap and looked up into the rafters, feeling like there was something he should say, but nothing came.

His eyes adjusted to the bare bulb, and he made out a coil of rope up there, and a wagon, and beyond that, in the front corner where the lines of the roof all came together, a wasps' nest as big as a grapefruit. He tried to image how he might go about taking care of it without getting stung, but nothing came.

Nothing came.

It was the start of something new, sipping gin in the garage and reading the morning paper, letting all the small problems and complications inside the house take care of themselves, Calmer seemingly no longer weighed down with responsibility and dread, with his wife's asthma, with his wife.

Spooner was hit with an impulse to acknowledge his father's new life. He said, "Maybe you should get a dog."

And realized even as he said it that he'd mistaken capitulation for recovery.

PART SIX

Whidbey Island

SIXTY

A long time after Philadelphia, after his teeth had been capped and the caps had fallen off and been replaced with other caps, which also fell off and were finally replaced with implants, and he could smile over his implanted teeth without feeling the lumps of scar tissue in his lips, after he could sit and work again without the eerie, scalding pain crawling over his back, and could lie down at night without the pillow floating beneath his head, and without drifting back to the operating table and what had happened there, one day on an island three thousand miles away, in a place as far removed from the city of Philadelphia as you could find, Spooner looked up from a very bad sentence and saw his daughter flying up the driveway like fire.

It was three in the afternoon; the driveway was a sheer quarter-mile climb from the road to the house. The child weighed eighty-five pounds and was strapped into a backpack full of school books.

For the previous half hour, Spooner had been nosing back and forth over this same bad sentence, poking here and poking there, like some sweet old bitch trying to rouse the still puppy in her litter, and now he stopped, grateful for the interruption, and watched her make the last hundred yards, admiring the way she finished it all the way to the top, remembering that feeling of breaking into a sudden all-out run for home, for no reason except you could do it, and exactly pictured his own long, unhinged charge down the paved hill from the highway in Vincent Heights, past a dozen houses whose closets he had attended as the Fiend, and felt the wild pull of the hill itself, the feeling of running for your life, and then hitting the red-dirt circle at the bottom, too fast and out of control, past two more houses he had broken into, and here the road evened out a bit and he slowed, the wind cool in his hairline sweat, and he turned right at Granny Otts's driveway and headed straight up it, almost as steep as the roof of her house—yes, he had been on her roof—and across the yard to his own front steps, willing himself to run even those last eleven brick steps up to the porch and the front door, and then at the door turning back to admire the distance he'd come, hands on his knees and feeling the trembling in the muscles of his thighs, and feeling his lungs—too small to feed the engine pounding in his chest—looking back at the far hill, at the amazing distance, and seeing clearly that he had done something that could be seen and measured, something real, and in that same moment seeing that it was all as pointless as mud.

———

Thus reengaged with his childhood, Spooner did not notice his own child was sobbing until she had stopped at the walkway, a few steps from the front door, and taken off her backpack and sat down on top of it and dropped her face into her arms.

He watched a moment longer, giving her a moment to collect herself because she didn't like to cry in front of him, and then he couldn't wait any more and stood up, thinking maybe something had happened at school. He knew how little it sometimes took. The child was twelve years old and didn't cry much and never had, especially in front of him. Spooner was forty-seven now and loved her crazily, and went crazy at the sight of her weeping and always had, and she understood him and protected him as much as she could from the facts of her twelve-year-old life.

He walked out the side door, coming to her from around the house, giving her a little more time, and then from her blind side sat down in her lap. She screamed, laughing and crying at the same time, and he slid off her lap and put his arm around her and felt her smoothing out, and then waited another few minutes, until she could talk.

"What's up, doc?"

He'd been saying that when she was sad or hurt or scared since the day they brought her home from the hospital.

———

There were two of them over there now besides the old man, commuters, landscapers, and truck polishers by day, citizens of the wild side by night. Marlin Dodge—the old man's grandson—and Alexi Sug, Marlin's Ukrainian weight lifter who seemed unable to move without first considering the positioning of his body to best show off the cut of his muscles. The old man's aversion to the pair could not have been plainer, but he seemed obligated in some way to let them stay. On the few occasions he and Spooner had spoken about them, the old man referred to them as *the grandson* and *Atlas Shrugged*.

The grandson and Atlas Shrugged had been at the bottom of the hill digging postholes with a rented tractor when Spooner's daughter got off the bus, and the one driving the tractor—the grandson—had choked off the engine and called her over to tell her that he was going to kill her cat. The cat was named Whitlowe, and had been with them awhile, a small, limping, twitching ball of muscle whose X-rays had revealed a piece of buckshot still lodged in his shoulder. He was half wild and covered with scars, his ears ragged-edged, like they'd been chewed by moths. The animal was a stray who'd come into the yard two or three years ago and still would not allow himself to be touched except by Spooner's daughter, and followed her room to room in the house and slept with her at night, his chin resting against the top of her head on the pillow, his drool in her hair when she woke up. Last winter she'd tried making him mittens.

The evidence against the cat was apparently all circumstantial. Marlin had seen him loitering in the area of his koi pond lately, and lately his koi were being murdered in the night.

As Marlin spoke, Alexi had moved closer, finally standing over her, huge and sweating, so close she could feel the heat off his body. He enjoyed a certain pretense of danger, this Ukrainian, presenting the world a moody, reckless, unpredictable sort of gunslinger with something slightly

off upstairs, and when Marlin had finished speaking he said, "Do you
know how much koi fish cost, little girl? More than your allowance,
I bet."

Spooner had noticed that many of the landscaping set were same-
toolers these days, but this was the first of the breed Spooner had run
into who aspired to be menacing to society.

The grandson, on the other hand, was not a bodybuilder but what
used to be called stout, back in the days when girth and a good appetite
were in fashion, and most likely a bully all the way back to first grade,
and had apparently come to a certain menace of his own without the aid
of human growth hormone or steroids or hours in the gym with free
weights.

SIXTY-ONE

The trouble next door had begun in the spring, seven months previous, when Marlin first arrived. Before that, it was just the old man and his dog—a sweet, 160-pound beast called Lester.

Hiram Dodge was a quiet, courteous gentleman who had once taught literature at Peed College in Oregon but had fallen out with his department and then the college itself during those years when English departments everywhere were being turned over to the politically entitled. Not that he'd quit on principle. In the end, it wasn't about the vandalism of literature, as he called it, more that he was sick of looking at their faces. Faculty and student body alike. In the beginning there had been exchanges of unkind words with the politically entitled, which led in about two minutes to charges of racism and sexism, homophobia, etc., which old Dodge had dismissed with the back of his hand, which led to campus demonstrations and demands for his removal, and outraged alumni, and story after story in the sympathetic Portland-area media—sympathetic to the politically entitled, not to old Dodge—and thus, outcast and friendless and surrounded by snipers, old Dodge bought a puppy and named it Lester Maddox and took it with him everywhere he went, referring to the animal by name every chance he got, which prompted a decision by Peed College to offer Dodge an enormous buyout, and perhaps because he was sick of looking at them, and sick of the students and all their entitlements, and because he could see that the administration had made the offer knowing that he would refuse it on principle, he took the money and left.

———

Old Dodge was a reserved sort of fellow, polite but not by any means as lovable as his dog. Spooner ran into him down at the foot of the driveway now and then, by the mailbox, or alongside the road, usually with Lester, walking up or down the long hill to Bailey's Corner. He was an unusually clean-smelling old fellow, always fresh-shaven, shirts ironed and starched and worn buttoned to the neck and wrists, who knew the name of every weed growing in the yard and spent hours in the morning sketching the egrets nesting in the marsh at the lowest, wettest part of the grounds. His wife and daughter were gone, a car accident, and the same accident had left him with a scar that dropped like a bead of sweat out of his hairline and all the way to his collar.

The old man had declined Spooner's occasional invitations to dinner or cookouts, although his dog hadn't missed one since Spooner moved in, and these days the animal was putting in as much time at Spooner's as he was at home, especially when Marlin and the weight lifter were visiting. Often he spent the night.

———

The old man got up early. The southern, more rural end of the island was a good place for birds—there were hawks and owls everywhere, and an eagles' nest at the edge of Spooner's property, and two more nests in the trees farther south, and most days you could see them out sitting on the channel markers in the Sound, fishing the shallows or, when the wind came up, hanging like kites over the marsh, hunting rabbits and quail and the occasional toy poodle that wandered a little too far from the house. Spooner had once seen an eagle take a pigeon right out of the air—at least had heard the impact and looked in time to see the explosion of feathers where the bird had only just been, and another time, walking with Lester along the southern edge of his property, a pretty fair-sized, live rabbit dropped out of a tree and landed with a certain *oof* right at his feet. Spooner looked up and spotted the eagle staring down, and they stared at each other a little while and then, hearing something at his feet, Spooner looked back at the ground and saw that Lester had eaten the rabbit.

For all that, old Dodge was not much interested in eagles or hawks, and had thrown in instead with the egrets, which struck him as more elegant killers. He studied the birds before he committed them to paper, sitting in a lawn chair with a cup of steaming coffee in his lap. Beside him on the picnic table he laid out pencils, a sketch pad, binoculars, and a coffeepot.

There were currently fourteen egrets nesting in the lower, swampy end of the old man's property and he knew them all pretty well, one from the other, ages, physical idiosyncrasies, dispositions, rankings, and it seemed to Spooner that knowing them so well had led to a certain disappointment with whatever he drew, which is to say that even when the work was very good, it wasn't good enough. A very tough grader was old Dodge.

What he was trying for was not just beaks and bones and feathers—he was a good sketcher and could do that in his sleep—but the moods and personalities that delineated the birds one from another. They were strange animals, the egrets, dependent on one another socially but showing no interest at all when one of their own was reduced to a pile of feathers by the coyotes and was left on the ground near the marsh at daybreak.

Sometimes Spooner walked over in the morning when he saw the old man setting up, and the old man always seemed happy enough to see him, and happy to show him his work from the day before, which he treated with a kind of friendly contempt. Spooner thought of his own art teacher back at Peabody Laboratory, Daphne Stone, who would pass slowly behind her students, hands hooked together index finger to index finger behind her back, *very good, very good, excellent, Helen,* and would pause as she arrived behind Spooner, who always drew the same thing, the house in Vincent Heights, the sun, his family in the windows, the dog somewhere in the air, as big as the house itself, and put her hand gently on his shoulder. *"No, honey, that's not quite it."*

He thought sometimes it wouldn't make a bad gravestone: *No, honey, that's not quite it.*

If he was in the mood, the old man might point out the particular egret he was working on that day, or that week—Spooner did not know how long it took him to study an egret—or just bring him up to date on the general state of affairs down in the marsh. Who was courting, who was nesting, who was injured or missing. Sometimes there would be a bird perched in a nearby tree, away from the others, cast out or shunned for some unknown offense. Pissing in the nest, for all Spooner knew.

So you either get up to take a piss in the night and the coyotes eat you, or you don't and the missus throws you out of the house. Damned if you do, damned if you don't again.

For their part, the coyotes were everywhere that year, taking rabbits, house cats, sheep, deer, even dogs the size of Lester—one of the younger coyotes would come out of cover and lure the dog into an ambush—and once in a while even an egret, and the scattered feathers would be lying there in the morning, and the old man would scrutinize the other birds for signs of remorse or anxiety, but they showed nothing of the kind, and he would sit all morning watching them, perhaps thinking of his own losses, and in the end would head down the long slope to the marsh with a rake and a plastic bag, Lester moseying along a few steps ahead or behind, to remove the remains. In the end, it was old Dodge himself who couldn't get on with the day until the carcass was out of sight.

SIXTY-TWO

Lester was enormous. He slept in the old man's house one night and between Spooner and Mrs. Spooner, nestled in at some awkward angle, the next. It was impossible to realign him in the night, and as for scooching him over, you might as well try to scooch the federal government.

Shortly after Spooner had moved into his house, he had seen the animal eat the same three-pound London broil twice in five minutes. Hot off the barbecue the first time, swallowing it more or less whole, then pumping it all back out onto the patio, wet and still steaming and more or less intact—you could almost think it was a baby Lester—and waiting for it to cool off, testing it now and then with his nose. And five minutes later, ignoring the shrieks and gagging noises that passed through those in attendance like the wave at Yankee Stadium, he ate it again. Spooner found himself in awe, not just of the animal's appetite, but of his lack of inhibition. Of being so comfortable with who he was.

Spooner grew powerfully attached to Lester, and in his mind the beast somehow became the centerpiece of this place and time, the best place and time of Spooner's life. He had a beautiful house and a beautiful drain field and a beautiful daughter and ten acres overlooking the sound, and worked when he wanted to work, and wrote what he wanted to write, and still never looked at Mrs. Spooner without some damp thought of her medically diagnosed, slightly misaligned vagina, this never failing to stir him to smile, even though they had been together a pretty long time for it to have stayed so fresh and new.

And occasionally even felt fresh and new himself, even though his hands and wrists were so shot that most mornings he could barely manage his own shoelaces, and his elbow joint didn't function until noon, and his legs were brittle and undependable one day to the next, and his back wasn't worth a damn where it had been broken either. Strangely all that was of no more consequence most days than a little spit dancing in the frying pan.

As for the Devil's Pocket, he thought once in a while of the young citizens in the street with their bats and tire irons, but he also imagined them now, wallowing all these years in what they were, with their bad teeth (though admittedly their own teeth) and dead-end work and wives daydreaming of collecting insurance payments after they were killed on the job, and wished them nothing more or less than the lives they had made for themselves to live.

He thought of himself as through with that place and that night, and signaled as much to Mrs. Spooner as often as was practical, but you are never completely through with a night like that, and there was still a list of their names somewhere in his storage closet that he'd never tossed out, and he stumbled across it now and then, looking for something else, a reminder of what happens when you go in halfhearted.

———

The old man's grandson had arrived that first time in a sparkling white Ford pickup with oversize tires and decorative pin stripes that ran the length of the truck, and as many times as Spooner had seen the vehicle since, he'd never seen it dirty, never even a spot of bird shit on the hood, a condition that to Spooner's certain knowledge was impossible to maintain in this part of the country, but there it was.

For years Spooner and old Dodge had shared a well, splitting the small costs of electricity and maintenance, but these days the pump ran constantly whenever the grandson was home, from eleven or so in the morning until dusk, washing his truck, watering his flowers, emptying and refilling the fish pond he'd built, and Spooner knew enough about electric motors by now and about living on the island not to wait for the water pump to burn itself up and leave himself at the mercy of the only well-pump man on the island, who, hearing the sound of desperation in a caller's voice, would be two weeks minimum getting around to taking a look. Instead, Spooner called the island's well digger, who needed work at the time and came directly over and put in another well. Seven days, four hundred and ninety-four feet. Nine thousand, seven hundred and ninety dollars, tax included.

Only the beginning of Spooner's affection for Marlin Dodge.

The grandson's truck could be picked out of any parking lot on the south end of the island, not just for its cleanliness but also for its oversize tires and built-up suspension, which left the operator's seat at about the height of a tennis umpire's chair. It had California license plates, highway-patrol-like antennae, custom air intakes, glass-pack mufflers, a sound system that could blow you right out of bed. Still, it wasn't technically the noise that woke Spooner when Marlin came in late at night. That is, he did not wake up hearing the truck as much as feeling it, a faint shaking in the dark, the nurse trying to wake him up after surgery, a metaphor that would bring him wide awake and buzzing with dread even as the truck's mufflers and state-of-the-art sound system rattled the windows of the bedroom.

Not that it had been dead quiet at night before the grandson arrived, there was always some sound outside, owls, the wind, the coyotes. The coyotes in particular couldn't kill a mouse without commencing a celebration.

The noise and shaking grew as the truck climbed the driveway, and then died suddenly. The door would slam shut and Spooner would lie awake, waiting, listening to the ticking of the huge engine as it cooled, and then sometimes he would hear Marlin yelling at the old man, bully-ing him one moment, nagging him the next, like some Fishtown princess born to dispense misery wherever she went. You would never guess, listening to it, whose house it was. But even if old Dodge was physically afraid of the grandson, Spooner could tell that in some way he was still holding his own. Not shouting or arguing, just quietly refusing to give in.

In the beginning Marlin would appear one week and be gone the next. Sometimes he returned in the company of Atlas Shrugged, whose hair changed color every time Spooner saw him—platinum blond now—and who appeared never to leave the house without taking off his shirt and oiling his body.

Spooner had to admit they worked hard, the grandson in his sleeveless shirts and the boyfriend in his oily muscles, hauling in topsoil and gravel and bags of cement; shovels, wheelbarrows, rakes, and rented machinery lying all over the yard; they were out there all day sometimes doing what they did. He could appreciate that—how many times over the years had he made admiring remarks regarding some stranger's character on this very evidence?—but realized that in this case he would never get around his personal disgust. He could have overlooked the muscle boy's grotesqueries, both of body and mind, could have overlooked the grandson's upper arms, arms like the fat lady's thighs, dimpled and so white on the underside as to appear faintly blue, and could have overlooked the various gold chains they wore and the stud earrings and the tattoos (one ran vertically up Marlin's calf, displaying the initials USMC, and Spooner still hadn't made up his mind about that; it was hard to imagine, but these days you just never knew), and might even have been able to overlook Marlin's obvious desire to steal everything the old man had. At least, if he hadn't known the old man, he could. If he hadn't known the old man he might have assumed, looking at the way the grandson turned out, that somewhere along the line the old man had probably stolen most of it himself. Spooner had lived long enough now to understand that even if aging slowed you down and straightened you out, it didn't erase what you'd done, or who you were.

Still, all that he could have overlooked. What he could not overlook was the other thing, Marlin's navel. His sleeveless shirts were all snug around the belly; buttons popped off the shirts that had buttons, delineating this navel, which stuck out of the round swell of his stomach like a boil. It was possible of course that Marlin had been born like that and couldn't be blamed, and possible it was some herniated piece of viscera. Spooner had read somewhere that 3 or 4 percent of the population was similarly affected, but as open minded as he considered himself to be, he could not rationalize away his disgust. There are some things you can abide, and some things you can't.

Old Dodge was also disgusted by his grandson, and more so once the bodybuilder began showing up with him. He was also disgusted by the spectacle of the oversize truck rolling up the driveway at three in the morning, the bass thumping in the night air like some malicious heart, but for reasons of his own he was unwilling to throw him out. Spooner thought it was probably an obligation to the women in his life who were gone now, one of whom had brought Marlin into the world. Leaving him helpless to change a thing.

And for a long time the old man made himself scarce.

———

He saw old Dodge one afternoon paused on the hill leading to Bailey's Corner, paused and adrift in some thought while Lester worried over a patch of grass like he'd lost his keys.

The old man's face was often bruised these days, but it wasn't clear that anyone was hitting him. Old Dodge had looked fruit stained or punched up most of the time even before Marlin's arrival. He appeared unsure of his footing today, and held on to a road sign as he waited for Lester to finish looking over the patch of grass. *Blind Entrance 400 Feet.*

Spooner pulled his truck off the road a few yards ahead of the sign and opened the passenger-side door.

It was early summer, and the old man was wearing his shirt buttoned as always to the neck. A bruise ran down his forehead that seemed to have bled from the hairline into his eye, and he was carrying a twenty-pound bag of dog food on his shoulder, which Spooner had no trouble imagining the animal eating in a single sitting. Old Dodge had begun to decline

Spooner's offer of a lift to the top of the hill, but Lester loved to ride and got in as soon as Spooner opened the door, and sat up close against him, making room for the old man, waiting patiently for him to get in too.

Old Dodge set the bag of food on the floor and climbed slowly into the cab. The bag fell sideways as Spooner started back onto the road, and the old man reached down to set it upright, and for a moment seemed disinclined to straighten back up, as if he'd decided this moment and this place were as far as he wanted to go.

The dog, meanwhile, was delighted at the way the afternoon was turning out—a truck ride, a new bag of dog food on the floor; how good could things get?—and gradually leaned more deeply into Spooner's side and then licked his neck and jaw, then stepped squarely into his lap and into his line of vision, and now his damp pecker was resting on Spooner's bare arm. Lester stuck his enormous, sweet head out Spooner's window, and the wind blew open the flaps that covered his teeth, and for a little while you could almost think he was whistling.

Spooner leaned back to see past the dog, but old Dodge had turned his face away, and looked out his window a long time, as if there were something spellbinding in the ditch, and Spooner saw clearly the meaning of the old man's hiding the bruise.

Another afternoon, not long afterwards, he saw them, Atlas Shrugged and Marlin, in the driveway, in flip-flops, washing the truck.

Marlin had the garden hose. He was sporting a pair of Bermuda shorts, each calf a collage of swollen, blue veins, but otherwise milk-white, muscular, and hairless. Soviet legs, which perhaps explained the attraction. Spooner noticed another, smaller Marine Corps tattoo encircling Marlin's ankle: Semper Fi Forever. It seemed like everywhere he went these days, Spooner was witness to America's crying need for more copy editors.

Not to mention dermatologists. A constellation of acne sprayed across Alexi's powerful back and neck, and across his powerful shoulders, and his powerful forehead, which was lumped up like the worst headache in history. His own shorts were cut off at the lap, like a Times Square whore, and his tattoos, beyond the mandatory ring of barbed wire around each bicep, were dark blue panthers in repose across each of his shoulders, oblivious to their own beds of angry red pimples.

As Spooner watched, the bodybuilder suddenly bucked and barked and darted a few feet away from the truck, which had already had its daily bath and was sparkling in the sun, and half a second behind him came an arc of water from the hose, and he dodged away happily and arched his back and shrieked as a drop or two found him, and Spooner watched them play, the grandson with the hose, the bodybuilder with his body: the playful squirtings of love.

And until the day that Spooner's daughter came up the driveway crying, that was as much as Spooner had to do with Marlin and Atlas Shrugged.

SIXTY-THREE

The landscapers were still at the bottom of the drive-way, the scene precisely as his daughter had described it. Two piles of posts and one pile of cement bags were near them on the ground, neatly stacked. The grandson was on a rented tractor with a posthole dig-ger, digging postholes. He had dug half a dozen of them so far, perfectly spaced, and Spooner could see at a glance that they were at least twenty feet inside his (Spooner's) side of the property line.

The bodybuilder noticed him first and paused, glistening sweat, strik-ing one of his possibly involuntary poses.

The attachment to dig postholes worked off the back of the tractor and looked something like a five-hundred-pound corkscrew, and Spooner had a moment of apprehension when he got close enough to sense its weight, and perhaps for that reason did not step up onto the tractor and pull the grandson off his seat, as he had expected to do, but took a posi-tion directly in the way instead, shutting down the site, as they might say down at the union office.

The grandson stared at him a little while, waiting for him to move out of the way, and finally shook his head and turned off the engine.

Spooner noticed the bodybuilder was barefoot.

"The tractor is rented by the day?" the grandson said. "So if you don't mind . . ."

The bodybuilder turned at the hips and stuck the shovel into a pile of loose dirt, in one movement giving better display to his obliques, his barbed-wire biceps, and his black-panthered shoulders. Spooner was exactly a lifetime past waiting around to be hurt and made a note of where the shovel was. When it got past this stage, the first casualties would be the toes of Atlas Shrugged. After that, it might go in a hundred ways, but this much of it had been decided a long time ago, before he'd ever heard of Whidbey Island: He would never start from as far behind as he had in Devil's Pocket.

He spoke to Marlin, not the weight lifter. "What's this about the cat?"

It was the bodybuilder who answered. "It's dead," he said. "End of story. If I get him, I'll drown him; I like to get them by the neck where you can feel them die. I get off on that sick shit, you know? It's just the way I am."

He smiled, enjoying this part, showing off for Marlin. Spooner imagined how he must look to them, skinny and old, not much more to worry about than the old man. He would get to the shovel, though, and for a literal fact would separate the bodybuilder from some of his toes. The main requisite for something like that wasn't muscles, or even quickness, but simply a willingness in the moment, and Spooner would not have come down if he hadn't been willing.

Spooner stood still and waited, feeling an old, icy calmness settling in. Yes, the first step in negotiations would be cutting some toes off the bodybuilder. What happened after that happened after that.

"Just keep the fucking cat away from our koi fish, we got no problem," the grandson said, flat-voiced, as if Spooner were boring him to death.

The bodybuilder said, "Those things are seventy-five bucks apiece, Dad, and he's killed seven or eight of them now. Every time we look outside, one of them's floating around on top of the water."

Dad.

The bodybuilder changed poses, possibly in some state of sexual anticipation. "Next time, though, he's dead. That's a promise. Keep your fucking kitty cat inside." Getting pretty carried away with it now, all this posing.

Spooner spoke again to the grandson, who had finally stepped down off the tractor. He glanced at the grandson's boots, which looked new and had ornamental gold buckles, wishing he were barefoot too.

It wasn't that the cat was particularly innocent of murder—a cat is a cat—or was above slaughtering a koi or two for fun; still, if history meant anything, the killers were egrets. Every year hundreds of people of all sexual persuasions moved to the island, often after some sobering experience—retirement or divorce or running out of closet space in the city—reminded them that the clock was running. They came to the island to find themselves, or maybe get in touch with nature and wildlife, or just to smoke a little dope in the woods and take a class or two in creative writing. Glassblowing was also big. Everywhere you looked these days, somebody was advertising to teach you how to express your creativity.

Before any of that could happen, though, you needed a fish pond.

For reasons still unknown, this sudden longing for creativity and/or meaning in life predisposed the island's transplants to koi, and well-heeled newcomers often built elaborate indoor/outdoor facilities with electric filters and heating controls and underwater lights so the koi, a colorful member of the carp family, could be observed at night, and also for reasons still unknown, this predisposition was especially prevalent among the same-tool set, but regardless of your sexuality, the egrets would kill as many of those beauties as you could buy. Why? Well, the food chain came into it somewhere. The smaller fish, at least, the ones you could get at Island Pets for $9.99 and that were a few inches long, these were snacks. But koi also came in larger sizes and grew in proportion to the size of their pond, and for a couple of hundred dollars, say, plus a sixteen-dollar round-trip ferry ride, you could get something on the mainland that no egret in the world could get down its throat. The egrets would kill it anyway. For fun or target practice or just on principle—who besides maybe old Dodge knew what was in an egret's mind? What was known was that occasionally one of them would dive-bomb a koi pond without checking the depth and end up clogging the pond's water filter, often with a colorful, two-hundred-dollar member of the carp family still impaled on its beak.

"You're on my property," the grandson said.

And here Spooner said nothing at all, leaving the matter of property lines for later, after the fence was up. The grandson turned away from him then and climbed back up onto the tractor, and the engine fired and the posthole digger jumped a little forward, and Spooner jumped a little backward, and the would-be cat strangler picked up his shovel, and a moment later they were back at work.

Spooner stayed a minute longer, watching, and then walked back up the driveway, still humming with adrenaline, realizing how badly the afternoon could have gone if it had gone his way. Realizing that he could now be looking at a ride to the county jail in handcuffs, charges of assault with a deadly weapon, months of front-page stories in the local paper, which came out twice a week and would milk the incident like the last teat on the last cow in the world, not to mention huge lawyer fees, also milking the incident like the last teat on the last cow in the world, even the possibility of jail.

He knew he was lucky that it had stopped when it stopped, but the feel of it was still all over him, and in his heart he wanted to go back and hack off some toes. Not so much to hurt somebody, although that was part of it. What he really craved was that look of surprise.

For weeks Spooner watched the fence project progress, the grandson and his bodybuilder digging postholes and setting posts, mixing cement, hammering away at supporting rails. At least he supposed that was what they were called, supporting rails. It was solid, handsome work, and personalities aside, you had to admit the fuckers knew how to build a fence.

SIXTY-FOUR

On the day of the next incident, Mrs. Spooner had scheduled the island's septic tank pumper to pump out their tank. Routine maintenance. She oversaw these things as her part of the unwritten pact that kept the marriage so alive and strong. She kept the septic tank pumped and supervised all matters relating to the physical upkeep of the house. She also wrote the checks, and cooked, and kept files and warranties and troubleshooting manuals where she could find them, and did much of the troubleshooting and tooling around herself.

But marriage is a two-way street, of course, and Spooner had his end of things too. He was in charge of emptying the dishwasher, for instance, and unscrewing jar lids, and routinely offered to help in other ways except they both knew better than to let him near the tool box. They had come a long ways, Spooner and Mrs. Spooner, without his physical involvement in the places they'd lived, and in his heart of hearts, he still could not get his mind around the idea of something that didn't move, like a house, having so many moving parts.

———

The septic tank pumper was gray-haired and huge and over the years had developed a philosophy of life. Spooner had met enough of them now—septic tank pumpers—to expect as much; those chosen to pump sewage were always philosophers, or in the process of becoming philosophers, and not just *She'll be comin' round the mountain when she comes* types, but the real thing, studying the meaning of life over the days and months and years they spent gazing down into the abyss. Who was more entitled to an opinion? They occupied a dark, forlorn corner of the field of philosophy, these septic tank pumpers, not a cockeyed optimist in the bunch, but Spooner had long suspected that it wasn't the work turning them bleak, that it might in fact be the other way around. That they might well have been bleak fellows from the beginning, and therefore drawn to the work, and predisposed to—and perhaps in extreme cases even dependent upon—finding what they found when they lifted the old lid off the tank.

After all, such people had to eat too. They couldn't all be teaching college.

The Spooner family's septic tank man arrived an hour before lunch in bib overalls and within twenty minutes had pumped out enough of what was in the tank so that his apprentice could get inside it with the big suction hose and collect the bits and pieces of stubborn residue, which the boss squirted off the sides of the tank with Mrs. Spooner's garden hose. Spooner watched them work, remembering the words of various coaches on the subject of teamwork, recalling as he watched that teamwork's greatest campaigners were never the ones who had to get in the tank.

But this was the way of the world. Somebody does the work, somebody else gets the glory. They knocked off for lunch at one o'clock and sat down beside the open tank to eat, and Spooner ambled out to see if the family was getting enough roughage, bringing along a couple of bottles of beer.

The boss was sitting against a tree in his socks, his work gloves lying across his rubber boots. The apprentice was looking skyward, perhaps calculating a philosophy of his own.

Spooner said, "What about a beer?"

The boss looked at him as if he didn't understand the question.

"Or a Coke, or something to wash that down?"

The boss, judging from the pile of bones next to him, was eating a whole family of quail. He shook his head, and Spooner noticed his mouth was stuffed full. "State law," he said. "We're on the job."

Spooner nodded that he understood; the world had not finished yet filling up with rules. The boss ripped off some part of the quail and swallowed it without chewing, and then wiped his mouth and nose backhanded with his sleeve. "I need to talk to the missus," he said. "This could be a disaster."

Spooner trembled.

"This septic system is a disaster waiting to happen," he said.

Spooner took a step closer and stared down into the tank. It looked clean as a whistle. "Maybe I could tell her something for you," he said. "She isn't feeling too well right now."

Marriage, he had learned, in addition to the recently described division of work, was also a learning process, a process that never ended, and Spooner was still learning a mile a minute, knowing her a little better every day, the moods and cycles and flows, what made her laugh and what made her happy, and he knew to a certainty that talking to the septic tank pumper wasn't what made her happy. Plus, she loved quail as much as the old man next door loved egrets, and it felt to Spooner like his life pretty much depended on keeping the septic tank pumper and his wife apart.

The boss shook his head. "There's more grease in that tank than I've seen in a long time."

"Grease?"

The apprentice was still looking at the sky—maybe he'd seen all the earth tones he could handle for the day.

"Grease, it must of been a foot thick in there. Is she using the garbage disposal instead of taking out the trash?"

"No, we take out the trash." Actually, this was Spooner's job, in addition to jar lids and emptying the dishwasher.

"The only thing that should ever go in your tank is shit," the boss said, "if you follow me here. I can tell just looking at a person's tank if it's a healthy situation, and this is not healthy."

"We're sick?"

Along with dizziness and the scaling feeling across his back and the teeth that kept falling out and all the rest of the side effects, Spooner

had emerged from the operating room in Philadelphia as a closet hypochondriac. He knew symptoms of dozens of diseases that his doctors
had never heard of. Particularly muscle diseases, which had become his
specialty. Some time ago he'd had to quit reading medical stories in the
newspaper—he would develop symptoms the same day—up to and including obituaries, and now this.

The septic tank man shrugged. "You get to know these things after
a while," he said, and the apprentice looked over and nodded, apparently
having seen the same signs the boss had. "But the main thing is, the missus is got to quit dumping all this grease into the system. It gets into the
drain field and you've got a disaster."

Spooner loved his drain field in a way you cannot understand unless
you have lived on a lake where the spring water table is only a foot and
a half beneath the ground. He felt threatened, and his stomach made
preparations to toss lunch, and in that very moment, perhaps the truest
epiphany of his life, he realized what the problem was.

Before he could say a word, though, there came from next door
a scream, and then the sound of trash cans spilled across a driveway.
Spooner looked in that direction, but the maples were thick with leaves
at this time of year and cut off the view between houses. It was not so
unusual, though, to hear screams from next door.

The septic tank man seemed even more startled than he'd been by the
grease in Spooner's tank, and also looked in that direction but he couldn't
see anything either because of the trees, and by and by there was another
scream, this one a little longer than the first one and not as human, and
then there was the noise of someone running through bushes and small
trees, and presently the bodybuilder crashed through, bleeding from the
nose, huge and shirtless and scary, crying like a baby.

The grandson appeared a moment later, twenty yards behind, rolling
through the same opening in the brush like some bear chasing campers.
Out of breath and sweaty. The bodybuilder circled a little bit, his hands
on either side of one of the elm trees, and called the grandson a big fat
bully. Those exact words, *a big fat bully*. The grandson charged but pulled

up short, more of a bluff than a serious attack. No way was Marlin Dodge going to catch Atlas Shrugged.

"What in the world is that?" the septic tank man said. He'd been sheltered, of course, coming as he did from a large, well-known island family and spending his whole life here, on the southern, less sophisticated end of the island, with few associations beyond his family and his customers, and had gazed into septic tanks all his adult life and had never seen anything remotely as awful as what appeared before him now.

The grandson was edging toward the bodybuilder, trying to walk him down. The bodybuilder hung just out of range, keeping a tree between them, still crying his heart out.

They moved from tree to tree and deeper into Spooner's front yard, and Spooner wished the cat were here to see this. Whitlowe might be a serial fish killer, but he had self-respect.

"Love hurts," Spooner said to the septic tank man.

The bodybuilder overheard this and turned on him furiously, wiping his eyes and his nose. He yelled, "You mind your own business, you fucking bigot! All of you people make me sick!"

Spooner had a strange feeling that he was being used to bring the couple back together. At the word *sick* though, he was reminded of where he and the septic tank man had been in their previous conversation. "That's what's gunking up the system," he said. "I throw up all the time. Everything makes me sick."

The septic tank man thought that over and then checked the grandson, who was catching his breath, still stalking Atlas Shrugged but the Ukrainian saw what he was up to and maintained the distance of separation, coming farther all the time into Spooner's yard.

Spooner said, "You two want privacy, maybe you ought to take it back over to your place." Before that was out of his mouth, the front door opened and Spooner's wife came out holding a hammer, 109 pounds, including the hammer, all sighted in on one murderous 109-pound thought. She stepped over the yard-high wall that bordered the sidewalk, through the plants on the other side, and then past Spooner in the direction of their neighbors. Seeing this, the bodybuilder decided that he'd take his chances back where he came from, and turned tail, as they say, crashing back through the nettles and brush and the trees.

She centered on the grandson.

He pointed at the hammer. "That's already assault," he said.

Even on the island, everybody was a lawyer.

This announcement was shortly followed by a snorting noise from the septic tank man. He had been following the action from a certain remove and now seemed to sense where he fit in. "Why don't you bring your fat sissy self over here, and I'll show you what assault is, junior," he said.

Mrs. Spooner, meanwhile, was still holding the hammer. Spooner noticed the veins in her right arm, pumped up thick and blue like the arms of the missing bodybuilder.

Marlin looked at the septic tank man, a huge man, maybe Marlin times two. "You don't have anything to do with this," he said.

It wasn't clear if he was talking to Mrs. Spooner or the septic tank man, but neither one of them was listening. "I'm calling the sheriff," he said.

The septic tank man began to laugh. "Swishy, swishy, something's fishy," he said. Sixth grade? Seventh? Not for the first time, Spooner marveled at the sides he ended up taking.

"That's assault," the grandson said again, pointing at the hammer, and then he turned his back and began to walk in a slow, deliberate way toward his house.

Spooner gently took the hammer out of Mrs. Spooner's hand, wondering how it would feel to swing a hammer at somebody's head. She was still looking at the spot in the trees where Marlin had disappeared, and Spooner realized that this moment had been in the works since the day their daughter had come up the hill crying because Marlin had said he was going to kill her cat.

"He'll call the sheriff," the septic tank man said. "That kind always does."

Spooner thought he was probably right. The island was the only place he'd ever lived where the police actually arrest a woman for brandishing a hammer at trespassers.

"Self-defense," Spooner said. Getting everybody on the same page.

But the septic tank man shook his head. "I didn't see the missus do a damn thing," he said. "As far as I observed, them two sweeties just came onto your property to have a sweetie-pie slap fight, and she was inside the whole time."

Spooner looked the situation over and saw the septic tank man's point. He took the hammer into the backyard and threw it over the bluff, and when he got back to the septic tank he said, "It never happened."

"I would say that's just the correct legal note," the septic tank man said.

SIXTY-FIVE

Time passed, and by and by a deputy sheriff appeared through the trees in the same spot Spooner had first seen the body-builder. She was a big girl, bigger than Spooner but smaller than the septic tank man, and her holster and belt squeaked as she walked over. Pock-marked skin, no makeup, her hair, which was her best feature, combed back into a ducktail.

"Here comes another fancy one," the septic tank man said. Surely, Spooner might have argued in different circumstances, there was more to a human being than that. Some of the deputy's friends probably copulated in ways the septic tank man's friends copulated themselves.

The deputy was moving closer all the time, picking her way through the brush and nettles, stinging herself now and then, not looking like a person accustomed to the great outdoors, and finally stopped a few yards in front of them, separated from them by only an open septic tank and the stench of just-removed human waste.

"Which one of you is Mr. Spooner?" she said.

Spooner lifted his hand. "Here," he said.

"I have a complaint that you threatened your neighbor Marlin Dodge with a claw hammer."

Spooner nodded, as if this was exactly what he expected.

"He said you threatened him with a claw hammer. Do you have the hammer on the premises, sir?"

"Here?" Spooner held out his arms and turned around, showing her that he had no concealed tools whatsoever. Perhaps offering himself up to be searched. "No tickling," he said.

He put his arm casually around Mrs. Spooner's neck and felt the muscles in her shoulder jumping under his hand. Given the chance, would she bury the business end of a claw hammer in the deputy sheriff's skull?

"Nobody threatened the queer," the septic tank man said. "I was here the whole time, and so was my associate."

The apprentice nodded, and the deputy sheriff looked them over, and it was clear she didn't believe a word they said. "Is that your story too?" she said to Spooner's wife. It felt to Spooner like his wife's muscles were playing dodgeball in there. There was, however, no outward sign of the percolation going on under his hand.

"I ought to charge you all," the deputy said, not even trying to keep the disgust out of her voice. Looking them over one by one.

"I wisht you would, dearie," the septic tank man said. "I'll sue this goddamn county till it pisses blood."

"Sir," she said, "I will remind you that I am an officer of the law. You can't talk to a deputy sheriff in that manner."

"My ass," he said, taking the other side of the argument.

"What did you say? Would you care to repeat that?"

Yes, he would. "I said, 'my ass.'"

"You all heard that," she said.

"I'm going inside," Spooner's wife said.

"Stay where you are, please," the deputy said. "I need statements from everybody. We can do it here, or we can go to Coupeville and do it." Coupeville was the county seat, and Spooner's wife did not care what the deputy said or wanted her to do, she was going back into her house. "Ma'am?" the deputy said. "I'm speaking to you."

But Spooner's wife was already walking through the plants, then over the shallow stone wall bordering the sidewalk, and then inside.

The deputy turned back to the apprentice, identifying him as the weak link. "I'd like to speak to you over here, alone," she said.

"Stanley don't talk," the septic tank man said. And now that he mentioned it, Spooner hadn't heard the apprentice say anything. He'd just sat there most of the time looking up into the cloudless sky.

"Sir?"

"He don't talk."

"What is he, retarded?" she said.

"You heard that," the septic tank man said to Spooner, "she called him a retard."

And that fast, the man in bib overalls was holding all the cards. "He's mute," he said, and there was triumph in his voice.

The deputy saw that she'd made a monumental mistake. "I meant dumb, like deaf and dumb."

"The hell you did," the septic tank man said. "What's your name? I'm going to file a complaint with the county."

"Look . . ."

The septic tank man only smiled, having her by the short hairs as he did, and she stood there without a bullet left in her gun. A moment passed, the septic tank man grinning, the deputy staring at the ground, pretending to be analyzing the case. She looked up and said, "All right, I'm going to interview Mr. Dodge, and I'll be back later for all of your statements," but she wasn't coming back, anybody could see that, because she'd crossed the one line—insensitivity—that no deputy sheriff from this place could cross and keep her job.

She turned around and picked her way back through the trees and nettles to the yard next door, her bottom as wide as a U-Haul, and Spooner did not see or hear from her again for a long time.

The septic tank man looked in the direction of Spooner's house and said, "You've got to cut down on the grease."

———

Spooner looked into her face when they'd finished, seeing her in some new, more complete way, and later on, as she napped, her head cradled in his arm in a place that was putting it to sleep, he stared at the top of her head, and for the first time in his life he could not come up with the words to tell her how tender she was to his heart.

SIXTY-SIX

The bodybuilder moved out that same day, packing his things while the deputy made Marlin wait in the truck. She even gave Alexi a ride to the ferry. Marlin made no effort to interfere, and sat in his truck for a long time after they'd left.

After that, Marlin threw a party once in a while, but nothing as long or as loud as before. He continued to work on the fence, and slowly the line of naked posts climbed up from the road, and Spooner sometimes noticed the big white Ford pickup parked in the driveway splashed with mud or covered with pollen from the alders, as if Marlin didn't even care enough to wipe it down with a damp cloth. Self-deprivation, the universal language of heartbreak and remorse. Other victims went on weeklong drunks, or quit eating; Marlin Dodge quit washing his truck.

From what Spooner could see, he blamed it all on his grandfather, the quarrel, the unfinished fence, the dirty truck. One night Spooner heard him yelling, "Why don't you just fucking die?" And useless, he was always calling old Dodge useless. A thirty-eight-year-old man who had lived all his adult life off a trust fund that was left for him by his mother.

SIXTY-SEVEN

There was a deer in the driveway, most of a deer, at least.

Spooner hit the brakes before he hit the carcass, got out of the truck and saw it had been a doe, spindly and small, but an adult all the same. Covered with yellow jackets. It looked like she'd been hit out on the highway, something going fast enough to tear her inside out.

The animal was laid sideways across the driveway in a narrow spot with trees on both sides, hidden by the bend in the roadbed. Spooner couldn't drive around it, even with the truck. It was early Saturday morning, and Spooner was on the way to Bailey's Corner for the newspaper and some milk for the dog. Lester liked milk with his cereal.

He left the truck running and walked back up to the house and found a coat and a pair of gloves and a fifty-gallon trash bag, and managed to fit the doe into the bag without getting himself stung. He stuck the gloves inside the bag with the deer, and then threw the whole thing into the back of the truck and drove it to the recycling center, where he watched it slide down a wide shoot into a trash compactor. He pressed the compactor's starter, still preoccupied with the vandalism, not even hanging around to listen. He was usually interested in the noises of things being crunched and sometimes if an unusual item came in—a used-up watercooler, say, or a BarcaLounger, even the occasional television set—the girls who ran the place would call him at home and set it aside until he came by and could listen to it with them.

———

He did not mention the doe to Mrs. Spooner, but that same afternoon he drove fifty miles to the north end of the island and bought a light single-barrel .410 shotgun at the hardware store, something she could point and shoot. He showed it to her in the yard, how to load it, how to work the safety.

"Why do I need to know how to load a rifle?" she said. He told her again it was a shotgun and not a rifle, but when Mrs. Spooner wasn't interested in something, she didn't pay attention to the details.

"Because of the coyotes," he said. "They've been coming right into backyards all over the island for house cats."

The next afternoon they went into the meadow and he showed her how to shoot. He wanted Marlin to hear it for himself, wanted him to hear that they had a gun.

"It's the coyotes," he said to her again. "We could lose the cat."

PART SEVEN

Falling Rapids

SIXTY-EIGHT

By the end of that year, citizens all over the state of South Dakota were saying they might as well live in New York City, which in the state of South Dakota was not a compliment. Murder-wise, the world had gone upside down. First the number—four homicides statewide, against the annual average of .8—and even more alarming, none of the killings occurred on any of the state's various reservations but were all east-of-the-river, white-on-white affairs, not an Indian in the bunch. Three males, one female, the last to go being Dr. Merle Cowhurl, D.Ed., superintendent of the largest school district in the state. Cowhurl was pronounced a goner at 5:25 p.m., Christmas Eve.

Dr. Cowhurl was described the following morning in the *Morning-Ledger* as an exacting sort of fellow, a stickler for respect and discipline and the district's dress code, as well as a stickler for being addressed as *doctor*, and not just by members of the various student bodies but by the faculties as well. Such warm remembrances were pieced together in the half hour before deadline by a skeleton crew working the city desk of the newspaper and, in the way these things happen, came to serve as Cowhurl's legacy, and many people who'd never thought much of him while he was on the job thought better of him, reading that, thought he was exactly what the school district needed all along.

There were arguments of course regarding the crime itself. Some elements of the population, undeluged as yet by Mothers Against Drunk

Driving, refused to count Cowhurl's death as murder, would not accept a car accident as a homicide no matter how drunk the driver was, a legitimate enough point for another time, perhaps, but in this particular instance obscured the larger, more pressing question of how much of an accident the accident had been.

This much was inarguable: Dr. Cowhurl was run over in his own driveway by his own wife, Arlene, who at the time was behind the wheel of a cheerful, cherry-red, twelve-cylinder Jaguar convertible he'd bought her as an anniversary present only seven weeks before, in early November. The car had just 750 miles on the odometer and was still technically in the break-in period, when sudden starts and stops were not recommended by the manufacturer. The dealership was 60 miles away in Omaha, Nebraska, and the car had already been towed there twice, first when the fuel pump quit and then again after Mrs. Cowhurl pulled a little too suddenly into a parking spot at the Alibi Lounge and liquor store and bent the front end of the frame. Cowhurl had been furious at her carelessness and, as a lesson in personal responsibility, deducted the towing charge from her monthly allowance.

According to the medical examiner's report, Mrs. Cowhurl was operating the Jaguar at approximately eighty-five miles an hour, heading south on South Ninth Avenue, when she abruptly changed heading and barreled eastward across a neighbor's lawn, blowing through the tall hedge that served as a boundary between the neighbor's yard and the Cowhurls', and plucked him off the controls of a new self-propelled Craftsman snowblower, which he'd given himself that same morning as an early Christmas present.

As per the warning instructions in the snowblower's manual, Dr. Cowhurl was wearing goggles and earplugs when the end came, in addition to his usual outdoor gear: insulated hunting boots, earmuffs, mittens, and a parka. Thus the educator was all in all pretty well sealed off from the outside world, which in the following weeks his detractors would whisper had been his modus operandi since the day he took over as superintendent, and in any case probably never recognized what was coming even if he'd sensed it in time to look up, as Mrs. Cowhurl attacked out of the setting sun, which as it happened was also the direction the snowblower was throwing snow at the time, into a fierce, cutting wind rolling down out of Canada, which in turn was throwing the snow back into Dr. Cowhurl's face.

Two weather fronts were closing in on the northern part of the state at the same time that afternoon, and the twenty-two-year-old television weatherman had predicted a once-in-a-lifetime storm, and the old-timers had been predicting more or less the same thing for three months—saying all along that a mild autumn promised a hard winter—and with this convergence of predictions plus the timing of the storm itself, the event was named even before it was delivered: the Great Christmas Eve Blizzard, not that it was anything compared to the Great Easter Blizzard, which occurred back in '49 and froze to death half a dozen drunks downtown yet didn't cause the cancellation of a single church service in town, or even postpone the traditional Easter-egg hunt in Keisler Park. But then, people in those days were made of harder stuff—ask anybody out at Sunset Convalescent—even the children, and the Easter eggs were real eggs, not some chocolate/marshmallow thing wrapped in tinfoil.

But Christmas Eve:

The cherry-red British convertible meanders peacefully up Ninth Avenue, twelve English cylinders humming sweetly together beneath the hood, Mrs. Cowhurl behind the wheel in sunglasses and a scarf. A sound then, something like clearing your throat, and the machine seems to slightly buck, and an instant later it is moving at eighty-three miles an hour, a speed it is still going a few seconds later when it slams into the six-inch curb at the edge of her neighbor's property, bending the Jaguar's frame (five thousand minimum for that, as Mrs. Cowhurl's previous jounce into the curbing down in front of the Alibi was much gentler and cost $1675) and then goes airborne, crossing the first twenty feet of the neighbor's yard in sudden and complete silence, the mighty twelve-cylinder Jaguar engine having seized shut with vapor lock just previous to leaving the ground—the sad truth is, reliability has never been British Motors' long suit. At any rate, the automobile, with its huge twelve-cylinder engine, is more than a little nose heavy, and it lands as you might expect on the front tires and front bumper and skids in that posture across most of what is left of the neighbor's lawn, taking out a section of the hedge and then a section of Dr. Cowhurl himself, catching him just at the knickers, breaking both his legs, and, according to investigating officers on the scene, catapulting him twenty-nine yards into the branches of the fir tree in the middle of his front yard. Thus, twenty-nine yards becomes the official distance Cowhurl was flung, although a blind man can see that the whole lot itself is barely thirty yards wide and that the investigating officer has confused yards with feet. Still, the report is the report and twenty-nine yards is and will remain the official distance, just as the verb *catapulting* is and will always be the incident's official verb, at least the one that will be used by the *Morning-Ledger* and every radio and television station in the state whenever the incident is rehashed. Hundreds, perhaps thousands of stories, and Dr. Cowhurl catapults through them, every one.

Although no one claims to have seen the actual impact, it is surmised that Dr. Cowhurl rebounded slightly off the ground after he dropped out of the fir tree because a banana-shaped piece of his scalp is found wedged into the car's front bumper, accordioned by the force of impact—*accordioned* being another verb that will appear whenever the event is reworked in the press.

But a little scalping is the least of the damage, as a moment after the banana-shaped section is removed from his hairline, the automobile's left front tire rolls over his head, leaving a detailed if slightly elongated likeness of the doctor's profile in the snow—right down to the front teeth and earplug—and even if the skull itself looks remarkably intact to the eye, it is not so to the touch, and the medical examiner is surprised and not a little queasy when he lifts it later and finds that it is soft and hard in random places, like a thawing chicken.

The medical examiner is late to the scene, due to family obligations and the weather—it is Christmas Eve, after all—but once arrived wastes no time pronouncing that the automobile hit Dr. Cowhurl at a high rate of speed, as it takes violent impact to *retroflex* a human's patellae, not to mention catapulting him twenty-nine yards into a fir tree, not to mention squashing his skull and dragging him beneath the rear undercarriage all the way to the house, where the vehicle finally comes to rest. And that fast, *retroflex* joins *catapulting* and *accordioned* as part of the incident's official language.

A neighbor appears and reports that a moment after the Jaguar crossed his yard and took Dr. Cowhurl off his machine, Mrs. Cowhurl exited her vehicle, walked calmly into the house and opened the bathroom window, where she could be heard to enjoy a long tinkle, then, by her own admission, she combed her hair and put on fresh makeup and returned to the car, checking one way and then the other, before backing it out of the yard, over Dr. Cowhurl, and then parking it in the garage. Innocently hoping, as her attorneys would posit at her trial, that Dr. Cowhurl would not notice the damage to the car.

SIXTY-NINE

News of Dr. Cowhurl's sudden end spread through the city like the previous spring's epidemic of Dutch elm disease, which had claimed all the trees that once canopied South Ninth Avenue, and left the neighborhood looking frail and bald, something like the aftermath of chemotherapy. Yet the two blocks of South Ninth Avenue where Calmer lived had for fifty years been the city's unofficial center for Nativity scenes, and the tradition held fast, unaffected by the naked look of the neighborhood. As always, there were angry letters to the newspaper charging idea-stealing and copycatting, and hard feelings, and grudges, and a fistfight/wrestling match that had gone on for half an hour before the police arrived to break it up. Lawsuits were filed and half a dozen lawyers were already at work on the case.

But like every other year for the past fifty years, endless lines of cars had driven past the various Ninth Avenue depictions of the birth of Baby Jesus, some featuring live livestock, and now, as news of the death passed through the little city, the populace bundled up and headed back out into the teeth of the two-front storm again, even though it was Christmas Eve, when traditionally the Christmas-display looking was over and there were family dinners and stocking hangings and present-opening traditions to attend, not to mention church services to remind the children of the true meaning of Christmas.

Calmer watched the procession outside from the living room, sitting on the sofa with his feet crossed on the coffee table. Cars crawled past the house, children pressed wet-mouthed against the back windows. The Peace sign blinked pale blue from the roof across the street, the color growing brighter as the afternoon turned dark.

It was Calmer's first Christmas Eve alone, and his was the only house on the block without at least a token Nativity display, not even a wise man in the bushes in front of the porch. He had turned off the kitchen and living room lights before he sat down, and the only illumination in the place came from a tiny red glowing button on the hi-fi. It was enough to see by though, and he looked around the room thinking this was it, where they'd ended up, as close as he ever came to making her happy.

He had been carrying around a dose of the flu for ten days, a strain bad enough that he'd called off his regular holiday trip to Montana to be with Darrow and his family. He hated to miss the little girls—four of them, all rock climbers and long-distance runners; miracles—but more than that he hated missing Darrow with the little girls. In that version of his son, he saw himself.

Calmer had been at this same post yesterday when the meter ran out on Cowhurl, listening to Handel's *Messiah* on the hi-fi with the volume so high it shook the cups and saucers. Loud music had given Lily headaches. The wind had been whistling out of the north, gusting to fifty miles an hour, and between that racket and the *Messiah*, neither the sound of Cowhurl's new snowblower nor the sound of the crashing Jaguar had made it across the street, although the snowblower itself did. It was a top-of-the-line self-propelled model that continued on even after Cowhurl was picked off the controls, clearing a path twenty-seven inches wide out to the street and then across it, bouncing first into the curb in front of Calmer's house and then heading north up South Ninth Avenue, wandering from one side of the road to the other, finally reaching a small cul-de-sac called Whiting Court where it vanished. No trace. And you had to wonder how many citizens had been stabbed with the thought this morning as they celebrated the birth of the Savior that if they had only been a little quicker last night getting out of the house that fucking snowblower could be sitting in their own garage right now.

But back to Christmas Eve:

Calmer had sensed a stir outside and tried to ignore it, afraid to go to the window on the chance it was carolers, but the movement continued and eventually not knowing what was going on began to intrude on the music, and he left the sofa and went to the front door and peeked out just as the first police car pulled into Cowhurl's driveway. Even at this distance the flashing lights were half hidden in the storm. A house or two farther up the block, he thought, all you would see would be the reflection of the lights in the snow whirling above the car.

Minutes passed and there were other lights, an ambulance, then a fire truck, more police, members of the press, and finally the county medical examiner. Calmer was still at the door watching when Cowhurl's wife was taken from the house and escorted to a police cruiser. She was wearing a fur coat and overshoes, smiling for the photographers when she saw they were taking her picture. There was an officer stationed on each of Mrs. Cowhurl's arms, holding on, but this was years before women's lib found its way to the Dakotas, and handcuffs were not deemed necessary.

SEVENTY

Christmas Day, Calmer pulled the curtains away from the front window and sat down on the sofa and sipped at an eggnog he'd made, laced with rum and nutmeg. The Robert Shaw Chorale was singing Christmas carols on the hi-fi, and he gazed trancelike across at Cowhurl's yard. Thirty inches of snow had fallen overnight, and except for the yellow crime-scene barriers and the footprints and tire tracks of various officials and official vehicles that had come back early Christmas morning to gather evidence, and the lone police car stationed in the driveway, you would never guess that anything out of the ordinary had happened over there at all.

Peace . . .

Peace . . .

About one-thirty, two of Cowhurl's three grown sons arrived together, one in an overcoat, the other in a parka. The one in the overcoat was a doctor of education, just like Cowhurl; the other was working toward his D.Ed. degree up in Fargo. There was a third son, Calmer remembered, who had seemed like a nice kid but was no student. Neighborhood reports had him up in Canada, living in Toronto with a colored girl. Later that week, when the boy failed to show for the funeral, a neighbor remarked to Calmer that it was no wonder the poor woman went crazy on Christmas Eve, with a son like that.

———

Although he was interested in the events across the street, Calmer took no pleasure in Cowhurl's slaughter, and instead, by nature and habit, put himself in the position of the sons. Seeing them arrive, he'd considered walking over and knocking on the door—something he had not done once in the years since he'd been demoted, had not spoken once to the man in all those years—but in the end couldn't think of what he might say if they invited him in. The sons knew who he was and must have been given some version of what had happened.

Half an hour later, Calmer finished off his third or fourth or fifth eggnog of Christmas Day and, feeling like some exercise for the first time since he'd gotten sick, put on his parka and mittens and went outside to shovel snow. The temperature had turned warm when the first front blew through, up into the high thirties, and then dropped again overnight, leaving a crust of ice three inches thick beneath the snow, which could not be shoveled but had to be chipped away piece by piece. An afternoon's work, at least.

Contrary to habit, he did not estimate the job or plan the work, just began where he began and went on from there, sweating even as the wind continued to blow a steady thirty miles an hour from the north, and when he'd finished his own sidewalk and driveway, he crossed the street and began on Cowhurl's. First the walk that ran parallel to the street, then the one that led to the house.

The wind rose and the temperature fell, and gradually the alcohol wore off and he stopped sweating, and his undershirt was soaking wet and cold as the snow itself.

His toes had gone numb even before he'd crossed the street, and now his fingers hurt like ten little ice cream headaches. Again and again, he took off his mittens and stuck his fingertips in his mouth, and before he'd finished there was no feeling even in that, and his eyelashes were thick with frost.

He was chipping away the last few yards of Cowhurl's walk when a car pulled into the driveway, a man and woman inside, and for a long moment they sat where they were, staring at the house, not a word between them, and seemed as far away from one another as it was possible to be and still be in the same car, and in time they got out and walked past Calmer to the house, single-file, their faces vaguely familiar but buried in their collars and scarves. They were together but in that way married people are together when it's all over and every man for himself. Calmer stepped politely into the snow to let them pass, and they went past without a nod.

He finished the job just as the last bits of daylight dappled the late-afternoon sky, and started home, wondering if there was any eggnog in the house, thinking he should have one because it was Christmas.

SEVENTY-ONE

As Calmer crossed the street for home, though, a car turned onto it, coming left off Twenty-sixth at the end of the block, and he stopped for a moment and watched the snow dancing in its high, double beams. He looked away then, suddenly dizzy, his eyes losing the shape of the street itself, the sense of near and far. He leaned against the handle of the shovel, afraid of falling, and tried to remember if he'd eaten anything today. The thought crossed his mind that his heart might have momentarily stopped—not a heart attack but something in the way of a musician who finds himself out of step with the orchestra and takes a few beats off to come back in on time.

The car began to slow, and Calmer gathered himself and moved slowly out of the way. He was almost to his front door when he heard the tires sliding across the ice and then gently bouncing into the curb—a heavy, wet noise, maybe the same sound Mrs. Cowhurl's Jaguar had made running over Cowhurl's head, although he was pretty sure it hadn't sounded like that to Cowhurl—and there were two cheerful toots on the horn and then the hum of the automatic window. Calmer turned, his feet stinging like the dickens, and tried to make out who was behind the wheel. He had a powerful urge to pee.

The car was low to the ground, and probably some shade of yellow under all the dirt. Ice was frozen a foot thick in the wheel wells, and the brake lights lit up the fog coming out of the exhaust.

"Calmer?"

He recognized the voice even before he bent to the open window and saw the face. Larsson lit a cigarette and laid his arm out the window, nineteen years old again, chatting up some girl on the sidewalk, hugging his door as he tried to talk her into taking a ride.

He was wearing an old letter jacket from the university, and a leather cap with fur earflaps. The car was a Cadillac, and the turn signal on the dashboard blinked on and off, throwing two distinct reflections off the lenses of his bifocal glasses.

Calmer looked into the car, and the warm air blowing out the window carried a waft of liquor. He thought again that he might like an eggnog.

"Some business," Larsson said, glancing over in the direction of Cowhurl's place. The Peace sign was still blinking from the roof, and Larsson pulled at his cigarette, burning a perfect circle in the dark. "Some business," he said again, and Calmer turned without a word to go back into his house and pee.

"Calmer?"

Calmer kept going; Larsson was as dead to him as Cowhurl. "You spare me a few minutes, you think? It doesn't have to be right now. Maybe tomorrow?"

He'd waited months to hear from Larsson after he'd been demoted and put back in the classroom, his salary cut in half, believing that Larsson would come to him with something else. He'd promised him as much when it happened. *Don't let's us make a big fuss, Calmer, you got my word all this will get worked out.* And Calmer was a long time—he was embarrassed at how long—seeing what Larsson's word was worth.

"I don't see the point, Larsson," he said now. Surprisingly matter-of-fact, but these days, what wasn't surprising? Who could have guessed that he would enjoy cooking and cleaning for himself, enjoy leaving a drink on the coffee table without a coaster while he tickled up a fire, playing the hi-fi too loud, going whole weekends without answering the phone or the doorbell? Or that Christmas alone would be so peaceful?

"We need to talk, Admiral," Larsson was saying. "We got a disaster on our hands."

"We?" he said.

"Everybody. The whole school district."

"You've got the wrong house," he said, and started inside again.

"Criminy sake, Calmer, I need a few minutes of your time."

Calmer said, "I have to pee."

"You and me were friends once," Larsson said, "still are, as far as I'm concerned. What do you say, I come by early tomorrow and pick you up? They got a champagne brunch at the club, I promise to have you home before the games start." The games, as if Calmer cared about the games.

And *promise*, as if Calmer had no memory at all. Or maybe it was Larsson who didn't remember; maybe that was the secret of success. Calmer felt unfaithful to Lily even giving him the time of day. Worse than that, in some way he still liked him.

He wondered if Larsson had seen him crossing the street and stopped on some impulse to make peace. Larsson would believe he could do that, throw his arm around your shoulder and make you forget he'd ruined you. From what Calmer knew, he'd been doing it all his life. Big-shot jock at college in Vermillion, big-shot banker—he owned the bank where Calmer's house was mortgaged—president of the school board, member of the state board of regents, the board of the Flatt Valley Hospital district, president of the United Way. A big shot with the Methodist Church and the alumni association, a big fund-raiser for the university. He'd cut ribbons and shoveled first shovels of dirt all over the state, and his picture was in every issue of the alumni news, and in the *Morning-Ledger* three, four times a month, always the same message: *It all comes down to teamwork, pulling together for the common good.*

And in spite of all that, in spite of what he was and what he'd done, Calmer liked him, couldn't help liking him even if there was nothing about him he liked. And it wasn't only Calmer—everybody in town had a tender spot for Dean Larsson, just as everybody who'd ever come in touching range of Merle Cowhurl despised him.

Larsson had been the first person to interview Calmer about the job in Falling Rapids, the meeting commencing at Larsson's office at the downtown branch of his bank and ending up a dinner and several drinks later

at a place called Minerva's, and on the way out of that eating establishment he'd hung his arm around Calmer's shoulder and told him that as
far as he was concerned, he was exactly the ticket. Brains and common
sense both, the rarest possible combination to find in the field of public
education.

He'd said, "Anything you need to make this happen, Admiral, you let
me know." From the beginning he'd called him Admiral, impressed with
Calmer's career in the navy.

Calmer peed, holding his pecker like a cigarette because his fingers were
still too stiff to hold it the usual way. They were also too stiff to rezip his
zipper and so he went into the living room and stirred the fire and stood
in front of it awhile, opening and closing his hands. He'd never made fires
when Lily was alive—asthma again—but now, October to March, he had
one going all the time. From the fireplace he watched Larsson maneuver
his car backwards into Cowhurl's driveway, close up behind the car that
had come in while Calmer was shoveling the walk. Larsson got out, ducked
under the crime-scene tape and went to the front door, weaving in the
wind like a drunk. He knocked and whoever answered noticed the wreath
still hanging on the door and took it down, and while Larsson waited to
be asked in, a rectangle of light was cast from the house out across the yard
like the doorway to the underground shelter back on the farm in Conde,
where Calmer's family had once waited out tornadoes.

Calmer walked into his kitchen and stopped dead. A carton of eggnog
had been left out on the kitchen table, and next to it was a bottle of dark
Bacardi rum.

He stepped back out of the kitchen and looked upstairs, listening, wondering if one of the kids had come home to spend Christmas after all.

Calmer made the eggnog and took it to the front porch and sat down
in the rocking chair. The crime-scene tape enclosed the entire front of

Cowhurl's property and extended to the spot in the neighbor's yard where the Jaguar had first left the street. A lone cop had been left sitting in his cruiser outside to protect the scene, but he was asleep now, the engine running.

For a long time it was quiet.

Christmas night.

Calmer realized that he was sad, wishing that Lily had lived this long at least. The best Christmas of her life, wasted.

The porch was screened in. He'd spent the weekend before she died building plastic windows to insulate the space for winter. She'd wanted real windows, custom-made, but the truth was she didn't like being out there anyway, where the cold stirred up her asthma and due to the bushes the only view to be had was directly across the street.

The wind had all but quit, and stars were visible in the sky—from the looks of things, the temperature would drop another twenty degrees tonight—and the Peace sign still blinked on and off, casting its blue light across the snow.

Calmer sat on the porch and drank eggnog and thought of Lily. He'd seen her happy without reservations exactly twice in his life—the night JFK was elected president and the day Richard Nixon quit the White House—and both times they'd drunk highballs in the kitchen and she'd ended up singing old Theta sorority songs. He thought of the pure, pitch-perfect sound of her voice, and for the first time in a long time he missed having her there with him in the house.

Oh, there would have been singing tonight.

SEVENTY-TWO

Dean Larsson came for Calmer a little after nine o'clock in the morning, looking like he'd slept on his face, his blue eyes shot with blood and his skin creased and scraped raw by the cold. He had on fresh clothes, though—pressed blue jeans and cowboy boots with silver toes and a homemade Christmas sweater that hung on him like lawn sod. Knitted into the sweater was a snowman with the feet of a chicken. The snowman's arms were twigs and stretched straight out, spanning Larsson nipple to nipple. The name Frosty was stitched into the fabric with an exclamation point, and underlined, but at a slightly down-hill angle from Frosty himself, suggesting another plane, as if the famous snowman happened to be passing by as the word <u>FROSTY</u>! was sliding down an adjacent hill.

Calmer met him at the front door and left him there while he put on his overshoes and coat, thinking again of Lily. It wasn't hard to imagine what she would say, that he was letting them push him around. She would have called it obscene, just having Larsson on the property.

In the car on the way to the country club he smelled alcohol in Larsson's skin, percolating up under the Old Spice. He was bigger by a hundred pounds than when Calmer met him, and made fun of himself over it in public. He drove one-handed and vaguely out of breath, smoking a cigarette and sipping with the same hand at a cup of coffee that he held between his thighs. If the coffee was laced, Calmer could not tell. Larsson's stomach rubbed against the steering wheel when he turned corners. He caught Calmer staring at his stomach and nodded along, patting it fondly. "Been living off the fat of the land so long, I turned into it," he said, and in spite of himself, Calmer felt an odd affection. The trouble, he thought, was that with Lily gone there was nobody around to hold him to his grudges.

A live ash dropped off the end of Larsson's cigarette and onto his stomach but he seemed unconcerned about setting fire to the sweater. The tires chomped snow and ice, and Calmer looked out the window and a little later he heard Larsson sigh.

"That was some business," Larsson said.

Calmer wondered if Larsson remembered it was the same thing he'd said last night, twice. Most likely he was just feeling around for something to break the ice, and *some business* was all that came to mind. Ordinarily he would have talked sports. Larsson could tell you his shooting percentage, batting average, yards per completion, and rebounds from every year he ever played anything, seventh grade to his last season at the university, remembered the won-lost record of every team he ever played on, and seemed even to remember the games themselves, all of them, inning by inning, play by play. Seventy-four years old and still coasting on what he'd done when he was fifteen.

Larsson blew smoke and sighed. "Jesus Christ," he said, "Christmas Eve you're out shoveling your own damn driveway and the missus gets a bee in her bonnet to run over you, and in a goddamn Jaguar automobile you just gave her for your anniversary? And then goes inside and has a squat and then comes back out and runs over you again? And then parks the damn car? And as far as I know, there wasn't even any reason. At least Merle wasn't diddling anybody I know of."

He looked over, maybe asking if Cowhurl had been diddling anybody he knew of, or maybe even if Calmer had some idea of what the state of relations between Cowhurl and the missus was. People were always saying she used to be quite a package until she let herself go, but that was before Calmer had met her. Lately, she'd been putting on weight, and looking at her you might not have seen how she could get in and out of a Jaguar in the first place.

They both knew Cowhurl had had an affair with a secretary up in the administration building—she had some strange name, it seemed to Calmer—and had taken her along to conventions in Denver and Minneapolis and Des Moines. Blushing, that was it. Darcy Blushing. A tidy girl, always straightening things up, wrapping everything in rubber bands, the kind of girl who made the best of what she had, always tuning and pruning herself into the little pat on the bottom she was. She was also the type of girl other girls didn't like, and as far as Calmer knew, she had no friends in the office of either sex, and had no use for friends—unless you counted her special friend, Dr. Cowhurl, whom she used like all-purpose cleaner. She was smart and careful and had a memory like a bank vault, and knew a thousand things she wasn't supposed to know, and when the time came, she knew enough to toss Dr. Cowhurl, D.Ed., and the whole school board over the railing like a sack of kittens. And when the time came, the financial settlement came out to a little over nine hundred dollars for every day the woman had been employed. Enough to buy a school district of her own.

Calmer had never told Lily about the settlement, not knowing what she might do with the information. She might call a talk show.

The school board paid up, of course, and that, as far as Calmer knew, had been the end of Cowhurl's wandering eye. On the other hand, that spring Calmer was fired or demoted—whichever way you wanted to put it—with no settlement, and he was a long time out of the loop by now, and to this day people who worked in the administration office were afraid to be seen with him, afraid it would look like they weren't part of the team.

The car was blowing hot air off the windshield and into his face, and Calmer unbuttoned his coat.

"What I think this might be about?" Larsson said, "he spoiled her. It's always a fine line between happy and spoiled. I've been married to the same female forty-four years, and I'll deny this in federal court if you ever repeat it, but you got to make them earn what they get. You just give them any damn thing comes into their head, they forget who's boss. Next thing you know you've got talking in the huddle."

He looked at Calmer again and winked.

"I grant you the woman's crazier than a loon, but that's a given. You know she shoplifts? Anything that isn't nailed down. Been sticking a rib roast up under her skirt at Compton's every week for years, holding it in there between her thighs while she checks out, I guess. Old Marty, he just sent Merle the bill every month, no harm no foul. But what I'm getting at, you've got to keep hold of the reins. Some way or the other, you got to have hold of the reins.

"Or you get talking in the huddle," Calmer said. *Please let Lily be listening.*

"You're fucking with me, Calmer, I know that. But mark my words, the next thing you'll hear, she'll be laying on the couch while some fifty-dollar-an-hour psychologist is working up a case of temporary insanity. And she'll get away with it, all because Cowhurl didn't have hold of the reins."

The year previous to the Darcy Blushing settlement, the school district had expelled a C-minus student at the new high school for getting herself in a family way. Calmer had fought Cowhurl over the expulsion, bitterly and personally, and when Cowhurl expelled her anyway, saying students had to be taught to take responsibility for their actions, Calmer had gone over his head to Larsson.

Responsibility.

In the end, Calmer tutored the girl himself, got her through an equivalency test for a high school degree, and she was living in Denver these days, married to a tire salesman, and sent Calmer a card every Christmas with pictures of her children and the pets. This year's card was sitting open right now on the dining room table, along with five or six others from students he didn't remember, even when he pulled out the yearbooks and looked at the pictures that went with the names.

SEVENTY-THREE

Larsson drove the Cadillac into the country club parking lot, parked, and reached into the backseat for the black Stetson hat he'd lately taken to wearing, and then got out of the car. He left his keys in the ignition. The lot had been plowed that morning, which had only made the layer of ice beneath the snow slicker and trickier to navigate than if they'd just left it alone.

Larsson moved over it carefully, a step at a time, his arms held out seagull-style for balance, grinning at himself as he slipped, stopping three times to shake hands with other members of the club who were also on the way in for the day-after-Christmas brunch. Some of them read his sweater out loud.

"Frosty!" they said.

Calmer was a few feet behind, invisible to Larsson's rich friends.

The dining room at the country club had picture windows overlooking the first tee box and the ninth green, and even with all the snow you could make out the general shape of the fairways by following the tree lines. Ice had caught on the underside of the branches and pulled them down, like earrings, and the branches hung motionless in the sun as if gravity itself had frozen in the night. Calmer squinted into the glare coming off the ice and noticed half a dozen children in the distance, riding sleds and some sort of metal saucers down a hill, carefully avoiding the flat area at the bottom, where the green was.

Country club children, already programmed to the inviolability of putting surfaces.

They went to an unoccupied table, Larsson marking it for himself
with his hat, which he hadn't put on his head since he got out of the
car, and then he led Calmer to the middle of the room where the buf-
fet had been laid out, about twenty-five yards of it—fruit, biscuits,
waffles, pancakes, a dozen steaming trays of eggs and bacon and sausage and breakfast steaks, gravy with sausage, gravy with bacon, gravy
with chicken gizzards, six or seven different kinds of potatoes. There
was a separate table of fish—perch, fried catfish, clams, trout, an
enormous salmon, head intact and smiling in spite of a body eaten
down to semi-skeletal, giving it the look of an airplane fuselage under
construction.

A few yards beyond the smiling salmon, also smiling, was an old black
man in a chef's outfit who was cutting thick, dripping slices of ham and
roast beef to order, and beyond him was a smaller table set with boiled
eggs, pickled herring, and pickled pigs' feet, this mostly for the unusually
large number of members who'd made their money in the bar business
and preferred a traditional holiday breakfast.

Larsson was an eater. He took two empty plates, filling one with flapjacks and sausage and maybe two pounds of eggs Benedict, and the other
with clams, waffles, hash-browned potatoes, and some of the salmon.
In spite of his Christmas binge, Calmer was not much of a drinker and
could hardly bring himself to look at the food on Larsson's plates. Or for
that matter at the grinning, half-eaten monster salmon at the end of the
table. There were whole towns in South Dakota that couldn't eat that fish
at one sitting.

Presently, they returned to the table, back to Larsson's hat, and he said
a quiet blessing over his food and then covered the eggs with ketchup,
then covered that and everything else on the plate with maple syrup. He
poured syrup until the ketchup began to float.

Calmer had taken three pieces of bacon, a slice of toast, and a glass
of orange juice. He drank half the juice and then on an impulse handed

it to one of the waitresses and asked her to fill it the rest of the way back up with vodka.

And then he did it again, and the second one came with a little umbrella. Larsson smiled at Calmer and smiled at his friends as they passed by the table, and some of them stopped a moment to ask after his wife or tease him about the sweater.

"We go back a ways, you and me," he said to Calmer when they were alone again.

Calmer found he had no opinion on that, and said nothing.

"Goddamn, but it goes by, doesn't it? Time, I mean? Things change, people come and go, and here we still are . . ."

Calmer began to feel the vodka and loosened his overshoes and put his feet up on one of the empty chairs and sat watching Larsson eat, with no particular thought in his head except that drinking screwdrivers was not a disagreeable way to spend the morning. His feet were hot and beginning to burn, as they always did for a week or so after frostbite.

Larsson signaled the waitress.

Calmer pried his stocking feet out of his overshoes and could not have felt better if the warden just took off the leg irons. He set them back where they'd been on the chair. "You mind?" he said.

"You know, honey," Larsson said to the waitress, "I don't see that a little shot of Irish in this would leave me any worse off than I already am. That man's not even a member and he's having all the damn fun."

While she was gone Larsson moved his plates to the side—both of them clean as a whistle, the last streaks of syrup wiped up with the last of the flapjacks—and set his elbows on the spot where they had been. He leaned in, and Calmer was afraid he might reach for his wrist and call him *honey* too.

"Well, get to the point, right?" Larsson said.

Calmer shrugged. Larsson burped. Larsson said, "Merle was a decent sort, Calmer, not the warmest human being I ever met, but a decent administrator." He stopped, rearranging it in his head. Calmer waited, saying nothing. "The plain fact is, the man made some mistakes, and now he's left us to clean up the damn mess." Larsson's voice took an unexpectedly hard tone as he said this, and then a long empty moment ensued, Larsson staring at him like he expected Calmer to object. The waitress brought Larsson his Irish coffee.

"Look, I know you didn't have much use for the fella; shit, maybe you don't have much use for me neither."

"What did he do?" Calmer said.

Larsson smiled at that. "That's the old Calmer," he said, "here's the problem, here's how we fix it." He checked the room, making sure nobody else was on the way over. "The worst of it?" he said. "There's been some . . . *statistical irregularities* in the testing."

Calmer stared at him, waiting.

Larsson said, "The rest is probably nothing that can't be handled in-house," and seemed to think that over, as if for the first time. "There's money missing from the general account, but my thinking is, I don't see any reason to tarnish anybody's name if we don't have to."

To Calmer the conversation had begun to feel like somebody stealing your car and then calling you up to see if the transmission was still under warranty. Calmer sipped at his drink and wiggled his toes and considered the tapered shape of the human foot.

Larsson said, "So why's the old fucker coming to me, right? Well, you're the only one I know that might have a handle on this. The first I heard about it, a friend of mine in Pierre, a man fairly high up in the state government, called up as a personal favor to warn me that we've got a red flag on the statewide achievement tests."

In the same year they'd squashed him, Calmer had noticed an unlikely improvement in the standardized tests over at Jefferson, in fact had asked the principal over there for breakdowns of the scores. He tried to remember what year that would have been.

"We got skewered results," Larsson said. "Whole classes getting ninety-eighth, ninety-ninth percentile in math, all of them over at Jefferson, the same three or four teachers—and the dumb bastards, one of the classes was even remedial math."

"*Skewed*," Calmer said. "*Skewered* means skewered."

"That too," Larsson said.

Jefferson was the old high school. The principal, Lobby Johnson, had come up through the ranks of the athletic department, spent a dozen years as the school's head football coach, and by now had thirty-odd years with the district, twenty-four of them in lockstep with Cowhurl. There had been hard feelings when Calmer was chosen assistant superintendent ahead of him, and Cowhurl had told Calmer on the day he was appointed to leave Lobby Johnson and his high school alone, that he would oversee what went on over there himself.

Calmer hadn't cared much for this arrangement but went along with it, leaving Lobby Johnson and his high school to Cowhurl, and for his part, Lobby Johnson went about running his school like a football team and harboring his grudges against the school system and against Calmer, and when the time came he was first in line to compose a letter of complaint. This marked the beginning of the end for Calmer; Cowhurl and the board had decided to get rid of him and were building a case, soliciting complaints—nothing official, just a phone call at home, an informal talk over lunch—covering themselves in the eventuality of a lawsuit.

But Lobby Johnson at least had never pretended that he and Calmer were friends. There were others who wrote complaints who had been friends of Calmer, some who owed him their jobs, the most surprising of the bunch being a middle-aged assistant principal who lived just up the street and had been promoted into his position on Calmer's recommendation, and for years had dropped into the house for a Saturday- or Sunday-afternoon beer. He was a disciple of Calmer's ideas on school discipline, which came down to one idea really, that if you wanted a kid to behave like a human being the first thing you did was treat him like a human being.

With Cowhurl and the board suddenly after Calmer's scalp, though, the assistant principal had a change of heart, and wrote a letter complaining that Calmer disrupted the smooth operation of his school with his—Calmer's—unannounced visits to see for himself how the students were being treated. Calmer, he said, was undermining discipline.

Like the others who turned against him, the assistant principal, for all his kitchen visits, had never said a word to Calmer about it before.

The waitress brought more drinks.

Calmer said, "What about the money?"

"We can put you on a consultant basis," Larsson said. "Say, two thousand a week, against a minimum of ten thousand."

Calmer looked at him blankly, gradually realizing he was being offered a job. He'd thought Larsson wanted a favor.

"Twenty-five hundred," Larsson said, "but that's all I can squeeze out of the discretionary fund."

Twenty-five hundred dollars a week? He tried to remember what he used to make back before he'd been demoted. A hundred a week? No, that was Milledgeville. Or maybe Prairie Glen. A lot of figures came into his head, but the only one that was anything like twenty-five hundred a week was the fifty-eight hundred that he'd paid for the house in Vincent Heights. He remembered the room he'd built off the back steps for Margaret's bedroom, and the old woman next door always talking about her birds, but now that he thought about it, it seemed to him that she'd lived with them too. And then there was that kid, running around breaking in to houses all over the neighborhood. What had become of him?

They had a few more drinks, which seemed to clear things up, in the way more drinks will sometimes do. Calmer saw no reason in the world not to drink screwdrivers every morning of his life.

"I can't go outside the district," Larsson was saying, "bring somebody in that's got to be brought up to speed. But I found out what's going on, which means sooner or later somebody else is going to find out, which then leaves us at the mercy of any small-time politician in the state who wants to be governor and goes blabbing to the papers. Besides that, I've got to hire a damn superintendent, and the whole mess has to be cleaned up by then, to keep whoever's next clear of this, completely out of the picture. You can see that."

Calmer nodded.

"And I can't use somebody we already got to look into it; it's the same fucking problem, who do I trust to keep his mouth shut? Hire some local lawyer and the next thing you know he's running for governor too."

"Tell me about the money," Calmer said.

"All right, three thousand a week against a guaranteed fifteen, but that's all I can do."

"No, the money you said was missing from discretionary spending."

Larsson scratched his head and smiled. "You would have done this for the good of education, wouldn't you?" Calmer didn't answer, and Larsson continued to smile.

"I don't know how much," he said, "don't even know for a fact who all took it. It's a side issue here, though. The problem's the test scores."

Calmer shrugged, seeing no reason to remind Larsson that he'd seen it coming. That he'd gone to Cowhurl and warned him.

"At this point I got no idea how long it's been going on or how high it went. That's going to be important, I think, how far back this goes."

The waitress brought Calmer another screwdriver, and he thanked her and gave her a ten-dollar bill. The biggest tip he'd ever left in his life. He took half of the drink down at once, noticed that he could no longer taste the vodka.

She came by again a few minutes later, possibly trolling for another ten-dollar bill, but this time Larsson asked for his tab. He held the pen awkwardly to sign, the way Cousin Arlo and his family held spoons when they ate.

Calmer started for the bathroom but meandered over to the bar instead and stood a little while staring, transfixed as the bartender doctored up three Bloody Marys, sticking a stalk of brownish celery into each glass before she slid them across the bar to the waitress. The waitress stood beside him while she waited, smiling.

She said, "You remember me, Mr. Ottosson?"

He smiled at the girl and shook his head.

"Carolyn Dickerson? You were the best teacher I ever had." Teaching, there would always be that. They'd squashed him—ruined him, he'd thought for a long time—but here was some kid he didn't even remember, calling him the best teacher she ever had.

"Thank you," he said, and the room seemed to pitch, and a moment later he was dripping sweat.

"Mr. Ottosson?" she said. "Are you okay, hon?"

Hon.

He smiled again and excused himself and moved past her, walking through the double glass doors outside onto the practice putting green in his socks. The cold felt good against his head, which was wet with perspiration, and then, without feeling it coming, he threw up over the snow. His eyes watered and his sinuses stung, and when his vision cleared, he bent over and picked up a little clean snow and rubbed it across his face.

The waitress had seen him vomit, and she came out now and took his arm. "Are you okay?" she said again. Beyond her, he saw Larsson collecting his boots and hat and coat at the table, hurrying, and beyond Larsson, the brunch crowd, hushed and watching. The best teacher she'd ever had. What did anybody here have that was worth more than that?

SEVENTY-FOUR

They gave Calmer the office that had been Cowhurl's, and the secretary who had been Cowhurl's, Alma, and authority to interview anyone in the district, up to and including members of the board themselves, as well as access to personnel files and all the district's financial records.

It led to misunderstandings, his moving into Cowhurl's office, and Calmer would rather have taken his own old office, but it was already occupied, as it happened, by a woman who'd been Lobby Johnson's assistant principal when Calmer was demoted into classroom teaching. The woman was one of Cowhurl's bunch and had written a letter for him claiming Calmer's lack of organizational skills was devastating faculty morale, and then written several others along the same lines that were signed by various members of the staff.

The office itself was vast and yawning, a place for meetings maybe, not for work, and likewise the desk. Calmer hadn't seen a shine like that since the visit to the funeral home to pick out Lily's box. There were no bookshelves in the room, or books, not even a dictionary, and the secretary didn't seem to understand who Calmer was or why he was there. She also appeared unsure of what stage of mourning the place was supposed to be in, and answered the phone in a hushed voice, as if family members might be just out of earshot, saying good-bye to Merle.

He made do with what he had. He brought in a few books and some copies of the *Atlantic* and the *New Yorker*, and put up a map of the world on the wall opposite the bank of windows, and hung his Think sign on the wall behind his desk. Alma was afraid of him, afraid of everything, and for a long time she started whenever he stepped out of the office. He saw that she was uncomfortable being asked to do things and preferred to be told. Cowhurl had called her when he wanted her and never looked up from his desk when he gave her orders: *Call Mrs. Cowhurl and tell her I'll be late for supper.*

Calmer would say, "Alma, would you see if you can get me Lobby Johnson?"

In Alma's long experience the nicer the boss was to you, the closer you were to being fired. And under this cloud her days passed, as they had always passed at work, but then something strange: slowly, almost unnoticeably, she began to think of Calmer in a different cast than any of the others, began grudgingly to trust him, and then to like him, and then one morning found herself looking forward to his coming through the office door.

Calmer worked carefully, beginning with a simple time chart he drew of all the standardized testing the district had done over the last dozen years, horizontal lines across the top designating months and years, and vertical components dropping out of them at regular intervals, showing the test scores, school by school. Names were added, teachers and students alike, and sometimes one of these names was familiar and would pull him off his spot to some other time and place, and he would occupy the old landscape a little while, complete with Lily and his old job, and realize only later, perhaps walking into the empty house, where he was on the time chart himself.

Before beginning the interviews, he built probability models for all the episodes of aberrant testing and could tell you, within ten million or so, what the odds of an entire class of remedial math students scoring in the ninety-ninth percentile of a standardized test were. The process was mostly trial and error, something like guessing your shoe size and then trying on the shoe, but it imitated the sound of scientific research, even to science teachers, and put together with the now undecipherable chart on the wall, it provoked confessions right and left.

Still, there were mornings Calmer could not remember why he was getting dressed for work or what work it was he was supposed to do. One afternoon he walked into his old office instead of Cowhurl's, and the current occupant—he had no idea who the woman was—dissolved into a fit of weeping and began some kind of confession of her own, and Calmer had no idea about that either, and while she was still sobbing he made his apologies for the interruption and left.

Another day he caught himself backing into his old spot in the faculty parking lot of the junior high school where he'd taught English for the five years before he'd retired. He smiled at that one, the absentminded professor.

In the end—five and a half weeks of interviews, 116 subjects—he built two more models, one giving the district every benefit of the doubt and one making the opposite case, and from these figures, he calculated best-case and worst-case scenarios of the school district's standing statewide without the cheating. Either result—the district in the top 40 percent of the state's schools or right in the middle—was ruinous politically, Flatt County being the richest, best-equipped, best-paying school district in the state, voters expected the best test-takers to come out of it and any bond issue the school board might have been contemplating for the next five years was now dead in its tracks.

It took Calmer two more weeks to recheck his work and write the report. Thirty-one pages, single-spaced. Alma probably could have polished it off in a couple of hours—when she got going out there it sounded like a hailstorm on the roof—and had knocked gently on his open door several times that day, offering to take the job off his hands. He saw that she was getting used to him now and was both anxious and resigned at the prospect of his leaving, knowing that work would go back to what it had always been when they brought in Cowhurl's replacement.

As for the report, Calmer had promised Larsson confidentiality and was good to his word, and so he typed it himself, all day and half of the next. He called Larsson then and heard the flat dread in the man's voice when Calmer told him it was finished.

"I'll have them cut your final check first thing in the morning," Larsson said.

It came back to Calmer that he was being paid. A hundred, was that it? The number sounded right, and Christ knew he could use an extra hundred, but when he thought about that, he couldn't remember what he needed it for. Maybe something for Lily, he thought. Maybe something for Lily.

A moment passed, Calmer and Larsson each thinking his own thoughts, and finally Larsson broke the silence.

"No one sees it but you and me," he said.

"That was the agreement."

Another long pause, and then, "How bad is it, Calmer?"

SEVENTY-FIVE

Out of long habit, Calmer woke up early, an hour at least before dawn, and went into the kitchen to make breakfast. Two fried egg sandwiches, pickles, some peas he'd set on a shelf in the refrigerator. There was an open glass of orange juice in there too, and he paused, thinking of having a little vodka with it, but there was a long, busy day in front of him and he didn't want to start it with a logjam in his thinker.

He sat down to organize the day's work, but nothing came.

He noticed the folder lying on the counter and remembered typing something yesterday. Something long. He stared at it a moment, blank, and a moment passed and it all came back to him at once. The Cheever story, the one about the man swimming home in the suburbs. Calmer felt a small wash of relief; the memory lapses were beginning to worry him.

He stared for a moment at the folder, thinking of the beautiful piece of work inside—fantastic and ordinary at the same time, seamless, unpredictable sentences. And it occurred to him that something as ordinary and fantastic as the story itself had happened as he'd copied the words, in those moments they were in his own hands, taking them off one page and transcribing them onto another, which is to say that for a little while they had been his in the same way that they must have been Cheever's when he first wrote them. The thought crossed his mind to have the class try the same thing. Not the whole story but a page or two. Old-fashioned, but what could it hurt?

He picked up the folder, thinking that he'd better get going if he meant to Xerox twenty-three copies before class.

———

Three hours came and went and found Calmer sitting casually at his old spot on the corner of a desk situated at the front of room 110 at Toebox Junior High School.

At ten minutes after eight, the classroom door opened and the school's principal, whose name Calmer didn't remember, walked in, a young woman a step or two behind. Ten minutes previous he'd escorted this same woman out, thinking she was a substitute teacher who'd stumbled into the wrong classroom.

As the interruption came, Calmer was discussing the style differences between short stories and novels, and was pleased with the way things were going so far, the class unusually attentive for the first period of the day.

Then the door opened and he saw the principal and the young woman and remembered the startled expression on her face a few minutes earlier. He'd said, "Thanks, I'll take it from here," and escorted her out the door and pointed the way to the principal's office, and assured her that someone there would know where she was supposed to go. Afterwards, he'd thought he heard her running up the hall.

The principal moved in closer and asked quietly if he might have a word with Calmer outside, and Calmer followed him back through the door and into the hall to sort out the misunderstanding.

———

He gave the principal no trouble at all, leaving peacefully, apologizing for the mistake, inside out with embarrassment. Still, he rode an old, sweet, familiar feeling all the way home, the feeling of having a class of kids in the palm of his hand, and was as surprised as anybody when he stepped into Larsson's office later that afternoon to deliver the report and found him apoplectic. He threw Calmer's check at him across the desk.

"I hope you realize what you've done," he said.

"Actually . . ." Calmer said, and it was a day or two before it came back to him, that he had in fact distributed to each student in room 110 of Toebox Junior High the same thirty-one-page report he'd given Larsson, detailing the district's long-term and ongoing cheating scandal on standardized tests, and the theft of $177,500 from the district's discretionary account, traceable to the office of the superintendent, Dr. Merle Cowhurl, D.Ed.

PART EIGHT

Whidbey Island

SEVENTY-SIX

The grandson's honey came back home to him in the light of the moon, in the spring, in a looming 450-horsepower automobile known as the Viper, which loomed a pale white color that evening, the color of skim milk maybe, or an albino. The car had California plates and crept up the driveway like a growling stomach, and at the top of the driveway near the garage, it maneuvered in backwards next to the grandson's pickup, which was also white, of course, but more the color of whole milk. The pickup, however—witness the grandson's broken heart—had been allowed more or less to return to nature, at least sat as muddy as any pig-shit pickup on Whidbey Island, Spooner's included, with underinflated tires, a cracked windshield, and good Christ, was that a crease in the tailgate? Still, the Viper backed in and stopped a yard or so from the truck, facing the opposite direction, like a filly offering the old stallion a sniff of her cookies.

And perhaps not coincidentally arranged for a quick getaway.

The grandson's honey emerged from the automobile slow and glistening like some reptile climbing out of the New York City sewer system. The Viper was a very low-slung car. He was still shirtless, with a tanning-salon tan and cutoffs cut to the pubis, and even in the moonlight you could tell that he'd been taking his supplements and lifting faithfully in the gym. You could also see how somebody in New York City might have flushed him down a toilet. He reached back into his racer to toot the horn.

The grandson appeared at the door and one moment stood pole-axed, and the next broke into tears and a wild scamper over the pineconed sidewalk—the grandson was barefoot but in this moment oblivious to pain—bound for his honey. The scene made Spooner think of *Splendor in the Grass*, although he couldn't have told you what *Splendor in the Grass* was if his eyesight depended on it—a movie? A line of women's dainties? Soap? It didn't matter; there was an undeniable splendor lying over the landscape, and perhaps something grassy too, although this was not a fresh-cut grassiness, as the old man stayed indoors and the grandson had not touched the yard all spring. But lawn maintenance aside, it was still pretty clear that this was one of those situations you hear about, often from sports commentators, where the whole is greater than the sum of the parts.

Spooner witnessed the episode in its entirety, having driven home from the grocery store with the Viper's blue headlamps in his rear window, and when the reunion commenced, splendor in the grass or not, he had mixed feelings. On one hand, he was a sucker for happy endings and for love stories, especially the kind where love overcomes great odds of distance and time, but at the same time, part of him had been hoping the bodybuilder was, well, dead—mixed feelings in this case being more or less analogous to the book-world term *mixed reviews*. When a writer tells you his novel has received *mixed reviews*, it means that after the book was trashed and his heart was broken in every newspaper and magazine in America, the weekend critic at the *Pekin Daily Times* said it was a heart-pounding race to the finish.

Calmer had been in the guesthouse a few months now, still settling in, and in spite of his age seemed to have lost interest in nothing. He and Spooner took walks every morning, always at his instigation, timed to the rising sun, which this time of year was a few minutes earlier every day.

The walks themselves followed the cliff that ran from Spooner's place to the southern tip of the island, two, two and a half miles each way, and included three or four fences to climb and half a dozen detours over deer trails, some of which dropped below the edge of the cliff, and there were places where a trail would emerge from the brush and Spooner would be staring straight down five hundred feet to a stretch of dark, massive, cold-looking stones.

The sight of the drop always stopped Spooner in his socks, but Calmer would already be moving ahead, oblivious to the height, confident and sure-footed and strong. Spooner's worry was not that Calmer would stumble off the cliff, rather that he would walk off into oblivion and not even notice. Calmer had arrived from South Dakota in some stage of dementia, distracted and restless in a way Spooner had never seen him before, his interest pulled one way and another by his line of sight, as if the whole world was a new place. This was the category of things that worried Spooner, and even when he—Spooner—worked or slept, occasionally even when he was *in delicto* with Mrs. Spooner, in the back of his mind Calmer was always falling. The upshot was that at the end of the day Spooner would climb into bed exhausted from keeping track of his stepfather and would wake up the same way for the same reason. And in this condition, of course, was much more likely than Calmer to end up as spillage on the rocks.

Calmer, on the other hand, slept very well. He realized something was going on upstairs, but his intelligence was intact. He could see why Spooner was tagging along every morning, and even if he was too polite to say it, would have preferred to take his walks alone.

But back to splendor in the grass:

The grandson and his bodybuilder cuddled awhile in the driveway and then took it inside. As for what went on in there, well, as the scientists say, we just don't know. Spooner imagined them dressing up like Royal Canadian Mounties, and then afterwards, perhaps that monkey thing, preening each other for mites. But that was only speculation and ignorance, and perhaps even homophobia raising its ugly head. The fact of the matter, as Spooner had already gleaned from the Sunday Styles section in the *New York Times*, was that same-tool love wasn't very much different or more preposterous than love by the prong-and-socket style nature designed, and after the boys next door finished with the part of it that was different—and Spooner counted on the *Times* to leave this last bit of uncharted territory uncharted—the grandson and the bodybuilder most likely cuddled and promised each other never to fight again, just like any other couple making up.

And during the cuddling perhaps also pledged to have the old man put away somewhere, where he would no longer be an encumbrance to their relationship, and while admittedly this was a pretty foul plan, it was not unheard of in the prong-and-socket world either. For his part, old Dodge stayed holed up in his room with his dog, except when the dog couldn't stand the domestic tension anymore and went next door to visit the Spooners.

Mostly Dodge holed up alone. He saw the mail that came into the house though and listened to the grandson's end of phone conversations, and was aware that Marlin was in it now with a local attorney to have him declared incompetent to handle his own affairs.

The old man's eyes were going bad, along with his hearing and the circulation in his feet, and he'd given up forever getting the egrets down exactly right on paper, although this was not just the problem with his eyes but a feeling lately, coincident with the arrival of Marlin and the bodybuilder, that he had somehow participated in the contamination of nature.

The old man had perked up though when he noticed that a fellow about his own fit in the world was staying in the guesthouse next door, this maybe three months ago, and guessed it was the stepfather Spooner had mentioned from time to time, back when he'd dropped by for a word in the mornings. Dodge thought about those visits quite a bit, about the days when he'd had the house to himself. The visits, the morning coffee, a few hours trying to get the birds down just right, a walk with the dog to the grocery store, maybe a romp in the yard. The days had seemed to pour naturally, one into another, with some peaceful accomplishment always in the works, night and day.

Then into this peacefulness strode Marlin, uninvited—as he supposed the boy went everywhere in life—and then his foul-breathed friend with all his muscles and bluff, and that fast, the place he'd made for himself was ruined, and lately he thought more and more of giving in, letting them have it and finding someplace else for himself.

The old fellow had been sitting in the yard when Dodge first saw him, wearing a baseball cap, reading a book. He was there about an hour and returned the next afternoon to the same spot, and the afternoon after that, and every afternoon unless it rained. Old Dodge considered putting on his shoes and pants and walking over to introduce himself, but even the thought left him tired, always too tired, and he didn't know what he might say anyway, and then one day the fellow simply appeared outside with a pail and a squee-gee, and commenced cleaning the slug slime off Dodge's bedroom window, and a few minutes later they were sitting across from each other at the picnic table, drinking beer, pleasantly shooting the breeze.

The fellow's name was Calmer Ottosson, and before long he was com-ing around once or twice a week, always when Marlin and Atlas Shrugged were gone for the day, and he was not only a reader, it turned out, but pretty well read.

Over old Dodge's quiet objections, Calmer washed the windows when the slugs scummed them up, and in spite of an openness that was unusual among the intelligent men of Dodge's acquaintance, particularly those in academia, it was a little while before they were comfortable together, before they could comfortably discuss the particulars of their lives or the business of getting old, or could just sit comfortably together and not talk at all. Unlike Calmer, old Dodge didn't keep abreast of politics or current novels, hadn't looked at a book or magazine or even a newspaper in months. It wasn't just his eyes; the truth was he could only hold a thought for a few seconds these days without somehow drifting back to Marlin and the bodybuilder. He daydreamed of setting fire to the house and burning up his grandson with it.

SEVENTY-SEVEN

Spooner's guesthouse was divided into three parts. The north side was the guest quarters—a bedroom, a bathroom, and a sitting room—and the south side was the office where Spooner worked, which also had a bathroom although Spooner preferred to walk outdoors and use the bushes. Although Mrs. Spooner preferred that he didn't.

Between the office and the guest quarters was a long, narrow room with a small kitchen on one end and a pool table and some exercise equipment on the other, and a couple of comfortable leather chairs with good lamps for reading. Calmer spent most of his time in this room, reading, napping, teaching himself to play pool, fascinated as the laws of physics materialized in front of his eyes. He was eighty years old, and this was the first pool stick he'd ever had in his hands.

After their morning walk, Calmer and Spooner—and Dodge's dog, if he was visiting—ordinarily repaired to the guesthouse, where Calmer would drink a glass of milk and shoot pool for an hour or two and then nap in one of the leather chairs, and Spooner and Lester would close themselves into the office to work. The place was well insulated, and Spooner would only notice the sound of the pool balls clicking when it stopped, meaning Calmer had put away his cue and gone into his bedroom to rest, and in the sudden quiet Spooner would hear even fainter noises—the sound of the Union Pacific over on the mainland, two miles straight across the water, rolling north to Canada, or a swarm of birds passing through the trees, also on their way north, and every forty min-utes or so the muffled sound of the icemaker dropping ice into the col-lection plate in the freezer, and the faint concussions of pistol shots from a mile farther up the hill, where one of Spooner's neighbors ran a gun shop out of his garage.

All these small sounds were familiar and Spooner was at home and comfortable and working pretty well one afternoon when the door to his office flew abruptly open and she was standing there, Mrs. Spooner, the old nostrils flaring—never a good sign—and, strangely for someone so clearly in the mood to talk, unable to enunciate even a single word.

He waited and by and by found himself wondering about the expres-sion *cat got your tongue*. Was it just Spooner, or does that strike you as a little gory for what it is meant to put across? Spooner had begun noticing expressions like these not too long ago, and they were everywhere in the language, lying right out in the open, like little headless bodies on the patio after the cat—speaking of the cat—has been out all night hunting. Where did they come from? *Explode onto the scene. Stop dead in your tracks. Pants on fire.* Was it the Old Testament?

Was it the Irish?

For her part, Mrs. Spooner simply pointed, stabbed her finger yonder, toward the front of the house, and with this physical action found her voice, issuing those two basic words as fundamental to the mysterious male/female equation as the monthlies itself. She said, "Do something."

Spooner got up and went with her, noticing that in spite of the obvi-ous excitement in the air, the dog, who enjoyed an occasional woof in the yard as much as the next Lab, remained lying on his back, his rear legs both suspended in the air, following the Spooners only with his eyes. He was tired. But then, already today he'd eaten a loaf of bread and a pound package of Morrell's bacon that Mrs. Spooner had laid out on the coun-ter for breakfast, then accompanied Spooner and Calmer on their regular walk to the foot of the island, and now seemed to have scheduled a little me time to sleep it off.

Spooner and Mrs. Spooner, meanwhile, walked together in the direction she had pointed—was still pointing—and although she was walk-ing beside him, it was not a regular side-by-side thing, the way they had once gone into the First National Bank of Collingswood, New Jersey, to be married, but more the way you and the beast napping in the office might walk if you were holding still another pound of Morrell's bacon in your hand, and in this fashion they—Spooner and Spooner's woman—progressed yonderly through the guesthouse to the double doors leading outside. And reaching the doors, looked out.

There, she pointed, *there*. And the two chattiest deaf people in the world had never spoken more clearly with their hands.

It could be useful to mention here that Mrs. Spooner, in spite of her lovely bottom and a wide-ranging and fascinating internal life, had not come into this world with a penchant to nurture. Her ancestors were obviously hunters and trackers, bred to eat the stragglers, not nurse them back to health.

In spite of this, she held Calmer in deep affection, and not only for his small kindnesses and acts of chivalry and his level head when things went upside down and her husband's—Spooner's—obvious and deep at-tachments to the man who had raised him. More than any of that, Calmer was established in some way in the middle of her daughter's heart, and she cared as much for the child's heart as her own.

Still, there sat an eighty-year-old man with undeniable signs of de-mentia cross-legged on an army blanket down in the meadow with his rifle, dressed, bottom to top, in the following manner: black shoes, dark socks, boxer shorts, white T-shirt, German military helmet, circa World War I.

Calmer aimed the rifle up into the air and squeezed off a shot and then lowered it and waited, scanning the meadow (was a duck supposed to fall out of the sky?) and then reloaded and fired again.

Spooner had never seen Calmer shooting into the sky before, but he understood straightaway what was going on. The image of a towheaded Calmer sitting alone in an unplowed field in South Dakota firing this very same gun into the air, trying to bring one back in right on top of himself had been with Spooner since the night Calmer had told him the story. Spooner had been in bed shivering with fever after he'd sat in the anthill, Calmer trying to find some way to recast what Spooner had done into something different from what it was. Perhaps trying to recast Spooner himself into something different.

"It's nothing," Spooner said to his wife. Rifle shots were no more out of the ordinary on the south end of the island than cookouts.

"He's in his underwear," she said, "shooting a gun."

Mrs. Spooner had an underwear phobia, part of a larger phobia connected to invasions of her privacy, and kept the bedroom shades drawn at night, and the bathroom shades drawn day and night, even though there was nobody out there to look in but the raccoons.

Spooner started down toward the meadow, maybe two hundred yards from the guesthouse, and Calmer fired off another one. "You have to say something to him," she said.

"I will, I will."

He meandered downhill in a head-of-household style, like there wasn't much more to this than unscrewing the pickle-jar lid. He fought an urge to run—not away but right at Calmer, to get it over with—but if he'd learned anything living the accident-prone life, it was that you never run downhill at someone with a rifle who doesn't know you are coming, and who one of these days isn't going to remember who you are.

Calmer was working the bolt action again, reloading. Spooner hurried the last few steps and began to speak but saw that Calmer had plugged his ears with Kleenex, so instead of speaking, Spooner moved around to the side where he would be visible out on the periphery of his vision, and waved.

Calmer brought the gun up and fired it again and then watched the meadow a few seconds, then looked over at Spooner, opening the breech to reload, as if he'd known he was there all along. He handed him the German helmet, which Spooner accepted and put on Mrs. Spooner's head as she arrived.

"The school bus is coming along soon, Dad," Spooner said, and where that came from he didn't know but it seemed to him that he'd hit one out of the park.

Calmer checked his watch and then nodded and stood up from his cross-legged position all in a single motion, not using the gun or even his hand to push off the ground, and Spooner watched in open admiration, forgetting for the moment that Mrs. Spooner was there expecting him to lay down the law and that in certain moods she was pretty limber-bodied herself, in fact in the right mood would climb all over you like a porch monkey looking for a hidden banana.

For now though he found himself trying to remember if there was ever a time in his life when he could have gotten up like that, or even a time he could have sat with his legs folded up in front of him in the first place.

Calmer smiled at Mrs. Spooner and patted her in a friendly way on top of her German helmet. He gathered up the blanket, folding it miraculously into a perfectly even rectangle, and then headed up the hill.

SEVENTY-EIGHT

The following week there arrived via certified mail a letter from Hillary Levin & Associates, a two-woman Langley firm representing Marlin Dodge. Ms. Levin was the most famous and successful attorney on the south end of Whidbey Island, specializing in divorces and anti-discrimination suits brought on behalf of aggrieved minorities, and while the divorce end of the business stayed pretty flat—she did not represent men in divorce cases, except in the cases of same-tool domestic partnership split-ups—the aggrieved minority suits side of things was expanding nicely, outpacing even the discovery of new aggrieved minorities.

She had city-girl mannerisms—was probably the fastest walker in Island County—and city-girl manners, and would pass the citizens of Langley on the street without a word in response to the occasional *Good morning, counselor*, and on the one and only occasion she and Spooner had been invited to the same party, he'd caught her staring at him all night, lethal as a castration machine, with an expression that said, *Everything in good time, sport.*

So it was no surprise to Spooner that Ms. Levin's letter did not strike a warm or conciliatory tone but simply laid out the complaints of Marlin Dodge, her client, and threatened immediate action if such complaints were not satisfactorily addressed.

One: intimidation. An elderly occupant of Spooner's home had on at least two occasions fired off a rifle in the front yard, for no apparent purpose except the intimidation of Marlin Dodge, and/or to cause Mr.

Dodge and his household unnecessary clamor and discomfort, possibly as reprisal for his nontraditional lifestyle. And here Ms. Levin also noted that Spooner had in the past threatened Mr. Dodge with bodily injury, at one point brandishing a hammer, causing Mr. Dodge to seek protection from the county sheriff's department.

Two: trespassing. The previously mentioned elderly occupant of Mr. Spooner's household had several times trespassed onto Mr. Dodge's property, climbing over the fence Mr. Dodge had erected to afford himself and his domestic partner, Alexi Sug, some measure of privacy and protection, and in so doing had upset Mr. Dodge's aged grandfather, Hiram Dodge, who suffered not only panic attacks but manic depression and some degree of dementia and disorientation.

Three: stolen livestock. The Spooner household had all but stolen Mr. Dodge's grandfather's beloved black Labrador retriever, Lester Maddox, holding him in the Spooner residence and/or on their premises for days at a time, with the animal's absence adding daily to Mr. Dodge's grandfather's growing state of confusion and agitation.

And that was it.

Sincerely, Hillary Levin, Esq.

It was lunchtime and Spooner put the letter in his pocket and opened the refrigerator and looked around for something for Lester. The dog had gotten up when the shooting stopped, hungry after his nap. Spooner spotted a ham in the back, wrapped in aluminum foil, maybe a pound of meat encasing a bone about the size of an exhaust pipe. As always when he saw a healthy-looking bone, Spooner felt a pang of regret that he couldn't somehow use it himself.

———

Lester sat beside him in the front seat on the drive into town, all the meat gone off the bone and working what remained, left to right, the way you might read the newspaper.

———

Ms. Levin was wearing pleated trousers with enough slack up front where she was beginning to bulge for a makeshift pouch, about what you might need for feeding the chickens. She was reclined in her office chair with her feet crossed and resting on top of a beautiful cherry desk.

She looked up, offering him not even the courtesy of appearing surprised.

"Do you have an appointment?" she said, and set a cigar in an ashtray. And it was a real cigar, not some white-tipped, unisex cheroot.

Spooner had never been a cigar smoker himself and stared at the gooey end, thinking of the female apparatus. "I just dropped by," he said, "to say that your letter arrived, and your client, Mr. Dodge"—and now he consulted the clock—"has until, let's say, three o'clock this afternoon to take down his fence."

SEVENTY-NINE

Spooner did not enforce the three o'clock deadline, but not over some sudden impulse to be reasonable. More, it was that old problem of not having the right tools for the job, meaning the task ahead was too big for a hammer, and so three o'clock came and he was not only waiting for the tool situation to improve—his friend Thorson was due home anytime and would lend Spooner what he needed—he was also waiting for the grandson and Alexi Sug to show up because, after all, this was for them too.

He sat peacefully on the front steps of the guesthouse with Calmer, talking about an afternoon back in Milledgeville when they'd all gone downtown, Margaret and Spooner and Darrow and Calmer, Calmer carrying Darrow upside down, as always, when an enormous red-haired woman blew out the front door of Trout's Sundry Goods and Liquor and bawled him out in the street for carrying a baby like that. Calmer remembered the woman right down to her print dress and white gloves. And they talked and time passed and pretty soon, maybe four-thirty, Thorson rolled up the driveway towing his bulldozer, which they had agreed over the phone was the logical step up from a hammer, and they all had a beer or two together, and finally the grandson and the bodybuilder appeared in their driveway, shoulder to shoulder in the looming albino-white Viper, and Spooner stood up and dusted off the seat of his pants and said, "Well, off to work."

He started at the top and drove the bulldozer downhill, splintering and unearthing fence posts whole, still attached to the cement they'd been buried in, two, maybe three hundred pounds each, just *chewing the scenery*, he thought, and hoped he might get to use that phrase when Ms. Levin took the matter to court.

The noise as the posts and rails snapped and crackled, loud as it was, was pretty much smothered beneath the noise of the bulldozer. Spooner saw Marlin and the bodybuilder when they came out the door, saw their expressions as they gradually understood what they were seeing. Marlin said something to the bodybuilder, who disappeared into the house and was back in no time at all with a video camera. It was the sort of thing Spooner never thought to do, to his considerable regret. Here, for instance, were years of pleasurable viewing lost forever through lack of foresight, but then even if he'd thought of it, how long would it have taken to find the camera? A month? Did he and Mrs. Spooner *have* a video camera? The bodybuilder turned the camera over to Marlin and stood by, flexing, while Marlin recorded the destruction of his handmade, home-made fence, rail by rail, post by post.

Spooner reached the bottom of the fence line and turned the machine around, lifted the blade a few inches and slanted it forward to collect the debris. It took longer cleaning the mess up than it had making it, but that of course was the oldest story in the world.

Nevertheless, time flew, as they say, and much too soon the job was finished, and the fence wire had been rolled into the shape of a wasp's nest and stood five feet taller than the bulldozer itself and twice as wide. The nest-looking sculpture was engulfed in a haze of dust and smoke, and suspended within it, like ornaments in a Christmas tree, were pieces of freshly splintered post rails, unearthed beer bottles, the jawbone of a deer, half a doormat, and an entire sign that had once been affixed to the giant maple at the entrance to Spooner's side of the driveway.

Seacliff.

Yes, Spooner's house had once had a name.

The previous occupants had come from a community just outside Se-attle called Mercer Island, a land of deep pockets indeed. They were dot-commers of some sort, just retired, all decked out to live in the woods and give the country life a stab; not terrible people, but the kind you would not be surprised to find out named their houses. And they had come not just for a stab at the country life but at rekindling the old spark, which had been extinguished over the years of counting money on Mercer Island. (This information, by the way, did not come to Spooner through the usual island channels, that is the real estate gossip you have to listen to in this neck of the woods to buy a house; but directly from the woman herself. As for the husband, he excused himself when she started in on it and went outside, and a moment later Spooner saw him behind the wheel of the new Land Rover in the driveway, reading the *Wall Street Journal*.)

The Mercer Islanders were in the early stages of divorce, and the woman wept a bit when she said she would have bittersweet memories of the place and would take comfort in knowing it would be in good hands, a family with all its connections intact. Everybody smiled—the Spooners, the woman, the real estate agent—and Mrs. Spooner, this completely out of character, even held the woman a moment as she cried, and on reflection, it was perhaps not the most sensitive thing Spooner ever did when, on an impulse fifteen minutes later, he stopped on the way out at the driveway entrance and levered the Seacliff off the old maple and tossed it into the bushes.

Spooner maneuvered Thorson's bulldozer back and forth, tidying up, moving the entire mess up the hill to a spot just this side of the grandson's driveway, where lay the property line, and left it there, the dust settling over the ground, the garage, and the looming albino-white Viper. And for a moment perhaps experienced that feeling Hemingway wrote about all the time—that he'd *worked well*.

This feeling of self-congratulation lasted all day and into the evening, even after he and Mrs. Spooner went out to buy groceries and saw that in all the excitement he had bulldozed his own mailbox.

Later, after dinner, he walked over to the guesthouse to say goodnight to Calmer. "There'll be trouble now," he said.

Calmer said, "I wasn't thinking this was a good time to borrow a cup of sugar." Smiling, way ahead of him, and yet in the morning, an hour after their walk, Spooner stepped outside the guesthouse to relieve himself in the bushes and saw Calmer next door with a pail and the squeegee, on a ladder, washing the old man's bedroom window.

And saw that sweet old Lester had been chained to a tree.

Spooner checked the driveway; the Viper was gone. He wondered if Calmer had considered that before he went over. More likely, the slugs had slimed up his windows and he'd gone over to clean off old Dodge's after he'd cleaned off his own.

He watched Calmer work, moving at a speed as familiar to him as the stroke of his voice, the same speed he ate and shaved, patient but slightly hurried, as if there were always more to do than time to do it. Spooner made no move to retrieve him. How was that supposed to go, anyway? *I thought we agreed you'd stay in your own yard?*

He'd heard of something like this before, of course, parents turning into the children and children turning into the parents, but he didn't see how such a change was possible without starting over from the beginning, as if everything that had passed between them didn't count.

Calmer finished the window and carried the ladder into Dodge's garage—in a house fire, he'd put away his tools—and presently Dodge came out of the back door in his underwear, carrying a couple of beers, and Spooner went back to the typewriter.

The dog was another matter, something that couldn't be set aside so that he could work.

How would Lester sleep? It was his practice by now to squeeze between them, facing Mrs. Spooner, and usually upside down with his nose nestled into the backs of her knees, and from this position any sound in the night would set off his tail—an enormously thick and heavy appendage—into big, loopy circles, whacking Spooner glancing blows across the ears. Spooner assumed there was some similar arrangement with the old man, although he doubted that the old man occasionally rolled over in the night, as he did, half asleep and hoping for a little late-night affection and poked the dog in the hip blade instead of Mrs. Spooner.

No, he did not expect that the animal would sleep much chained to a tree in the yard.

Spooner could not stand to see a dog on a chain.

EIGHTY

The next morning out along the cliff Calmer suddenly stopped, staring at a clearing ahead tucked beneath the top of the cliff. There was a single tree here, sprouting out almost sideways, its roots tangled and exposed, a jerry-built-looking sort of tree that appeared so faintly attached that a canary might bring the whole thing down.

A moment passed and Calmer scratched his ear. "Those kids scare me to death," he said. "Oh, I suppose they're strong enough. They're like monkeys, really, every one of them, but still, it frightens me. They should stay on the path." And he surveyed the steep, loose patch of dirt beneath the tree now, looking for the girls.

"Darrow's kids?"

Calmer nodded. "That stuff looks all right, but it breaks off under your feet." Spooner looked at him, realizing that he'd been out there himself, testing the footing for the girls.

———

Days passed, a week, then two, with Lester chained to the tree. Night and day. A pail of water was set out for him in the morning, but once the animal had lapped the trunk a few times the radius of his circle was so short that he couldn't reach it.

Sometimes when the grandson and Alexi were gone, Spooner saw the old man come out of the house and untangle him, looking around as he worked as if he were afraid of being caught.

———

At night, in bed with Mrs. Spooner, Spooner awoke to an eerie howl-ing next door, a sad, unnatural noise that woke Mrs. Spooner too, and they lay together listening in the cool, clean sheets, no trace of dog breath or dog flatulence in the room, no press of dog elbows pinning their own legs to the mattress, or violent shaking as some small itch tingled into the beast's consciousness and was obliterated by the wild thumpings of whichever hind leg could be used to get at it, or yips and twitching as he dreamed his retriever dreams; and they lay together in the quiet, settled room, Spooner and his wife, in clean, smooth sheets, and could not get back to sleep for missing him, for thinking of him over there chained to a tree.

———

She was up first in the morning, just at dawn, brushed her teeth and combed her hair and put on a pair of jeans. She walked out into the backyard in her slippers, rolling the bedroom's sliding door open as qui-etly as she could. He heard the noise though—these days even when he slept, he was never all the way asleep—and got up too, stepped barefoot outside onto the cold patio tiles and watched Mrs. Spooner bending over the dog, trying for a little while to untangle the chain's metal knots but in the end simply unhitching the collar and leaving it there, still attached to the chain.

He was a skeleton of his former self by now—which is to say that you could tell he had bones—and lapped at a pail of water Spooner got him from the utility room, and ate a couple of sandwiches that Spooner made out of some of the leftovers that had taken over the top two shelves of the refrigerator in the animal's absence, and then the dog and Spooner went back to bed, each to his regular spot, and after Mrs. Spooner had made breakfast for their daughter and walked her down to the road to catch the school bus, she came back to bed too, and they all slept together until noon.

Saturday afternoon, with Mrs. Spooner and Spooner's daughter gone for the weekend to Seattle and Spooner unable to get anything done, tar-babied to one sentence after another, he heard the distinctive pop of Calmer's .22 from the meadow.

Grateful for the interruption, he went to the door and then sat down on the steps and watched Calmer and old Dodge taking turns down there, trading the rifle and the helmet and fresh beers back and forth, the shots echoing from the hills across the road as if someone were shooting back.

Spooner sat down and watched, and listened to them laughing, and he ached to be down there with them, for a little while to be one of the coots himself, drinking beer in the meadow, laughing. It just made you want to retire.

Presently the grandson emerged from the house next door and stepped out onto the patio. He was next to naked—nothing on but his Jockey briefs—and his stomach was huge and smooth and perfectly round, and on it rested a pair of awful-looking saggers that from this distance called to mind the faces of housebound, indolent children.

The grandson took a step or two forward, gingerly, as he was barefoot, and called out to the old man, scolding him the way you would scold the dog—*Get back over here, goddamn it*—but the old man seemed not to hear, and when the grandson called him again and danced out a few threatening steps farther, Dodge calmly handed his beer to Calmer, took the rifle, and fired off a shot in the grandson's general direction—a shot in the dark, you could say, the old man being at least half blind without his glasses—that was exactly as likely to kill young Marlin as lightning.

The deputy arrived half an hour later with the coots still in the meadow. The deputy had been here before, a year or so ago on the day Mrs. Spooner had chased Marlin and the bodybuilder off with a claw hammer, and now she stepped out of the squad car, saw the rifle and instantly dropped behind the fender on her haunches, covering her head. It made Spooner's knees ache, just the sight of somebody that size on her haunches.

She called out to them from behind the car to put down their weapons.

The grandson had apparently seen the sheriff's cruiser first and was already out there beside her, telling his side of the story. He had dressed— shirt and shorts and loafers without socks—and pointed across the meadow as he spoke, striking some classic tattletale's pose that Spooner recognized from a lifetime of trouble with teachers and city editors.

Spooner jogged down the hill toward the deputy on legs that had been rebuilt seven times in various operating rooms across America, legs like an old dog's, and set about to defuse the situation. It was a mark of his new maturity that he thought to defuse the situation rather than exacerbate it, although even as the word *defuse* passed through his mind he found himself thinking of fuses and that little white string dangling out of Mrs. Spooner's nest the day previous, after she'd emerged from the shower to dress for the trip into the city, and he considered and rejected working this image into his conversation with the deputy.

He nodded politely at the deputy and then glanced out into the field, as if he'd just noticed the geezers with the rifle. "There's been a misunderstanding, I think," he said, dripping maturity. "They're just plunking at some cans and bottles."

The deputy jumped at the sound of his voice and then screamed at him to get down. "Get your ass down! Now," pointing at the ground to indicate the correct direction. Pointing, in fact, with her black, semiautomatic pistol, and screaming *"Down, goddamn it! Are you deaf?"* A passerby might think he was witnessing the world's harshest puppy training.

And then she turned and screamed in the other direction, bawling at the old men to drop their weapons.

"They can't hear you," Spooner said. "They put toilet paper in their ears."

"I'm telling you for the last time," she said. "Get down."

The grandson shifted his weight, dropping off his haunches to a knee. "It's partly my fault, officer," he said to the deputy. "I should have seen this coming."

She glanced over at him quickly, then rose a little and peeked through the windows to check on the old men. She moved to the side, trying to duck-walk up toward the front of the car, but took only one step and then lost her balance and rolled a little ways downhill. How do ducks do it, anyway?

She sat up, got to her knees, specks of grass and dirt on the back of her shirt, and used the door handle—holding it with both hands—to maneuver herself back up to her haunches. Overweight as she was, the deputy was as comfortable haunched as Spooner was sitting down. Spooner had read somewhere that this was how women of certain tribes delivered their babies.

The deputy took half a dozen deliberate breaths—huge flap-happy lungs pressing into the name tag on one side of her shirt and the badge on the other—and wiped at her forehead, her whole face glistening like a fresh turd in the desert, and it was hard to say if she was catching her breath from the effort to pull herself back up, or if she was trying to collect herself and calm down. It was also hard to say what she had in mind regarding Calmer and old Dodge; for all Spooner knew she was readying herself to charge the bunker.

Instead, she cracked open the cruiser's door and crawled back inside, low to the seat until she was wedged in beneath the dashboard, and called on the radio for backup.

It was what they needed, all right. More deputies.

"My grandfather suffers from dementia," Marlin said, even as the deputy was signing off. Perhaps believing that if he kept the lie alive a little while it would sprout and have a life of its own.

The deputy crawled backwards out of the car, still keeping low. Her hat had fallen off when she lost her balance, and rolled a pretty good distance out into the open. The sheriff's insignia on the crown caught the sun and twinkled.

The grandson was saying, "This time we're going to have to do something, get him in some kind of supervised living facility where he'll be safe." The deputy gave no sign that she'd heard. "That other one," the grandson said, indicating Calmer, "I don't know what his story's supposed to be."

Spooner looked down at the grandson and said, "You're something, aren't you?"

She said, "Sir, I'm telling you for the last time," good news to Spooner, who didn't like being nagged even under the best of circumstances—that is, by the unarmed—and without giving it another moment's consideration he walked out into the meadow where Calmer and the old man were still drinking beer and enjoying the afternoon.

Spooner took the toilet paper out of one of Calmer's ears. "Let me have it for a second, will you?" he said.

Calmer checked to make sure the safety was on—you can't be too careful with firearms, he'd been saying that for as long as Spooner could remember—and handed him the rifle, and old Dodge, who hadn't realized yet that he was in the middle of a police emergency, handed Spooner a beer, which he polished off without pausing once for oxygen. He'd never been much of a beer drinker but could have been except for the taste.

The deputy arrived from behind then, armed and dangerous. "Facedown! On the ground now!" she said. "Do it!"

Calmer got to his feet and pulled old Dodge up after him.

"I said on the ground!" Still screaming. Calmer smiled politely, with no intention whatsoever of lying on the ground.

The deputy looked quickly at the grandson, who had followed along behind and arrived on the crime scene last. "Which one of them fired at you, sir?" she said.

For a moment the grandson couldn't seem to make up his mind who he wanted to finger. "Him," he said finally, and indicated Calmer. "It was him." But now she stared at him a moment, perhaps beginning to smell a rat.

"It was *he*," Calmer said to the grandson and then addressed the deputy. "Madam," he said, "no such thing occurred."

And there was some kindliness for her in his voice that had nothing to do with the words themselves, some consideration of her situation perhaps, of the embarrassment at being stuffed into this absurd outfit that did nothing but exaggerate her obesity and awkward, mannish appearance, and she seemed to just give up, sagged and let the gun drop to her side, and in that surrender, you could see the powerful sway of Calmer Ottosson's kindness.

As for Spooner, he was picturing the scene that could erupt if she got more careless than she already had and maybe shot off her own toe. They could have their own Ruby Ridge, Spooner and Calmer and old Dodge, and for a long second this not only seemed possible but logical, where he and Calmer had been headed from the start.

She holstered her firearm, though, turning her back on the grandson, who continued to press the issue as if he had not noticed her change of heart, and then, unaccountably, she was on the verge of tears.

Calmer laid a hand on her shoulder and walked her a little ways back to the cruiser. He picked her hat up and dusted it off, and she wiped at her eyes and then got in the car and backed carefully down the driveway.

And then she was gone, and Spooner sent Marlin home and went back to work, and Calmer and old Dodge sat back down and picked up shooting and drinking where they'd left off.

EIGHTY-ONE

Spooner found Calmer early in the morning, half an hour or so after sunrise, sitting out in front of the guesthouse reading Friday's *New York Times*. He'd folded the paper into quarters, the edges lining up exactly, and was staring at a story about an opera singer—at least there was a picture, upside down to Spooner, of someone in pigtails and a set of horns alongside the article.

Weather-wise, it was already a perfect spring day in the Great Northwest, gray skies and a mist in the air, although Calmer hadn't seemed to notice, and he sat in a windbreaker with his legs crossed and mud on his shoes and the bottom of his trousers, looking at the page as if something about the opera singer worried him. Beverly Sills? Was that Beverly Sills? There was some age, Spooner thought, when women couldn't bring off the horns-and-pigtails look anymore.

"Beverly Sills?" Spooner said.

There was a peculiar, unsettled cast to Calmer's expression this morning that Spooner hadn't seen since Lily was at large.

"They came and . . ." Calmer hesitated, trying to come up with the name. "The fellow next door, they came by earlier and got him. The police and a lawyer and someone from the county." He paused again, remembering it. "They said they'd be back for his clothes."

They looked at each other, the suddenness of what had happened still in Calmer's face.

Spooner sat down on one of the big rocks that lined the walkway between the two houses, feeling obligated to explain and soften some fact of life, except there was no such fact, just this small morning impasse that constituted the present moment.

Calmer said, "He was pretty quick, but they had him outnumbered," and picturing that, Spooner remembered a panicked grosbeak that had gotten into the garage last weekend, careening wildly into one window after another, leaving little dustings of feathers in the air every place it hit while Mrs. Spooner closed in from below with her butterfly net to save it.

The moment passed and Calmer looked back at the newspaper. Next door, a truck turned in to the driveway, most likely Marlin was returning from wherever it was that they'd deposited old Dodge for storage, but Calmer did not look up at the sound, already absorbed in the article on Beverly Sills.

The grandson got out of the truck and went in the front door, and then a little time went by and the garage door opened, and he emerged with a car jack and his toolbox.

And now Lester also appeared from around the side of the guest-house, pine needles sticking to his coat and his nose, and he had a seat beside Spooner, his tongue narrow and raised along the side edges, like the brim of a Texas Ranger's hat, and there were specks of dirt and pine needles stuck to it too, and to the ragged black ribbons covering the lower teeth in back, and Spooner began picking the pine needles off, cleaning him up.

"She said there'd be a hearing," Calmer said. Spooner looked up and found him staring at the house next door. "The woman from the county. She said there'd be a hearing into his competence."

EIGHTY-TWO

The grandson went back into the garage and came out this time rolling two tires along in front of him, one with each hand. He stopped and let the tires roll a little ways of their own accord until they slowed and wobbled and fell into each other, coming to rest not far from the truck. He went into the garage again and came out with two more. Half of the people on the island had pickups, and this was the first Spooner had ever seen or heard of any of them changing out winter tires for summer. People with cars did that sometimes, but not trucks. He recalled asking Dodge what Marlin did for a living, back when the grandson first showed up, and the old man had chewed it over a moment and said, "Marlin keeps a very shiny truck." In point of fact, he lived off some monthly stipend left to him by his mother, and the truck was the closest thing to a job he'd ever had.

Marlin came out of the garage again, carrying what looked like brake liners. He blocked the back tires with pieces of firewood and got down on his hands and knees to look for the right spot to set the jack, then pulled himself back to his feet, like some arthritic old knight just knighted by the queen, and set the jack, and then gradually, an inch at a time, lifted the far front quarter of the truck off the ground. The fender came up first, the axle hanging beneath it, and it rose half a foot or more before the tire left the ground. He continued his jacking until there was a foot of clearance, tire to driveway, stopping now and then to check how much room he'd made for himself to work.

Calmer made a small, humming sound, as if something had surprised him, and he brought the paper closer and began the story about Beverly Sills, which to Spooner's knowledge he had already read twice in the last twenty minutes.

EIGHTY-THREE

He woke with the sun on his face, in a chair, still half in some dream regarding women with cow-horn helmets. The cloud cover had burned off and he was sweating in spite of a pretty stiff breeze that had come up off the water. He stood and took off his jacket, then noticed that a newspaper had been blown apart and lay in sheets around the yard.

Calmer went about the yard picking up the sheets of paper, hurrying against Lily coming out of the house and seeing the mess and worrying herself into another asthma attack. She had it in her head these days that Cowhurl was vandalizing the place, and there was no talking her out of it. Ever since he'd been fired—demoted—she felt them watching every minute of the day; keeping secret records. *Just waiting for us to make a mistake,* she said.

The fact was that a pack of stray dogs was running loose, tipping over Calmer and Lily's garbage cans Thursday nights—Friday was trash collection day—scattering their stuff up and down the street. He remembered the panicked way she got him up the first time it happened, like the garage was on fire. There was no calming her down, no telling her it was only garbage and that everyone else's garbage cans, including Cowhurl's, had been tipped over and strewn over the neighborhood too.

And so these days he took the garbage out Friday mornings, at first light.

The newspaper had been blown to kingdom come and he spotted another sheet of it, out past the garage, pressed against some bushes along the driveway. The paper seemed to breathe as the wind blew and died. He picked it up, checking around to make sure he'd gotten it all, and began to ball it up with the rest but then stopped when he noticed her picture, a little heavy these days but still a package of songbird he found very appealing, and he folded it carefully and stuck it into his pants pocket, thinking it might be something good to read in front of a fire later, and only then remembered that they couldn't have fires. Remembered Lily's asthma.

The breeze came through the trees whistling, and branches dead all winter cracked and fell through other branches and landed with surprising force—as he watched, one of them as tall as a man fell out of an alder and stuck a foot deep into the earth, quivering like an arrow.

The wind rose and fell, and tree limbs cracked and broke, and small single clouds rolled at remarkable speed across the sky, and yet for all the movement there was also an absence of movement, a blossoming unease.

The kids.

And for a long moment he couldn't catch his breath.

Where were the kids?

He looked at the alder branch, still upright in the ground, and in that instant he might as well have been speared himself, bug-style and pinned to the felt in some museum. How long had it been since he'd seen them? He tried to remember where they'd been, if they'd been together. Then a moment resembling relief. Margaret was across the road with the Ennis girls. He remembered now. She'd told them where she was going, which left the other one, the one you always had to worry about anyway. Calmer quieted himself, was still until he could think. It wasn't necessarily so bad. The kid could be in a tree or on the roof or setting fires somewhere. Or have broken in to somebody's closet and at this moment was pissing away into their shoes. The "Fiend," they'd called him.

He thought of the car. The car. Oh Christ, the car.

He checked the driveway, already knowing it wasn't there, and then looked north, out toward the two great, dead maples that stood near the property line, and then beyond them, to the bottom of the hill. It was more or less what he'd expected now that he thought about it, the car coming to rest at a strange, tilted angle, and he dropped his chin onto his chest and started out across the yard running.

He thought of himself and his father in the front seat of the old flat-bed, idling at a train crossing on the dirt road to Aberdeen, his mother in the backseat in a dress and sun hat. The dust blew in, the train blew past, so close that he could feel the rattling in his legs.

And he pounded through the trees and brush, all the fear set aside, one thing at a time. Christ, was he still inside there? Underneath?

There was wind to consider—if a gust caught her sideways as he moved in close to the dock—no, wait, not that.

He thought of Ennis flying out the back door and then next to him at the running board, putting his back into it too, to set the car upright. Calmer had never said it to anyone—who would he say it to but Ennis himself, and Ennis was a man who suffered to be told good morning— but a second before Ennis grabbed hold, Calmer had put together the shaking in his body and the shaking he'd felt hundreds of times when an airplane began to stall, and realized that like an airplane, he had loaded some mechanical part of himself beyond its limits and set off a series of failures in the various systems that kept him up. Which is to say he'd known he was right at the edge.

It was what the boy was after every day of his life.

———

Calmer cleared the small stand of trees twenty yards from the car. He began to call out the boy's name—not that he expected an answer—and then stopped. The name had slipped his mind.

Wait, calm down. There was an inch or two of clearance beneath the running board, and he got down on his hands and knees and peered into the darkness, hardened against what he might see. His eyes corrected for the darkness, and he glimpsed the shoes. And followed them to the legs and the legs to the body, everything bigger from this angle than it should be, an illusion. Still, what was there was there, the twisted, strange angles aside, it was what it was, and he knew he could never let her see the boy like this, ruined. That would be as heartless as the news itself.

Something moved.

"Don't worry," he said, "it's all right now. Everything's all right." He hurried to the front of the car, to the thing that had to be done, and, facing away from the wreck, bent his knees until his hands found the hard, narrow edge of the low side of the bumper and lifted with all his strength.

The car seemed to stir, almost as if it had come awake, and then a violent force tore the bumper out of Calmer's hands, skinning the pads of his fingers down to the tips, and there was a scalding pain and a wild, ringing clamor, and for a little while the throbbing in his head seemed worse than the throbbing in his fingers. Strangely, he thought he'd heard a voice. At the moment the car was torn from his hands, he thought he'd heard a single spoken word, and realized he must have spoken it himself.

He looked at his hands, which he held down and away, the fingers spread, like a girl drying her nail polish, and the blood followed the line from his palms to the tips of his fingers, and then beyond the fingers, dripping off the lowest points, the half inch or so of empty, loose skin dangling below each of the nails. They had the look of gloves pulled inside out. His head and hands throbbed, and all of it floated in a wild clamor, and it was a long time settling down.

And again he remembered the voice. Not the boy's—it was a man's voice. His own, he thought, it must have been his own voice. A single word: "Hey . . ."

EIGHTY-FOUR

Suppertime, Spooner knocked at the bedroom door. Calmer had been in there all afternoon, hadn't come out even to meet Spooner's daughter as she got off the school bus. He never missed that, walking her up the driveway carrying her books, talking about her teachers or what one of her friends had worn to school. What was *cool*. Lester had also been missing all afternoon, and it was close to time to eat. The dog had a hard rule about missing meals.

Spooner looked quickly out the back door, checking that the animal hadn't been chained again to the tree, and then out the front. No dog, but Marlin was still in the driveway under his truck, working.

Spooner knocked again and then tried the door, which was unlocked— Calmer never locked the doors here on the island and took some small pleasure in not having to, returning to a time and place where no one broke in to houses.

Spooner poked his head in and saw Calmer asleep in bed. It was strange to see him in bed while it was still daylight—in the old days he was always up, in Georgia and Prairie Glen and South Dakota, always going, daybreak until nine or ten at night, and even when he stopped for a few minutes to have a drink or a smoke, he was looking around for something to do while he rested.

These days he went to bed early and napped an hour or two on the couch, and it seemed possible that an enormous exhaustion had built up over the years, over the decades, and was finally coming due.

Well, Calmer had earned his naps.

He'd covered himself with a light blanket, looking small underneath it, but he had always seemed smaller to Spooner when he slept, as if some of the air had been let out, and was always turned on his side and curled down into his knees, covering whichever ear wasn't buried in the pillow with the meat of his forearm, like a soldier waiting for the next incoming shell. Looking at him, Spooner thought of the scene at the funeral home, how he'd curled up about like this in the box, and for a while no one had known what to do until Darrow had leaned in for a closer look and Calmer had gotten out and stretched, complaining about the hardness of the casket's floor on his back.

Spooner thought passingly of the missing dog and then noticed that Calmer's hand was wrapped in a towel, and then that blood had soaked through underneath, where it covered his palm.

The towel was loose and slightly overhung the tips of Calmer's fingers. It looked like a lot of blood, but then it didn't take a lot of blood to look like a lot of blood. There was more of it on the floor leading to the bathroom and Spooner went in there, and it was splashed over the sink and the edge of the bathtub, and soaked into the shirt Calmer had been wearing earlier and was now stuffed into the hamper. The wastebasket held a pile of bandages and tape, stiff and almost black with dried blood.

He went back to the bed and gently rolled Calmer's shoulder. His eyes opened, clear and alert, and he sat straight up. He checked his wristwatch, and at the movement the towel dropped off his hand—his left hand— into his lap. He looked at the hand, one side and then the other, skin dangling off the end of his fingers and the fingers themselves, raw and caked black at the edges, like they'd been burned. He took the other hand out from under the blanket, and some of the towel came up with it, stuck to his palm.

"Well, for the love of Pete," he said. He took the blanket off his feet, maybe to check that his toes were intact. The hand attached to the towel began to seep blood, not so much from one place or another, just all over.

Spooner said, "Good Christ. You burned up your hands."

Calmer held up one of the hands between them—the one not stuck to the towel—as if to suspend judgment until all the facts were in. Then he moved it up to his nose and sniffed. "I don't think so," he said. "There's no odor." Interested in the puzzle, if not the injury itself, but then, even back when he was razor sharp, Calmer might reach for a pepper shaker or a pencil and notice a fingernail had been smashed or was half torn from the bed underneath it, and would need a minute or two to remember that he'd closed it that morning in the car door.

He pulled the towel the rest of the way off his right hand, and there was a peeling sound as the cloth separated from the wound, and in the moment before blood began to pool, Spooner saw what looked like a series of shallow excavations. The pads of Calmer's palm were missing, as well as the three billowed areas of each finger. While Calmer watched himself bleed, Spooner walked back into the bathroom, shut the door, and did the thing he could be counted on to do in moments like this. He was still bent over the toilet when Calmer came in behind him, ignoring the regurgitation, and went to the sink. He put his hands under the faucet, the water as cold as it would come out, and hummed to himself as it ran.

Afterwards, together, they wrapped his hands in clean towels and headed for the hospital, which was in Coupeville, thirty miles north on the highway, but first Calmer insisted on apologizing to Mrs. Spooner for ruining supper, and Mrs. Spooner in turn insisted on seeing his hands, then said nothing at all for a moment when she saw them, and in this silence was everything that could be said.

Over Calmer's protests that it was nothing, they all went together to the hospital, she and Spooner's daughter in the backseat, Spooner and his dad up in front, the Spooners out for a family outing, and Calmer remarked that it was good to have everyone together like this and that they should do it more often.

The doctor advised keeping Calmer overnight, but Calmer only smiled and, using one of the same hands the nurse had just bandaged, shook the medical man's hand with a grip that had drained a million cows of their juice—you could see the surprise in the doctor's face—and patted him audibly on the shoulder blade, saying thanks, but he wouldn't want to take a hospital bed from somebody who might need it. His blood pressure and heartbeat and respiration were all steady and strong, good for a man half his age, although he was running a low-grade fever—100.7. He still hadn't mentioned pain or acted as if he were in pain, even when the nurse moved his fingers around to bandage them one by one.

While that had been going on, Spooner's daughter had turned white and fainted, and Calmer sat with her in back on the way home, holding her a little while and then pretending to faint at the sight of cows along the road.

EIGHTY-FIVE

It is not entirely accurate to say Spooner found the body. At least not in the sense of finders keepers. In the sense of finders keepers, the body was found by Lester, who, in the weeks he'd spent chained to the elm tree in the grandson's backyard, had lost perhaps thirty pounds. Thus, he could now urinate from the classic three-point stance and was beginning to look like he had a rib cage, and seeing this new, sleek version of the beast, Mrs. Spooner had gone to a veterinarian and bought a fifty-pound sack of diet dog food and instructed Spooner not to give it to him all at once, and in other ways laid down the law that Lester, for his own good, was through as a recreational eater.

Meaning that ever since his rescue, Lester had been served only the daily recommended diet for animals his size (the new, sleek size, not his previous 160–180 pounds) twice daily, feedings he finished in seven or eight seconds, and even though he would look up at Spooner afterwards with that *you're shitting me* expression, he was in all other ways his old happy self, from the moment he woke up every morning wedged into his old happy slot between Spooner and Mrs. Spooner, knowing in his own way that he was integral to the whole sweet, happy mess.

———

The sun set on the trip back from the hospital and cast the driveway in a dark gloom, steeped as it was on either side with maples and firs and alders, bringing horse blinders to mind, or the Lincoln Tunnel, and then two eerie lights appeared straight ahead, and Spooner stood up on the brakes.

Lester was standing neon-eyed along the tree line, just outside of the beams of the headlights, and the instant Spooner recognized him—even before he saw that something was wrong with the shape of his body—he realized that in all the excitement a near-calamity had occurred: Nobody had fed the dog.

Spooner got out and walked to the animal, crossing through one headlight and then the other, throwing shadows two directions at once. The dog looked steadily into the lights, not having picked up yet on Spooner's aroma. His tail wagged cautiously, not in its usual big happy loops, waiting to see what this was coming out of the dark.

Then Spooner spoke his name, and in the instant the word *Lester* was released into the air the dog closed the distance like Spooner was chicken pot pie.

There was something lopsided about the animal's shape, and Spooner lay him down in the driveway in the headlights and knelt down with him, afraid that he'd strayed out onto the road and been hit. He pressed his fingers into him lightly at first and then more deeply, watching the dog's expression for some sign of pain, but the animal only groaned sweetly and thumped the driveway with his tail. You got the same thing when you asked Calmer about his hands.

Mrs. Spooner was out of the car now too, and behind her their daughter. "Is he all right?" Mrs. Spooner said.

"He seems all right," he said. "I was afraid something hit him." And ran his hand over Lester's coat again, top to bottom. "He's swollen through here, but he seemed to be moving okay."

Having heard Mrs. Spooner's voice, Lester could not contain himself another minute and scrambled to his feet and buried his nose in Mrs. Spooner's cookies, as he always liked to do by way of greeting.

"Good God," she said, "look at his stomach."

And that was it, all right, his stomach. *Distended*, as they said. Not the way it had been distended before, when he was 180 pounds, but stretched and taut, like he was pregnant.

"Good God," she said again.

Then, as if to ease her worried mind, Lester backed up a step and tossed it all up, and even in the glare of the headlights and the darkness of the night, there was no mistake about what he'd had to eat while he was waiting for supper.

EIGHTY-SIX

The local paper made Marlin Dodge a front-page story and did what it could to come up with a hero. The paper had been sold recently to a small chain and it was a business now, and heroes and pictures of heroes sold newspapers, and as a rule the paper did not like to run tragic stories without one, a little good news with the bad. In this particular case—"South Whidbey Man Dies Under Truck"—the editors had settled on Lester. "Dog Summons Neighbor to Scene of Accidental Death." Which Spooner, still a newspaper man at heart, did not think quite caught the gist of what had happened. Not that he was going to contradict it.

The paper ran a large, flattering picture of Lester across the top, side by side with a less flattering picture of Marlin Dodge.

"Dead at 42" it said below Marlin.

Beneath Lester it said, "Too Late to Save Master."

"Well, you saved a little," Spooner said to the dog. "You didn't eat his head."

The tragedy was replayed the following week, but with a new slant. Coyotes.

Aberrant behavior, the coroner called it, possibly due to a growing competition for food. "This could get a lot worse before it gets better," he said.

EIGHTY-SEVEN

Old Dodge came home. The county dropped the hearing into his competency—not a word of apology—and Spooner hired a dump truck to take away the nest of ruined fence, and Calmer and the old man resumed their afternoon visits, sometimes down in the meadow drinking beer and shooting Calmer's single-shot .22, and even though Mrs. Spooner still worried about the rifle, and Calmer occasionally got up from supper to see if Lily needed anything in the bedroom, the grandson's death had somehow returned the place to its natural ambience, only sweeter now for the reminder that time was running out.

But if time running out made things sweeter, it also worked another direction, and Spooner, a man by now of some reputation for going his own way, who had over the years taken pretty dramatic steps to be seen in that way, craved the good opinion of his stepfather more than he could ever admit, and felt the chance to find out where he stood with him slipping away.

He had thought when Calmer first arrived that the answer would be obvious, or at least he would find a way to ask the question. But there was a forty-year precedent at work against that and Spooner remembered like yesterday the awful silence that would fall over the kitchen after any utterance, no matter how innocent, of this general subject was floated out over dinner.

And in the way things happen, forty-odd years had come and gone and with the exception of the one awful letter from his mother, nothing was said. On the other hand, remembering the letter, Spooner sometimes conjured up a life where everyone poured out his heart at dinner, and the mother cried over her dead husband and brought out pictures of her wedding to show what she'd looked like back before she'd been cheated out of life, and glimpsing this scene Spooner rethought everything and had no objection to this code of *omerta* after all.

Still, he wanted to hear from Calmer. It didn't concern him much that what Calmer said wasn't so dependable these days, only that time was running out for him to say it at all.

As far as Spooner could tell, this need to know where he stood with Calmer had materialized in the hospital in Philadelphia, on the operating table, where somehow he'd lost the ordinary capacity to see himself from a reliable, consistent perch. Such capacity, when he thought about it, described one half of the two working parts of conscience, and even if conscience wasn't exactly what was missing, he knew that he had his finger on the right page in the catalog, and over the years had fixed on Calmer, the most ethical man he'd ever known, to tell him how he was doing.

The preoccupation with time running out was a new development, probably traceable to the night in the driveway when he presided over the disgorgement from Lester's stomach of a huge, wet, perfectly intact chunk of Marlin Dodge's calf, still bearing three and a half letters of the four-letter tattoo, USMC. Spooner had been confused and worried at the time, floating around loose in that world of blind spots that lies in the throw of a car's headlamps, and as he stared at the heap Lester had disgorged, he—Spooner, not Lester—briefly mistook the lettering, taking it for a USDA stamp of approval.

Realizing his mistake, Spooner had taken off his jacket and carefully wiped the animal's chin clean of Marlin's goop and then taken his face into his hands, gently, but bringing into play a certain man/dog authority that was unusual between them, and looked into Lester's dark eyes, holding his attention a long moment and then directing it to the evidence at their feet—the smoking gun of all time—and quietly, firmly, enunciated the word *no*.

EIGHTY-EIGHT

The bandages on Calmer's hands had to be kept dry and changed every forty-eight hours, and the trips to the doctor's office left him tired and edgy. "You don't take a thirty-year-old horse to the vet," he said. "They keep telling you it's all for your own good, but in the end, it doesn't make any difference what they do. You live for a while and then you die." More and more, Spooner saw him receding into the old make-do days where he'd spent so much of his life.

They were on the way home from Coupeville. "You have to treat an infection. That can make a difference," Spooner said.

Calmer turned in the seat and stared at him. "Listen," he said, "you should know this by now. There are people you can't trust—doctors, lawyers, even your own family."

Spooner thought he saw where things were headed. He remembered the conversation outside the house in Falling Rapids after Calmer had been demoted, he and Phillip and Darrow sitting in lawn chairs, Phillip saying that they hadn't heard the other side of the story—the whole scene as clear to him now as Calmer's shadow had been behind the screened kitchen window. A small bad moment, yes, but a throwaway, he would have thought, in the sadness and disorder of that awful year. He saw though that he'd misjudged it.

"He didn't know what he was saying," Spooner said. He felt Calmer's eyes resting on him, waiting, attentive. "He was what, sixteen, seventeen years old? With a brain like . . . It's like you opened up a box of Cracker Jacks and found a million dollars. No, wait—a tit. Everybody else gets a whistle or a little plastic gun, and he gets a tit. It doesn't even fit in his pocket, you following me here? He'd not sure what he's supposed to do with it, he's not even sure he's supposed to have it."

Calmer continued to wait him out.

"So the way these things can go, he said something just to be part of things, that's all, something as a matter of fact that he'd heard from you. *Listen to both sides . . .*"

It was quiet a minute and Spooner took two or three false starts at what came next, gradually seeing that a tit in a Cracker Jacks box wasn't the metaphor it had been cracked up to be when it first skipped into his head.

"Let's forget the tit in the Cracker Jacks," he said finally.

Calmer smiled and held up one of his bandaged hands. That fast, his good mood was back. "Ah, but 'the moving finger writes,'" he said, "'and having writ moves on; nor all your piety nor wit shall lure it back to cancel half a line.'"

Spooner would have loved to say something in that vein back, to remind Calmer that he was also a literary man these days, but all that would come to mind was the part of Humpty Dumpty where the egg couldn't be put back together.

EIGHTY-NINE

It took longer to reach the end of the island than it usually did, Calmer walking more slowly, stopping every forty or fifty yards to look around, as if marking his place. It seemed to Spooner he might be favoring his left leg, but it was pointless to ask. Calmer would as soon admit that his leg hurt as admit that he didn't like what Mrs. Spooner had made for supper.

They sat on the bait shop's steps, drinking seventy-five-cent beer, and presently Calmer patted himself down and found a pencil in his shirt pocket, and in spite of his bandaged fingers wrote a series of numbers across a napkin.

Four, six, nine, thirteen, nineteen, and after that a blank space for what came next. It was the old game from the years in Milledgeville, Calmer and Margaret and Spooner sitting at the kitchen table after supper, Calmer making up the numbers.

At first it had gone like this:

2, 4, 6, 8, ___ or 3, 6, 9, 12, ___

They hadn't gone too far with that before a disagreement came up that you might say spelled out the future. Calmer wrote down, 1, 4, 9, 16, 25, ___, and Margaret had the answer—thirty-six, six times six—before Calmer even put the five on twenty-five.

Part of the game was the right number; the other part was the reason.

Spooner sat looking at the answer a little while, just staring at it until Calmer began in his patient way to show him where it came from. But

Spooner knew where it came from; he was thinking of something else. "It can be any number," he said.

It was still only a month or so after the wedding, probably before it had begun to sink in with Calmer what he had on his hands.

He said, "How now, brown cow?" which set Margaret off giggling, as it could be counted on to do.

Spooner said, "You could have a different rule."

"But not in the middle of the game. One rule for all the numbers in the line. You can have any rule you want for the next line."

Still Spooner stared at the numbers.

"What other number could it be?" Calmer said.

Spooner shrugged, picked his birthday. "One," he said.

Calmer crossed out thirty-six and wrote a one on the end of the sequence, looked at Spooner, and raised his eyebrows in an exaggerated way. "And what, pray tell, is the rule?" he said. Talking Shakespeare now, the way he sometimes did.

"Whatever the number is, that's the rule."

"But how would one say it? How can it be expressed?" Calmer had not talked to them yet about equations, didn't see any reason to muddy the water with the word before they understood what it was for.

Spooner said, "The rule is the last number is one."

Calmer studied him a moment and then smiled, and when Margaret looked up at him to see if that was fair, he shrugged, as if Spooner was right. "The anarchist," he said.

And here they were, forty-odd years later, Spooner and Calmer sitting on the bait house steps, playing the old game. He picked the pencil carefully out of Calmer's fingers and wrote, 25.

Calmer said, "Magnifico!"

The truth was that Calmer had a partiality for prime numbers, and once you knew that, the rest of it was simple addition.

"You remember what we were talking about yesterday?" Spooner said. "I wanted to be sure we understood each other about that."

He waited, but there was no sign that Calmer remembered anything at all.

"Your kids turned out fine, Dad, especially Phillip."

Calmer shook his head and smiled at the misunderstanding. "No, we weren't talking about him. The other one, in the city."

"Phillip's the one in the city," Spooner said. "He lives in Manhattan, in an apartment on Lexington Avenue."

Calmer cocked his head, rethinking it. He killed the last warm swallow of foam in the bottle and made to get up and leave.

Spooner sat where he was. "Right?" he said.

Calmer assumed a familiar, patient expression, then lowered his voice in a way that it was understood what he said wasn't for any of the others to hear. "The other one," he said. "The one in Philadelphia."

———

Calmer got up and went to the trash can to deposit his empty bottle. Spooner followed along after him, like a catfish just whacked with the fish whacker, and in this condition they commenced the second half of the morning's walk, the more difficult half, mostly uphill, following the natural rise of the cliff. Calmer was out in front, unusually deliberate about where he put his feet, as if his shoes were too small and it hurt him to step.

And Spooner followed along behind, wondering if Calmer was doing the arithmetic now, figuring out who he was.

———

Calmer took his regular nap when they got home and later Spooner saw him out in the meadow with old Dodge. They were down there together almost every afternoon these days, sometimes even in the rain.

NINETY

It was time to change the bandages again, but Calmer had gone into his bedroom after the morning walk and hadn't come out, even for lunch. He'd been slower out along the cliffs again, and reluctant to talk when they sat down at the bait shop.

Most likely, his hands were hurting. Spooner hoped that it was his hands, not what he'd said yesterday about whom you could trust. He was still running a fever—it was half a degree higher, actually—but there was no pus in the dressings when the nurse cut them off up in Coupeville, no streaks of infection running up his arms.

He'd had two beers and a Coke at the bait shop, and then turned on the hose when he got home and drunk from the nozzle a long time. Spooner gave him another hour, and then another, and sometime close to two-thirty he tapped on the door and looked in.

Calmer was lying on his back, reading. There was a shine to his skin, and the light from the reading lamp collected in a damp line of sweat across his forehead. Calmer had propped up one of his legs on a pillow. Lester was next to him, resting his massive head across Calmer's chest, and as Spooner moved closer the animal swept his tail slowly across the sheets, wrinkling them one way, smoothing them out the other.

"Let's run up to Coupeville and get the bandages changed," Spooner said.

Calmer looked at his hands, at the bandages, and then rested one quietly on top of the animal's head. Lester's tail moved across the sheets again.

"Let's let it go this once," he said.

Spooner took in the width of the dog's skull—Christ, what a head—and then Calmer's T-shirt, dark with sweat. "You feeling all right?"

"Sleepy," Calmer said. "Just sleepy," and closed the book and laid it down over on the other side of Lester.

There was a chair under the window and Spooner sat down, then got back up and went to the icebox for a couple of bottles of beer. Calmer gave his a taste and set it down on the reading table.

"No good?" Spooner said.

"Just some water, if you don't mind."

Spooner went into the other room again and filled a glass with ice and water, and this time when he got back Calmer had closed his eyes.

Spooner set the water glass on the bed table and sat back down. He stared at the ceiling, remembering the mangled body under the truck axle, wondering if Calmer had tried to lift it off his chest. But if that was it, why hadn't he just used the jack? From what Spooner had seen of it, the nature of Calmer's disease didn't affect reasoning or intelligence; his memory was what it was after. He would have seen what needed to be done.

"You still don't remember how it happened," Spooner said, indicating Calmer's hands, but Calmer only smiled, as if he were waiting for him to get the joke.

Presently, the smile faded. "I wish I could help you," he said.

NINETY-ONE

Spooner found him, still in bed with the dog; it was a little after seven o'clock. He'd brought over a glass of crackers and milk at bedtime and left it on the reading table, and it was still there, untouched.

He opened the door and let Lester out, and the dog went to Mrs. Spooner's garden and commenced a four-minute urination.

———

The coroner told Spooner it was impossible to estimate how long ago Calmer had been shot, but then made an estimate after all, for the newspaper. He said it could have been a month. The bullet was in next to the femur, about halfway between Calmer's knee and his hip, the entrance wound from the front. The infection had gone into the bone.

"He would have lost the leg anyway," the coroner said, and then offered up another opinion that would also make its way into the paper. "A gunshot wound," he said, "can be extremely dangerous."

NINETY-TWO

Margaret had been in Boston and took the first flight west. Darrow drove from Montana with his wife and kids in the old VW van, all his eggs in one basket. Phillip was in London, doing some kind of accounting that nobody in England knew how to do, and he caught a nonstop flight to San Francisco and then a flight north, arriving in Seattle half an hour before Cousin Bill, who had bought a trombone and was starting his first lesson when Spooner ran him down at his music teacher's house out on Beaver Island.

The marine forecast had called for a warm, calm day and they were all pretty good swimmers, but Phillip, who had not gotten to the top of the New York City accounting world by taking chances, strapped himself nevertheless into a life jacket before setting foot in the boat.

The boat itself was a rowboat—Darrow's suggestion instead of the fishing boat Spooner had arranged to borrow. And it was a better idea, the sound of the gulls, the quiet of the water, the oars breaking the surface, in and out, like breathing, and only a week before, as it happened, Spooner's friend Dr. Ploof had received a forty-year-old rowboat via UPS, bequeathed to him by a patient who'd skipped town years before owing him a little over eight thousand dollars.

As to the matter of casting Calmer's ashes into the sound, Spooner's understanding of the way it worked was that the ashes would be washed from the sound into the ocean, and from there into other oceans, and from

them into other sounds and rivers and inlets and outlets, and in the end
Calmer would merge with all the various waters of the world and trickle
here and there all over kingdom come, and in this way gradually disappear
into the currents of water and time.

And one of these days, it might rain a little Calmer too.

NINETY-THREE

The ashes were in a box in Spooner's lap. He was stationed toward the back of Dr. Ploof's eight-thousand-dollar rowboat, on the same seat with Margaret. Darrow sat in the next seat, rowing,
and beyond him was Phillip in his life jacket, watching over his shoulder
as America disappeared, and Cousin Bill, who, although more of a sailor
than a paddler, was quite a water-going man himself and was anxiously
waiting for his turn at the oars.

They'd put the boat in near the bait shop at the south end of the
island, stopping inside to buy beer for a last toast, and paddled a mile
or so out, beyond the bay to open, deeper water where the wind picked
up and the current began to take the rowboat south. According to the
marine forecast, the surface temperature of the sound was thirty-eight
degrees—so cold that the inch or so that had already leaked into the
bottom of Dr. Ploof's rowboat was numbing Spooner's feet—and the
wind off the water dried the sweat off Spooner's face and scalp, and then
began, a little at a time, to chill him, and he wondered if he should have
brought a sweater.

They went out into it, farther, a little farther, and a little more, and
when it finally seemed like far enough, Darrow, his lips edged blue by now,
like everybody else's, turned the little boat into the wind and waited.

And everywhere in Dr. Ploof's rowboat were freezing Whitlowes,
waiting for Spooner to make his move.

Spooner reconsidered the dark, square box in his hands. It was
heavier than he'd imagined it would be, and there was more of it. He

opened the top and fixed his eyes on the contents, not really contemplating his stepfather, as the other passengers may have thought, but quietly imagining the box they'd need to haul his own ashes out to sea. At this point in his life, Spooner had accumulated titanium rods running down the inside of both femurs, ceramic hips, a small metal plate under his scalp, fourteen implanted teeth, three screws in his bad ankle, one screw in his good ankle, and Jesus only knew how many screws holding his elbow in place. He imagined the sounds of the scattering of his ashes, the plopping as the screws hit the water, the splashing pieces of titanium.

He glanced again into the box and Calmer was smooth as brownie mix. Never any trouble for anyone.

And the family was waiting.

The wind seemed to pick up again, blowing Spooner's shirt flat against his chest, and there were clouds on the horizon now, and the temperature dropped a few degrees in not many minutes and pretty soon, marine forecast or not, it could have been October. He ran his hand over his chest and his nipples were like BBs. Still, no one spoke, no one hurried him at all. And he sat looking at the ashes, trying to feel what he was feeling more clearly, looking for some better connection prior to chucking the remains of the greatest man he'd ever known, or at least the greatest man who had ever known him, into the Puget Sound.

And then he saw it, what was going to happen. Saw Calmer's remains blowing back into their faces, the ashes sticking to everything wet and floating around in what was by now half a foot of water in the bottom of the boat, saw them tasting the ashes in their mouths and all of them spitting over the side, and saw that this whole idea of throwing Calmer away was too much like emptying a half-full can of Coke out a car window at eighty miles an hour anyway and, reconsidering the whole scene, began to think of the ceremony as littering. He saw that it would be better and more dignified to simply set the box into the water and let it sink—it was two or three hundred feet deep here at least—and allow the currents to do the dispersing out of sight.

He closed the top and then leaned over the side, the boat rocking dangerously at the motion, and set the box in the water.

It was a heavy little box, but then, so was a Chris-Craft.

Which is to say it didn't sink.

There was not a word from his cousin or his brothers or sister—on reflection, Spooner sometimes pictured this scene as another family's: he as the full-grown, still-lovable Mongoloid child, doing his best but mucking up the works for the thousandth time even as the siblings retreated into an old silent agreement, sheltering him from knowing that he has mucked up the works again, from knowing the one thing he does know, absolutely, that he is *special*.

It was Cousin Bill who finally commented. "Oh boy," he said.

The little box bobbed in the chop that had come up with the breeze, and drifted away from the rowboat, southeast, toward Seattle. And there was a thought, Calmer's ashes washing up intact in West Seattle. Spooner turned and looked at Darrow, who was smarter and would have an idea— and at the risk of undermining not only that statement but the countless other references to Darrow's superior intelligence, it is perhaps not unfair to remind you whose idea the rowboat was in the first place—waiting to hear how they were going to re-collect Calmer's ashes.

"What did you just do?" Darrow said. Nothing accusatory in the question, that wasn't the tone, although you couldn't call it strictly informational either.

Spooner said, "My thought was that it would sink."

Cousin Bill, meanwhile, climbed to the bow and began making the same sort of motions with his hands that you make for someone parking in a tight space. He was a water-going man and knew a few things about currents and tides, and seemed now to have taken charge of the ship. Darrow took no offense at being replaced, and for a few minutes he followed instructions, pulling hard on one oar and then the other, his strokes smooth and rhythmical, and for a little while you could actually see what the expression *having an oar in the water* was all about.

For their part, the civilians—Spooner, Margaret, and Phillip—sat where they had been sitting, trying not to look one another in the eye, wary of unspoken messages passed at such an emotional moment, knowing that something might be said with a single glance that could never be taken back. The word *stupid* floated in the air like colored balloons after the flashbulb goes off, but nobody uttered a word.

And Dr. Ploof's eight-thousand-dollar rowboat continued to fill with the Puget Sound, and just prior to drawing even with the box of ashes, Cousin Bill looked back to make sure the crew was ready to make the retrieval, and noticed the water. "Bailer," he said, "we need a bailer." He leaned far to the right—Spooner's side of the boat—his fingers just brushing the box, and then he was past it, empty handed.

Spooner, who had the better angle, leaned out and also touched the box, but it was slippery and too big to be plucked up with the tips of his fingers, and he was angry suddenly, as if he—or Calmer—were being teased, and he reached for it again, this time with both hands, wanting this thing settled straightaway. Darrow flattened one of the paddles against the current and pulled with the other, bringing the side of the boat around in the direction of the box of ashes, and it is likely that if Spooner had just waited a second or two longer the ashes would have come to him, right to the side of the boat, and it is also likely that his reaching would not have caused the rowboat to flip over—although not completely upside-down over, just out from under the passengers—as it did, as rowboats sometimes do.

But it's a second-guesser's world and always has been, and on that subject it is also the kind of world where the only human with enough sense to wear a life jacket is the human who doesn't go overboard, which is to say that when Spooner came back to the surface and cleared his vision, what he saw first was Phillip, alone in the rowboat, leaning carefully over the side to collect one of the paddles. Margaret and Darrow were behind the boat and slightly to the other side, swimming in. He did not see Cousin Bill but heard a certain familiar hooting from behind the craft, indicating wild amusement, which, taking into account the personalities involved and the amount of amusement available—thirty-eight-degree water and a half hour's ride back to the island, in the unlikely event that the boat didn't sink—narrowed it down pretty well to Bill.

Not that any of this registered particularly as what it was, since even though there were sights and sounds to burn in these first moments in ice water, there was not much in the way of meaning. A whole new world, but too much to take in all at once. Or perhaps you could say it was like the world at your moment of entry, the On/Off switch is switched on and there you are, brand-new and bawling and out of focus and not knowing shit from Shinola—although if you want to get technical about it, Spooner hadn't known what Shinola was before he went into the water either.

Later, after his brothers had pulled him out and he'd had a chance to warm up and dry out and think it over, he was struck with the idea that the first half minute or so in ice water probably wasn't much different from the first half minute after you homogenized your elbow, or maybe went headfirst into a boiling vat of collard greens, or were sucked out of an airliner. That apparently the human signal operated inside a pretty narrow frequency, now that he thought about it, and beyond that frequency nothing came through but static, one noise as meaningless as another.

Margaret was the first of the victims back in the rowboat, pulling herself up as easily as one of those prepubescent Russian gymnasts mounting the parallel bars, and then leaned forward until gravity tipped her onto the floor, where she splashed into maybe eight inches of water. She got to her feet and took charge, took the oar from Phillip and paddled one side and then the other, like a canoe, and Phillip made his way cautiously to the front, and then stopped for a moment, collecting himself, preparing for the rescue.

Darrow came on from behind him, however, tipping that side of the boat almost to the water line, and yet Phillip, who was standing up and hadn't heard him coming, again managed to stay dry. Cousin Bill arrived third, handing up the six-pack to Phillip before allowing himself to be dragged on board.

Then for a little while Spooner was alone in the water, treading water, he supposed, although he couldn't say what his arms or legs were doing, or particularly feel where they were, and when he looked up into the boat, the faces were indistinguishable, one from the other, like strangers leaning in over the crib.

He glimpsed the box then—the sun's reflection off it, at least—and moved to retrieve it, and was shortly surprised to find himself actually heading in its direction, yet even as the gap narrowed he felt time slowing, distinctly slowing, until it almost stopped, like one of Calmer's old puzzles, the closer you get, the slower you go, and presently the water lost its hard bite and turned warm on his face and pulled Spooner its own way, but before he gave in and allowed himself to be dragged back into the rowboat and saved, he persisted a little longer, one last chance, making corrections off the dancing light up ahead, and for a little while you might say they were right back where they started, he and Calmer, and where they had always been, which is to say, just out of reach.

ACKNOWLEDGMENTS

It seems I have been remiss. As far as I know, this is novel number seven and up until the present moment I have never undertaken to compose one of the love notes that often accompany a work of long fiction, thanking all the people who made it possible. There was such a note that accompanied *Paper Trails*, a collection of short nonfiction that came out a couple of years ago, but then it was pretty much a matter of being shamed into it, as my friend Fleder had not only come up with the idea for the book and the title for the book, but had also been the one who waded through the thousand-odd columns and chose which ones to use and where to use them, and so in the end I thanked him for helping—I still love that, *helping*—and thought, well, that's that.

But it wasn't, which brings me around to the reason I don't— didn't— write acknowledgments, which is that you can't just say *thanks, Fleder*, and move on. Pretty soon, you are not just thanking Fleder, you are also thanking publishers for publishing and editors for editing and typesetters for typesetting and loved ones for putting up with your temperamental, artistic moods during the long, difficult years it took you to wait for Fleder to finish the work back in New York. You are thanking your dog and the postmistress and your agent. Think about that, your agent.

It was Fleder himself who brought the matter to my attention. He is modest to a fault, and looked at the bare-bones acknowledgment for his work in *Paper Trails* and said, "Wait, you can't just thank me."

"Who else?" I said.

He said, "Well, what about Esther?"

And I said, "ICM already got fifteen percent of the book, and it is not entirely impossible that they did even less of the work than I did." Notice I said this to Fleder, not to Esther herself.

And Rob said, "You're not going to thank Esther? Have you made some decision never to come back to New York?"

And in my world that is what you call a point well taken. You damn right I thanked Esther, in fact, I suddenly feel like thanking her again—I wonder if she'd like her feet washed—but before we get puckered up for where all this will inevitably lead, it may be useful to first discuss the rules.

One rule, actually, and it is simply that there is a difference between people who are paid to be helpful and nice and those who are nice for free, and generally speaking the coming acknowledgments will be more heartfelt regarding the volunteers as opposed to the professionals, especially those volunteers who made it through when the novel was 250 pages longer than it is now.

Among those in the eight-hundred-page category is Padgett Powell, as far as I'm concerned the most underappreciated novelist/short story writer of our time, who spent hours hunting through the text for titles and in fact came up with three or four that were better than anything I came up with, but were all in some way *of* the material as opposed to being *about* it. One of his suggestions, for instance, was *The Accidental Quality of Things That Are True*, or something a little better than that, and even though the phrase was taken directly from the book itself, it nevertheless failed to settle with my breakfast. Why? Who knows? It may be my preference for a good American name like, oh, Esther Newberg, over the Native American version, *She Who Rips Throats for Pleasure*.

By the way, Esther, I've been thinking about you a lot lately, how much I appreciate everything you've done.

But what I was saying before I was interrupted with that spontaneous appreciation of Esther was that when someone of the talent of Padgett Powell takes the time it takes to ladle through eight hundred pages of a first draft of your soup, you have been complimented in a way you should not forget.

Also on the subject of underappreciated talents, I should mention that my friend Dr. Ploof also accepted the manuscript in the long form, commented a few days later that he liked the beginning very much and then did not raise the matter again, which I took as confirmation of my suspicion that the story was too long, and immediately set about removing 250 pages from the manuscript, and considered adding pictures. The most useful criticism, by the way, does not come neatly thought out and typed for you to read in the Sunday Books section of the *New York Times*. The very best criticism isn't written at all, or even spoken. It is simply there in the awkward silence as you and the doctor sit safely buckled into his pickup in the moment before he turns the ignition key, each of you diverting the conversation by nursing some old shoulder or knee injury that has come alive during the ascent into the cab, and the silence goes on and on and now you are sitting there watching helplessly as the natural moment for some complimentary remark on the manuscript passes into the ether. Criticism of this sort causes you to think, to cast a fresh eye over a whole project, to understand what you have done in larger terms, and perhaps understand it so well that you throw a third of it away.

And one night a year or two from now when over a bottle of wine the doctor confesses, as he surely will, that he lost the manuscript the day you gave it to him, you will thank him anyway because the doctor, as always, has left you a more thoughtful person and in his own way may have improved the book.

The book by the way is a novel, not in any sense a memoir, but is nevertheless based loosely on events and characters from my own life, which prompted me to send early copies to all the relatives who show up in the pages—both my brothers, Tom and Arthur, my sister Kitty, and my cousin Bill Vann. Actuarially speaking I am probably slated to go first (Bill is a little older but comes from better stock) and it occurred to me that opening the novel up to familial objections/comments before its publication might cut down on unsightly graveside celebrations later on.

Tom in particular understands the structure and sound of good sentences, and not only can pick out the ones that aren't good, but can also see how to fix them. This talent—editing—has pretty much gone the way of pinsetters these days, especially in the book business, and I would be very surprised to find another writer anywhere who gets to run his stuff past two sets of eyes as good as Tom's and Dr. Deborah Futter's, who is in charge of me over at Grand Central Publishing, and while technically this violates the rule of acknowledgments—that is, she is paid to save me from myself whereas Tom, Kitty, Arthur, Cousin Bill, Dr. Ploof, et al. are not—she is bent enough off true to pass for a member of the family, and sometimes I cannot help thinking of her as a volunteer. And even though she doesn't seem bent enough to be one of mine, Dianne Choie, also of Grand Central, should be acknowledged because without adult supervision where would any of us be?

My sister also read the long version, and she is not only the most literary member of my family but maybe our best writer, and her approval of vast tracts of *Spooner* have loaded my six-shooters for the long process of copyediting that still lies ahead, a process I have always found to be a nasty, two-week walk down memory lane with Miss Kilmer, an obese grammarian back at the University of South Dakota who once returned a term paper I submitted without even the courtesy of a failing grade, just the notation *This Is Entirely Inappropriate*, and ever since I have daydreamed that if only they'd let me take my sister with me to college, Miss Kilmer would never have gotten away with that.

My youngest brother, Arthur, recently gave up a partnership at Price Waterhouse to teach high school mathematics, and in spite of that has a very accomplished sense of order and time, and pointed out for me all the places the novel violated the normal rules thereof—i.e., Spooner ages three years while the rest of the world ages twelve—and made helpful suggestions in regard to how one might go about fixing the problem. His main suggestion, in fact—to have all the characters age at the same rate

without regard to issues of maturity—not only seems to have straightened out much of the confusion but has also given me a brief glimpse
into the workings of an orderly mind—Arthur's—and I think we all
know that a writer can never get enough of seeing the world from a different perspective.

Also in the category of nice-for-free readers of the eight-hundred-
page version is my friend Fleder—you remember Fleder, the author
of *Paper Trails?*—and even though I was a little disappointed with his
contribution this time—the man didn't offer to write even the first
draft—and none of his suggestions for a title seemed exactly right to
me either, one of them became the title nevertheless. So as I publicly
thank Fleder again, I will also take this occasion to acknowledge that
this far in my career as a literary man, Fleder has named or, in this
case co-named, at least three and maybe four of the books I have produced. (Can anybody here remember who named *Paper Trails?*) I might
also mention that a warm, unsolicited note regarding the manuscript
from his wife set me humming for weeks. She is Marilyn Johnson, an
intoxicating and faultless woman as far as I am concerned, except for
one night a couple of years ago in the town of Deadwood, South Dakota, when she suddenly refused to allow her husband to play with me
anymore unless I stopped proposing small bets on the color of undergarments worn by the cowgirls who stumbled into old Saloon No. 10,
leaving us nothing to do but drink, gamble, and watch the streets for
sightings of Kevin Costner and David Milch. Mr. Costner is a movie
star and owns the town's most expensive restaurant, and David Milch
is the Hollywood genius who produced and wrote much of the HBO
series *Deadwood*. Mr. Milch's story was an interesting one to me, at least
as it emerged from maybe half a dozen profiles written about him
back when *Deadwood* was in its heyday, and it goes like this: Mr. Milch
had pined to do a western ever since he was an important writer on an
Emmy-winning network cop series and could just as easily have been a
novelist, if I remember the story correctly, and after years of research
and reading everything available on the old west decided to focus his

talents on the town of Deadwood in the 1870s. But hold your horses, Tex. As Mr. Milch has explained it, he didn't read *everything* after all, he read everything except the novel *Deadwood*, and was not only able on his own to come up with the same setting and feel and characters that populated the novel, but somehow intuited a footnote-in-history sort of character named Charlie Utter into pretty much the same human being who is the central character of the novel. Except Mr. Milch gave him an English accent, and if that's not Hollywood genius I don't know what is.

Needless to say, I have been meaning to compliment Mr. Milch on his series and his genius for quite a while, but having missed him the night Mrs. Fleder put her foot down on the business with the cowgirls' undergarments, I guess the best thing to do now is just sit back with the rest of the viewing public and wait for him to do it again.

But I digress. We were talking about Esther. Thank my lucky stars for Esther.

And speaking of lucky stars, what to do with Mrs. Dexter? Oh, I'm afraid we have caught our petticoats on the old horns of a dilemma this time. Does she qualify as unpaid? Thirty-one years together, sickness and in health, childbirth, PMS, menopause, and still in some mysterious way I don't know the woman at all. This much I can say absolutely: Mrs. Dexter is not remotely inexpensive. On the other hand, she obviously doesn't do the things she does for money. She is probably over there in the house as I write, ironing my underpants so that there will be no chance of old Magoo popping out for a visit if some visitor should materialize out of the desert. Mrs. Dexter has spent twenty years getting me to wear something over my underwear, and not just now and then, but every time I so much as run to the grocery store. She teaches that consistency is the key to success, and I have come to realize over the years that she is telling me something even bigger than the story of underpants, she is telling me about life and writing.

The woman in fact may have already given me all the criticism a writer ever needs: "*Think about it Peter,*" she said recently, even though she knows I hate being spoken to in italics, "why do you think they call them *under*pants?"

Mrs. Dexter and I have a daughter, Casey, who inherited many of her mother's wonderful traits but never picked up the knack of speaking in italics, and she also gave the book high marks, and claimed it was not just because I am her father, and the truth is that with the possible exception of Mrs. Dexter herself, there is no one I care more about pleasing.

Which for some reason brings me to Esther. I wonder if Esther needs something buffed. Which for some reason brings me to Cousin Bill, and I guess that we all know what Cousin Bill wants buffed.

But then perhaps the less said about Cousin Bill and buffing, the better, and thus let us matriculate (to use a word that belongs to Padgett Powell) on over to the nonprofessional readers of the shorter version, Dr. Catherine Robinson and Ms. Betsy Carter. Dr. Robinson said it was an honor to look through my stuff for errors but I have not heard back on that yet, and all I can say is that it is a hard thing, waiting for the call with the results from the doctor. Ms. Carter, meanwhile, pronounced the work lovable although she did take exception to the use of the simile *teeth like Chiclets*, used twice in the same paragraph, which I found and changed, not liking it much myself, although the real problem Ms. Carter and I have lies in the matter of perception. She hears *teeth like Chiclets* and thinks of a big white anchorman smile, and I write *teeth like Chiclets* thinking of the feel of teeth loose in my mouth after they have been knocked out of the gums. She is entitled to her opinion, of course, but the truth is that all the high living in New York has caused her to lose touch with the common people.

Oh, and James Ellroy. If it's all right to thank him before I thank Esther again, Mr. Ellroy didn't read this one for me, but back in the days before I was a writer of acknowledgments I authored a novel called *Train*, which was set in Los Angeles in the 1950s, and telephoned Mr. Ellroy out of the blue one afternoon and asked questions regarding that city that must have called into question why someone who didn't already know this stuff would even try to write about it, and Mr. Ellroy was not only patient and friendly and gave me all the time I needed, he also knew what he was talking about. This is a very rare sort of phone call for me, and a pretty persuasive argument for going back to answering the phone, and these days the phone never rings with good news without my remembering Mr. Ellroy's consideration and patience. This has happened maybe twice since the publication of *Train*.

And as long as we're headed backwards, I should also mention Bob Loomis, my editor back at Random House in the days before I wrote acknowledgments, who was honest and gracious with me through five novels and deserved to be thanked personally and graciously for that when I left, and wasn't. And not only that, I think he was the one who suggested Esther to me when it was time for my previous literary agent—a handsome, very snappily dressed up-and-comer in the business whose name I couldn't remember even during those few months he represented me—to leave the premises. Somehow when I thought of the future with this fellow I thought of living with a goiter, and the truth is, even if he were still my agent I cannot imagine myself thanking him for anything except perhaps once saying that he had worked too long and too hard—he may have been twenty-five at the time—to represent a one-time novelist who was not ready to commit to him for the duration, and saved me the half hour or so it would have taken to fire him diplomatically. And I know that sounds harsh, but at least I didn't have him whacked, which I am sure could have been arranged with a two-minute call to Esther, whom I've been meaning to thank for several paragraphs now but haven't found the opening.

And so we come to the end of this song of appreciation only to realize there is one more category, those volunteers not just unpaid, but who have gone to some personal expense to make this book possible, a category of one as it happens, the former heavyweight fighter Randall Cobb, whose left arm and by implication his career were done damage that could never be repaired one cold night twenty-odd years ago in a since-gentrified neighborhood of Philadelphia when he waded into as unpleasant a setting as that city has to offer and saved enough of my brain from the bats and tire irons of the outraged citizenry that I could later tie shoe laces and write books, which all these years later it turns out is everything I need (along with Mrs. Dexter and the offspring, some scenery and a dog or two) to be happy.

And Esther.

Don't let me forget Esther.